Horde

Book Five of the Outsider series.

by
Aiden Phoenix

Copyright © 2023 Aiden Phoenix

No part of this book may be reproduced in any form or by any electronic or mechanical means including information storage and retrieval systems, without permission in writing from the author. Except for the purposes of making reviews or other cases permitted by copyright law.

ISBN: 9798853592599

Cover created by Aiden Phoenix.

This book is a work of fiction. Names, characters, locations, and events are products of the author's imagination. Any resemblance to any persons living or dead, locations, or events are coincidental and unintended by the author.

Table of Contents

Prologue: A Closer Look....5
Chapter One: Horde....24
Chapter Two: Camp....40
Chapter Three: Attack....58
Chapter Four: Spoils....76
Chapter Five: Reprieve....94
Chapter Six: Redoubt....114
Chapter Seven: Thorns....132
Chapter Eight: Deal....149
Chapter Nine: Home Ward Bound....168
Chapter Ten: Home At Last....186
Chapter Eleven: Personal Reunions....203
Chapter Twelve: Surprises....219
Chapter Thirteen: Back to Routine....235
Chapter Fourteen: Winter Days....252
Chapter Fifteen: Guests....271
Chapter Sixteen: A True Party....291
Chapter Seventeen: Beneath the Mountain....309
Chapter Eighteen: Blind....324
Epilogue: Sleepover....344

Welcome to Collisa!

Collisa is a new world brimming with opportunities for adventure and growth. It is also brimming with chances for romance and fun. This is the story of Dare and the life he builds for himself with the women he meets and falls in love with.

As you can guess, it is a harem tale, with all that includes. Be aware that it features varied and explicit erotic scenes between multiple partners. It is intended to be enjoyed by adults. All characters involved in adult scenes are over the age of 18.

Prologue

A Closer Look

Dare drifted awake as he felt Marigold moving softly in his embrace.

After a bleary moment he realized she wasn't trying to slip away to relieve herself or anything like that, and cracking his eyes open saw by the faint light filtering into the tent that it was barely dawn. So he settled back down into a half-asleep state and just enjoyed the feel of his gnome lover's warm, plump, deliciously soft little body pressed against him.

The tiny maid had stated outright she'd volunteered for this scouting mission to be his bedwarmer, but if he'd still had any illusions about her sincerity the last week had dispelled them. She'd proven to be insatiable, jumping on him the moment they retired to his tent each night, and ready for another round (or several) the moment they woke up in the morning.

She'd even tried to find time to sneak him away for some fun while they were scouting the monster horde threatening Terana province. Guaranteeing that if they didn't tire themselves out in their duties, by the time they collapsed in each other's arms at the end of each night they were more than ready for sleep.

Not that Dare was complaining. At all.

Not only was Marigold incredible in bed, she was also fun to be around. An excellent conversationalist with a sharp wit and (usually naughty) sense of humor, she was also so full of energy, relentless positivity, and cheerfulness that he felt incredibly drawn to her.

The thought of finishing this scouting mission and her returning to her duties to Baroness Marona at Montshadow Estate made him feel a bit wistful.

He'd miss her.

Although on the plus side it was more motivation to visit his noble lover and see her and Belinda at the same time. As well as Marona's other beautiful maids, many of whom had made it clear they were interested in him.

Of course, returning back to his life depended on whether they could defeat this monster horde and save the province. It numbered in the hundreds, and was getting dangerously close to the town of Terana and Marona's forces gathered outside it.

Which meant today was the day to take greater risks and try to get vital information about their enemies.

Dare was drawn from his grim plans as he realized Marigold's soft movements had become a bit more urgent. She was breathing harder as well, almost gasping, and a couple times seemed to be stifling moans. But it wasn't until he heard a soft, incredibly erotic squelching sound that realization dawned.

He couldn't help but chuckle. "Starting without me?" he teased, hand trailing down to brush her fingers buried deep in her sodden sex.

His lover giggled and nuzzled against him, kissing his shoulder. "Force of habit." Her voice, breathy from her self-ministrations, sounded a bit wistful. "It's only recently that I've had the freedom to seek lovers. Before that I had to learn to take care of myself."

This was the first he'd heard much of her past, since aside from a few offhand comments about growing up in the underground gnomish settlement of Deepwater, she hadn't spoken much of it. And certainly no hints before now that it had been less than idyllic.

Were there troubles in her past she hadn't told him about?

If so Dare didn't press; if she felt comfortable opening up she would. He leaned down and kissed the top of her head. "I'm happy to take care of you when I can," he murmured solemnly.

"You sure are." She made a contented sound and took his hand, pressing it against her velvety folds, then gasped softly as he began to gently caress her. "That's why this last week has been so wonderful. You've spoiled me so good . . . I've had more and better sex than in the last six months combined. Maybe even the last year!"

"In that case let me make sure you're set for the next year," Dare growled, ducking beneath the blankets covering them and beginning to kiss his way down her plump body. He savored her warm, silky soft skin as he briefly teased her breasts and large plump nipples, then along her soft tummy and even softer shaved mound.

His gnome lover giggled. "I hope I won't have any more dry spells, now that you'll be around to fuuuuuuuhhhhh!" Her words cut off in a breathy moan as his lips found her plump, sopping labia and began gently nibbling them.

Dare smiled slightly and began putting all his skill to work giving her the pleasure he'd promised.

Marigold made the most adorable squeaking sounds of pleasure as his tongue thrummed against her clit, her pillowy thighs clamped around his ears and small hands firmly pushing his head against her sex.

"Keep going," she panted, squirming in delight. "Goddess, yes! Just like that!"

He was more than happy to comply, occasionally pausing to slide his tongue through her folds to gather up her flowing nectar. It tasted of sweet feminine musk with a hint of cinnamon, making his cock throb eagerly at the prospect of the pleasure to come.

His plump gnome lover lasted another few minutes until he felt her tense and clutch at him desperately. He flicked his tongue even harder against her bud to carry her over the edge, and with a squeal of pure ecstasy she squirted all over his face.

As she quivered in bliss Dare kissed his way up her smooth shaved mons, across her plump tummy and to her large breasts. Where he played his lips over her large, pale pink areolas as he kneaded her warm pillowy flesh with his hands.

She got back to squirming and making those delightful squeaks, especially when he sucked an eraser-sized nipple into his mouth and nibbled it teasingly.

"Now!" the pink-haired maid finally panted, urgently reaching down to tug on his hips. “I need you in me.”

Her gorgeous blue eyes were probably the widest of any woman he'd ever seen, like an adorable begging puppy in a cartoon. He couldn't have said no to that pleading look even if he'd wanted to.

Which was very much not the case; his throbbing manhood wholeheartedly agreed with the idea of being inside his sexy gnome lover, and he eagerly climbed up to press his tip against her silky soft, sopping labia.

His thick, nine inch cock was a startling juxtaposition to his gnome lover's tiny pussy, and it seemed impossible that it could fit in. She was even shorter than Zuri, inches shy of four feet and a good two and a half feet shorter than him.

In fact, at one point just for fun he'd laid his erection on her belly with his balls resting on her mound, and discovered it was half the length of her torso, the tip almost reaching up to rest between the tiny woman's breasts.

Yet thanks to the world system that allowed races of different sizes to safely have sex and bear children, when he pushed between Marigold's folds he slid inside her with ease, plunging all the way to her cervix in one smooth motion with over half his length still outside her body.

Although what was inside her made an obscene bulge along her mound and lower abdomen, his tip clearly visible even beneath her plump belly. It was hot as hell.

Even better, in that strange way of the world system, even though he could move within the tiny gnome's pussy with ease, the sensations of their fucking were the same as they would normally be, aside from without the pain of course.

Because of that Dare felt like her walls were strangling him tighter than even Zuri's vise-like grip. It was such an indescribably pleasurable sensation that even after almost a week straight of fucking the tiny maid morning and evening (and sometimes during the day if they could get away from their companions), it still took all his self control not to explode inside her within half a minute.

And he had experience with Zuri and Rosie, who were both nearly as tight. Not to mention plenty of experience in lovemaking with over a dozen other women he'd been with since coming to Collisa.

Soon after they'd first met Marigold had told him no pussy was as tight as a gnome's, and in his experience she was absolutely right.

For her part, she'd described it as being gloriously stretched to her limits, every part of her sensitive love tunnel and clit stimulated simultaneously from the pressure, with all the pleasure it entailed.

And unlike Dare, who had to fight mightily to rein in his overwhelming pleasure so they could fuck for even a few minutes at the pace the eager little gnome preferred, she basically climaxed nonstop the entire time. Rising to higher and higher peaks until he erupted inside her, pumping her full of his seed.

At which point the pink-haired maid switched to a different position and urged him to keep going, plump body squirming and jiggling with his thrusts as her strangling walls rippled around his length and her eyes rolled back in pure rapture.

She knew he could fuck right through one or even two orgasms before needing a break, and even then usually only a short one. She made full use of his stamina; for all her prim, proper maid composure in public she was an absolute wildcat in the sack.

On top of the vigorous sex she loved to be spanked and have her long hair pulled, as well as her nipples pinched and her clit mauled. And she was just as quick to slap his ass to spur him on to greater efforts, and claw his back in pure ecstasy as she was overcome with pleasure.

That morning they fucked for almost a half hour until she was a limp, quivering ball of jelly in his arms, adorable round face relaxed in the ultimate expression of blissful satisfaction. “Fuck my tits to finish off,” she mumbled dreamily. “I want you to come all over me.”

Dare pulled out of Marigold's gaping pussy, their combined juices flowing from within her pink depths, and climbed up to straddle her chest. Settling his erection in the valley between her pillowy breasts, he began to thrust as she eagerly pushed them together to engulf him in a soft embrace.

Still slick with her juices, his cock slid across her silky skin with ease, a sensation nearly as good as fucking. Even better, she was so tiny and he was so long that with every thrust she was able to bob her head down and kiss and lick his tip, or even take his entire head into her small mouth.

After the insane pressure of her little pussy he was able to slow down and enjoy himself now, and Marigold finally used her elbows to push her boobs together so she could use her hands to jack him off as he kept thrusting eagerly. Under her expert care it didn't take long before he groaned and erupted all over her eagerly upturned face.

After a few spurts he pulled back to coat her jiggling breasts, then even farther to spray her plump little tummy and mons. Then, with a final gasp, he collapsed beside the tiny gnome and gathered her into his arms, affectionately stroking her soft skin. She was warm, flushed and glistening with perspiration from their exertions in spite of the chill of an autumn morning.

"Damn, you make me feel so good," Marigold purred, nuzzling his chest. "When I finally have to go back to the mansion I'm going to be so lonely in my bed. I don't think I'll be able to replace that glorious cock of yours even if I use everything in the broom closet and vegetable crisper."

Dare was used to her astonishingly lewd mind by this point, and chuckled as he lovingly stroked her silky pink hair, which fell in a luxurious waterfall all the way to her ankles. His fingers brushed her body through it from shoulders to calves along the way, exploring her luscious curves. "I'll be sure to visit as often as I can, then."

His little gnome lover sighed contentedly and somehow wiggled to cuddle even closer to him. "Best. Week. Ever," she said with a dreamy smile.

He grinned and kissed her sweaty forehead. "It's been incredible," he agreed. "I thought the Prevent Conception scrolls

Zuri gave me before leaving would last me weeks, but I'm already almost out."

"Mmm," she murmured, big blue eyes looking up at him mischievously as she stroked her fingers over his rock hard abs. "Keep fucking me like this and I won't want to stop when you run out, even if it means getting knocked up."

At his expression she giggled in delight. "Kidding. I'm sure our babies would be adorable, but I'm not ready to be a mother just yet."

Dare let out a breath he hadn't realized he'd been holding, not sure if he was relieved or disappointed. Which was absurd, since he already had more children either born or on the way than most people would ever want, and his six fiancees insisted they were just getting started.

And yet he found himself overjoyed with each one, eager to be a father.

Still, his relationship with Marigold was more fun and excitement than anything deeper. They'd been together for a week and made love dozens of times, but his feelings for her hadn't grown and deepened like they had with Zuri, Pella, Leilanna, Se'weir, Sia, and Ireni. And the pink-haired maid seemed to feel the same.

She was fun and he was happy to have her as a lover, but somehow he didn't see her joining his harem or being a mother to his children. At least not right now.

Maybe in the future.

The pink-haired maid idly rubbed her belly, spreading his cum over her skin. "Belinda told me this is better than lotion," she murmured. "Maybe I should spread it all over my body and leave it on when I dress."

Dare's cock couldn't help but twitch at the thought, and at the sight of it she grinned wickedly. "Ooh, you like the idea of me walking around all day absolutely filthy with your seed?" She giggled, then with a reluctant sigh wriggled out of his arms. "Maybe some other time." She dug in his pack for one of Zuri's Cleanse Target scrolls. "Come on, let's go clean up."

Marigold pulled on his shirt to go outside, which was as good as a dress on her tiny body, while he wrapped himself in his cloak. He also wadded up the bedding to clean, then together they ducked out of the tent and headed for the stream.

The camp was still quiet at this hour, the tents of the two messengers, Hayan and Ellina, still and undisturbed. Only Ilin was in sight, seated by the fire in a meditation pose, a blanked draped over his shoulders his only concession to the night's chill.

Dare wondered if the Monk would sit in the middle of camp like that even in the dead of winter.

The man was meditating, as he usually did whenever he had a spare moment. That or doing an intense exercise routine every morning and evening. Dare usually joined in, but even though Sia had gifted him with an incredible body when he came to Collisa, and he considered himself in peak physical shape, he was rarely able to make it through the entire routine. At least not without pauses to rest.

Ilin, on the other hand, had been vigorously working his body and mind from a young age, and usually finished exercising looking as if he could do it all over again. Even his meditation was a mental exercise, looking inward to his body and balancing his inner lines.

Marigold tugged Dare's hand insistently, shivering in the cold, and together they hurried to the stream flowing nearby. “If this goes on much longer I'm going to start having you heat me water in the kettle for this,” she complained as she stepped into the ankle deep, icy flow.

He grimaced as he joined her. “I'd be fine with that. Maybe I'll get a kettle going before we start having fun each morning.”

She giggled. “If you did that, the water would all boil away before we're finished.”

He wasn't sure he'd been given many better compliments than that. “Ready?” he asked, still holding the wadded up bedding.

The tiny gnome pouted, but with a determined set to her plump lips nodded as she hugged herself for warmth. Dare wrapped an arm around her and they both dropped into the frigid water, bracing against the cold as she read off the spell on the scroll through chattering teeth.

The chilly water surged around them, turning bluish-purple as it whisked away all the dirt and filth, leaving them, their clothes, and the bedding cleaner than the best shower or washing machine. And much quicker, thankfully.

The moment the spell faded they surged out of the stream, shivering as they fled to their tent. Which thankfully still held the warmth of their bodies. Once there they stripped out of their wet clothes and set them and the bedding outside for Marigold to hang up to dry, then dried each other off.

Before Dare could begin to dress she pressed up against him for warmth, so they cuddled together for a minute or two to warm up before getting ready for the day.

He took a lot less time to dress than she did, pulling on clean underwear, pants, shirt, coat, leather armor, and cloak while she was still laying out her adorable black and white maid uniform. "If you're done getting ready sometime before noon," he teased, playfully swatting her round bottom as he ducked out the entry flaps, "I'll have breakfast cooked in fifteen minutes."

"You try arranging hair down to your ankles, making yourself presentable, and putting on a complicated outfit while crouching in a tent!" she called after him. Then she giggled. "Actually, I'd love to see you wearing a uniform like this."

While Dare appreciated the parting sally, and found the mental image funny, as he straightened and took in the camp he felt the weight of the situation settle down on him once more.

In camp, with someone on watch, he could do his best to relax and enjoy his time with Marigold. And he could honestly say that he was glad she'd accompanied him for much more than the fantastic sex; her cheerful presence kept him from brooding on the situation, the danger his family and their home faced.

She lifted his spirits and let him face his task with optimism and purpose.

A monster horde grew with every spawn point it passed and absorbed monsters from, growing in numbers and strength with shocking speed. It was a peril that, left alone, could eventually threaten entire provinces, entire regions, even entire kingdoms. In fact, there was an entire continent that had long ago been lost to monsters and never reclaimed.

And one was rampaging straight for Terana, the town Dare and his harem lived a day's ride from and where many of their friends and lovers lived. Over the last week it had come within days of the town, and with each passing day it grew stronger from Terana's spawn points.

They were running out of time to stop it.

He was out here with Ilin, Marigold, and two messengers to scout the horde's location and strength, kill its scouts to slow its progress, harass it and thin its ranks if they could, and clear the monster spawn points in the direction of the horde's movement before they could join it.

That had involved him and Ilin, the only high level combat classes in the group, needing to clear spawn points with monsters three, four, and even five levels above Dare's. Which made them dangerously high level for the Monk.

It was a risk Dare never would've taken in other circumstances.

But they'd done it anyway, taking minor wounds in the process, knowing that if those monsters joined the horde it would probably be impossible for Marona, Baroness of Terana Province and the mother of Dare's unborn child (one of them at least), to beat the monsters with her ragtag army.

Odds weren't great they'd beat it even so, and he'd yet to identify the strongest monsters in the center of the horde, far from where he could see them with his Adventurer's Eye. But their efforts were bearing some fruit as his noble lover gathered her army, doing her best to prepare for the battle to come.

Or to evacuate her town, if they couldn't stop the horde.

Shaking his head to dispel the grim thoughts, he made his way over to the fire and got water boiling for coffee and a pan heated for pancakes.

"Are you two always this noisy in the morning?"

Dare jumped half out of his skin and sheepishly whirled to where Ilin remained in his meditation pose, eyes closed and expression placid.

Normally the Monk could meditate through just about anything but actual danger to the camp. Which was why Dare could fuck Marigold a dozen feet away without embarrassment no matter how loudly she squeaked, since his friend would neither hear it nor take note.

Which was more than he could say for the messengers, who'd moved their tents so far away they practically had their own camp. They even had their own fire.

"Sorry, didn't mean to interrupt your meditation," he said. "We've got a bit longer before we'll break camp if you want to get back to it."

Ilin grinned, although his eyes remained closed. "No worries, my friend, I wasn't meditating." He tapped a spot on his forehead between his eyes. "I was doing mental exercises to see the world around me without physical vision."

Dare blinked. "Clairvoyance? That's something Monks get?" This was his first time hearing about it.

His friend snorted. "Of a sort. I gained access to the Third Eye at Level 30."

"Oh, right." Dare supposed he *had* heard about it, it just hadn't registered at the time.

While the leveling in the last week as they scouted out the monster horde had been poor at best, clearing various spawn points and hunting monster scouts that were usually lower level than them, Ilin had still managed to reach Level 30 yesterday.

And Dare had gained 33 the day before, although there hadn't been much that was exciting for him that level.

30, though, was a big one, like every ten levels was. And while the main gain for it for any class was the +5 overall stat boosts from Power Up, the Monk had still picked up a few neat goodies. In the impromptu celebration when Ilin described his new abilities, he'd mentioned Third Eye but hadn't elaborated.

"So what sort of cool stuff can you do with it?" Dare asked, grinning. "Can you see really far?"

His friend shook his head, eyes still closed. "At higher levels, certainly. When I first get it, however, my Third Eye doesn't extend much farther than 20 yards, depending on whether I open my Locks." He grimaced. "Although without proper training of the mind it's scarcely better than a parlor trick. As with so many other of my class's abilities that require constant training and discipline."

That certainly seemed to be the case, and it made sense that his friend would be practicing his new ability, and likely would do so for many hours to come.

It was a common saying on Earth that to master something took 10,000 hours of practice. That very much wasn't the case on Collisa, where the ability system usually held your hand. Many abilities actually took over your body to perform the moves, allowing you to do them in the fastest and most proficient way possible. Thanks to that most classes could perform superhuman feats without much practice, occasionally even beyond the usual limits of their body.

Monk abilities didn't act for you, however, they simply unlocked the body's capability to perform the move. So in order to use their abilities Monks had to constantly hone their body and mind through training and meditation.

Dare was proud of what he was able to do as a Hunter, but he could admit that an inept moron who chose the class would still be able to use abilities with the same proficiency as him. So while they would still suck ass, they wouldn't be completely useless.

A lazy or undisciplined Monk, however, would be absolutely pathetic. On the other hand diligent Monks had the potential to be explosively powerful, more so than other classes of the same level by a clear margin.

Although one downside was that their full power could only be accessed for short periods of time, and tended to come at a price to their bodies if they opened their inner Locks, which allowed them to surpass even the physical limitations of a Monk's well honed body.

"So what does Third Eye do?" Dare asked as he leaned forward to get the first pancake cooking.

"It improves my chances of spotting something hidden through magic or other means, and also lets me look beyond physical barriers to see what is hidden from the eye. For instance, I can look through walls, and see people in Stealth or magical invisibility." Ilin patted the ground beside him. "Come. You can't learn the ability, of course, but it's a good exercise for honing the mind."

With a shrug Dare settled down crosslegged next to his friend and closed his eyes. "All right, so what do I do?"

The Monk's voice came deep and resonant. "Imagine you are opening an unseen eye in the center of your forehead. The sight it gives you is black and white and of muted details, like afterimages after you close your eyes. You can turn this eye in any direction, even behind you or directly upwards or downwards, and see what lies in that direction. But you must think of a place to look, unlike your usual sight. Picture it like focusing on a specific spot, with all other details fuzzy . . . there is no simply looking in a direction and seeing what you see."

Dare frowned. "So I'm remembering what I've seen around me and picturing it as if I'm looking at it?"

"And using your imagination to fill in the details," the Monk confirmed. "If you had access to the Third Eye then your imagination would be supplying accurate details, so long as your mental focus was sufficient."

With a shrug Dare imagined opening an imaginary eye and staring forward, at a ghostly afterimage of the fire flickering in front of him. Then he moved his gaze beyond it to the plains stretching out ahead of them, and the woods in the distance.

Then, grinning to himself, he turned his imaginary eye to look behind him, through the cloth of his tent to where Marigold was dressing. He could imagine her pulling on the various layers of her black and white maid outfit, skin rosy and glistening from her recent dunk in the cold water.

Ilin coughed, sounding amused. “As a rule, it's considered rude to use the Third Eye to invade the privacy of others except at great need.”

Damn, the man was as perceptive as always. Although Dare just grinned. “Good thing it's just my imagination, then.” He opened his eyes, abandoning the exercise. “So you can do this while you're meditating to provide extra security for the camp?”

“Yes, that is one of the uses it can be put to.” His friend also opened his eyes, sighing. “Speaking of security, I was obliged to keep watch most of last night after Marigold retired to your tent at the end of her shift. Young Hayan brought a blanket on his watch and ended up falling asleep, failing to wake Ellina for her watch as well.”

Motherfucker. Dare's contented mood after the morning's lovemaking shattered as the grim reality of their purpose out here crashed home again. He shot to his feet, looking around, and the Monk obligingly pointed off towards Hayan's tent.

So the asshole hadn't just fallen asleep with a monster horde only a few hours away and put them all at risk, but he'd been aware enough of his actions that he'd crawled into his tent to be more comfortable.

Marigold emerged into the chilly dawn air, wearing her black and white maid's uniform along with thick white woolen stockings and a heavy fur coat and cloak. Somehow in spite of camping out in the wilds for almost a week, not to mention the fact that she'd fucked vigorously last night and this morning, she looked clean and composed with every strand of her ankle-length pink hair in place in a braided circlet. Her French maid uniform was also spotless and neatly pressed, as if it had just come out of the laundry.

And she'd managed the transformation in the short time he'd been chatting with Ilin and starting breakfast; she was a Level 8

Clothier, with whatever abilities that entailed, but he would swear she had some sort of magic to her.

Or maybe just a ton of training as a maid in a proper lady's mansion.

She made a few quick adjustments to her ruffled half apron and bonnet, then with a spring in her step glided over to join them. Although her smile faded when she saw Dare's expression. "What's wrong?"

"Do you have the newest report for Lady Marona prepared?" he asked her.

The plump gnome nodded. "Sure, aside from a few quick notes."

"Good, I'd like to add a note as well." Dare motioned curtly towards Hayan's tent. "We'll send him."

She quickly retrieved her portable writing desk and materials, and settling down in the collapsible camping chair he'd made her got to work scribbling a few final details from their activities and discoveries over the last few days.

Once she was done he added a brief message for Lady Marona. "Look forward to seeing you soon, and hope you and the baby are safe. Don't shoot this messenger, but be sure he receives whatever punishment is suitable for someone who falls asleep on watch. Don't send him back to me."

Normally Dare wouldn't pass the buck when it came to leadership, including unpleasant necessities like calling out subordinates and enforcing punishments. But he wanted to make sure Hayan actually delivered the report back to the baroness, and if the idiot realized he was in trouble he might dump the message or snoop around in it and destroy Dare's note.

If more needed to be done over the matter in the future, he'd do it.

After wrapping the report in a waterproof skin, Dare walked over to Hayan's tent and dragged the messenger out by one foot as he squawked in surprise and thrashed.

The young man blanched as he woke up enough to realize what

was happening. "Master Dare!" he stammered. "I-I'm sorry about falling asleep-"

"Forget about it," Dare told him curtly, shoving the report into his arms. "Pack up and get ready to ride back to the Baroness's camp with this report. You can skip breakfast since you should reach it by midmorning and can eat there."

Also there was no way in hell he was making pancakes for the asshole who'd put him and Marigold in danger with his lack of discipline.

Hayan hurried to obey, looking relieved that he didn't seem to be in trouble. Although his relief would likely be short-lived once the report was delivered and read.

While he was packing up Ellina, the other messenger, crept out of her tent with a chagrined expression. "I'm so sorry, Master Dare!" she blurted, rushing over and bowing low. "I slept right through my watch shift-"

"It's all right," he assured her. "You weren't awakened for it." Ideally she would've noticed something was wrong and gotten up anyway to start her shift, but he could hardly blame her for her lapse in the middle of the night. "Although I hope you'll be extra vigilant about your shifts moving forward," he added as he offered her a pancake.

The young woman nodded solemnly. "I will, I promise."

Hayan finished packing up and rode away on his horse, in the direction where Marona had set up her small army's camp several hours in front of the monster horde. The rest of them settled in to eat breakfast.

"So," Marigold said brightly as she reached for another pancake, "now that we've had our fun this morning, what's the boring stuff planned for today?"

Ilin and Ellina both seemed a bit irked by her cheerful demeanor, considering they'd been sent to scout and delay a monster horde that threatened their homes and loved ones. But that was just the lighthearted gnome's way.

She took the threat seriously, she just didn't let it dampen her spirits.

Dare wished he could share her bright outlook. Not only did he have to worry about the horde itself threatening his family, but also the possibility that Ollivan, the knight who'd been determined to make an enemy of him during a hunt against a raid rated monster about a month and a half ago, would use the distraction of the rampaging monsters to attack Nirim Manor.

So he had more reasons than simply that the monster horde grew bigger and more dangerous with every passing day to want to take it out quickly and get back home.

"First of all, we take out the spawn points in the horde's path for the day," he said firmly. "Then we clear out the scouts making for Terana, after which I'm going to do it."

His companions exchanged worried looks. By "do it" he meant sneak in close and do his best to identify all the high levels in the horde. But since the horde followed different aggro rules than usual monsters, able to aggro anything in their line of sight or other senses, the attempt would almost certainly result in the monsters spotting him, aggroing him, and chasing him en masse.

Dare and his companions had already had this discussion more than once during the last week of scouting. They thought it was reckless and suicidal and served no purpose, since with a telescope or even just their eyesight they could get a good enough view of the monsters to identify them.

They didn't know that Dare needed to get to within double the distance of his perception circle to use his Adventurer's Eye on the monsters at the center of the horde. Which meant he was going to need to be practically on top of the weaker monsters at the edges.

Or, well, Ilin knew, he just thought it was a stupid idea.

Dare had assured them that he could easily run away if or when the monsters aggroed. It might even be a good way to lead the horde off in a different direction away from Terana, which they hadn't risked attempting yet.

Or at the very least a clump of monsters might split off to chase him, which he and Ilin could then whittle down.

"I can't argue with the value of the information you'll gather," the Monk said reluctantly. "But while rare, there are monsters fast enough to catch up to even you. Especially if you go long enough for Cheetah's Dash to wear off. You might end up run down and overwhelmed."

It was the same argument he'd made before, and while Dare didn't discount it, he wasn't going to let it deter him this time. "Then I'll have to hope I'm strong enough to kill whatever's fast enough to catch me. That, or I manage to get in and out without being spotted."

His friend frowned, but raised no further objections.

Dare swallowed the last bite of his pancake, washed it down with the rest of his coffee, and stood briskly. "All right, friends," he said. "We've got a busy day, let's strike camp and get to it."

Chapter One

Horde

Dare cautiously raised his head from his hiding spot and stared down at the mass of monsters surging along in the distance, inexorably moving towards Terana at the quickest pace the slowest among them could manage.

Which wasn't fast, but it wasn't slow, either.

There were probably four hundred monsters in the horde, ranging in in Level from 1 all the way up to over 30. And that was just the strength of those on the outskirts; he had yet to get close enough to the center of the mass to identify the strongest monsters with his Adventurer's Eye.

Although he hoped to change that today.

If he'd needed any warning that the horde was here to cause devastation and ruin, the path of destruction they left behind them proved it. Trampled grass, uprooted trees and bushes, even ugly slashes in the dirt and sod. As if they simply relished in destruction and would turn their gleeful carnage on the ground itself if no better targets were available.

Needless to say, the animals of the wilds had all been smart enough to flee the noisy, destructive mob. Although if the sound hadn't frightened them the sight of the things would've done the job.

Monsters in their spawn points could be nightmarishly hideous and terrifying, like giant spiders or chimeric abominations of animals and humanoids. Some Dare had even avoided based on their appearance alone, even though in video games he'd happily taken a warhammer to ghoulish corpses at close range, watching the carnage he wreaked without the slightest hint of queasiness.

Real life was different. And while Collisa had many features similar to the games he'd loved in his old life, in the more than half year he'd been here he'd found it was every bit as real as Earth.

Which was why a horde of hundreds of monsters, ranging from giant rats, to massive elemental automatons, to creepy undead horrors, to things that were almost humanoid but wrong in the details, was particularly frightening to look at. Especially since unlike normal monsters the horde operated by different rules.

For instance, Dare could walk right up to a spawn point in open view of monsters, and as long as he wasn't in the aggro range of their perception circles he was just fine. Whereas at the moment he and his companions were hiding behind some bushes a mile away, in the clear knowledge that if one of the monsters below spotted them the entire horde could come charging their way.

Which was why they were ready at a moment's notice to flee westward, in a different direction from Marona's small army shadowing the horde from a distance of several hours, always keeping themselves between the hundreds of monsters and Terana behind them.

At this point the town was only days away, and the horde grew with every passing hour; the sooner they could act, the better.

He finally ducked his head. "Seven spawn points in the horde's path that we need to clear today," he whispered. Unfortunately they couldn't clear the spawn points within the line of sight of the horde without being aggroed, which meant in spite of their best efforts at least a few spawn points got overrun by the monster horde every day.

Sometimes the horde annihilated those monsters and moved on, slightly higher level and with better loot as a result. But more often at least some of the monsters in the spawn point joined the horde's ranks.

Which was why clearing them was so necessary; without Dare's and Ilin's efforts over the last week the horde would be easily twice as large as it was. Particularly since they were also hunting down the horde's scouts to further thin its ranks.

With no further delay they slipped back down to where their

horses waited and mounted up. Dare set a brisk pace away from the horde, towards the first spawn point.

The closer they got to Terana the lower the level of the monsters, thanks to the way spawn points worked. It meant most of the monsters they faced were in the 26-29 range now, fairly easy pickings for him and Ilin.

The monsters in this spawn point were outliers, though, Level 29-31. The fact that some spawn points could produce slightly higher level monsters, and the unpredictability of the abilities the monsters might have, made adventuring dangerous for most, with many adventurers meeting their end before they even got to Level 30.

For most, but not Dare.

He'd been blessed (literally, thanks to his benefactor Sia who'd brought him to Collisa in the first place) with the Adventurer's Eye, which gave him vital information about the monsters he was fighting such as their level, hit points, mana, stamina, damage capabilities, and the attacks and special abilities they'd use in a fight.

Thanks to that he was able to enter every fight armed with the greatest weapon of all: knowledge.

These monsters were called Degenerate Ardins. Basically large frogs with an odd, long-limbed appearance, many standing on two feet. According to Ilin, ardins were an animal found in swamps, rivers, and lakes far to the south, but those were usually green or grey and mostly harmless to people unless threatened.

These ones were tar black, including their empty eyes, with wicked claws and fangs and a sense of *wrongness* about them. Hence the degenerate part, he concluded.

They weren't going to be a delight to fight, since they had good mobility on land. And he assumed insane mobility in the water. Among their abilities were Jump, Spring, and Scurry, and they also spat a substance that caused an allergic reaction, with itching and rashes and with too much exposure anaphylactic shock.

Thankfully their damage was low in most other cases. But they were still going to be a pain.

Especially, as Dare discovered on the first pull, since they came in groups of four. Unexpected adds; another way adventurers died out in the wilds.

He wasn't planning to die here, though. He coolly used Rapid Shot to down the monster he'd pulled, just in time for his Prey's Vigilance ability to kick in and throw him slightly to the side to avoid an incoming gob of spit. Two more were right behind the first from the other ardins, and he used Roll and Shoot to avoid them and loose an arrow at his second target.

That was about the time when the three frog monsters used Jump and Spring in quick succession to close the distance between them, and he found himself facing an attack from the long, lightning quick tongue of the nearest ardin.

Before he needed to worry about taking evasive action Ilin appeared from the side, slamming into the monster in a vicious flying kick that sent it tumbling away. The Monk followed up with a flurry of punches and kicks, and Dare helped finish the monster off with two arrows to the head.

The other Degenerate Ardins were close behind the first two, but Ilin managed to draw them away in a flurry of motion as Dare focused on finishing them off from a distance.

Once they were down he rejoined his friend in the midst of the bodies to help loot. The Monk was rubbing his arm, where a lucky tongue strike had landed, and Dare frowned. “You okay?”

Ilin chuckled and rapped on his biceps. “Skin of Iron.”

He was talking about an ability improved through constant conditioning that allowed him to flex his muscles at the moment of impact to severely reduce blunt damage. Dare wasn't sure if it worked like that in real life, ie if he could do the same if he practiced the trick, but it made a great defensive ability for Monks. Although thankfully most of their class's survival was based around evasion, not taking any hits at all.

His friend's hit points were slightly diminished, but nothing that wouldn't heal in an hour or so. And since he showed no other sign of discomfort or negative status effects Dare trusted there was nothing to worry about.

Forewarned about the extra adds, the next pulls went more smoothly. To the point that after the third one Ilin smiled fondly. “This reminds me of when we first met, hunting the kobolds with Zuri.”

True; those monsters had come in groups of four as well. Dare felt a brief pang, missing his goblin fiancee and their daughter Gelaa.

Most spawn points tended to have between 30 and 40 monsters, with obvious exceptions like monster camps, large camps, mega spawn points, dungeon entrances, and other oddities. This one had an even 32, meaning they cleared it in 8 pulls.

After that it was on to an easier spawn point with lower level monsters that came as solo pulls. Ilin barely had to step in for that one, letting Dare take everything out from a distance.

Then there were swarms of giant wasp things that died quick but offered lower experience and shit loot. And so on and so forth, until they'd finally cleared the seven spawns. After that all that was left was to hunt down any scouts, then he'd be free to do his foray closer to the horde.

He'd found hunting the scouts to be a disappointment. They usually came in groups of 6 to 12 enemies, but although they offered double experience and improved loot since they were part of the horde, they were almost all under Level 10.

In fact, they'd been using it as an opportunity to get experience for Ellina, who was a Scout, or an archery class that specialized in mobility and ambush, and Marigold, who was a Sorcerer combat subclass. It was pretty easy for Dare and Ilin to kite or even tank the low level monsters while the two women took them down from a distance, and only took a bit more time.

The patrols were infrequent enough that Dare didn't even need to have his gnome lover switch to the four hour at a time sleeping schedule to maximize her mana regeneration. Although in spite of that, thanks to the experience bonus the two women had both gained a few levels in the last week.

Neither had seemed particularly determined to level, but the opportunity to make such quick, easy progress filled them with delight. Which had led Ilin to wryly observe, “You just can't seem to help wanting to power level people, can you?”

True, Dare did have a tendency to want to help everyone he met find a safe and efficient way to hunt monsters.

Today the only patrol they encountered was a group of Level 12s. They were familiar to Dare, Boarites that brought a nostalgic recollection of his days leveling near Lone Ox when he'd first arrived on Collisa.

Once Marigold and Ellina had finished downing and looting the monsters, he turned to his companions. “Okay, you keep shadowing the horde from in front to warn Marona if they suddenly change pace or direction. I'm going to go scout them.”

To his surprise Marigold ran forward and threw her arms around his waist. “Be careful!” she cried, kissing his hand while looking up at him with her wide blue eyes. They reflected genuine concern.

Smiling, Dare dropped to one knee to wrap her in his arms and kiss her full lips. “I'll be back soon,” he promised her. “The monsters won't even see me.”

She hugged him for a little longer, then reluctantly let him mount up and ride away.

He circled around to approach the horde from the north, then left his horse waiting about a mile away and approached on foot. Not only did he want to make sure his mount stayed safe while he scouted, but if he *did* have to bolt away at best speed he wanted to have the horse ready at a good distance so he could mount up and get out of there.

Since he wasn't a Stealth class he hadn't bothered to practice sneaking around very much. Especially since he'd discovered early on that the moment you aggroed a monster it would discover your position, making a beeline for you even if you were hidden.

Sure, with intelligent creatures that sort of sneaking outside of Stealth could still be useful, and even more so *with* Stealth. But aside from a few regrettable but unavoidable confrontations with some of the vilest people Dare had ever met, he'd been spared needing to fight anything but monsters and animals.

Still, he at least knew enough to stay behind cover and find folds in the ground where he'd be hidden in the grass.

Tense and ready to act in an instant, he moved closer and closer to the monster horde. The tumult that made a muted roar at the distance he usually remained from the hundreds of monsters resolved into individual shrieks, squeals, bellows, roars, and snarls.

The sounds clawed at his ears until he wanted to cover them, unnatural and unnerving and so loud and pervasive they had a pressure of their own. Imps cackled as they darted and dodged between the hooves and feet of larger monsters, the limbs of automatons squealed with every movement, huge, lumbering brutes snorted and growled warnings at those around them.

And over it all came the bellowed orders of the more powerful monsters leading the horde, an unrecognizable but foul tongue that turned Dare's stomach.

It was awful to listen to that racket while not being able to see it, but he couldn't afford to chance being seen when he risked a look. That didn't stop him from imagining the entire horde coming towards him instead of away, so even if he somehow managed to avoid being seen or aggroing any of the enemies, he'd still end up trampled under hundreds of feet, paws, hooves, talons, or whatever else they used to get around.

Finally, though, he reached a spot where the grass was short and dry and the ground flat, offering no hiding places. He had a choice between painstakingly retracing his steps, letting the horde get farther away so he'd have an even greater distance to creep, or risking a look now.

Fuck. Maybe he should've scouted out a good route to sneak up to the horde *before* the horde reached that spot. Or tried the tactic of hiding in their path and letting them walk right up to him.

But it was too late now. He might get spotted as he tried to turn around and back away, and he'd already gotten this close.

So, taking a breath, Dare unslung his bow and fitted an arrow to the string, using Rapid Shot to put four more arrows in his hand holding the bow. He waited until the ability's cooldown was done, just in case, then with a final breath rose up high enough to look at the horde.

He immediately began picking out individual monsters and checking them with Adventurer's Eye, starting with the obvious officers and big bruisers at the periphery.

Level 10. Level 12. Level 18. Party rated Level 24. Which the pragmatic part of Dare couldn't help but file away as a target if the opportunity presented itself; any party rated monster that gave experience would give him progress towards his Protector of Bastion achievement, and he still had 6 to go.

Dare had yet to be spotted, at least as far as he'd seen, so he began checking the beefier monsters and their leaders deeper inside the horde.

Level 21. Level 28. Level 24. Level 32. Level 29 party rated (that was going to be a bit more of a challenge).

To his frustration he still wasn't close enough to see the monsters at the very center of the horde, which mostly seemed to be a type of orc.

There were dozens of the brutish creatures, similar to the orc he'd seen that was a member of the Marshal's Irregulars in Jarn's Holdout. But unlike that one with his rusty reddish-brown skin, these were a sickly pale yellow with blackened veins running through their flesh.

Although whatever afflicted them didn't seem to have weakened them, but if anything made them stronger. Their muscles bulged impossibly, as if on the verge of ripping apart with a sudden movement, and they stalked through the horde with a sort of feral fury that often exploded into vicious ferocity at the slightest provocation.

Dare watched one of the orcs tackle a much larger troll, hammering it with its gauntleted fists until the troll was a broken ruin beneath it. Then it stood and made a show of pissing on its victim, bellowing a cry that was half victory and half challenge to the surrounding monsters as they shied away.

Jeez.

But the one that stood out to him was by far the biggest of the orc-ish monsters. It stood easily a foot taller than the others and was half again as wide, swinging a massive double-bladed axe as easily as if it was a bamboo stick.

From the way the huge orc moved and interacted with the monsters around him he seemed intelligent, and since even the stronger monsters in the area cowered in his presence he was probably the leader of this horde.

Dare needed to use his Eye on him.

As he was debating moving closer his luck finally ran out, and the clamor of monsters closest to him crescendoed. The ones on the periphery began jumping up and down and pointing his way, or outright charging him.

For a moment he paused, torn, then with a curse he activated Cheetah's Dash, increasing his movement speed by 25% for up to 2 minutes with no stamina usage increase, and sprinted towards the horde. Towards more and more monsters that were breaking off and charging his way, like a leak in a dam that swiftly grew to a flood. And all the while he looked frantically with his Adventurer's Eye.

Okay, the monsters in the center were called Cursed Orcs. Shit, all between Level 34 and 37. And the leader, the leader . . .

Dare's Prey's Vigilance kicked in to dodge a hissing fireball, and he loosed an arrow at the Level 6 Fire Sprite that had cast it at him, practically obliterating the low level monster. He saw more projectiles coming his way, most so low damage they'd itch or scratch at worst.

Then in the midst of the mass of charging monsters, he spotted the giant orc leader pushing his way towards him with furious bellows. The orc stepped past an enemy Dare had already identified, into range of his Adventurer's Eye, and-

"Cursed Orc Warchief. Monster, Party Rated. Level 38. Attacks: Earthquake, Sundering Shockwave, Cleave Enemies, Full Circle, Rush, Leap, Terrifying Aura, Bellow, Warchief's Roar, Chop, Crush, Tackle."

Hoo boy, that guy was a chonker. Although on the plus side at least he was only party rated, not raid rated; at that level he would've been able to stomp the majority of Marona's army in one attack.

They would've had to evacuate Terana and flee the horde's advance while calling for aid from heroes throughout Bastion. Even as it was the Warchief would be a challenge, but not an impossible one.

Dare snarled as an arrow slammed into his arm, barely taking away 1% of his hit points and not even applying a bleed effect. It still stung like a bitch, though, and he used Roll and Shoot to reverse direction, coming up to his feet facing the other way as more projectiles fell in a rain around him.

He took off like an arrow, fumbling in his pouch to put on the goggles Ireni had given him as he sped up to nearly 40 miles an hour, flying across the plains. Fleetfoot combined with Cheetah's Dash's (movement specific) agility boost allowed him to easily navigate the rough ground, without falling flat on his face at speeds that would've seriously injured or even killed him.

And he made full use of them.

After a few hundred yards he risked a glance back. He was mildly surprised to see that the Warchief wasn't pursuing him, but was roaring for the monsters around him to get back to the horde and continue on their way. Or at least so he assumed, given the movements of those who obeyed their leader, which was most.

The orc was obviously no fool, and wasn't about to let his forces be divided in pursuit of one lone scout that was obviously too fast to catch.

That didn't stop the few dozen monsters who'd first broken off to chase Dare, who continued to run after him as if they didn't hear the shouted orders or didn't care. In fact, even if it might be reckless there was an opportunity there, and he slowed his headlong sprint to let the monsters catch up, causing them to hoot and pursue with even greater enthusiasm.

Thirty or so monsters ranging from Level 5 to Level 20. No threat at all to Dare, but every one he killed might be a life saved when Marona's army faced the horde, since she'd recruited fighters as low as Level 10.

So he nocked an arrow and began downing the nearest monsters, killing them one after another with a single shot.

The entire time he kept an eye on the monster horde, in case the Warchief sent more and stronger enemies after him. But to his further surprise the huge orc seemed to have dismissed him, all his focus on keeping the monsters around him in motion.

Or wait, no.

It was subtle at first, especially since so much of Dare's attention was focused on the low level pursuers he was scything down. But as he watched the horde he noticed the dense blob of monsters beginning to stretch out, specific types clumping together. Which in some cases meant monster packs left their leaders behind, or leaders left their packs.

It took a few seconds before he realized what was happening: the Cursed Orc Warchief was ordering his faster monsters to leave the slower ones behind.

Fuck. The intelligent monster must've realized Dare was a scout and might be trying to lure the horde away, and in response was charging full steam ahead for whatever force was out there sending scouts.

Or the town they were defending, if that force was out of place and couldn't manage to stop them.

Dare finished off the last of the monsters pursuing him and

bolted for his horse, leaving behind the majority of his arrows as well as the loot on their bodies.

At their current pace the fastest monsters would reach Marona's camp sometime tomorrow morning. He needed to get there as soon as possible and warn her.

* * * * *

To Dare's relief Ilin, Marigold, and Ellina were aware of the monster horde's increased pace and had kept ahead of it. They looked relieved to see him, but also urgent about the change in circumstances.

"Whatever you did certainly riled them up," the Monk called as Dare reined his horse in beside him. "What now?"

"I got the information we need," Dare replied grimly. "And since it's mostly the monsters Level 20 and higher that have the movement speed boosts and abilities, they're the ones at the head of the horde charging for Baroness Marona's camp. I think it's time we head there to give warning and see what she wants to do."

The others seemed almost relieved at the decision, and gratefully joined him in increasing their pace to the fastest ones the horses could maintain for the six or so hours to Marona's army.

"What did you find?" Marigold asked, reining in her sleek mountain goat beside his horse. She had out her slate writing board and looked ready to write notes. "Tell me everything you saw, all the insights you had."

Dare noticed the others gathering around to listen as he quickly reported his findings. When he finished their expressions were grim. "Around 30 monsters in their high 30s, and their leader is party rated," Ellina said. "Lady Marona may have ten fighters over Level 30 in her entire army, including you two."

Yeah, this was going to be brutal. In most cases he'd say a single adventurer was a match for multiple monsters, even fighting them at the same time. Personally he'd put himself up against several equal level monsters as an even match, and in a party he thought they could take out far more than they could individually.

But outnumbered at least three to one with enemies that would swarm them en masse was something entirely different.

He just hoped his noble lover had managed to gather more and stronger fighters since the last report from her camp. Or better yet that her pleas for help from nearby towns had been answered, even though in most cases there wouldn't have been time for that yet.

Both hopes were disappointed when they crested the final rise and came in view of Marona's camp.

The army she'd gathered was pathetic compared to the raid party Dare and Ireni had joined to fight the Magma Tunneler about a month and a half ago, which had featured nearly 40 heroes ranging from Level 30 to 37.

In contrast, the baroness had a bit over a hundred fighters in total, less than a dozen over Level 30, maybe a few dozen over Level 20, and the majority in their high 10s at best.

To be fair, that was pretty respectable for a small town like Terana and the surrounding province. Even in a frontier region like Bastion, where people needed to be hardier and faced more danger in their lives.

Still, Dare couldn't help but miss his fiancees, all in their high 20s or low 30s; they would've been invaluable in this fight.

At the same time thinking of the women he loved, with Pella, Leilanna, Se'weir, and Ireni carrying his babies and Zuri caring for their young daughter Gelaa, he was very relieved they were staying far away from this fight. Especially in the face of a monster like the Cursed Orc Warchief.

Marona's army might be sufficient to deal with the horde, which only numbered a few hundred of mostly lower level monsters, with only a few dozen enemies over Level 30. The difference would come in that all of her fighters were intelligent and could work together and follow strategies, while the Warchief would have trouble doing anything with his monsters but sending them in a rush.

Still, it was going to be brutal. And a lot would rely on how Dare and the other higher level fighters were able to influence the battle.

Particularly in keeping the Warchief and other dangerous Cursed Orcs away from Terana's vulnerable lower level fighters.

One Earthquake or Sundering Shockwave from that party rated monster could kill dozens of people if they weren't careful.

They passed the healer and support section of camp on the way in, and Dare saw Lady Amalisa Kinnran hurrying to meet them, smiling in relief. “Ilin, Dare!” she cried, ready to greet them both with hugs as they dismounted. “I'm glad you're okay.”

Amalisa was the daughter of the nobleman who'd been Pella's master, as close as family to Dare's dog girl fiancee. When the young noblewoman's own brother had kicked her out with nothing, Dare had invited her to come live at Nirim Manor.

Which had delighted Pella, and added even more joy and brightness to their home.

“How have things been here?” Ilin asked as the young noblewoman stepped back from him. The usually unflappable Monk looked a bit awkward at her show of affection; good to see he wasn't completely made of stone.

Amalisa grimaced. “We're trying our best to get geared up and earn some levels so we can survive what's to come. But there's a lot of fear that it won't be enough.” She gave Dare a closer look; as a member of his household they hadn't kept his Adventurer's Eye secret from her, so she knew he could judge the strength of the horde better than anyone. “Will it be?”

He noticed that the sweet young woman had gained a level since he'd last seen her, and was now Level 18. Which meant she was a full 20 levels below the Cursed Orc Warchief; the monster would kill her in one hit even through the protective barriers she could cast.

Over his dead body. He forced a smile. “If we work together and fight our best, it will be.”

She didn't seem reassured, and Ilin gave her a comforting smile. “Don't worry, I'll be standing between you and anything that would do you harm.”

To Dare's surprise that seemed to reassure her, and she flashed them a brilliant smile before hurrying back to her duties.

He wanted to check on Rek'u'gar, the younger brother of his hobgoblin fiancee Se'weir, and the 18 goblins the young man had brought with him to fight the monster horde. They were members of the Avenging Wolf tribe who'd settled on his lands, under his protection and responsibility, and he wanted to make sure they were being treated well and were sufficiently prepared for the battle to come.

But it would have to wait on giving his news to Marona; honestly he should've rode on past Amalisa as well, but things weren't so urgent he couldn't spare her a few moments.

Their arrival in camp caused a bit of a stir, since most either recognized them as the high level scouts their baroness had sent to keep an eye on the horde, or at least high level adventurers and therefore capable of helping to turn the tide of the battle.

Thanks to that stir Marona was waiting for him outside what he assumed was her war tent, along with several officers who would effectively be raid leaders for the distinct groups of fighters like tanks, melee fighters, ranged damage, and healers and support.

In private the mature noblewoman was Dare's lover and the mother of his unborn child, and he'd seen her softness and warmth. But in public she was every inch the proper, competent, respected Baroness of Terana. He fully supported her in that role and was proud to call her his lady, and indeed glad that it was her province his family had come to call home.

So he was at his most formal as he dropped to one knee in front of her. “My Lady,” he said, bowing his head.

“Master Dare,” she said solemnly as she gestured for him to rise, all regal authority. “You must have urgent news to return to camp.”

“I do, my Lady,” he said as he regained his feet. “I've learned important details of the monster horde, including their leadership.” At his words Marigold hurried forward to give Marona her notes. “As well, I regret to inform you that the horde has increased its pace, leaving the slower monsters to follow behind and approaching with all haste. I fear my scouting may have stirred them to action."

The baroness grimaced. "So we'll have to meet them on the field sooner, but face fewer enemies. A mixed blessing." She turned, motioning curtly towards the nearby war tent. "Come, fill us in on everything you've learned about our enemy. We need to plan our next move."

Chapter Two
Camp

Dare, Ilin, and Marigold trailed in after the noblewoman and her officers. The war tent was dominated by a table covered by a large map of the province, which had since been covered by a smaller and far more detailed map of the specific area they were in.

A dozen chairs surrounded the table, enough for them all to sit. Although the gnome maid took a position behind her mistress, ready to serve her needs.

Dare quickly filled the group in on his findings over the last week, and particularly the day's events. The news of the high level Cursed Orcs leading the horde, and their party rated Warchief, caused a stir of unease among the assembled men and women.

"Can we even meet such a force?" an older man Dare's Eye identified as a level 36 Priest asked anxiously. Dare vaguely recognized the healer from Lord Zor's raid, the man who'd taken over leading the support when Lady Ennara perished to the Magma Tunneler's fires.

"That's what we're here to determine, right Master Jurrin?" Helima, Captain of Terana's Guard, replied in a determined voice. She was a Level 30 Warrior, in her late 30s and weathered from a harsh life, but still lovely and with appealing curves only highlighted by her muscular figure.

Jurrin shook his head dourly. "The Cursed Orcs alone could wipe us out, even without the rest of their horde."

Marona's expression tightened at the pessimistic words, but rather than answering she looked to Dare for his opinion, both as the scout bringing the information and as one of the highest level adventurers in her camp.

He took his time considering the question, as he had since

scouting the horde. Based on his answer she might choose between fighting or fleeing. All the people in this camp might die based on his words, or Terana would burn as its people left their homes and most of their belongings they couldn't carry on their backs to the monsters.

It was a serious responsibility. "Ilin and I managed to fight enemies up to Level 38 when we were clearing spawn points ahead of the horde," he said slowly. "But those were one or two at a time, not all at once. I'd have to know what high level adventurers we have in camp, their levels and classes, before I could tell you for sure."

The baroness glanced to the aging Priest. "Dare, allow me to formally introduce you to Master Jurrin, the raid party leader for our eradication force . . . the highest level fighters we have." She looked at the older man expectantly.

Jurrin frowned at him, obviously not impressed. "Your pardon, my Lady, but if he's given his information is his judgment any more valuable than mine?"

"We'll only know once we hear it," she said placidly. "Especially since you yourself seemed unsure of our chances."

The Priest flushed, looking even more irritated. Although he turned his irritation on Dare, not his baroness as he answered, voice stiff. "Along with you and your companion, a Hunter and a Monk I've been informed, we have myself as a Level 36 Priest, Captain Helima of course as a Level 30 Warrior, a Level 34 Fighter, a Level 32 earth Mage, a Level 29 Invigorator, a Level 31 Quickblade, an unspecified Level 35 melee fighter-"

"Sorry," Dare interrupted, frowning. "Unspecified?"

The Priest scowled at him. "As in he did not specify his class."

Marona cleared her throat. "That is generally the practice of those who pick classes considered either cowardly or more often selected by criminals. Such as Stealth classes." She paused. "Although some simply choose not to divulge their class, since they believe it puts them at a disadvantage."

"Or makes them look a fool or a rustic," Jurrin said with a sneer, a not so subtle dig at Dare's own choice of class as a Hunter.

Which honestly he still didn't see; Hunters might not have the ability to hit multiple targets with their attacks like Archers, or better range, accuracy, and armor penetration like Marksmen. But in return they got better mobility and survivability, which any rational person should value much higher.

After all, that had pretty much been his reasoning when he'd chosen Fleetfoot out of the three broken advantages Sia had offered him before sending him to Collisa, and he not only didn't regret the extra 34% speed, he still considered it stupidly overpowered compared to the other options he'd been given.

Besides, being a Hunter hadn't stopped him from topping the damage charts in Lord Zor's raid when they'd hunted the Magma Tunneler. Hunters could do the same single target damage as the others under most circumstances.

The baroness cleared her throat again, more sternly this time. "You were listing our available high level fighters, Master Jurrin."

"Ah, yes." The man had the grace to look a bit chagrined. "Finally we have a Level 28 Druid and a Level 33 Summoner."

Dare rubbed his chin thoughtfully. So a raid party of 11, which was better than he'd expected, honestly. Although the levels were lower than he'd like.

At least the weakest people were healers and support, who could get away with being a bit lower level than the rest of the party since level had almost no impact on them, aside from their hit points and the strength of their support spells.

Although if Helima hoped to tank monsters 8 levels higher than hers, even as an off tank, she was in for some trouble.

"So if I've got the classes correct, that gives us a main defender in the Fighter, an auxiliary defender in Captain Helima, three healers and support in you, the Druid, and the Invigorator, three melee damage dealers, and three ranged damage dealers."

Ilin cleared his throat. "Actually, while Summoners control their constructs or familiars from a distance, most of their pets fight from melee range. Since without their pets they're basically limited to defensive magic for themselves, many raid leaders classify them as melee damage dealers."

"Which is pointless since this isn't a raid, it's a monster horde," Jurrin snapped. "The monsters won't follow normal patterns so it'll be more like a battle between intelligent creatures."

"In some ways," the Monk said blandly, turning his placid attention on the Priest. "But once the battle is joined they'll charge us head on and use their abilities like any monster would, aside from the Warchief and any he directly gives orders to."

"Not to mention that raids are organized under basic logical principles," Helima added in a mild tone. "Defenders in front, melee damage on the flanks, ranged damage as far back as possible, and healers and support at the very back."

"Except if we're meant to hunt the highest level monsters in the horde, we'll probably have to carve our way through the weaker enemies to reach them," the Priest snapped irritably. "We can't have such a stratified formation in the middle of a battlefield."

An uncomfortable silence fell. "He's got a point," Dare said. "The melee damage would probably want to defend our own flanks instead. Or our Mage could raise walls of earth around us to give us a straight shot at our target." He wondered if the earth Mage in question was his friend Morwal's master Gerar, back in Terana in its time of need.

Jurrin slammed the table with his palm. "My Lady," he said tightly. "The scout has given his report. Perhaps it would be best if he was dismissed so we may plan this battle?"

What was this guy's problem?

Was it Dare's apparent youth he found objectionable, since Sia had given him the body of an 18 year old? Maybe his class choice? Or even that the man knew Dare was Marona's lover and thought he was benefiting from nepotism, rather than being here by his own merits.

Marona raised an eyebrow. "Were his ideas poor ones?"

"His very presence is an offense!" the Priest growled. "I say nothing of his status in your household, but he has no status in the Adventurers Guilds, no achievements of note to his name, is relatively unknown, and is barely more than a mere boy!"

He stood to loom over Dare, face dark with rage. "Tell me, lad, how do you manage to get to Level 33 while still a teenager? Three levels below mine, a place I've spent over 30 years earning. I've been leveling almost twice as long as you've been alive!"

He waved an accusing finger in Dare's face. "You would've had to have started as a child of 12 years and been dragged along through leveling by adults actually doing the work. And more than a few, all working in concert for your benefit. You're most likely a noble's brat being fed levels so daddy can have a hero to brag about."

"Master Jurrin," Marona said quietly but firmly.

"My apologies, my Lady, but I *must* speak!" he snapped. "For the sake of Orin, my old friend. Your paramour is a pampered child who's never had to achieve anything through his own merit, and now he pretends to know war and wants a seat he hasn't earned at this table? Giving advice where lives are at stake?"

He pointed at Dare again. "Go to your mistress's bed and wait her pleasure, boy! That's why you're even in this tent at all."

"That is *enough*," the baroness said in a soft but commanding tone, smoothly rising to her feet. "Old friend, it is not Dare alone you insult now. Excuse yourself until you have your temper, and more importantly your tongue, back under your control."

She turned to Dare. "I'd ask you to excuse yourself as well. And you, Master Ilin." She inclined her head. "Thank you for your brave service."

Jurrin looked as if he would protest, but Dare immediately stood and bowed low. "My Lady." Ilin joined his bow, and together they left the tent.

The Priest stormed through the entry flaps a few moments later, shot them both a withering glare, then strode away between the tents to duck into one of the nicer ones.

"Envy is an ugly thing," the Monk said mildly, looking after him.

Dare shrugged. "At least he's not trying to rob me or kill me outright. As long as he doesn't insult Lady Marona again, I have no quarrel with him. I'll either prove my worth to him or he'll remain a blind fool."

He glanced back at the tent. "Besides, he's Marona's friend, and obviously a close one she's had for many years. If they have an issue it's better for them to deal with it, unless she asks me to step in."

Ilin chuckled. "Unusually reasonable. I suppose the truly exceptional rarely feel the need to prove themselves to their detractors."

It probably helped that even if Dare looked like a teenager, he'd been 27 when he died on Earth. Old enough to have calmed down from his wilder youth, when someone like Jurrin getting in his face would've made him flare up and push back just as hard, saying and doing unwise things.

Too bad that in spite of the Priest's age, he hadn't learned his own lesson about being the adult in that sort of situation. And he'd embarrassed Marona because of it.

Dare shrugged again. "I spent enough time in my younger years arguing with irrational idiots to know that there are more productive things to do with my time. There's a saying where I'm from . . . don't feed the troll."

His friend paused, then leaned closer and lowered his voice. "On Earth?"

Dare blinked. It hadn't been too long ago that he'd revealed to his fiancees, as well as Ilin and Amalisa, of his true origins. He was going to need to get used to talking about Earth with people besides Ireni and Sia.

Although it was a nice thing to get used to, being able to share that part of himself with the people he cared about. "Yes.

Specifically the internet."

Ilin gave him an odd look. "I thought there were no trolls on your world."

Dare laughed at that. "They take a different form, and are usually more a nuisance than a threat. The feed on attention of any kind, even the most vitriolic, and wither and vanish when ignored."

"Ah, don't feed the troll." His friend chuckled, then sobered. "Although Jurrin seems more a jealous man looking out for his friend, albeit in misguided ways, than a person such as you describe."

"Right." Dare sighed and turned away from the tent. "Let's go find Rek and see how the goblins are doing."

* * * * *

Rek and his warband seemed in good condition and even better spirits.

Several of them had gained levels, while all of them handled their weapons better and moved in more disciplined formations. They'd apparently been treated well enough by the rest of the army, at least considering the usual treatment goblins could enjoy from other races, and they had no complaints.

Dare described what he'd seen of the monster horde to the young chieftain, and they briefly discussed strategy and the battle likely soon to come. He also listened to the hobgoblin's concerns and what the goblins needed in the way of supplies and equipment.

Some of that Dare could get himself with his hunting and leatherworking. Although it turned out he didn't have time right then, because Marigold came running to tell him that Lady Marona wanted to see him in her war tent.

Time to go sort things out. He hoped.

A few of the baroness's maids, including Belinda, were waiting outside, along with a handful of runners. But while the beautiful dragon girl gave him an inviting smile that promised future excitement, she ushered him right past the others and through the entry flaps without a word.

Marona was there waiting for him, but Dare's happy smile faltered and he did his best not to tense when he saw Jurrin standing off to one side, arms crossed. For his part the older man glowered but said nothing.

“Master Dare,” Marona said formally, although her eyes were warm and apologetic. “Master Jurrin would like your assurance that you'll follow his commands during this battle.”

Okay, no hint of apology from the Priest; Dare was expected to be the bigger man here.

Fine, if his lover asked it of him. Besides, it was just smart to follow the leader so they all lived through this, even if he didn't like the guy.

He inclined his head at Jurrin. “I give you my word, as long as you don't give any dishonorable orders.”

The man snorted. “That's a given.” There was an uncomfortable pause, then Marona pointedly nudged her friend and he cleared his throat and continued. “I'll, ah, make best use of your abilities in this battle, for the sake of Terana. Our personal feelings need have no bearing.”

That was probably as good as Dare was going to get. “All right. What's the plan?”

The Priest grimaced. “We'll gather together the raid and prepare.”

“That's right,” the baroness said gravely. “We get the battlefield ready this evening, get a good night's sleep, and in the morning the monsters will be upon us.” She looked off in the direction of the monster horde with an expression of fierce determination. “We'll face them then and destroy them.”

Dare couldn't help but grin. “We will, my Lady.”

Text appeared in front of him. “Quest accepted: Battle for Terana. Under the leadership of Baroness Marona Arral, assist in the destruction of the monster horde. Rewards vary based on contribution.”

His noble lover wouldn't have seen his personal notification, or possibly even realized she'd issued a quest; as Sia had explained it, quests were automatically issued by the system for important or novel tasks, or occasionally even mundane ones.

Whatever reward the issuer offered was usually listed as a quest reward as well, but almost always the only reward the system added to the quest was an experience bonus. Although some truly heroic quests were publicly acknowledged through the world system, and there were achievements for completing enough quests of various sorts.

Anyone could theoretically issue one, although it was more likely the world system would assign a quest to tasks given by important people like the leaders of communities, nobles, heroes, notables, and advocates of deities.

In fact, it was possible Dare himself had issued quests before. Although Sia had only laughed when he'd asked her.

Thus far he'd accepted every quest he'd been offered, since they'd all basically represented a chance for extra experience. If quests could have downsides, aside from sometimes needing to go a bit out of your way to complete them, he hadn't seen one yet.

Marona inclined her head at his words and turned to Jurrin. "I'll excuse you to your duties, my friend."

The man hesitated, obviously not wanting to be excused and giving Dare a suspicious glare. But finally with a stiff nod he turned and swept out of the tent.

The moment he was gone Marona stepped forward into Dare's arms, pressing her soft body against his as she stood on tiptoes to press her lips to his. "I'm sorry about that, my paramour," she murmured, stroking his back as she looked up at him with her lovely dark eyes. "To say Jurrin was not acting himself is a vast understatement . . . I have never seen him behave that way."

Dare tenderly ran his hands through her soft dark hair, streaked with strands of silver. "He was looking out for your welfare."

She sniffed. "I'm not in need of that sort of looking after." She kissed her way up his neck to claim his lips again, as soft and sweet as she'd been stiff and formal around others. "Thank you for being so courteous, even so."

"He's your close friend, and I trust your judgment." He let the matter drop and rested a hand on her tummy. "How are you two holding up?"

His lover grimaced. "Aside from the fact that a ravening horde of monsters is descending on my camp, and we're all that stands between it and my town?" She slumped against him so he was supporting most of her weight. "I'm exhausted," she admitted frankly. "And wound up like a spring and being pulled in a thousand directions at once by my duties."

Dare held her gently. "Can I come to you tonight?" he asked. "I give great massages . . . back, shoulders, feet, anywhere you're tense. And I think we'll both sleep better cuddling."

"Oh gods yes, please do." She sighed and pulled away, with effort restoring her composed, noble bearing. "Thank you, Dare. I'm glad you're back."

"So am I." He gently cupped the back of her neck and gave her one last kiss. "What can I help you with?"

Marona smiled grimly. "Kill the damn monsters threatening my town." With a rueful smile she stepped back to the table to look down at the map. "And give your goblins a refresher on mixed unit tactics . . . we've been trying, but military strategy for them seems to be to hide behind a rock and shoot arrows at the enemy, or charge in waving a club."

Dare chuckled. "I will. Rek's smart, even if he didn't have the benefit of a formal education."

She nodded, stepping past him to pull back a tent flap. "Tonight, then."

As he left the tent the maids and runners waiting outside streamed in, along with a couple of the officers from the earlier meeting, apparently back with urgent issues.

Not far away Ilin, Jurrin, and Helima stood with several other men and women, the party the Priest had selected to take care of the most powerful monsters in the horde. The Monk was introducing himself to the others, in his usual quiet way making friends.

Although from the looks of things a few already knew him, probably from his charitable work in Terana and his tireless efforts to get an orphanage built in the town.

Before Dare could join the group Jurrin pulled him aside and invited him to the raid party. He had to admit he hesitated a bit before accepting, since doing so would give the man so much of his personal information.

But he had nothing to hide, and Marona trusted the Priest for a reason. So he joined the raid, taking in the information that popped up about the ten other people in it. Limited, for a party member rather than the leader, but he got their class and their general reputation in previous parties they'd been in.

Including red flags like abandoning or betraying their party, although thankfully none of the people here had anything like that. Knowing their reputation was useful, but Adventurer's Eye gave him more, and in much greater detail.

He also noticed Jurrin's "unspecified class" wasn't a member of the raid, which likely didn't please the Priest. Dare had a feeling he would be even less pleased if he learned the Level 35 was a Darkblade, an obvious assassin class with abilities like Stealth, Poison Edge, and Garrote.

It was hard to think of a scenario in which the man had chosen a class so suited to preying on others and wasn't a criminal of some sort. But it was possible, Dare had no knowledge of any crimes the Darkblade might've committed, and more importantly they needed his help in the coming fight.

Still, he'd warn Marona about the man's class.

"Hmm," Jurrin murmured, obviously looking over Dare's information. "Rather mundane background, I must say. Not at all what I expected. Standard gear, perhaps slightly on the fine side. Humble considering your supposed station. And your choice of class

. . ." He shook his head. "You must have some quality that impressed the Baroness. Forgive me if I don't see it . . . unless she was charmed by your appearance itself."

"You'd be a fool to believe Lady Marona so vain," Dare said a touch coolly.

Jurrin flushed. "I do not," he said, voice stiff. "Which is why I will work with a relative unknown, whose only previous experience I've personally seen was being kicked out of the raid group of a prestigious man."

Dare angrily opened his mouth, but before he could respond the Priest held up his hands. "I'm aware of the circumstances, or at least what I saw and heard from others. You may not remember but I was there in that raid with the other healers and support, and even in the same party with your redheaded lover."

Jurrin's eyes narrowed as if in memory of the event. "And for what it's worth, I can applaud you on behalf of my Priestess sister . . . don't fuck with healers."

The words came as a surprise considering the man's hostility; a sign he was warming up to Dare? Or more likely echoing a sentiment that Dare himself shared, gained from his extensive experience in multiplayer RPGs back on Earth.

Tanks were the big swinging dicks of a group, sure. The proud few whose role was vital in a party or raid, bravely facing off against terrible monsters who would kill their companions in a couple hits. Piss off a tank and you were out, simple as that, because everyone knew it was you or the tank and they didn't want to lose the tank.

DPS, on the other hand, were generally agreed to be a dime a dozen. If you didn't make the cut there was a line of other damage dealers waiting to fill your spot. Or if you looked at a raid or party leader the wrong way, or drew the ire of the tank, you could be replaced in a heartbeat.

Healers, though, were the unsung heroes of the fight. The ones who went into battle with very little defenses and waged their own quiet fight to keep their companions alive.

Ie, they held your life in their hands. And while most would never consider letting someone die on their watch, even someone they disliked, that was something you'd be wise to remember. They were deserving of respect and weren't nearly as helpless as they seemed, even when they were often defenseless.

If for no other reason than because when push came to shove, their companions would rush to defend them. Even DPS would put themselves in front of a monster to protect their healer. And while healers usually didn't toss around their influence like tanks did, in an argument between the two it was a tossup who the group would support.

"Don't fuck with healers," Dare agreed.

With a last appraising look the Priest turned and led the way back to the party, where he introduced Dare and then introduced the others to him in turn. To be honest the names came so quick that he had a feeling he'd be calling everyone by their class in his head, at least until he could hear the names a few more times and get them cemented.

"I've never met a Monk before," the Invigorator, a woman in her late 20s, said, twirling her hair in her fingers as she looked Ilin over with open curiosity. "Aren't they really hard to master?"

"Indeed, ma'am," the Monk said with a solemn bow. "It takes extensive training of the body, mind, and soul. A lifetime of dedication and discipline, often using techniques passed down through generations by a skilled master." He bowed politely to Jurrin. "Now, if we're done introducing ourselves?"

"I believe so." The Priest inspected the Monk with a frown. "Since you're one of our lowest level melee classes, and by far the most lightly armored, I have to ask . . . are you fit to stand against enemies up to 8 levels higher than you?"

"For a brief time, if I'm willing to open my Fifth Lock," Ilin replied. "You will have to leave me behind if I do too much damage to my own body. Healing will only do so much, I'm afraid."

"That's hardcore," the Invigorator said, twirling her hair a bit faster and also biting her lip; Dare had a feeling she might be barking up the wrong tree. "You'd be willing to break yourself like that?"

"For a good cause, ma'am, without hesitation."

"Don't question a Monk about their willingness to make sacrifices, Estellis," the Fighter said with a laugh. "I've heard they swear not to drink or have sex." He shook his head in disbelief. "I'm not sure I could do something like that, even in exchange for a powerful class."

"I'll trust your judgment on that, my friend," Ilin said blandly.

Estellis looked disappointed. "You swear not to have sex?"

"Indeed." The Monk looked serene, but Dare knew him well enough to spot an equal mixture of amusement and wistfulness. "A vow of celibacy. Keeping the body and mind focused."

"I can live without that kind of focus," the Fighter said, clapping Ilin on the shoulder.

Jurrin cleared his throat. "Friends, tomorrow we battle a monster horde, and I'm confident we face a fight like nothing any of us have ever encountered before. Perhaps we should prepare?"

The group quickly quieted and grew solemn as they followed the Priest out of the camp, around laborers frantically digging trenches and earthworks as well as creating stakes and wooden barricades.

Hopefully the fortifications would make a difference in tomorrow's battle; the world system tended to respond poorly to trying to cheese monster fights by attacking them from a spot where they couldn't reach you, or using terrain to funnel them together and limit their movement.

But if the rules for monster hordes were different, then Dare could trust that Marona and her officers were right in believing that the rules for engaging them would also be different.

For the rest of the evening he, Ilin, and the rest of the raid practiced working together, with Jurrin calling out threats while the party shifted formation. They even had the healers and support cast their buffs, barrier spells, and heal where damage was declared.

Dare was gratified when the raid leader even asked the earth Mage, who was in fact Morwal's master Gerar, to practice swiftly raising walls of dirt around and behind them, covering their dash towards their targets at the center of the horde.

Although the Priest didn't give him credit for the idea, assuming he hadn't thought of it himself before Dare suggested it.

The training was similar to what he'd done with Zor's raid, except with far more consideration for the chaos of battle and unexpected problems. Dare quickly found that he ran out of arrows faster than expected, unfortunately without a camp follower like Felicia there to toss him more.

He didn't need Jurrin to tell him he'd need to bring more full quivers with him tomorrow, even if they made movement more cumbersome. Although at least he had his belt that reduced carry weight by 20 pounds.

Still, the Priest seemed satisfied enough by Dare's ability to loose arrows quickly and on target, as well as responding almost instantly to changing situations and new orders.

They kept training until full dark, at which point Jurrin called them all together for a few final words. "Tomorrow we save our home, or die in the trying. Make whatever preparations you deem necessary, then get a full night's sleep. Drink if you feel the need, but not overmuch."

As the raid dispersed Helima sought Dare out. "As I recall you still owe me a few drinks," she said lightly, putting a hand on his arm. "And I don't know about you, but I could use some relaxing before whatever comes tomorrow." She gave him a wide smile. "I didn't bring my manacles, unfortunately, but there's always rope."

He was tempted, no question. But he regretfully shook his head. "You know I want to, Helima. And I've put you off far more often than you deserve. But I promised Lady Marona I'd attend her tonight."

The tough guardswoman's eyes softened. "Then I'm more than

happy to be put off yet again. Offer whatever rest and comfort you can to our Lady, she works twice as hard as any of us."

Moving with surprising speed in spite of her heavy plate armor, she caught him and pulled him in for a fierce kiss, promising future passion. "But you'd better show me your full skills as a legendary lover to make it up to me," she said with a teasing smile as she pushed him in the direction of Marona's tent, hard enough to send him stumbling a few steps. "And we *will* be using the manacles."

Grinning like an idiot at the kiss and the prospect of what the future might hold, Dare made his way to the goblin portion of camp and briefly talked with Rek about tactics for the next day's battle. The hobgoblin understandably wanted reassurances that his people wouldn't just be used as front line throwaways, as goblins often were, and Dare gave his word that they'd be treated like any other fighters.

He intended to press the issue with Marona and the various officers with goblin fighters in their parties, too.

Finally, he washed himself, changed into clean clothes, and made his way to Marona's sleeping tent. She wasn't there, however, and his second guess proved correct that she'd be in the war tent, still working herself to exhaustion.

Miss Garena was there as well, and Dare corralled her. "Can you guys handle the rest if I take Marona to bed?" he murmured.

She looked surprisingly relieved at the suggestion. "Please do." Then her normally stern expression became even more so. "As long as you plan to help her rest, not tire her out further?"

"I will," he promised, ducking into the tent.

He found the baroness up to her elbows in reports, bags under her eyes as she listened to Belinda read her a list of supplies. He came up behind the draconid maid and hooked an arm around her slender waist, guiding her towards the entry flaps.

"Time for the Mistress to call it a night," he told her firmly.

Both women looked at Dare with wide eyes as he ushered Belinda outside, then returned for Marona, who arched an eyebrow at him. “You're ordering my maids around, now?”

“Only when it's important.” He ducked down to scoop his lover out of her chair in a princess carry, making for the entry flaps.

He half expected her to protest or at least tell him to put her down, but she simply looped her arms around his neck and rested her head on his shoulder with a soft sigh.

As he stepped outside he noticed Miss Garena looking at him with eyebrows raised in mild surprise, and the other maids whispering and giggling. He ignored them as he made for his lady's tent.

Once there he ignored Marona's mild protests that she could do it herself and undressed her, then bathed her with a cloth, soap, and a bucket of warm water thoughtfully provided by the maids. After that he dried her off with a towel, then laid her down on her stomach atop her surprisingly comfortable camp pallet and began kneading her shoulders until he felt the tension ease from them.

Dare moved on to her back, then her glutes, down her thighs and calves, and from there moved to her arms. Then he turned her onto her back and repeated the process in reverse, so focused on helping her relax that he didn't dwell on the view of her gorgeous small breasts, flat tummy, and smooth shaved mound. Finally he massaged her hands, then her feet.

The entire time she moaned softly in contented appreciation, putty in his hands as he did his best to work the tension out of her tightly wound body. By the time he finished the beautiful noblewoman was relaxed and peaceful, eyes drooping.

He gently gathered her up into a sitting position, playfully ignoring her murmured noises of embarrassment as he fed her the hot meal the maids had also diligently provided.

“I don't know whether to feel like a baby or an invalid,” she said with an adorable pout as he brought the spoon to her lips.

“Feel like a beautiful and very exceptional woman who deserves to be pampered after a hard day,” he said, kissing her soft shoulder.

Marona made a contented noise and cuddled against him as she chewed. When she finally swallowed she looked up at him, dark eyes soft and warm and very, very sleepy. “Would you like to make love?” she murmured.

Dare smiled. “I would like that.” He stroked her soft cheek, noting her drooping eyelids. “But what I'd like even more is to sleep peacefully with you the whole night through.”

“Mmm, that *does* sound wonderful,” she mumbled around a huge yawn. “But are you sure? I could at least use my mouth . . . I've been wanting to do that with you, and anyway after you've been so good to me I want to be good to you, too.”

“You are. Always.” He set the plate aside and shifted to lie down with her, pulling the blanket up to cover them both. As he tenderly stroked her back she cuddled against him and closed her eyes, her breathing soon becoming deep and even in sleep.

He held her for a few minutes as he wound down from his own day, luxuriating in the feel of her soft body and happy he'd been able to do something to ease her burdens.

Finally, content in this peaceful moment rather than dwelling on the battle to come in the morning, he drifted off as well.

Chapter Three

Attack

Dare woke to find the bed cold and empty beside him. Which was a stark contrast to the heated voices outside.

"I'm just saying you need to consider the practicalities of this, my Lady," Jurrin said stiffly.

"How's this for a practicality?" Marona said, not sounding quite as composed as usual when in public. "He eased my burdens when I needed it most." Her voice hardened. "Which is more than I can say for some yesterday, with their childish antics."

"If you wish to speak of childish antics, what about being carried through half the camp like a blushing bride by a man almost young enough to be your grandson? Do you know what sort of rumors are flying now?"

There was a brittle silence for what felt like a very long time, until the Priest coughed uncomfortably. "I'm just saying."

"Perhaps you should say less and hear more," the baroness said, the words very precise and cold as frosted glass. "Yes, when I was so exhausted I could barely sit up straight he was kind enough to carry me to my tent. Any rumors that arose from it are the fruit of wagging tongues who have more important things to be worrying about, with the monster horde only hours away."

"Of course, my Lady," Jurrin grumbled, although he didn't sound particularly contrite. "In any case, I need to assemble my raid and Master Dare seems to be nowhere to be found. If you happen to see him, could you send him to where we trained yesterday?"

A few moments later Marona ducked into the tent, already fully dressed and wrapped in a warm fur cloak. She saw Dare's eyes open and sighed. "Sorry to wake you."

"Sorry to overhear your conversation," he replied with a rueful smile, sitting up.

She laughed. “Because you didn't want to eavesdrop, or because of what was said?”

“Yes.” He held out his arms, and she slipped out of her cloak and settled down to share a warm embrace and kiss.

“Mmm,” his lover mumbled against his lips. “I meant it, you know. The way you took care of me last night was wonderful, and lying in your arms was the best sleep I've had in a very long time. I needed that more than I realized.”

Dare stroked her back. “I'm glad I was able to ease your burdens.”

“Mmm.” She abruptly planted a hand on his chest, pushing him flat his back. In that position his morning wood stood up proudly beneath the blankets.

She looked at it and licked her lips, grinning. “I believe we were talking about something last night.”

He grinned back. “If it pleases my Lady.” He started to reach down and unlace his pants.

“Ah ah ah.” Marona pulled the blankets aside and caught his hands, pushing them away. “This gift I'm unwrapping myself.”

Dare was more than happy to lay back, hands behind his head, as his lover freed him from his pants and began stroking him with both hands. Her skin was soft and warm in the chill morning air, smooth as if she'd just put on lotion, and he was soon rock hard and straining his hips upward with pleasure under her gentle ministrations.

“Your pardon if I'm a bit clumsy,” she murmured as she lowered her head to press her soft lips to his tip, silver-frosted dark hair spilling over his hips and thighs. “It's been a while since I've done this.”

Then the baroness opened wide and took him into her mouth until his tip bumped the back of her throat.

“Marona!” he gasped, dropping a hand to her head to gently stroke her hair. “That feels incredible.”

She made a contented noise, further adding to the pleasure of her warm, wet mouth, her soft tongue playing over the underside of his glans. Then, with a soft gagging noise, she pushed her head farther down until his tip popped into her throat in a fresh surge of pleasure.

Dare felt her swallowing desperately to curb her gag reflex, and had to say that even if it had been a while for her, she definitely knew what she was doing; the baron had been a lucky man.

Which went without saying.

Marona looked up at him lovingly, dark eyes glistening with tears from the effort of taking him in even deeper, starting to hum again as her swallowing throat massaged his shaft. He could see her slender neck bulging from his girth, an incredibly erotic sight, and brought his other hand down to hold and caress her head with both.

She couldn't manage to get him all the way in and finally pulled herself off his cock with a gasp, wiping away saliva and mucus before diving in again. Her head began bobbing up and down his length, esophagus opening to him again and again as she hummed and swallowed and used her hands to maximize his pleasure.

The sight of the serene, elegant baroness between his legs, her big brown eyes red, face flushed, and saliva and mucus leaking from her mouth as she gagged on his cock, was one of the most erotic he'd ever seen. The pleasure finally overwhelmed him, hips beginning to jerk with his impending eruption.

"I'm coming, Marona!" he panted.

His lover made a pleased noise and pushed herself as far onto his cock as she could, hands firmly jerking his saliva-coated base as he shot his first spurt down her throat.

Dare saw her swallowing greedily as he emptied himself into her welcoming warmth, watching the visible bulge of his tip jerking with every jet he released. As the pleasure surged through him he came more than usual, filling her up, and was still coming when she pulled herself off him with a gasp, so his last shots covered her beautiful face.

Marona beamed up at him and licked her glistening lips. "That was delicious," she said with a low laugh. "Just the breakfast I needed."

He gathered her in his arms and kissed her softly. "I love you," he murmured, stroking her hair.

"And I love you." She rested her head on his shoulder contentedly for a moment, then with a sigh of regret sat up again and reached for a cloth to clean herself off. "And now we both have duties to attend to."

Dare felt his chest clench at the reminder, and with a solemn nod began to dress.

It was a bit luxurious to have a tent tall enough that he could stand, and he made full use of it as he put on his armor and checked his gear. He was surprised when Marona moved to help him, making small adjustments to his clothes and armor and smoothing his tousled hair.

"I've arranged for you to have as many arrows as you'll need," she said, intent on her work. "And if you want a horse to carry them, at least as far as where you must leave it behind, I've arranged for a well trained one that should stay calm in the face of monsters."

An entire horse loaded down with arrows seemed excessive, and he chuckled. "That's more than enough to kill every monster in the horde by myself."

His noble lover stepped back, looking up at him anxiously. "Anything to make sure you return to me, my love."

Surprised and deeply moved, he pulled her into his arms again. "I will," he said, kissing her head. "If I have to wade through an entire sea of Cursed Orc Warchiefs, I will."

"Good." Looking embarrassed by her moment of vulnerability, she pulled a thin, silken white scarf from where it had been concealed in her bodice, still warm from her skin, and tied it around his arm above the elbow. "Take this as a sign of my favor."

"Thank you, I'll treasure it." Dare pulled her into another embrace and a long, lingering kiss, then with regret ducked out of her tent and started briskly for the field where his party had trained last night.

Ilin was there, along with most of the others. Dare noticed the Darkblade chatting up the Druid, seemingly innocuous, but something about it made him uneasy. Like the man had been looking his way before he looked back.

"Heads up on our unspecified friend," he told the Monk in a low voice. "He's a Darkblade."

His friend grimaced. "Generally an unsavory sort, although unless we know he's committed a crime we can't do much but keep a wary eye out. Especially since we'll need his poisoned daggers in the fight to come." He jerked his head towards Jurrin. "Does he know?"

"Not yet, although I told Lady Marona." Dare made his way over to the Priest, who glowered at him. That didn't stop Dare from quietly sharing his findings about the Level 35 assassin class.

To his relief Jurrin believed him, although the man seemed suspicious about how Dare had come by the information. In any case he shared Ilin's view that they couldn't do much but be vigilant. And that they certainly needed all the help they could get.

The raid leader excused himself to address everyone. "All right, people!" he snapped. "We've trained, we've planned, now let's go over it one last time." He waved at the trenches, earthworks, and staggered rows of spikes and wooden barricades arrayed in the path of the oncoming monster horde.

"In less than two hours the horde will hit our defenses here, which will be manned by the Baroness's lower level forces. Ideally the monsters will be funneled into kill zones with our defenders in their mid and high 20s plugging the gaps, while the damage dealers hit them from behind and the sides and the healers and support try to keep everyone alive. We wish them the best, but we're going to leave them to it."

He turned and motioned curtly to a hill off to the right side of the battlefield, with a copse of trees growing around its northern side. "We're going to hide there and wait for the horde to engage the Baroness's defenses. Then we'll sweep in from the side and carve our way to the center of the horde with the help of our Mage's earth walls, to where the Cursed Orcs and their Warchief are waiting. It'll be our task to kill them, and any other high level monsters we come across, before they can reach our army and wreak havoc."

The Fighter raised his hand. "Question. If we're going to be in the center of the monsters drawing their ire anyway, why let them get close enough to risk the lowbies?"

The Darkblade snorted derisively. "Trust a defender to consider himself and everyone else invincible. We can't take on hundreds of monsters, mostly lower levels or not . . . even if they were all lower than Level 10, we'd face death by a thousand cuts."

"Not to mention we'll be hard pressed just to kill the party rated Level 38 Warchief, let alone all his nearly as high level Cursed Orcs," Estellis said. The Level 29 Invigorator looked pale at the prospect of going up against such powerful enemies, but determined as well.

"Right," Jurrin said firmly. "We'll kill any monsters that get in our way, and if the ranged classes can pick off any monsters above Level 20 that might pose a threat to our Lady's army on the way, so much the better. But our main focus, our *only* focus, is the Warchief and its Cursed Orc lieutenants. A lot of innocent people are going to die if we can't deal with them."

He looked around for questions, but there didn't seem to be any; they all knew what they needed to do.

They moved to the copse where they'd wait to spring their flanking attack, and for the next few hours they practiced signals, did a few mock charges, but mostly rested and prepared for what was to come.

The Priest and Invigorator both cast their buff spells, which was the main tool in the Invigorator class's arsenal, hence the name. She could cast a variety of buffs that were useful for any class, but only one on each person.

Still, the buff she gave Dare boosted his speed and agility, making him feel surprisingly powerful.

She also had a spell to regenerate health, although slowly enough that it probably wouldn't have much use outside of party and raid rated monsters, in dungeons, or to help wounded adventurers recover between battles. Which might make the difference in a protracted battle against the monster horde.

Estellis would be incredibly useful in any group, but aside from her few personal defense abilities she was mostly there to strengthen the rest of them. Which meant she could theoretically sit out of a fight entirely and still provide a useful contribution.

Commendably, she intended to accompany them anyway to make whatever difference she could.

The sun was halfway to noon when the horns of Marona's sentries began to blare out, warning that the horde had been spotted. The signals were shrill and frantic, especially when it became obvious that the monsters were rushing towards Terana's small army at full speed.

Dare clapped Ilin and Helima on the shoulder and moved to stand with the ranged and healers, weighed down by 160 arrows in eight quivers and expecting he'd need every one.

This was going to be like nothing he'd faced before on Earth or Collisa, and he could admit he was afraid. He just hoped he'd live through the battle to return to his family.

* * * * *

Hundreds of monsters flowed past the copse of trees towards the fortifications, showing no sign they were aware of the eleven people hidden within.

Although Dare and his companions, watching from their concealed positions, were certainly aware of them.

He was closer to the ravening horde now than he'd been even when scouting it. Thanks to his Eagle Eye's 10% bump to visual acuity, close enough to see the warts on the faces of the nearest imps as they fluttered past, around the legs of beast hybrids and humanoid beasts and undead and horrors spawned straight from nightmares.

And they were all headed right for Marona. Who was safe at the rear of an army and ready to flee to safety if absolutely necessary, but even so.

Dare's grip on his bow tightened in grim resolve; this stampeding mass of foulness and destruction threatened his lover and their unborn child. Threatened his fiancees and *their* unborn children, and baby Gelaa and seed Eloise, and the home they'd all created at Nirim Manor.

He'd use every arrow he had to kill these things, then switch to his spear until it broke, then his knife and even his fists if there was no other option.

The front of the horde drew near enough to the fortifications and its defenders to be in range of the longest ranged classes, the Marksmen and air Mages and a few others. Physical and magical projectiles flew out from behind the earthworks to slam into the monsters, injuring some and even killing a few of the lowest level ones.

Closer, and more spellcasters and archers joined the barrage, thinning the monster ranks. But slowly, not enough to make a dent on the seething horde.

"Now!" Jurrin called, just loud enough for the party members to hear, and they all burst from the trees and sprinted forward.

Gerar was already casting his Earthen Walls, and he got the timing nearly perfect. Just as Ilin and the Fighter and Quickblade slammed into the nearest monsters, two dirt and rock barriers burst from the ground and roared into place, bisecting the horde for twenty yards in front of the raid party. They entered the narrow corridor as the earth Mage began casting the spell again, face strained with effort.

Dare had no need to waste any arrows on the weaklings he and his companions were tearing through. The melee fighters were more than capable of clearing the way to the Cursed Orcs, and those in the raid who had area of effect attacks were better suited for it anyway.

Instead, in the brief time he had before he got in range of their main targets targets he raced up the southernmost wall and ran along the top of it, focusing on downing the higher level monsters leading the packs going for the rest of Marona's army. They mostly fell with one arrow anyway, and with them dead the horde became far less organized, and in some places their charge even faltered.

Of course, from up there he found himself the focus of ranged attacks by dozens of monsters, and even some friendly fire. He kept loosing arrows until the last moment, then leapt back down to run beside Gerar, who was wheezing as he finished casting the next pair of walls and immediately got to work on the third.

And hopefully last; they were nearing the center of the horde.

Behind him he heard chittering and screeching as monsters scaled the wall or simply punched through, taking up the pursuit. He turned to shoot down the faster ones before they could catch up, although none were really a threat.

Above the clamor of the monster horde he heard the clash of weapons and screams of pain and fear from voices that clearly weren't monsters. The sound spurred him on, thinking of the desperate, low level army behind the earthworks fighting for their lives.

Including Amalisa, and Rek and his warriors.

Bellows of challenge up ahead heralded the Cursed Orcs pushing their way between the earthen walls, clashing an assortment of crude weapons together over their heads. Helima and the Fighter moved ahead, shields ready to meet them, while the rest of the party spread out behind the two tanks, with Ilin moving around their flanks to keep the other monsters away from the more vulnerable healers, support, and ranged casters.

It was a delicate balance, staying close enough to watch each other's backs but far enough that the Warchief's area of effect attacks wouldn't catch them all. Dare ended up back on one of the walls, raining arrows down on the Cursed Orcs ahead. He got a good view of the two tanks getting overwhelmed by the monsters, the healers and support struggling to keep them up as they downed one of the pale monstrosities, only for another to take its place and keep up the pressure.

He kept moving to avoid monster attacks as he turned his full focus to downing the most dangerous enemies on the battlefield, satisfied to watch first one Cursed Orc then another fall to his arrows.

Then the world exploded.

Dare wasn't sure if it was Earthquake or Sundering Shockwave, but it blew up the battlefield around them. His Prey's Vigilance kept him from the worst of it, but he still found himself flying off the wall into the mob of monsters on the northern side, who immediately began swarming him.

Disoriented and shaken, he fought to his feet against the swarm of bodies. Thankfully he had a lot of help from Quill Shot; with the blows raining down on him, his 1% chance to instantly loose an arrow from his passive ability went off multiple times.

It was actually kind of broken against a swarm of lower level enemies.

Even though he felt the cumulative agony of dozens of weak attacks, death by a thousand cuts as the Darkblade had warned, with his hit points being whittled down at an alarming rate, he killed half a dozen monsters in the space of a few seconds.

That cleared enough space around Dare to finally find his feet and begin dodging the incoming attacks. He was tempted to let the hits keep coming so he could scythe through these monsters with Quill Shot, but the effect was too slow and sporadic.

And more importantly, his health was dropping quick and none of the healers or support seemed aware of his plight. He was covered by agonizing scratches, gouges, and burns, stinging bites on every exposed area of skin, and more than a few attacks that had gotten through his leather armor.

As he fought desperately he used Snap whenever he had a spare moment, his hand lifted overhead emitting a brief flash of moderately bright light to signal his location to the rest of the raid.

Unfortunately, while the attempt brought no aid it *did* bring more enemies, drawn by the odd light.

Just as Dare was starting to worry he heard a bellow, or more accurately a Warchief's Roar. The monsters around him abruptly backed away and began surging south towards Marona's army again, leaving a clear space around him as they streamed past.

He couldn't help but think the sudden reprieve wasn't a good thing, and sure enough he spotted the massive Warchief pushing through the press toward him, even if it meant flinging monsters aside. Easily nine feet tall and broad as a car, all piled muscles on the verge of bursting beneath sickly, veiny skin, it was the stuff of nightmares.

"Human!" the Cursed Orc roared in a thick, bestial voice, pointing its massive battleaxe at Dare as if it weighed nothing. "You think I did not Notice you?"

Fuck.

Thus far, being Noticed by Collisa's deities for basically figuring out how to turn a Healer ability into a frag grenade hadn't done much for him, aside from get him screwed by a Succubus. Although if it was going to cause monsters, or at least intelligent ones, start making a beeline for him then that would seriously suck.

Although it presented an opportunity, too.

The Warchief was by far the biggest threat on this battlefield. If Dare could get it to chase after him that would create an opening for the rest of the raid to kill the other Cursed Orcs, and begin hunting the rest of the horde after that.

And hey, maybe he could do some damage to the big bastard while he was at it. If he found an opportunity he could even try to kill it.

So he activated Cheetah's Dash and began running back towards the copse of trees at an angle, which allowed him to draw and loose arrows at the Warchief as he went.

His damage was pretty respectable, but against an enemy five levels above him it was significantly reduced. That, combined with the party rated monster's ridiculously large health bar, meant that each arrow felt like it did nothing.

Cumulatively, though, he could see the Warchief's health slowly dropping.

The Cursed Orc leader was no typical monster, though, and even if it seemed determined to hack him to pieces it wasn't going to just blindly chase him until he shot it full of arrows. Instead it roared orders to the monsters around it, sending the swiftest, those with abilities that slowed their targets, and of course the ranged ones all chasing after Dare.

Some of those monsters stood between him and the edge of the monster horde with the copse of trees beyond it, enemies he'd need to deal with if he wanted to get to clearer ground.

So he used Savage Claw, his only melee ability besides Hamstring, to swiftly sling his bow over his shoulder and bring out his spear in an attack that dropped a Level 14 bugbear. The spear was a better weapon for attacking enemies at close range while running at high speeds, and he practically lanced a few monsters as he passed them.

He misjudged the force of his blow on his fourth target, and as his spearhead pierced right through the neck of the diseased horse monstrosity he was attacking, killing it instantly, the weapon got stuck. He had a choice between either abandoning it or wasting valuable seconds yanking it free.

The debate was short-lived as the Warchief Bellowed behind him, knocking the monsters around him to the ground and Dare himself to his knees at the sheer force of the sound.

On instinct he used Roll and Shoot to throw himself forward, only for the ground to buck beneath him and send him flying farther than he'd expected.

He twisted in midair to see the Warchief slamming its axe into the ground with such force that it quaked for dozens of yards in all directions, making monsters squeal and flail and even causing them injury.

The massive Cursed Orc didn't seem to care about friendly fire, though, all its focus on Dare.

He landed clumsily, rolling and nearly losing his bow, and came to his feet to see the Warchief Leaping towards him, covering over ten yards in an inhuman display of power. He barely had time to throw himself to the side using all the speed of Fleetfoot and Cheetah's Dash as an axe as tall as his own body came smashing down where he'd been.

Not missing a beat, his enemy released its axe with one hand and backhanded him. Dare barely had time to turn aside and lift one shoulder before the blow caught him on the arm and back, sending him flying once again as his vision went black around the edges.

Well, this wasn't going well.

"Use your bones for toothpicks, human!" the Cursed Orc snarled somewhere back where he'd been as he slammed into the ground and rolled. "Make sausages of your guts!"

Fuck this.

Dare did a kip up and Pounced to a monster at the ability's maximum range of 10 yards, *away* from the Warchief. He didn't even bother to finish off the badger-like monstrosity as he sprinted at full speed to put some distance between himself and his enemy.

A glance over his shoulder confirmed that the Warchief was using Rush to pursue him. Thankfully between Dare's peak athleticism, his minor speed boost from Power Up's stat increases at Level 30, Cheetah's Dash, and most of all Fleetfoot, he was able to easily outpace the huge monster.

Behind him he felt the ground shudder and dirt and small debris pelted his back, maybe from Sundering Shockwave, but he was just out of range. The Warchief's furious roar confirmed the miss.

Rapid Shot came off cooldown and he spun, loosing arrows at his enemy as he ran sideways. He didn't want the Cursed Orc to give up on chasing him and return to the battle, at least not until he got some signal that the rest of Jurrin's raid had cleared the other major threats and were on their way to help him.

Assuming the old bastard deigned to come to his aid. Cynical, and probably unworthy to think of the cantankerous Priest. But better for Dare to assume he was on his own unless Ilin, Helima, or maybe Gerar came to help.

Although he kept his desperate speed he veered slightly to bring him closer to the monsters at the back of the horde, some of whom turned to try to engage him. They were mostly weak and could be a useful resource in the fight as he continued to run and gun, or at least run and bow.

Monster speed boost abilities usually had short durations and short cooldowns, which was good because Cheetah's Dash ran out just as the Warchief's Rush did. At which point the intelligent monster did something unusually clever and used Earthquake *behind* him, propelling his huge body through the air almost as far as a Leap would.

Shit shit shit. Bad enough the brute was stupidly powerful without it getting cute with its abilities.

Dare used Roll and Shoot to put some distance between them, loosing the arrow as soon as he came back to his feet. From nearly point-blank range, as it turned out, as the Cursed Orc somehow managed to be behind him, enormous axe again swinging down.

Prey's Vigilance saved him, twisting him sideways so the blow roared by close enough to brush his nose and toes. This time Dare was wise to the backhand and Pounced again, finding another monster at 10 yards from the horde he'd been sticking to the periphery of.

"Scurry and leap, you little shit!" the Warchief snarled. "You're not fast enough."

Dare tried to reassure himself that wasn't true, and if he needed to he *could* get away from the party rated monster. He was continuing to keep ahead of it and loose arrows when he could, and almost had it down to half health. In return so far his enemy had only given him a few bruises.

As if the universe was stepping in to punish him for his

optimism, his luck finally ran out soon after. Prey's Vigilance popped up only to be immediately wasted on a quill shot by a monster in the nearby horde, and even worse Dare's automatic dodge came right as the Warchief again Leaped at him, so he couldn't react in time to completely avoid the swinging battleaxe.

Fire burned across his hip as he stumbled away, feeling the hot wetness of blood flowing down his leg. It wasn't an official movement debuff but it *did* hinder him and cause a burning pain with every step. It also took a healthy chunk of his health and, obviously, applied a bleeding effect.

Godsdamnit, he'd just *known* an ability that automatically took over his actions was going to screw him over at some point. Usually the world system picked the ideal way for Prey's Vigilance to dodge the attack, or maybe he'd just assumed so since he'd never really tested it.

Out of desperation Dare dodged towards the Cursed Orc.

Against a normal monster it probably wouldn't have worked, but intelligence meant pattern recognition and his enemy fucked up by assuming he'd keep trying to dodge away like he had been. He still almost got a massive boot to the face as he rolled behind the huge monster, but somehow he came up with the Cursed Orc's back still to him.

With his spear gone he had to resort to his fallback knife, slashing it across his enemy's leg with Hamstring to slow it down by 25%. The Warchief roared, more in fury than pain, and before Dare could get to the other leg to Hamstring it as well that massive axe slammed down into the ground in Sundering Shockwave.

He found himself flying through the air again, although in this case it seemed like it might be a good thing since it carried him *away* from the monster trying to hack him into pieces. He was even able to twist in midair and land with some semblance of grace.

Aside from the searing pain from the wound on his hip, that is.

Cheetah's Dash was still minutes away from being off cooldown, but he used Roll and Shoot to get some more distance as well as loosing an arrow at his enemy. Then he turned and sprinted away again, keeping close to the horde and hoping against hope his defensive cooldowns would come off their timers before the orc . . .

Oh, right. Dare glanced back to see that the Warchief was chasing him using Rush, but had yet to use Leap. Pounce wouldn't work if you had a movement speed debuff, and it looked as if the same applied for the party rated monster's ability.

Better yet, it was slowed with Hamstring and was struggling to keep up even with Rush.

He took full advantage of his enemy's weakness, counting down the seconds until the Hamstring effect faded to run and shoot more arrows with Rapid Shot. He managed to whittle the Cursed Orc's health down to around 35% before the debuff ended, and was starting to feel optimism that he might do more than just survive.

He might actually kill this monster all by himself.

As Hamstring's effect fell off the Cursed Orc Dare braced himself to use a defensive cooldown for when the giant monster Leaped. But instead his wily enemy used Earthquake again to throw itself through the air, and as it approached the ground it threw back its head and Bellowed.

Dare stumbled, dazed. He knew the battleaxe was coming his way but had no time to stop it. Worse, he knew he could no longer rely on Prey's Vigilance to produce the best results for him.

And the Cursed Orc Warchief knew it too.

Dare automatically ducked beneath a surprisingly feather-light blow from the monstrous battleaxe, which immediately twisted back around for a swift second blow as he was struggling to recover. He knew he couldn't completely dodge it.

But he didn't have Fleetfoot for nothing.

Agonizing fire scored across his chest as the axe tore through his leather chestpiece and sliced a furrow across his ribs. But as it swung away Dare caught the haft just beneath the wickedly sharp blades with one hand and hung on for dear life. With the other he slung his bow and reached into the reinforced pocket on his belt.

The Warchief grunted in amusement as Dare was yanked off his feet, as easily as if he weighed nothing thanks to the giant monster's immense strength. His enemy swung the axe high, obviously planning to slam him into the ground beneath it, and for a moment he was over the brute's head.

Dare threw the object in his hand straight downwards and shouted, “Grow!”

His magical legendary chest expanded almost instantly to its full size, the force of Dare's most powerful baseball windup combined with gravity and the weight of about a hundred lead bars inside hitting the Warchief with the force of a speeding truck.

The monster didn't even have time to make a surprised noise as it was crushed under thousands of pounds moving at around 70 miles an hour. Dare wasn't sure if it would've one-shot the Level 38 party rated monster, but it sure as hell did 35% of its hit points worth of damage.

Not to mention mashing it to paste.

Physics was an unforgiving bitch.

Chapter Four

Spoils

Dare found himself flying through the air, twisting to try to cushion his fall. His efforts weren't helped by the text that appeared in front of him, distracting him and causing him to tumble clumsily when he hit the ground.

"CONGRATULATIONS!

"You have defeated the leader of a monster horde and averted a dire threat to Terana and to Bastion and perhaps all of Haraldar. May all sing your praises."

"Party rated horde boss Cursed Orc Warchief defeated. 80,000 bonus experience awarded. (Experience doubled for horde monster kill, and doubled again for defeating its leader.)"

"Completed 5/10 towards Achievement Protector of Bastion: Slay 10 party rated monsters in the region of Bastion."

"Trophies gained: ALERT, some trophies destroyed. Gained Monstrous Battleaxe. Loot body to acquire."

Almost on top of those alerts came a far larger and brighter one, along with a raucous notification noise that made him jump in surprise as he lay sprawled on the ground.

"**Global alert. For balancing purposes the legendary enchantment "Shrink" has been modified: Shrink's "Grow" function may no longer be activated in the case of enchanted item's imminent collision with a living target.**"

Motherfucker. Dare lay on the ground, hurting and broken, and laughed ruefully; the gods seemed determined to take away all the toys he thought up.

He wondered if imminent collision would apply to the crushing trap he'd created above Nirim Manor's gate. That wasn't really imminent since it didn't happen until *after* the chest grew and caused the tunnel's ceiling to collapse, crushing everything beneath it.

Although he was sure the moment he tried it the chest would be further nerfed.

Oh well, at least it would still work to operate the pump at Nirim Manor so they'd have running water. And he could break down doors or break through walls with it if he didn't mind damaging it; it had no durability stat, but he had to assume it could still break if he used it as a magical wrecking ball.

And of course he could always use it for its actual purpose, to carry loot.

Dare pushed painfully to his feet and staggered over to the dead Cursed Orc and the chest on top of it. “Shrink,” he mumbled, then picked it up and tucked it back into its special pocket. Heavy as it was full of lead bars at full size, it was meant to easily carry gold which was way heavier than lead, and when shrunk weighed just a few pounds.

He was just glad he'd agreed with Leilanna's insistence he bring the item with him, when he'd wanted them to keep it at home for their convenience pumping water and as a defensive measure in case Ollivan attacked.

He just hoped they wouldn't need it, because he sure as hell had.

Dare grimaced at the dead Warchief, or what was left of it. Honestly he could've thrown the chest right at the start and might've won the fight right then and there. But against an intelligent enemy he hadn't wanted to risk missing and having his trump card wasted, since the horde leader was definitely clever enough that it wouldn't have fallen for the same trick twice.

So he'd held out for the perfect opportunity. Most of the other times the Cursed Orc had gotten close enough to try throwing it, Dare had been fighting for his life and hadn't had a moment to react. Honestly it had been desperation and good luck as much as planning that had let his last ditch effort succeed as well as it had.

The Warchief could've just as easily shaken him off the axe

rather than trying to lift it overhead to crush him to the ground like that. And then what would he have done?

Oh well, it had turned out as well as he could've hoped. Aside from the fact that he was at 30% health with two bleed effects and a bunch of wounds.

Gritting his teeth against the pain, Dare held the gash across his chest with one hand and with the other reached out to loot the Cursed Orc Warchief. He got two notifications back to back.

"Alert: because you did full damage to this monster and received no healing or other aid from your raid during the fight, loot priority passes from raid leader to you. By loot rules it is yours to share as you wish, or not."

"ALERT, some items destroyed."

Fantastic.

Dare got 312 gold, 23 silver, 8 copper from the horde leader, as well as a Master quality item called a Home Ward, a dark wooden box about the size of his fist covered in elaborate gold ornamentation. He also got the Monstrous Battleaxe, which he definitely didn't relish lugging home.

That was it; whatever else had been on the boss, it was gone now. Served him right for getting cute cheesing world system mechanics, although on the plus side he was still alive to be annoyed about it.

He jumped again as another notification appeared in the center of his vision with a dire alert noise. "**You have gained Noticed 2**."

Fan-fucking-tastic. If demon chicks had been invading the kingdom to fuck him and monster horde leaders making a beeline for him across a battlefield, what was being even more Noticed going to do? He wasn't naive enough to believe it was a good thing to draw the attention of powerful beings.

Aside from Sia, that is. Dare loved her attention.

Speaking of which, he wondered what she thought about all this . . . he supposed he'd have to see when he got back to Nirim Manor, since she could only speak to him while dwelling within Ireni now.

In any case he'd be back with his family soon, as long as the rest of the battle was going well.

Which he should be getting back to, to help deal with the rest of the horde. Also he needed to find a healer, or at least bandage his wounds before he fainted from loss of blood.

But as the adrenaline of the fight faded and exhaustion and the pain of his injuries surged, he took a moment to just bask in the thrill of his accomplishment as he stared at the Warchief's crushed remains.

Dare had just killed a party rated monster five levels above him, all by himself.

It had taken forever, and he'd had to cheese an enchanted item to do it. Also he had no idea how the rest of the battle was going. But with the leader of the monster horde taken care of, the rest of them shoul-

Prey's Vigilance kicked in and the ability threw him to the side, twisting in time to see a dagger flash by his shoulder.

It was the Darkblade, his weapon true to his class's name with the oily black substance coating it: Poison.

The dagger flashed again and Dare threw himself backwards with Roll and Shoot, coming up and loosing an arrow at the assassin.

The man shifted to the side so it flew harmlessly past, using either evasion or a defensive ability of his own. "Coin flip to fail against Stealthed enemies, my ass," he growled, obviously referring to Prey's Vigilance's weakness against Stealth. Which thankfully hadn't happened here.

Without another word the nameless assassin surged forward, weapon low and ready.

He was fast, and his movements had an odd blur that made him hard to follow with the eye. But what he didn't have was Fleetfoot and Cheetah's Dash.

Dare sprinted away from the dangerous man, keeping a constant eye on him in case he tried to throw his dagger or any other poisoned weapon. The Darkblade growled a curse and took up the chase, surprisingly fast compared to most people Dare had seen, maybe even faster than Pella.

In other words, still not nearly fast enough. He could outpace the assassin even with his wounds.

Once he got far enough away he switched to a sideways run and activated Rapid Shot. "If you're here to rob me of the Warchief's loot, most of it was destroyed," he called as he unleashed his barrage of arrows in quick succession.

The assassin smirked as he blurred, avoiding all but one, which he parried with his dagger. "I'll loot you, certainly, after I've completed my contract."

Contract? Dare could only think of one person who'd send an assassin after him, assuming that little shit Braley down in Kovana hadn't suddenly grown some balls.

Ollivan.

Cold clarity washed away his haze of pain and blood loss, and he fit another arrow to the string. "So the knight sent you to kill me?"

His assailant smirked wider. "You think I would betray-"

Dare drew and loosed while the Darkblade was talking, and the man barely managed to twist away from the arrow. His smirk disappeared in a snarl. "You son of a bitch."

Dare wasn't about to be lectured on dirty tactics by a backstabber with a poisoned blade. As the Darkblade rushed forward again Dare prepared another arrow. It took some effort, but he was able to use Snap with the hand holding the bow as he drew and loosed.

The assassin flinched at the sudden light blazing right where he'd been focused on the arrow, and this time he failed to dodge in time. The arrow slammed into his hip, chunking off some of his hit points and spinning him around with a snarl of pain.

Dare loosed more arrows as the man struggled to recover, but while he managed to score another hit the assassin again almost dodged, and the arrow gouged a deep furrow in his side.

His assailant cursed and danced back, blade blurring to parry another arrow. Miraculously he managed to recover and dodge the next few arrows as he broke off the shaft buried in his hip. “Should've listened to my patron,” he hissed. “You're a dangerous bastard if you're not killed quickly.”

“Ollivan sent you, didn't he?” Dare demanded. He readied an arrow but paused to use it.

The Darkblade laughed. “Very unprofessional, telling the target who hired me. Besides, you weren't the only one he sent me after. They should be easier targets.” With another low laugh, the sound fading unsettlingly, the man blurred and vanished from sight in Stealth.

Dare's fiancees and children back at Nirim Manor.

With a sudden surge of terror he drew and loosed where the assassin had been, then cursed as the shaft passed through thin air. He loosed more arrows, trying to make a grid pattern around where the Darkblade could've gone as he fled.

The more coolheaded part of him warned him to stop, focus. Stealth was all well and good, but invisible people still made noise. Still left footprints or made a furrow through long grass like that on the plains around them.

And at the last extreme, if he couldn't find the bastard he could still outrun him to get to Nirim Manor first. After delivering a warning to Marona of the danger, in case the assassin went after her as well. He could convince her to come with him so he could keep her safe as they went to warn the others, or at least to ride to safety on her own.

Assuming he couldn't find the Darkblade. Who might be invisible but was also wounded and-

Blood! Another telltale to point Dare to his Stealthed enemy. He began searching the ground more intently for those sorts of clues, a skill he hadn't practiced much in the past. Which was a lack he cursed now when the lives of his loved ones depended on it.

The Darkblade obviously knew the weaknesses of Stealth, and

was taking care. But even the utmost care wasn't perfect when you were just a few steps away.

Dare spotted the grass only feet to one side of him crushed in the imprint of a footprint and desperately leapt away. Too slow; the air rippled and he saw the outline of an invisible dagger plunging towards his heart.

Prey's Vigilance was still on cooldown, as was Roll and Shoot, and even with all his speed he'd been too slow.

The man had told him he was leaving to make Dare lower his guard, and he'd fallen for it. He only had time to grieve his failure, and hope his loved ones at home would somehow be forewarned of the assassin and find a way to stop him.

Just before the dagger-shaped ripple pierced his armor another blur, not of Stealth but of pure speed, appeared and caught where the Darkblade's arm would be. The man's Stealth shattered as Ilin, veins bulging and skin flushed an unhealthy purple, whirled and flung the assassin twenty feet to slam into the trunk of a tree.

The Monk surged forward again, crossing the distance at speeds Dare would struggle to manage with Cheetah's Dash, and nowhere near that explosive acceleration. The Darkblade shakily tried to push to his hands and knees, but didn't even have time to push off the ground before Ilin did a flip kick that focused all of his momentum and power into his heel, driving it into the back of the man's neck.

Dare heard a sickening *snap* and the assassin went limp, paralyzed but obviously still alive.

Almost immediately afterwards Ilin dropped as well, the normally stoic Monk letting out a strangled grunt of pain.

Dare bolted to his friend, dropping to his knees beside him but keeping a wary eye on their enemy, in case he had some tricks even while paralyzed.

“Are you okay?” he asked, helping the Monk up into a sitting position.

Ilin gave him a strained smile, the blood on his teeth and frothing the corners of his mouth probably not a good sign.

“Opening the Fifth Lock takes its toll,” he wheezed. “Especially at this level and with my imperfect mental and physical control.”

Dare shook his head in amazement. “Looked pretty perfect from where I was standing. You fucked him up almost before I knew what was happening . . . I'm guessing you were able to see through his Stealth with your Third Eye?”

His friend chuckled, expression pained. “Would that I had already mastered the skill to use it in battle. I'm afraid I found him the same way you did . . . by the disturbances even an invisible man makes to the world around him.”

If Ilin had spotted that from any distance he had to be insanely observant. As in, even more than Dare had thought. “How's the battle going?” he asked, glancing back towards the horde. Or where they'd been . . . the few monsters in sight were milling around the earth Mage's walls, while the rest had probably continued on to attack Marona's fortifications.

The Monk spat blood and smiled wearily. “We eradicated the core of the horde, all the Cursed Orcs and the powerful monsters under them. Once I was sure the party's ranged and support were safe I left them to mop up while I came in search of you.” He grimaced and motioned to the man sprawled nearby. “None too soon, it seems . . . Ollivan's hireling?”

“Not sure who else it would be.”

Ilin grunted. “I'll be fine, go take care of him.”

Dare gently set his friend back down and stepped over to the assassin. Although he kept a wary distance, mindful that that one of the Darkblade's abilities was Last Gasp, which sounded a lot like some sort of break a false tooth and breathe poison gas at your enemy type of trick.

The paralyzed man glared up at him with hate filled eyes, breathing shallowly through gritted teeth; his smirks were nowhere to be seen now. “I may have failed this contract,” he spat, “but the Guild will succeed in the end. They always do . . . you and your whores are dead. Especially the ginger slut.”

Dare's vision briefly went red. But infuriating as the words were, they seemed like an obvious ploy to goad him into finishing the assassin off. Which he wasn't about to do just yet. “I think they'll lose interest when I kill your employer before they even know you've failed.”

And he *was* going to kill Ollivan. Whatever hope he'd had of a peaceful resolution, or more ideally a lawful one, had vanished with a poisoned blade at his back. Threatening his family.

He didn't care if he ended up in a dungeon for it, the knight had to die.

Although he'd do his best to not get caught; Gelaa and Eloise and all his other children shouldn't have to grow up without a father because of a monster like Ollivan.

The Darkblade wheezed, either laughing or struggling to breathe. Maybe both. “They'll know. The Guild knows instantly when one of theirs dies, wherever it happened in Bastion.”

“Then I guess we'll have to keep you alive.”

“Like this?” the man said, rolling his eyes down to his paralyzed body. “No thanks.” His jaw clenched, and he spat.

Dare was already several feet away in Roll and Shoot, the poisoned spit splattering harmlessly on the ground behind where he'd been. As he came to his feet he saw the nameless assassin convulsing in death throes as his poison took effect.

He cursed and stepped over to the man again, looking down as he went still, eyes staring sightless at the sky. He didn't mourn the Darkblade's death, only how much more he could've learned from him. And, if the assassin's claim was true, that it had sent a warning to this Guild of his.

“Well shit,” Ilin said with uncharacteristic grimness.

Dare swayed on his feet, sick with dread for his loved ones and weak from pain and blood loss. He cautiously approached the assassin again, wary of more nasty poison surprises, and began patting him down. He was searching for tattoos, sigils, hidden notes, anything that might give him clues about this Assassins Guild.

But to his frustration he found nothing suspicious at all. Which he supposed he shouldn't be surprised about since no assassin wanted to give away what they were.

To his disgust, he couldn't even find where the Darkblade hid the poison that coated his dagger.

Without a backwards glance at his assailant he limped over to the Monk, grunting with effort as he hauled the shorter but surprisingly compact man to his feet, half carrying him. "Come on, we both need a healer."

"No argument there, my friend," Ilin mumbled, struggling to help support his weight. He gave Dare a long look, dark eyes grim. "What are you going to do about this?"

Dare stared grimly northwest, in the direction of Redoubt. "Warn Marona, make sure the horde is fully dealt with. Then find Ollivan and kill him, and settle things with this Assassin's Guild. One way or another."

"Tall order." Ilin briefly gripped his shoulder, the gesture lacking his usual easy strength. "You don't have to ask, my friend . . . I'll get Marona and Amalisa and any others who might be in danger back to Nirim, and use my Third Eye to keep constant vigil against more assassins until you return or send word."

Dare felt some of his tension ease at that reassurance. "Thank you. More than words can express, thank you."

The Monk grimaced, jaw tight. "I just wish there were two of me, so I could aid you in this. You should have someone to watch your back."

Dare shook his head. "I need speed right now. I mean to go light, just my gear. I've never tried to travel long distances at the full speed I can manage, always held to a slower pace by having horses with me, or companions. But I think if I push to my limits and use Cheetah's Dash whenever it's up, I can reach Redoubt sometime tomorrow."

Ilin whistled. "I'd say that's impossible without powerful magical artifacts or spells, but I have no doubt you could." He suddenly perked up, looking ahead.

Dare followed his gaze and saw Jurrin and the rest of the raid approaching from around one of the earth Mage's walls. Although the Druid was nowhere to be seen, and he felt a brief pang as he wondered if she'd fallen in the battle.

The rest of their companions met them not far from where the Cursed Orc Warchief had fallen, and to Dare's relief the Priest immediately cast healing magic first on him, then on Ilin.

He was still exhausted and felt like shit, but at least he wasn't bleeding to death. As for his friend, the Monk couldn't be fully healed with magic from damage due to opening his Locks, and had to recover naturally from it.

As long as he didn't push himself so far over his limits the damage was permanent, which hopefully wasn't the case here.

Jurrin had checked the Cursed Orc Warchief as he cast his healing spells and now looked pissed at them. Although at least he had the grace to finish doing what he could for them before giving vent to his outrage. “What is the meaning of this?” he demanded, glaring at the dead party rated monster, then at the two of them. “You've already taken the loot?”

Dare shrugged. “It's mine, according to loot rules. I soloed the monster.”

Several members of the raid snorted or even openly laughed at that.

“It's true,” Ilin said, looking offended on his behalf. “He'd already slain the Warchief when I arrived.”

Jurrin's outrage only deepened. “What obvious rubbish. I don't know why your friend is willing to support your lies, lad, but our dead companion over there would likely tell a different tale. How dare you insult his memory by stealing his contribution to-”

Dare didn't have time for the man's stupid belligerence. “The only thing he contributed was a poisoned dagger meant for my back,” he snapped, striding over to the assassin's body and carefully picking up his black-coated weapon.

He tossed it at the Priest's feet. "He was a Darkblade, just like I warned you. By his own mouth sent to murder me and anyone associated with me." His voice hardened. "Such as our Lady."

Gasps rang out from the raid, and Jurrin stared at the dagger, face pale. He licked his lips. "You could've murdered him and pl-"

"Oh come off it, Priest," the Fighter growled. "That monster corpse is flat as a flapjack . . . whatever went down here was the stuff of epics. I'd hesitate to call it a great coincidence that the notification we received about a balance change to the ##### ###### came just after all the monsters in the horde suddenly became disorganized and leaderless."

Estellis nodded. "Besides, he wouldn't have been able to loot the monster if he'd had help from another party or raid member, even if he killed that member. That's not how loot rules work."

"The Darkb-I mean our unspecified class companion wasn't *in* the party!" the Priest snapped. "He wouldn't have been affected by loot rules."

"That doesn't change my point!" the Invigorator shot back. "And the fact that he wouldn't show you his class is because he was assassin who tried to kill Dare!" She waved at Dare and Ilin. "I think they've done a heroic thing, and protected the Baroness twice over."

Dare appreciated the support, but he'd already wasted enough time here. "We need to get to Lady Marona and tell her what's happened," he said curtly. "I won't claim any loot from the assassin, although I'd warn you to be cautious in searching him in case he had any poisoned surprises."

Without waiting for a response he started across the battlefield, still supporting Ilin with his shoulder. To his surprise Jurrin didn't try to call him back, him and the rest of the raid spreading out to inspect the dead Warchief and cautiously search the Darkblade.

"Speaking of loot," Ilin murmured as they walked towards the earthen walls, "what did that big brute drop?"

Dare shook his head dourly. "Some gold and a Master quality item. Unfortunately using the legendary chest to crush it destroyed some of the loot, as well as some of the trophies." He produced the Home Ward to show his friend.

"Balance and harmony," Ilin said, staring at the gilded box in awe. "Your luck continues to astound."

"I'm guessing it's good?" Dare asked, turning it in his hands. He hadn't taken the time to inspect it before and did so now, at which point he realized why the Monk was so amazed.

The Home Ward's description said: "Master quality item. Once bound to a location gain the ability Home Ward Bound: Once a day become ethereal and move yourself, a full pack, a mount, and a companion and their pack or up to 150 pounds of baggage, directly to bound location from up to 100 miles away. Cast time 10 minutes, travel speed 2 miles per minute."

He cursed in amazement. "Fast travel?"

"Of a sort. You become ethereal and immune to harm and travel directly to your destination in a straight line. Quite a fun experience, I'd imagine." The Monk clapped him on the back. "I'd wager with your speed you could manage a hundred miles in a few hours if you left your horse and pack behind and pushed to your limits, but with this you can go the distance in an hour and bring everything with you."

Dare turned the box in his hands, inspecting its elaborate ornamentation. "How rare is something like this?"

Ilin chuckled. "At this level? I haven't heard of one dropping. In the higher levels, 45 or so, you might see a similar item drop off 1 out of 200 party rated world monsters or dungeon bosses. Maybe 1 out of 20 raid rated monsters."

"So I'm guessing it's valuable?"

"To travel up to 100 miles in an hour, when for most it would take three to four days on foot and two or three days on horseback? Not to mention offering an escape if you can manage to barricade yourself from attack for 10 minutes." The Monk shook his head in disbelief. "You could ask 10,000 gold and it would sell immediately. Double that, and no doubt find a buyer in time."

Their conversation died as they rounded the earthen wall and came in view of the earthworks and trenches.

The defensive line where Marona's army had held back the horde looked like something straight out of a nightmare, with slain monsters and gore scattered everywhere. Although thankfully the slain on their side seemed far fewer, maybe fifteen at most.

Too many, but it could've gone much worse.

The mood among the army was weary but jubilant, the threat that had loomed over their heads for over a week dealt with. They could return home to their families, and had their combat pay and a share of the loot to show for it.

Many had a gained a level as well.

Amalisa wove her way through the impromptu celebration and met them just past the earthworks. At the sight of Ilin she rushed to support his other side, innocent features going ashen as they filled her in on the assassin's attack and what he'd said.

Rek also found them in the confusion of the battle's aftermath, and Dare felt a surge of relief at the sight of him apparently unharmed, although covered in blood and looking shellshocked. He strode forward to clasp his soon to be brother-in-law's arm. "Good to see you well, Chieftain," he said. "How did your fighters fare?"

The young hobgoblin smiled wanly. "It was a glorious victory." From his tone he didn't seem sure of that. "I lost two warriors. Dak'u'Lo and Kag'u'Gori. Good fighters." His stoic expression faltered. "Good friends."

Dare rested a hand on his shoulder. "I grieve with you, brother."

Rek took a shuddering breath, straightening determinedly. "We will burn them soon, if you would honor them by attending."

"I would." Dare shook his head reluctantly. "But our troubles didn't end with the defeat of the monster horde, I'm afraid." He quickly filled the young man in on the assassin's attack and what the man had said before killing himself.

The chieftain listened grimly. "We'll redouble our watch at Nirim Manor," he said, expression hard. "No one will come near to threaten my sister and her child." He bowed low. "I regret hastening Dak's and Kag's pyres, but it is necessary . . . we'll leave for home within the hour."

"Thank you." Dare clasped arms with him again.

Amalisa went with the hobgoblin to help them prepare to leave, as well as getting ready herself. Dare and Ilin left them to it and continued on in search of Marona.

They found her looking over the wounded, those serious enough or with specific types of injuries that meant that even after they'd been healed they still required recovery time. Or would never fully recover, for crippling or disfiguring wounds; at least not without expensive treatments from high level healers or Alchemists.

The baroness looked weary but stood with shoulders raised, as if a great weight had fallen off her shoulders. Dare hated to bear her down with new worries, but there was no option.

His noble lover rushed to them with an expression of joy and threw her arms around him and Ilin both. "I knew you could do this," she said, kissing Dare's cheek. "Thank you."

Text appeared in front of Dare. "Quest completed: Battle for Terana. For your contribution in killing 13 low level marauders, 9 low level officers, 2 elite officers, and 1 horde commander, you receive 56,220 experience. Double experience bonus for monster horde kills is applied. As word of your heroic deeds spreads, your regard in Terana Province will grow dramatically."

Well, between that and the experience bonus for killing the Cursed Orc Warchief, on top of the experience he'd gotten for the actual monster kills, he was well on his way to Level 34 already.

Although it was hard to be excited about that under the circumstances. He gave his noble lover a strained smile. "I'm glad to see you safe, my Lady."

The baroness drew back and gave him a close look, her own smile fading. "What's happened?"

Dare sighed and motioned to the war tent in the distance. "Let's discuss this away from prying ears."

He knew his caginess was worrying her, but he could exactly reassure her that there was no reason for concern. As she turned and regally led the way to the tent he kept his eyes on the terrain around them, looking for the telltales of another Stealthed enemy. He could see Ilin doing the same.

Once they were inside he helped his friend drop into a chair at the war table, then slumped into one himself. Marona settled down beside him, hand on his leg. “Dare, what is it?”

He took a deep breath and took her hand with both of his as he explained his encounter with the assassin.

As he spoke he saw her back go rigid, jaw clenched in fear and fury. When he finished she pushed to her feet and began pacing. “The fool,” she spat. “He's like a spoiled child who breaks his hand punching a stone, so he draws his sword and hacks at it until his weapon is a ruin, and finally tries to roll it off a cliff only for it to roll back and crush him. The source of his own problems but constantly venting more and more fury at the target he wounds himself on.”

“I'm going to kill him,” Dare said flatly.

His lover turned to him, eyes blazing. “Yes, you are.” She stepped over and gripped his shoulders, looking down at him with fierce intensity. “And you're going to be smart about it.”

He appreciated her show of full confidence that he could get the job done. Which he intended to do, although he wasn't sure exactly how he was going to manage it yet.

He gently pulled her down into her seat again. “I need to know everything about Ollivan and his family, as well as anything you've heard about this Assassin's Guild.”

She pressed her lips together. “Most assassins worship Jozul, God of Dark Deeds. They're selfish and pragmatic . . . they'll do what they have to in order to fulfill a contract, but you're right to think that if you kill Ollivan the contract disappears and most won't go to any more effort to hurt us.”

“So they won't try to avenge a fallen Guild member?” Dare

asked.

She hesitated, then shook her head. “Not unless you paid the Guild some particular insult. Assassins die in failed assassinations, and most would blame that more on their associate's incompetence than on you. As long as the contract giver is dead they won't waste the time and coin, not to mention risk themselves, to go after us.”

“Which just leaves any assassins the Guild might send after us now, before they get the message that the contract is nullified,” Ilin said grimly. “You should come to Nirim Manor, my Lady. Along with anyone in your household an assassin might target to hurt Dare . . . I have the means of seeing through Stealth and intend to guard everyone until the danger is passed.”

Marona shook her head as she stood and moved to the entrance to the tent. She murmured something to a maid outside, then returned. “I appreciate the offer, but it's not necessary. Orin was understandably worried about thieves and other ne'er-do-wells trying to rob us or cause us harm, and paid for expensive Enchantments around Montshadow Estate to alert us to any intruders, Stealthed or not.”

She rested a hand on Dare's shoulder, looking down at him. “In fact, send your family there as my guests until the threat is dealt with. They're more than welcome.” She smiled at Ilin. “And with your Third Eye for extra security, we'll be even better protected.”

Dare nodded in relief. He hated to disrupt his family's lives at Nirim Manor, but it was probably the best option. “Thank you, Marona. I'm not sure what they'll choose to do, but the offer is much appreciated.”

The baroness gave him a comforting smile and squeezed his shoulder, then straightened briskly. “Another way to deter the Assassin's Guild is to spread this attempted assassination far and wide. They work in the shadows and prefer to avoid attention, and this is not only an embarrassment for them but will also bring the guards and nobility of Bastion down on their heads.”

Her eyes tightened. “Especially if I let it be known I was one of their targets. That's bound to make my peers nervous . . . nobles may make use of assassins against their enemies, but they won't like the idea they could become victims themselves."

Dare shifted, feeling the pressure to be gone and deal with this, before Ollivan or the Guild caused further threat to his loved ones. "I need a few things from you before I go. Mostly your help making it seem like I'm still here, hunkered down guarding everyone, rather than on my way to kill Ollivan." He smiled grimly. "Although I should outdistance any warning unless I can't manage to find him quickly."

"Of course, my love," Marona said. "What else?"

He looked down at his gear. "A short bow my level I can conceal beneath a cloak, along with hair dye and a sword."

Chapter Five
Reprieve

With their customary efficiency Marigold and Belinda got to work transforming Dare.

He couldn't have been in better hands as they cut his hair short and dyed it a mundane mousy brown, then showed him how to apply subtle makeup to make himself look plainer and stand out less. They also found some simple laborer's clothes for him to wear.

Gone were his expensive armor and fine clothes made by Zuri, in their place a serviceable linen tunic and pants that would comfortably be worn by anyone from laborers to adventurers. As well as a long, heavy wool coat to keep out the cold that similarly would be worn by farmers and travelers alike. And over it all an oiled canvas cloak for the rain that was stiff and uncomfortable but would draw no attention.

And more importantly, would hide the outline of his new short bow and the single quiver of arrows he kept hidden beneath it.

To Dare's pleasant surprise a new type of bow had become available at Level 30, which he hadn't been aware of. Or at least hadn't given a closer look to, given his disdain for short bows. But this one was a compact recurve that did away with many of the previous weaknesses of the short bow.

Although like all recurve bows, its superior stats came with a significantly higher price tag. Marona waved away any questions of cost when he brought it up. "Just bring it back in one piece," she said with a strained smile.

After belting a short sword at his waist and holding his spear like a staff, with no armor to distinguish him, he could've passed for any of a few dozen classes. Combined with his disguise Dare the Hunter was nowhere to be seen. Even better, Ollivan remembered him as being Level 30 and wouldn't believe he could've gained 3 levels in such a short time.

Anyone who could've reported different was either dead or in a dungeon.

While the maids worked, Marona filled Dare in on everything she knew about Redoubt and Ollivan and his family, a branch of the expansive and powerful Harling family led by Lord Valiant, Duke of Bastion. Ollivan was Valiant's nephew, son of his oldest sister who was reportedly his favorite sibling. And thus he passed that favoritism to Ollivan.

Although not without a great deal of embarrassment to the family.

The most recent word back from Redoubt was that Marona's attempts to discredit the knight had been largely successful, and after his servants had been caught out trying to burn down property that ultimately belonged to his uncle the duke, he'd fallen into disfavor.

What that disfavor entailed, the baroness didn't yet know. But it hadn't stopped Ollivan from hiring assassins to kill them, so ultimately it wouldn't be quick enough to stop the threat he represented.

As Dare checked himself in a mirror and packed up just the things he needed most, Marona pressed a map of Redoubt into his hands and pointed to a few locations. “Here's the house of Ollivan's parents, where he lives. And these are his two favorite brothels where he often spends the night, according to rumor.”

She fussed with his canvas cloak, trying to look confident for his sake but obviously worried for him. “Now that you have the Home Ward you can get to Redoubt and back in a brief enough time that no one will even believe you could possibly be there. Furthermore our entire camp here will be able to stand witness that you were here fighting the monster horde, then immediately turned southward for Nirim Manor with your companions and goblin conscripts.”

Dare nodded. “Thank you, Marona. For everything.” He tucked

the map away and gave her a hasty but heartfelt kiss.

Then, to his chagrin and everyone else's amusement, Belinda and Marigold lined up for their own kisses, hands clasped primly in front of them and lips pursed in silent expectation.

"For Eala," his dragon girl lover said solemnly as he kissed her. She was referring to her fellow maid, who Ollivan had raped while a guest in Marona's house. "Be careful, but end that scum."

Marigold nodded fiercely as she pressed her full lips to his. "For Eala."

With that Marona wasted no time pushing him towards the entrance to her tent. "Go quickly, and tell no one. We'll cover for you for as long as we can, and in the confusion after the battle you shouldn't be missed."

Dare went, joining Ilin, Amalisa, and Rek outside and mounting up.

Together they all departed the camp heading south by southeast, towards Nirim Manor. Once they were out of sight he took a quick look around, then bid his companions a last hasty farewell and dismounted.

Finally, after taking a moment to bind the Home Ward to this location, he activated Cheetah's Dash and ran due west, circling around the camp until he could make directly for Redoubt.

He didn't sprint, since he couldn't maintain that for long. But by now he had a good idea of his limits, and he was determined to push past them and still make it to full dark before he collapsed in exhaustion.

In spite of his grim purpose, in spite of his dread for the safety of his loved ones and his uncertainty about just how he was going to go about stopping Ollivan and the assassins, there was a certain catharsis in running. In feeling the wind stream past his face and the soles of his boots pound the sod under his feet. In counting down the seconds of the 5 minute cooldown on Cheetah's Dash and then feeling the afterburners kick in.

Dare was going fast. Ridiculously fast. As in a trip that should've taken seven or eight days on horseback, without remounts or killing the horses of course, should be manageable by late tomorrow.

When he slowed down to check his map and the landmarks around him, he judged that he'd manage almost half the distance today. And he'd started in the afternoon.

Low level monster spawn points he sprinted right through to avoid the delay of circling them. Animal predators that tried to ambush him he either outran or, if they were faster than him, gave him an opportunity to practice drawing his bow and arrows from their concealed cases beneath his cloak.

Dozens, then hundreds of miles thudded under his feet. Hills passed by to either side, rivers shimmering in the distance and streams appearing ahead to be jumped, then falling away. Beautiful vistas faded into the distance behind him, unnoticed.

Dare's lungs burned, his legs were jelly, his heartbeat was a fierce drumbeat in his ears. His breath came in panting gasps and he had to pause often to sip from his waterskin and soothe his rasping throat.

He didn't think he'd ever pushed himself this hard. Or at least not for nearly this long, hour after hour. Even when he'd carried Zuri and his pack as they traveled, they'd paused for rests and to eat.

Now he ate as he ran, choking it down around panting breaths. He gulped water as he ran. He only paused to relieve himself, and then only as long as he had to.

When his strength failed and he was forced to slow to a stumbling walk for a time to get his strength back, his mind was filled with images of Zuri, and Pella, and Leilanna, and Se'weir, and Ireni. Of baby Gelaa and his seed Eloise, innocent and helpless.

And before Dare felt ready, probably sooner than he should've, he lurched back into a run again.

As darkness fell his best efforts reduced him to a fast walk or stumbling run, barely faster than a walk. Even with Cheetah's Dash he wasn't making his usual traveling pace.

Part of him knew he should stop and sleep. That he'd be able to go faster in the morning when he was rested. That if he kept to a slower pace that didn't wear him out too soon, he'd go farther faster overall.

But still he pushed on.

Dare probably should've taken a clue about how his sheer exhaustion and borderline panic was affecting his mental state by the fact that when he reached a large forest that stretched across his path, he decided to dive into the darkness beneath the trees rather than stop for the night.

It was only when he felt his Adventurer's Eye give the familiar alarm that he'd entered a spawn point that he hastily backed away, until he was back outside the border. He stood there with his hands on his knees, heaving for air for all he was worth.

Caution finally made a reappearance and he straightened enough to Snap, briefly illuminating the darkness around him. He could see monsters in the spawn point, far enough away to not aggro thankfully, but aside from that nothing but dark trees all around.

Godsdamnit. He should've known better than to shut off his brain and push himself beyond reason like that.

Dare didn't do much hunting at night, and for good reason; that's when most of the animal predators came out in force, and also you couldn't see if you were about to stumble across a roaming monster. Also, he was in an area of Bastion that was fairly far from all nearby settlements, and the monsters around here were in their high 30s.

Which meant for the most part the animals were, too, since they instinctively hunted the most powerful monsters they were able to.

Cursing quietly to himself, he pulled out his bow and moved his quiver to his belt for easier access. Then, using Snap to light his way even in the brief flashes it offered, he began circling the spawn point in search of a clearing to set up camp.

When he finally spotted one up ahead, he entered a dream.

* * * * *

A scent filled his weary mind first, flowers and sweet clover.

Dare could also swear there was a soft glow ahead, warm and inviting.

More than that, the gnawing worry that had taken root in his gut since the Darkblade's attack slowly eased, and a sense of profound peace filled him.

He stumbled forward, leaving the dark forest behind. The clearing was larger than he'd expected, a hundred yards across at the least, with grass, clover, and flowers he didn't think should be blooming this time of year forming an inviting carpet beneath his feet.

The air was warmer than it should've been for an autumn night, fresh and sweet smelling, and the light in the clearing was a soft silver brighter than a full moon. Even though none of Collisa's varied and constantly changing moons were at that phase or in the sky together right now.

Dare looked around in wonder and took a deep breath, his aches and pains falling off him like a blanket, although his weariness remained. He could've happily collapsed right there and slept, without so much as a fire or tent or even a blanket, with full confidence he'd be safe and comfortable.

And yet that would be rude, for the Lady stood at the center of the clearing, waiting patiently.

Dare couldn't help but stare in awe as his feet took him forward. He would guess she was a dryad, but out of all the creatures he'd seen on Collisa she was the only one whose level he couldn't see, either with a usual inspect or with his Adventurer's Eye.

She was at least two feet taller than him, and while the obviously humorous term to describe her would be “willowy”, she was in fact so long in limbs and torso she almost appeared stretched. Like the trunk of a young tree.

Her skin was the rich reddish-brown of a cherry sapling's bark, smooth and unblemished, and rather than hair chains of cherry blossoms bloomed down past her feet, trailing behind her like the train of a gown.

The dryad was nude, as he would expect, breasts small but lush with dark brown nipples, and her curves subtle but unquestioningly feminine. Her features were at the same time young but ancient, soft and round but proudly sharp. All in all her appearance was alien, and yet compelling and perfect in her own right.

She was unquestioningly the Lady, not just of this clearing but perhaps of all this woods. Maybe even more. There was something about her that invited reverence, and he didn't hesitate to drop to one knee and bow his head.

“Lady,” he said, voice seeming rough in that beautiful place. “Your pardon for intruding here.”

“Nonsense,” she said, voice melodious as the purest notes of a dozen harmonizing flutes. Her tone was warm and gentle, and listening he felt as if he was wrapped in the purest sort of love. “All are welcome in my meadow. I am Rosaceae.”

“I am Dare, Lady Rosaceae.”

“No need for formality.” The tall dryad covered the distance between them in one graceful step and helped him to his feet, not so much ushering him as lifting him with surprising tenderness with a hand on his shoulder. “Come, lay aside your burdens in my domain and let me tend you.”

Tend him she did, guiding him to a stream of the clearest water, unexpectedly warm as if it came from a hot spring. Dare didn't even think to be embarrassed as she undressed him and bathed him. Her hands were gentle, reddish-brown skin unexpectedly soft and warm.

Of anyone he would compare the feel of her to Rosie, the other plant girl he'd met. Although Rosaceae bore regality and grace and a quiet, nurturing sort of power like a mantle.

Somehow, just with pure water, she cleansed him better than even Zuri's spell could. The bath refreshed and invigorated him more than he would've expected, his exhaustion easing just enough that he thought he could stay awake for a bit longer.

When she was done tending him she bade him roll in the soft clover to dry. Then she dressed him in a tunic of woven plant fibers, softer than silk, with slippers of the same cloth for his feet. At last she took his hand and led him away, still in his haze of wonder, leaving his things behind as they walked down the stream.

It didn't even occur to Dare to be suspicious of the profound feeling of contentment and welcome that suffused him, or the kindness the dryad showed him as a complete stranger and intruder on her domain. Such was the peace of this place that not only was it inconceivable that she might mean him harm, but he couldn't believe that any who came to this place would even be capable of it while in her presence.

They soon came in view of a table set for two, laden with not only a wide assortment of fresh fruits and vegetables but also roast meats and cakes. And to his surprise, he realized he and the Lady were not alone in the clearing.

Fussing with the cutlery at one of the place settings, seeming intent on getting it perfect, was one of the most beautiful women he'd ever seen.

She was a bunny girl. And while he'd heard all bunny girls were beautiful, and Clover, the one he'd been with before back near Lone Ox certainly had been, this woman was unimaginably more so.

Of course Dare was surrounded by beautiful women he was proud to call his fiancees, and had met many others whose beauty was undeniable. And all his beloved who'd met Enellia, the ethereally lovely butterfly girl, wouldn't hesitate to insist that she was unquestionably the most beautiful woman any of them had ever seen, which he would fully agree with.

Until now.

She was his age or a bit older, about Leilanna's height and dressed in the most elegant gown of shimmering silver. The color matched her soft, straight hair, which was in fact silver of a color he'd never seen before, even with hair dyes; it wasn't white or grey but shone with an almost metallic sheen, so hints of reflections from the meadow around her were visible.

Her hair was pulled up in pigtails hanging down to her waist, which made her seem unexpectedly cute and approachable considering her flawless beauty. As did the large wire-frame glasses she wore.

In contrast to her hair, the fur on her ears and on the cute little cottontail poking out from a hole in her gown was the purest white. Her skin was also pale as milk, more so than he'd ever seen in any other women except Clover, smooth and without blemish and looking unimaginably soft.

The bunny girl's beautiful gown was slit up to the waist to reveal a gorgeous pale leg, and hugged curves that could've been the ideal for feminine beauty. Her heart shaped face was perfectly symmetrical, sweet and youthful with big gray eyes, a delicate nose, and full red lips.

Even in this peaceful place Dare felt his mouth go dry in the face of such beauty, unsure what to say or do. With Enellia, Rosie had been there to help dispel the awkwardness, the playful plant girl making him feel welcome and at ease.

He had made love to many beautiful women since coming to Collisa, was engaged to marry six of them, and knew how to act with women as well as any man could claim. And at the moment he felt like a kid staring at his crush.

To his surprise, the impossibly beautiful bunny girl, dressed like an elegant lady, seemed almost as shy as he felt. But that didn't stop her from gliding forwards to meet him, big gray eyes shining behind her large glasses.

“Hi,” she said, biting her lip as she offered her hand. “I'm Lily.”

Dare tried to remember his usual poise and charm as he lifted it to press his lips to the back of it. Her skin was as amazingly soft as he could've hoped, warm and to his surprise slightly clammy; was she nervous? “I'm Dare. It's a pleasure to meet you.”

Her milky pale skin did nothing to hide the blush that crept up her neck and across her cheeks, and she bashfully fiddled with her glasses. “Dare. It's nice to finally know your name.”

Um, what?

As if realizing what she'd said, Lily blushed even harder and hastily took his hand, leading him to the table. “Come on, you must be starving. And you're practically asleep on your feet, you poor thing.”

Dare went along, feeling his own cheeks heat at holding her hand. As if he was still a shy kid and not the man who regularly wooed women and had a harem back home. “Aren't you going to join us, Lady Rosaceae?” he asked, turning to the dryad.

Only to pause in consternation when he realized that she was nowhere to be seen.

Sure, his attention had kind of been captured by Lily, but even so he would've noticed if she'd departed. Had she somehow disappeared?

The bunny girl laughed as she guided him into his seat. “Oh no, she has no need to eat. As a dryad she's a demigoddess, and operates on different rules than mortals.”

Dare made a strangled noise. “A what?”

She gave him a surprised look as she settled down in her own chair. “Haven't you heard of Rosaceae? She's the ancient ancestor of all florans. She's been alive for tens of thousands of years.”

Holy shit, he'd just gotten a bath from a demigod? If he'd known . . .

Lily picked up her plate and shoveled a heaping portion of salad onto it. “Come on, eat before it gets cold. I worked really hard to prepare this.”

Dare fumbled with his own plate to spear some slices of what he thought was roast duck, some fragrant mashed potatoes, and a smaller portion of all the other dishes on offer.

He felt a bit bad thinking it, but from the first bite it was clear that in spite of how beautifully laid out the spread was, the bunny girl's cooking had a ways to go before matching Se'weir's. It was good, delicious actually with hunger as a spice.

But on the subject of spices she could've used more salt and maybe some herbs and onions.

Still, she was looking at him so hopefully as he chewed that he had a feeling his approval of the meal meant a lot to her. Although he had no clue why such a perfect woman was so eager to impress him. Still, the food was good and he happily made appreciative noises as he swallowed.

"This is delicious," he said. "Exactly what I needed after the day I've had. Thank you, Lily."

The bunny girl blushed again and fiddled with her glasses. "You're very welcome." Trying to hide her pleased smile, she dug into her salad with more enthusiasm than poise.

It was cute.

As they ate a somewhat uncomfortable silence settled and Dare cleared his throat. "So do you live with Lady Rosaceae?"

Lily smiled dreamily. "Oh, wouldn't that be a wonder? Cunids and florans both live out in the wilds and see a lot of each other. I love the few plant girls I've met, they're such sweethearts, and we get along great." She giggled. "Even though we eat plants, we only do one sort of eating with plant girls."

Dare felt his face heat at the unbidden mental image of this beautiful woman with Rosie and hastily cleared his throat. "So you're a guest here too?"

She nodded. "For the last few days. Rosaceae has been such a gracious host. It's been a wonderful reprieve from all my traveling."

He ate a few more big bites, hunger warring with his desire to make polite conversation. "If you don't mind me asking, what sort of traveling are you doing? I'd heard cunids like to stick to their warrens and don't usually venture too far from settlements."

"Oh." For some reason the gorgeous bunny girl blushed furiously at the question, taking her glasses off and absently wiping the lenses on her elegant dress, then putting them back on. She looked back up at him a bit bashfully. "Well, I'm not very much like other cunids. Everyone in my warren always told me so. Mother says I take more after my human side."

That wasn't really an answer, so Dare listened attentively as he kept eating, hoping for more.

She obliged him as she nibbled at her salad. "I like to read books, and reading about the world always made the warren seem so small. Mother was always so wonderful about it, she'd visit the nearby villages and towns to get me new books to read, especially the romantic stories I love. She also got me these glasses so I could read them. And she never got on my case when I only seemed interested in reading, instead of doing other stuff cunids prefer to do. She was even proud of it, and always . . ."

He felt his eyes drooping and head beginning to nod as Lily's sweet, lovely voice lulled him to give in to his exhaustion. His fork dropped back to his plate as weariness overpowered hunger, and at the sharp *clink* he jerked back upright in surprise.

Then Rosaceae was there, soft hands lifting him up with astonishing strength to cradle him. In his drowsy state he was more than happy to rest his head on her narrow shoulder, feeling the soft rocking motion as she carried him away.

"Goodnight, sweet prince," he thought he heard Lily murmur, so quietly he was sure he must've misheard. His drooping eyes cracked open to look at the table, but the bunny girl was nowhere in sight.

She could've been a pleasant dream.

He was carried into a bower formed of the branches of flowering trees woven together, where he was stood up just long enough for the dryad to undress him. Then she laid him down gently on a bed of soft, fragrant heather.

As he slipped down into sleep he was distantly aware of Rosaceae's warm, soft body pressing up against him, pulling him onto a gentle embrace as the long curtain of cherry blossoms that was her hair settled over him like a blanket.

Suffused in her comforting presence he drifted off into pleasant dreams.

* * * * *

Dare woke gradually to find himself still lying on the bed of heather, Rosaceae's long limbs wrapped around him and his head resting on her soft breasts. He was distinctly aware they were both naked but wasn't embarrassed about it.

He wasn't sure if he'd woken her or if she'd been awake, but she began stroking long, elegant fingers through his short hair. “Did you sleep well?” she asked in her melodious voice.

“Very well,” he said, although he was still tired. He had a feeling he'd only slept four or so hours, and it was clearly still night. “What's going on?”

The dryad laughed lightly. “In the wild, with nothing affecting their natural sleep rhythms, most races sleep for a few hours after sundown, wake to spend a few hours in quiet reflection in the dark, then sleep again until morning.”

“Oh.” That sounded surprisingly pleasant, and while Dare still felt the urgency to make it to Redoubt as soon as possible, he couldn't exactly run at night and he still needed more sleep.

So he settled back against her, murmuring, “Why are you sleeping with me?” Part of him realized that might've been rude, even though he'd asked out of genuine curiosity.

She didn't seem offended. “Would you like me to leave?”

“No.” He chuckled ruefully. “I just didn't think demigoddesses liked cuddling. Also we're kind of strangers.”

Rosaceae laughed again, voice tinkling pleasantly in his ears. “Are we?” Her hand moved from his hair to his back, joined by her other as she began gently massaging him. “My distant descendant Rosie is your lover, is she not? And your seed Eloise waits in your garden to bloom next spring.”

Her voice turned even warmer, and fond. “It pleased me to see it. I and my daughters are built for solitude if necessary, but it gladdens my heart to think of Eloise growing up amidst family, with brothers and sisters to play with.”

Dare looked up at her rounded yet sharp features. “You know of them?”

“Yes. I see much of what happens where life grows strong, and of course I keep a loving eye on my children as any mother would."

He hesitated. "Are they all right? Everyone back at Nirim Manor?"

She tenderly kissed his head. "Yes, they are. Rest assured in what you have to do next."

The dryad's hands found their way to his glutes, kneading the tension out of them. Although the tension ended up moving somewhere else; to his chagrin he felt his cock, nestled against her soft hip, begin to stir and grow under her gentle ministrations.

He started to pull back, feeling his face heat. "Sorry."

"Why? Your body does what comes naturally as we lie together in freely shared intimacy." She trailed one hand over his hip to wrap her long fingers around his girth with a surprisingly tight grip, rubbing it firmly. "Would you like to entwine?"

Dare certainly would. But even as his hips bucked against her hand he hesitated. "I left my Prevent Conception scrolls behind." He shook his head grimly. "I wasn't planning to go looking for a good time while fighting to protect my family."

"I understand." Rosaceae kept stroking him. "But do not fear on that count. The release would help you sleep better, and I would very much love to see what we create together." She shifted, and he felt his tip press against her soft labia, sticky with her nectar. "Come, join with me."

The scent of cherry blossoms filled his head with her arousal, and he couldn't help but chuckle. "Who am I to refuse a demigoddess?" Running his hands through the silky vines of blossoms that were her hair, he kissed her breast beneath his head and took a dark nipple into his mouth, sucking softly.

As he did he twitched his hips and pushed into her warm depths, drawing a quiet sound of pleasure from his dryad lover.

He'd discovered that Rosie with her surprisingly tough yet supple plant body had the ability to accept any size balls deep in her small hole and still be incredibly tight, feeling only pleasure from the fucking no matter how hard and fast he went.

Rosaceae was just as tight, although when she said entwine she meant it. He found his arms and legs wrapped tightly around her just as much as hers were around him, only their hips moving together in short, sensuous movements.

Dare let himself sink into her gentle passion, feeling the frustration of his situation with Ollivan, his fury and fear and panic, all soothed away. He still worried for his family and was determined to protect them, but the sharp, hopeless bite of his emotions had faded to firm resolve.

His orgasm caught him by surprise, not only in its suddenness but in its intensity, and his whole body stiffened against her as he released his seed into her depths. She gave a quiet moan in turn, and he felt her silky tunnels clench around him, milking him to the last drop and even then continuing to ripple.

Afterwards weariness settled over him again, and as he softened but still remained inside her he drifted off to sleep again, both of them remaining firmly entwined.

Some time later he drifted awake to the pleasure of feeling himself beginning to harden in the dryad's warm slick tunnel, growing and expanding against her tight walls. She moaned and began to undulate her hips again, and he joined her for another brief but fierce coupling before again shooting his load into her depths.

The rest of the night went like that, sleeping peacefully with his cock enveloped by Rosaceae's sticky sex, half waking in a haze of pleasure to move within her as she mirrored his movements, and finally climaxing inside her as she milked every drop.

Then drifting off again.

Dare wasn't sure how many times, five or six at least. But the final time he woke to feel himself growing inside her the pale light of dawn streamed through the bower's leaves, and he could smell the tantalizing scent of frying meat and vegetables.

His dryad lover leaned down to softly kiss his lips, and he tasted cherries and honey as her tongue slipped into his mouth. She moved against him one last time, hungry and urgent, and he squirmed back against her for a few minutes until finally emptying his balls in several powerful surges of pleasure.

Then, a bit reluctantly, he let her go and climbed to his feet, pulling the soft tunic she'd given him over his head. “I need to be back on my way to Redoubt,” he said. “But thank you for this night of rest and wonder when I needed it most, Rosaceae.”

“I was glad to,” she said, stroking his back. “Please visit any time, you will always be welcome.” She paused, looking at him keenly. “In fact, return once your current task is done, since you'll be heading back this way.”

Eager as Dare was to get back to his family, that seemed like the least he could do. Especially if it meant a safe place to rest on the way back. “Thank you, I will.”

“Good.” With a faint smile she moved her hand down to squeeze his ass. “You have a really nice butt, by the way. Most women appreciate that more than you realize.”

Thinking of the times when his other lovers had mentioned the same, he supposed that was true. Although it was a bit surprising to hear a regal, ancient demigod say so.

When they emerged from the bower he saw Lily busy at a fire near the stream, maybe thirty or so feet away. And in spite of the fact that he'd already come over half a dozen times that night he still couldn't help but stare.

Last night Dare hadn't really taken the time to appreciate that she was the first bunny girl he'd ever seen or heard of who was dressed. Although to be fair he'd only met one other, Clover, before her.

Still, “dressed” was a dubious description for her outfit this morning.

She was wearing leather shorts that weren't much longer than underwear, and so thin and form-fitting that it brought to mind something his friend had once told him, “Her pants are so tight I can read her lips.”

Her top wasn't much better, a strip of the same thin leather wrapped loosely around her gorgeous breasts, so with every step it looked as if they would pop out. He could see her small, perky nipples poking out the material and couldn't help but stare for a moment before tearing his eyes away, cheeks heating.

The outfit left a lot of very sexy pale body exposed, and to avoid impolitely gawking he did his best to focus on her beautiful face.

Dare hadn't thought to do it last night so he did it now, inspecting her with his Adventurer's Eye: "Cunid, adult female. Humanoid, intelligent. Class Leatherworker, Combat Subclass Archer, Level 8. Attacks: Triple Shot, Flame Arrow."

Lily was still wearing her hair up in those cute pigtails and had on her large wire-framed glasses. That plus the big smile she gave him when she spotted them walking over made him feel more at ease.

"Good morning!" she said, looking between him and Rosaceae with a knowing expression. "Did you sleep well?"

"Like a baby," he said, smiling inwardly. *Awake every few hours.*

"Good!" The bunny girl turned to the table, holding out her arms. "I made breakfast."

Dare took in the sizzling skillet of meat and vegetables, the steaming omelets loaded with chopped onions and peppers, and a wild salad with chopped radishes and carrots. It all looked delicious, and smelled pretty good too. "Thank you, Lily," he said, settling down in the same chair from last night. "This is amazing. I don't know how I can ever repay you for your kindness in my time of need."

She smiled shyly, her prominent rabbit front teeth making the expression adorable.

Rosaceae stuck around this time, kneeling gracefully seated on her heels to be closer to eye level with them. Again Lily loaded her plate with salad and dug in enthusiastically, while Dare took good sized helpings of everything and ate it all, then had seconds.

After eating sporadically yesterday with the battle and then the run here, falling asleep with his meal half eaten, then the nocturnal exercises, he was ravenous. And while the food still could've benefitted greatly from salt and spices, it was delicious.

And he made sure to tell the bunny girl so, to her quiet but obvious delight.

Finally, though, Dare finished clearing his plate for the second time and reluctantly pushed it away. "Thank you both for your hospitality," he said. "But I need to get back on the road, so to speak."

Lily looked a bit disappointed and opened her mouth, but a subtle but sharp head shake from the dryad forestalled her. "And you'll visit again on your return trip?" Rosaceae said, almost more to the bunny girl to him.

He wasn't sure what the exchange was about, but nodded. "For a brief stop, or at most to stay the night if you'll have me. My family's waiting for me back home, and we were in some fear when I left . . . assuming I can sort out the situation I need to get back and reassure them that everything's all right."

"Of course," the dryad said warmly. "Go in peace, Darren Portsmouth. And may you have the greatest success in your ventures."

Dare blinked in surprise; he wasn't sure he'd used his full name with anyone since coming to Collisa, and he was sure he hadn't told her. But then again, she was a demigoddess who could observe the world through plants.

To his further surprise, as he stood from the table Lily leapt up as well and threw her arms around him, body soft and sweet against him. "It was good to meet you, Dare!" she said, backing away and playing with one of her pigtails as a blush spread up her pale, swanlike neck. "I hope things go well and I see you again soon."

"I hope to see you again, too," he said. With a last awkward bow to both women he made his way over to retrieve his clothes and gear.

It was with a bit of regret that he left the enchanted clearing behind, Rosaceae and Lily waving behind him. He was charmed to see that the dryad had lifted the bunny girl up to cradle in one long arm.

As he stepped into the trees he was surprised to feel a strong blast of icy wind howling against his cheeks. Even more surprising, he saw a few flakes of snow drifting through the canopy to settle on the forest floor.

Frowning, Dare looked up at the sky through the clearing, which looked clear and pleasant, then at the snowflakes finding their way through the tree branches in the dim, gloomy forest.

No doubt about it, this was the season's first snow. He was just glad he'd been lucky enough to avoid what had probably been a cold night in the warmth of the demigoddess's clearing.

And the warmth of her embrace.

His clothes were ostensibly warm enough for this weather, with his long wool coat and waterproof canvas cloak. But coming into the cold was always unpleasant, even if he was properly bundled up.

Oh well, he'd warm up soon enough as he started his run. He might even be shedding some layers of clothing once he began working up a sweat.

With a last wave back at the dryad and bunny girl, Dare turned away and ran northwest through the trees, mind shifting away from the demigoddess's peaceful refuge and back to his grim purpose.

Chapter Six
Redoubt

Dare got his first view of Redoubt in the midafternoon, although since it was built on an expansive plains it was still several miles away. Its walls were high and in good repair, the ramparts dotted with siege weapons, and it projected a feeling of safety in the wildness of Bastion.

It made a heartening sight as he ran the final miles across the plains, dodging spawn points until he finally reached the large road leading between Redoubt and Jarn's Holdout to the south. Once there he paused for a few minutes inside a copse of trees to reapply the makeup the maids had given him, restoring his plain disguise that had been washed away in Rosaceae's bath last night.

Then he did one last check of his appearance with the mirror Marona had lent him, making sure nothing was out of place, before stepping out onto the road.

He soon caught up to a caravan heading towards the city and offered to accompany them. The merchant and his guards seemed a bit confused by that, especially given the ease with which he'd overtaken them and the nearness of the city ahead.

Although they didn't complain about having a Level 33 with them to scare off possible bandits on the last stretch to the city. Even if bandits operating in view of Redoubt's walls would have to be pants on head stupid.

There was a respectable line waiting to get in, although like with other places in Bastion the Governor's insistence on fostering settling and trade, as well as a more welcoming environment for adventurers, meant that the taxes were reasonable.

The guards jotted down some notes and took a few coins from the caravan before waving them through, giving the wagons only a cursory inspection. Dare they simply nodded to politely as he passed, obviously an adventurer even if currently hiring himself out as a guard.

It was almost odd not to be given second looks for his physical appearance, thanks to the maids' makeup. He'd gotten so used to admiring attention from the ladies that he'd almost forgotten what it felt like to be an average Joe.

Not so helpful if you were hoping for a love life, but great for blending in.

Just inside the gates he paused to look around Redoubt. It wasn't as big as Kov by any stretch of the imagination, maybe 20,000 residents at most. However, as the capitol of a frontier region its travelers were as often adventurers or mercenaries as traders or settlers. That gave the city a rougher, more boisterous feel.

The streets showed some sign of planning at the beginning, laid out in square blocks. But since then the second stories of buildings had grown to loom over some of the side streets, turning them into little more than alleys. In a few places construction had blocked off a street entirely aside from at best a footpath where night soil was dumped.

To make things even more cramped and hectic, apparently vendor stalls were allowed on the streets here, not just in the market. Which led to some places where wagons could barely fit through, and traffic jams surrounded by a deal of boisterous shouting and cursing were frequent.

It seemed that while the Governor had lots of good ideas for encouraging prosperity and growth in Bastion, he was more lax than expected on civic management.

There were no sewers and obviously little effort applied to municipal hygiene, giving the air a rank smell that Dare hoped his nose would grow used to before too long; not everywhere could have running water, toilets, and septic tanks like Nirim Manor.

Maybe in the future.

The place seemed to be bustling, at least, and for the most part the people were relatively clean and warmly dressed. Many squares had public wells where citizens could draw water.

As he strode down the street leading from the south gate he looked around. Not idly taking in the sights of the city, though.

During the entire run to Redoubt he'd been planning what he would do here, how he'd go about eliminating the danger to his family. Ollivan might be the ultimate threat, but the Assassin's Guild was the more immediate concern, since they might be sending out another assassin after him soon.

Or possibly had already sent one.

Killing the knight would end the contract, but not immediately. Stopping the Assassin's Guild would end the immediate threat, but Ollivan might try some other way.

More significantly, a shadowy organization of murderers would probably be harder to find than the nephew of Bastion's duke. And might feature some very powerful and dangerous enemies, like the Darkblade had been.

Ollivan would be easier to find, but it might be harder to find an opening to kill him without getting caught. To say nothing of the danger the Warrior himself presented.

Around and around Dare's thoughts had whirled as he put the miles behind him. Hard to find assassins, dangerous enemies. A knight who might be constantly surrounded by bodyguards and lackeys, or always in public. An assassin possibly on the way, Ollivan planning further ways to threaten Dare's family.

On and on.

Until he realized he was an idiot and the answer was right in front of him. Honestly it almost felt like cheating, although even if unfair it was unfair in his favor, at the expense of scum, and he felt no guilt about it.

The assassins skulking about Redoubt no doubt blended in perfectly with the citizens around them, showing only the most secret and subtle hints they were part of a shadowy organization. Passwords and hand signs, dead drops and all the other skullduggery of their trade.

And they were all walking around with huge signs proclaiming their guilt hanging over their heads. Or at least huge hints that they were less than savory people. Invisible to most, but not to Dare.

So as he wandered the streets of the city, he actively inspected the passersby around him with his Adventurer's Eye. He was searching for the Stealth classes: Poisoners and Shadow Shifters, Darkblades and Stalkers, Darkspells and Enervators and Wardbreakers and Soul Thieves, Shadebows and Snipers.

Anyone who struck from the shadows or from far away with bow, blade, or spell, or killed by more subtle means such as poison.

It was a daunting task, looking at each individual in a city of tens of thousands. Although he narrowed his search by ignoring anyone below Level 15, which eliminated just about all the usual citizens. But even with them he had to inspect their level, which took time.

He also had to decide which part of the city to search first. The obvious answer was the slums, as a place where the criminal element could blend in. But with the way Redoubt had grown and overgrown, pockets of more haphazard construction occupied by poorer tenants could be found in a lot of places.

Also there was the fact that high level and highly paid assassins might be better served hiding in plain sight in one of the more prosperous districts. Which meant they could be anywhere.

Dare purchased a skewer of meat and peppers from a vendor, eating as he wandered the streets, both to ease his hunger and to make himself stand out less. There were a surprising number of people over Level 30 in Redoubt, most adventurers or guards but also a few crafters.

Those might be worth coming back to at some point, when the lives of his loved ones weren't at stake.

After about an hour he finally had some luck, spotting a Level 23 Shadebow coming out of a bakery. The Stealth archer was dressed in mundane clothes and had a pleasant look about him, exchanging laughs with the baker as he tore into a fresh loaf of bread with his teeth, a cloth-wrapped bundle under one arm.

He could just be an adventurer out of his gear and at his ease around town, but Dare noticed the man paid more attention than most to the guards patrolling the streets.

Since it was his first lead he followed the Shadebow, using Adventurer's Eye to track him so he could keep so far back that not even a professional should be able to tell he was being trailed. Especially not on these busy streets, where he might as well have been invisible.

The man's purposeful walk took him through increasingly poor sections of the city, the buildings around them becoming shabbier and more crowded with large families of tenants. Settlers, maybe, or day laborers. Probably some refugees, too, given the chaos on Bastion's northern border that thankfully hadn't stretched as far south as Terana.

Hopefully, for the sake of his family, it never would; they had enough problems to deal with.

Finally the possible assassin entered a part of the city dominated by tents, patchwork buildings made with bits of rubbish, and even people huddled together beneath canvas tarps that offered no protection from the cold, but at least some cover from the sporadic snow that continued to drift down from leaden skies.

The man, looking far too prosperous and cheerful for the misery around him, turned down a final narrow street, made his way down between ramshackle buildings to a shabby old tavern, and with a casual look around ducked inside.

So if he was with Assassins Guild then they really were located in the slums. And either in the basement of the tavern or it housed a secret tunnel that led to their hideout.

That was almost disappointingly predictable.

Dare noticed a young Level 11 Stalker lounging by the tavern's door, sipping from a flask and huddled in a heavy cloak against the cold. He had no reason to be outside other than because he couldn't afford shelter, which was obviously not the case, or because he was a lookout.

Okay then.

Dare walked right past the street and kept going, looking even more closely at everyone around him for other lookouts or suspicious characters. He didn't see anyone but stayed wary; he'd noticed people were watching him, most of their looks unfriendly. And considering his getup it wasn't because of his looks or signs of wealth.

Unfortunately, if people who picked criminal classes had a big sign over their heads for him, he had just as big a sign over his head for everyone thanks to being Level 33. Meaning unless he'd really fucked up his life he had no reason to be poverty stricken, since he could literally walk outside and clear low level spawn points for enough loot to afford at least a room and meals.

And the cold, miserable people around him were well aware of it.

In an odd way it was strange to not be too worried about the unfriendly attention, since unlike in a usual slums where he might have to worry about being mugged or hoodwinked, he was so much higher level than these people that he didn't have much to fear. And those who were higher level like him would have no reason to be here, either.

Even criminal organizations who might control these slums wouldn't waste their higher level enforcers on this place. So unless he really did something to draw notice he probably didn't have to worry about anyone coming after him.

Of course, it also meant that Dare was going to have a bitch of a time investigating that tavern. Which might've actually been one of the defensive measures the possible Assassins Guilt took; anyone who'd actually be a threat to them would draw attention the moment they entered the slums.

Meanwhile the assassins could cement their own presence here fairly easily and cow the downtrodden residents without much trouble. In fact, they probably *were* the criminal organization in charge here.

So he'd probably have to wait until darkness, where he could skulk in the shadows and people wouldn't be able to see him to note his level. Or at least, not humans; he'd noticed the slums had a larger than usual population of other races, many of whom had better night vision.

As for his own vision, his ability Eagle Eye gave him a slight benefit at night. Enough that as long as there was a moon in the sky and it wasn't cloudy, he could at least make out silhouettes well enough to use his Adventurer's Eye.

Dare briskly made his way out of the slums, deciding that until dark he'd move on to searching for Ollivan and trying to find an opening to take him out.

The transition from poor to rich was starker than he'd expected as he made for the mansion where Ollivan still lived with his parents, the buildings going from slums to modest residences within the space of a single street, then to shops and more prosperous houses.

And finally to walled compounds with guarded gates, large yards, and mansions where the nobles, prosperous merchants, high level adventurers, and other wealthy and prominent citizens of Redoubt lived.

The heart of government, wealth, and culture in Bastion.

Here Dare found he had the opposite problem from the slums; nobody batted an eye at his level, since he saw plenty of people in their 30s and even some in their 40s. Hell, he even spotted a dignified old man with long white hair and beard that was Level 56, his class Phasewarper.

Unfortunately, Dare's humble clothes drew more than a few sneers, and he noticed the guards paid him extra attention, eyes narrowed in mild suspicion.

Damn, he should've brought a finer change of clothes so he'd be better able to fit in no matter where he went. Although that was easily enough rectified by a visit to a tailor. It hurt a bit to spend gold when Zuri made things nearly as fine, and with a lot more love, but his purpose was too important to worry about cost.

Also, if his motivation for leaving his clothes behind was that they would make him more noticeable, he could actually buy the fashions of Bastion and look less like he'd come from somewhere else.

Ten minutes later he left the tailor shop in a surprisingly well fitted off the rack (so to speak) suit of pale tans and whites, with a long dark overcoat and thin raincloak. His other clothes were stuffed in his pack, which thankfully he'd mostly had empty so it all fit.

The fashion was to wear the coat unbuttoned, so he concealed his short bow beneath that instead of the cloak, which wouldn't have hid jack. His sword and spear were nice enough to pass even with finer clothes, and he drew a lot less notice as he resumed his walk to the Harling branch family's mansion.

Unfortunately, the place was well locked down with guards and forbidding spikes atop the walls. Although Dare might've been willing to risk infiltration even so if magic wasn't a thing.

But knowing there were things like signal wards and other magical defenses gave him pause; he didn't know enough about them to circumvent them, if that was even possible for his class.

So after spending a few minutes loitering near the gate, taking notes in his monster logbook about the classes and levels of the guards in case he'd need that information later, he abandoned the mansion as a prospect for now and moved on.

To the two brothels where Marona had said Ollivan often spent the night.

The sun was setting as Dare made his way to the red light district, which was close enough to the wealthy to be convenient but far enough away to be respectable.

Dare noticed a marked change in the city at sundown, with more decent folk and children retreating indoors and the streets becoming more boisterous. He even saw a few obvious prostitutes loitering near taverns and inns, trying to balance dressing provocatively with bundling up for the plummeting temperature. It was almost impressive how they strategically bared thighs, hips, and cleavage in a way that clearly hinted at their profession.

Terana had a night life, of course, but by public assent it was kept indoors or to the back streets. Marona didn't allow public indecency, drunkenness, or solicitation.

In Redoubt men staggered the streets with bottles in hand, laughing and singing snatches of song. Vendors hawked wares like Prevent Conception scrolls, hangover remedies, and the recreational drugs available on Collisa. Whores of numerous races lifted their skirts or tugged down their tops to entice passersby, or even sidled up to press against men who met their eye.

No doubt pickpockets were also out in force, and Dare wasn't about to follow a woman of the night into a dark alley and possibly get set on by a gang of thugs. Although at his level that was less of a concern.

As a frontier city that drew adventurers it was no surprise the region's capitol had more of a night life. And considering how haphazard the civic design and management seemed to be it was no surprise they were lax on vice as well.

Although it seemed the governor, mayor, or watch commander, or all of the above, recognized that as the center of civilization in Bastion Redoubt had a reputation to maintain for order and safety. The brightly lit streets chased away the growing darkness, even in most alleys, and patrolling guards showed a strong presence. The pertinent laws were also prominently displayed, as well as the punishments for breaking them.

That didn't seem to hamper anyone's fun, though.

If the market district of the city was boisterous, the red light distract was absolutely wild. It was by far the most separated and isolated of all the various sprawling districts, even the slums themselves, with the streets leading into it clearly marked by the namesake lanterns.

In fact, most of the lanterns and magical lights along the streets were red or pale pink, giving everything a garish hue.

Acrobats and contortionists performed on the streets for coins, wearing skintight clothing but still probably uncomfortable in the cold. Although a few had fires lit to keep them warm, and also for passersby to gather around to warm their hands as they watched the show.

Illusionists and magicians also plied their trade, and vendors beneath heat enchantments enticed the surprisingly large crowds wandering the streets with sizzling meat or fresh cakes. Or food intended to improve performance in bed, like oysters.

Dare wove through the crowds, keeping a sharp eye on his possessions as he made for the first brothel on his list, the Crate. Which was a strange name for an establishment frequented by nobles, unless it was some sort of euphemism.

Twice he caught pickpockets thanks to the improved reflexes afforded him by Fleetfoot, shoving them back but letting them scurry away since he didn't want to draw attention to himself by dragging them to the guards.

Although he did break a few fingers on the man who tried to draw a knife on him with his other hand. Which had to be the stupidest move ever for someone ten levels lower than him.

Finally he saw a sign ahead with a surprisingly well done painting of a crate on it. And it was an equal surprise to find that it wasn't hanging over a brothel after all, or at least not simply that.

In fact, it seemed to be a large and bustling tavern with customers coming and going. Including an unexpectedly large number of women, not just whores but laborers and even a few ladies who looked more wealthy.

Interesting. Dare followed a group of richly dressed young men through the doors, welcomed by cheery music perfect for dancing, and laughter and clapping from within.

He stopped short just inside, eyes widening.

In spite of what he'd seen so far in the red light district, and even the market district, he hadn't expected to be confronted by a naked woman dancing seductively on a stage in the center of the room, gracefully stepping around glittering coins tossed at her feet.

The aforementioned crate, he guessed, which explained the odd name.

Patrons crowded tables clustered around the stage, clapping and whistling and tossing coins. Although they seemed to be socializing just as much, quaffing ale and digging into finger foods like fried meats and vegetables.

Dare became aware of complaints from patrons trying to get in behind him and hastily stepped aside. Although before he needed to go looking for a table a gorgeous serving girl led him to a small booth near the stage, suitable for a couple or at most four people.

She was dressed far more conservatively than he would've expected, considering the girl dancing naked in the center of the room. Almost primly.

Thankfully, he didn't even have to ask her to satisfy his curiosity about the establishment, since as she took his order she happily explained what the Crate was all about.

It was obviously a strip club, and Marona had told him it was a brothel, but it operated in a way he'd never heard of before.

Specifically, any woman, whether a patron or a serving girl or even a vagrant off the street, could go up on stage and dance. If she pleased the crowd they'd toss her coins to encourage her to strip off her clothes, while if the crowd wasn't impressed they'd boo her off for another woman to take her place.

She could take the coins and leave at any point, although the tavern took half for providing the safe venue. The more clothing the woman removed, and the more obscene her movements, the more and higher value coins she was usually tossed.

Although of course her appearance was usually the biggest factor in deciding how well her dance went.

The serving girl also, while speculatively looking Dare over, hinted that the tavern rented rooms by the hour. Many of the women dancing for the crowd descended from the stage when a gentleman shook his coin purse and pointed at the ceiling, in a well known invitation to take the entertainment to a more private setting.

So a tavern, strip club, and brothel. That any woman could walk into off the street to earn coin if she was willing or desperate enough.

The woman currently dancing must've pleased the crowd well enough, because a couple gold glittered at her feet. Although the stream seemed to be drying up as the onlookers got their fill of eyeing her. Her last effort was lying on her back with legs spread, fingers delicately pulling apart her labia to expose her glistening pink interior in a shockingly lewd display.

The position of Dare's booth gave him an excellent view and he couldn't help but stare, feeling his cock begin to swell. He dug in his coin pouch and pulled out a silver to toss on the stage.

The obscene stunt drew eager approval from the appreciative crowd, and earned the dancing woman several more silver and another gold. After which she began gathering up the coins and her clothes, to a few disappointed groans.

A few men shook coin purses at her and pointed at the ceiling, but she only smiled at them coyly as she disappeared behind a curtain at the back of the stage. Presumably a place to dress and settle up with the tavern.

"You seem a cultured sort, so I doubt I have to tell you," the serving girl told Dare as she prepared to fetch his beer, "but it's something we tell all new patrons as a matter of course. Getting hard is fine, even expected, but try to keep it out of view under the table. None of the patrons want to see that. Same with exposing yourself or jacking off. No touching any girls here, even with their permission . . . take it upstairs or outside. No shouting, lewd or offensive comments, or other undue noise disruptions. No indecent propositions except to the dancers onstage unless you're the one approached."

She playfully waggled a finger. "And no warnings, just the boot if you don't follow the rules."

"I understand," he told her with a smile. She smiled back before hurrying off.

The next woman to take the stage was a patron, giggling and egged on by the shouted encouragement of her tipsy companions. She began to sway her hips in time to the music, running her hands over her curvy body through her fine evening gown as she turned in a circle to look at everyone leering up at her.

Far from looking embarrassed or shy, she almost seemed to be luxuriating in the attention.

The elegant woman looked wealthy, and Dare wondered if she was slumming and stripping in the club for the titillation rather than any hope of coin.

If so, she earned a fair amount of silver in any case. Although she only stripped down to her underwear before gathering her earnings and clothes and fleeing giggling behind the curtain, to a few grumbles from the onlookers who'd hoped for more.

The next dancer was one of the serving girls, a beautiful high elf, as slender and ethereally perfect as any picture of an elf Dare had ever seen from Earth.

Although of course she didn't hold a candle to Leilanna.

Her ascent to the stage immediately drew cheers and a sense of eager expectation, copper coins flying almost from the moment she set foot on the platform and began one of the most graceful dances Dare had ever seen.

He found out why the staff here was dressed so primly as he watched the elf make a show of slowly removing each item, playing the crowd for more coins which they were happy to toss. Copper and silver rained on the stage, and as she finally pulled off her bra to expose her small, perfect breasts and pressed a finger into her slit through her panties, gold made an appearance.

At that point a finely dressed gentleman cleared his throat and nodded to the ceiling. He didn't shake a bag of gold or make any overt offer, but the beautiful high elf looked delighted as she nodded to him and began gathering her earnings and various layers of discarded clothing.

There was some grumbling from the crowd about the lucky man cutting the show short, but the mood immediately bounced back as a sleek, black-haired catgirl from the crowd climbed up onto the stage.

She began doing graceful acrobatics while somehow losing clothing in the process, and soon copper began flowing again.

In most cases Dare would've been happy to watch the show all night, and throw his own share of coins and maybe even point upstairs. But like he'd told Rosaceae, right now he had more important things to worry about than getting his dick wet.

He needed to protect his family.

The serving girl brought his beer around, and after paying her he sat back and took a sip, pretending to watch the nimble catgirl while using his Eye to inspect the patrons in the tavern. He was looking for nobles or high level adventurers he could approach to casually inquire about Ollivan, and judging by the coins flowing onto the stage here the patrons had to be on the wealthier side.

There were a few good prospects, but he thought his best bet was a table of guards who were all around Level 30 sitting in one corner. Dare called the serving girl back around to order them a round of drinks, then when they received them and nodded his way he nodded back and sauntered over.

“My thanks for all your service to this fine city,” he said, grabbing a chair from a nearby table and motioning to an empty spot at theirs.

“A fine sentiment, citizen,” a grizzled older man said, waving. “Pull up a chair.”

Dare settled at the table and took a sip of his beer. “Redoubt really hops at night, doesn't it? Must make for exciting shifts.”

There were a few snorts from around the table. “Let's just say we never complain when we have the day shift,” the grizzled guard said.

“Holy shit,” another guard muttered, staring at the stage. “That's the sexiest pussy I've ever seen.”

Dare turned to see that the catgirl was now nude and apparently stretching and doing poses. The coins continued to flow as she contorted her supple body in ways even most flexible girls would struggle with, sable tail raised in a playful question mark and curling and waving with every motion.

It certainly did hint at interesting possibilities.

Pretty as she was, he thought Linia was far more beautiful. Although as he watched the show he somewhat regretted he hadn't tried some more acrobatic stuff with his orange dream catgirl lover when he had the chance, back in Jarn's Holdout.

He tossed the sable catgirl a gold, as much in thanks for giving him ideas in case he ran into Linia again as in admiration for her posing. When she saw it she smiled and turned to the guards' table to show herself off to them, rubbing herself and moving her lithe body provocatively.

"Fuck," the grizzled veteran said, shaking his head in disbelief. "You can get a night with a whore for that in some establishments. Must be nice to be an adventurer tossing around gold like it's copper."

Dare bit back his own curse at his blunder; he was trying to get on these guys' good side. "Had a good streak of luck recently," he said, motioning for the serving girl to bring them another round. "Any of you ever thought of taking up the life?"

The guards all snorted. "Thanks, I'd like to live to be as old as Macor here," a young guardsman said, jostling his grizzled companion. "I'll stick to the regulated guard training and patrolling the streets."

"And I've retired from my adventuring days," Macor agreed. "The wife likes to know I'll be home every night, and the greatest danger I'll face is having a pair of tits shoved in my face."

Dare laughed. "May we all face that danger," he said, raising his mug. There was a chorus of assent and laughter as other mugs clashed against his in toast.

He settled in at the table to drink and exchange gossip with his new friends, idly watching the stage. The girls who went up usually only danced for a few minutes, fifteen at most, but surprisingly there always seemed to be another woman waiting to hop on the stage when it was vacated.

The clear amateurs often left the stage with only modest (or perhaps immodest) earnings, especially if they weren't particularly pretty. Although cheerfulness and enthusiasm went a long way for even the homeliest and most clumsy dancers, usually earning them goodwill and coppers.

As for those clearly experienced in seduction, and attractive on top of that, they usually gathered up at least one gold along with the rest of their coin.

There were women of various races, although most were human. Dare saw everything from thrill seeking wealthy girls, to women of other more respectable professions here looking for extra coin, to clearly destitute women hoping for a good dance to turn things around.

Which they were delighted to succeed at tonight, since he would toss the most obviously struggling a gold and usually a few silver as well. To the point where the more poorly dressed women would usually turn to face him for their dance, and more than a few pointed up at the ceiling in silent invitation.

Although to be fair, they weren't the only ones who seemed willing to rent a room with him. Even the serving girls looked to him expectantly or gave subtle hints, probably because of his clothes since he still wore his makeup to make himself look more homely.

He responded to each hint and subtle invitation with a warm smile but firm shake of his head, ignoring the ribbing of the guards around him.

As the night progressed the mood in the tavern grew ever more merry, with the songs the musicians in the corner were playing becoming downright boisterous. The dances became increasingly erotic, and just about all the women who went up on stage stripped fully, and many played with themselves as well.

A few times multiple dancers went up together, especially the serving girls, generally drawing showers of coins as they all but fucked each other right there in the middle of the tavern.

It made a pleasant backdrop for Dare's subtle probing for information from the guards.

He figured that a man like Ollivan would be causing enough trouble to get noticed by the law, even if he was immune to punishment, and subtly shifted the conversation to gossip about the guards' interactions with the rich and famous.

Which they were only too happy to talk about; the rich tended to draw resentment, and that applied all the more if they were scum who committed crimes.

Ollivan fit that to a T, and it seemed like the guards had plenty of tales to tell about the knight; he may have been protected by his uncle the Duke of Bastion, but he wasn't protected from rumor and outrage.

Unfortunately, what Dare didn't learn was where he could find the bastard. In fact, Ollivan seemed to have disappeared from view after some recent scandal that Dare presumed was the attempted burning of Nirim Manor.

It looked as if he was going to have to poke around among the nobility or the adventurers, see if any of them knew what the man was up to. Although part of Dare was afraid that Ollivan disappearing meant he was on his way to Nirim Manor to cause trouble.

He hoped Ilin and his fiancees were keeping vigilant, because at the moment he was far away and in a good position to figure out where the Warrior had gone and what he planned.

Besides, if Dare *did* learn that Ollivan was making for his family, he could reassure himself that he'd be able to get there much faster than the knight, as long as the man didn't have too much of a head start.

Leaving the guards to their drinking with a final round of beers and a few clasped forearms and back slaps, he poked around the

Crate and chatted up some of the wealthier and higher level patrons. Although he had poor luck since most wanted to look at the women displaying themselves up on the stage, not talk to a random stranger who approached them out of the blue.

Eventually he found himself back at his table, debating leaving the Crate, pleasant as it was, to continue to Ollivan's other preferred brothel and see if he had more luck.

Also now that it was dark he might try sniffing around the Assassin's Guild, if that's what that tavern in the slums was. Or maybe even try to break into Ollivan's house and look for clues. Although that would be a last resort in a town where the guards were so vigilant.

He was still debating his options when a figure blocked his view of the stage.

Chapter Seven

Thorns

Dare looked up in surprise as a woman slipped into his booth across from him, looking furtive.

He judged her to be in her late 30s, although her somewhat homely features were drawn and lined by stress and grief that aged her, so she could've been younger. She was skinny and wore plain robes and a heavy cloak, clasped at the neck with a gold brooch in the shape of a bird.

"You the answer to my prayers?" she asked, nervously licking her lips and not meeting his gaze.

The hell? She wouldn't be the first invitation he'd gotten tonight, but in spite of her mousy appearance and furtive manner she was by far the boldest.

He took a cautious sip of his beer. "I'm not here for that, miss," he said politely.

She flinched as she caught his meaning and laughed hollowly. "I'm not either."

Frowning, Dare looked at her with his Eye, and to his surprise saw she was a Level 34 Healer. So definitely not a prostitute or grifter, since adventurers of her level should have no trouble earning money.

And from the way she couldn't meet his gaze and had reacted to the idea that he thought she was propositioning him, it didn't seem like her interest was romantic, either. "What are you here for, then?" he asked warily.

In reply she fished in the collar of her robes and produced an amulet engraved with the sigil of a blooming rose crossed by a long, wicked thorn. "Heliora, Goddess of Purity," she whispered. "You've heard of her?"

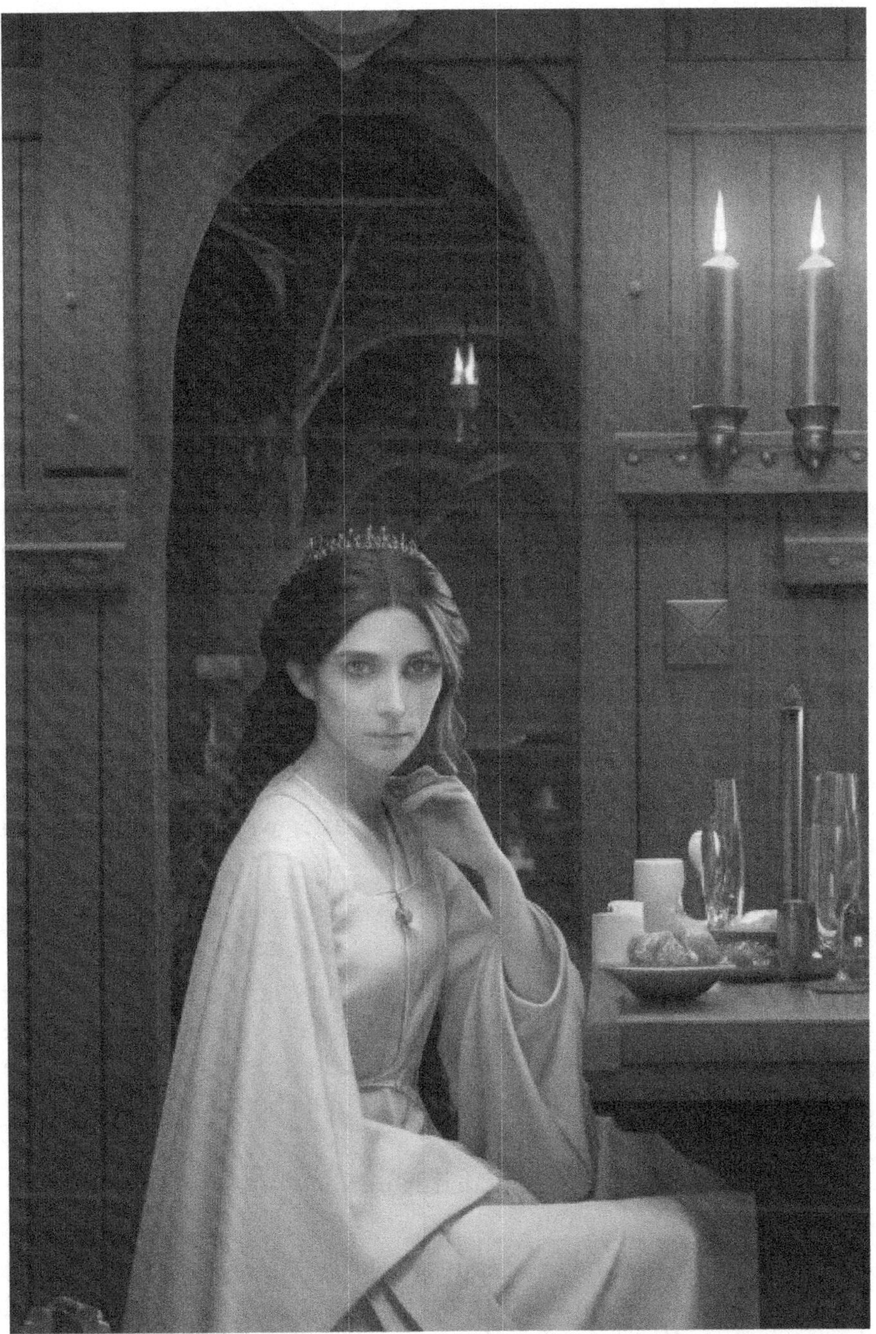

He hesitated. “Not sure,” he admitted.

The Healer laughed bitterly. “Yes, the rose doesn't bloom often in this harsh world, it sometimes feels.” She clenched the amulet in her fist. “So Heliora wields the thorn.”

The haggard woman finally met his gaze, eyes blazing. “And if you don't know her, she's Noticed you.”

Dare tensed at the obvious hint; the last time he'd been Noticed a party rated monster had chased him across a battlefield trying to cut him in two. “What does your goddess want of me?” he asked, even more warily.

“The thorn.” The Healer tucked the amulet back into her robes and sat with hunched shoulders, staring at the table. “Let me tell you a story of an Adventurers Guild Healer who, ignoring the explicit warnings of a close friend and all the rumors she'd heard, took a contract to hunt monsters for gold and experience with a noble Warrior.” She shuddered. “One who it turned out was not so noble in anything but title.”

He hissed through his teeth as the dots connected. “Ollivan?”

She flinched at the name but nodded slightly, eyes haunted. “I don't wish to speak of what I suffered when I went alone in the wilds with him. And I doubt you need me to, after what he almost did to your lover.”

Shit, so this woman really did know who Dare was. So much for his haircut and makeup. “No, I don't,” he said gently.

Her pale face set in quiet grief and fury at the memory of her ordeal. “He told me if I tried to run he'd have me thrown from the Guild for breach of contract. That if I tried to report his deeds to the magistrates it would do no good, and in punishment he'd expose my infidelity to my husband.”

That motherfucker. It sounded like exactly the sort of vile deeds the knight would carry out.

The Healer hunched miserably, a tear slipping down her gaunt cheek. “I did anyway. Went to my husband and explained how I'd been abused. Went to the Guild representatives to testify of his misdeeds. Went to the magistrates in pursuit of justice."

Dare felt sick as he guessed how this story would end. He almost wanted to stop her, tell her she didn't need to say any more.

But she kept going inexorably. "My husband called me a whore, my contracts an excuse to bed noble adventurers behind his back, and that I'd only come to him out of fear of discovery. He threw me out of my home without so much as a chance to bid farewell to my children, and told me if I returned he'd call the guards on me. As for the Adventurers Guild, they feared to displease the Governor and tossed me out on my ear.

"And the magistrates?" She laughed harshly. "What a fool I was to believe in a world where justice existed for highly placed nobles."

He clenched his fists; he understood that frustration and fury all too well. "I won't speak of justice, or even of vengeance. Only a need to protect myself and my family."

The Healer nodded. "As well you should." She snorted bitterly. "Immune from the consequences of his vile deeds as Ollivan seems, he erred in trying to burn your house. His uncle and the rest of the nobility have turned their backs on him, at least for the moment. Likely he'll worm his way back into their good graces soon enough, but he has no desire to wait."

She waved vaguely around them. "In this very tavern, and others in Redoubt, he's been heard to drunkenly boast that he would spend his entire fortune to hire assassins and mercenaries to have revenge on you and anyone associated with you."

The poor woman shuddered again. "But he doesn't have much of a fortune at present. The whole reason he wanted to go out hunting monsters with me was to earn coin for his dark deeds, as he told me often enough while he brutalized me. And why he took my share of the loot and treated me even more harshly when I protested."

"I'm sorry," Dare murmured.

She spat on the floor by their table. "Don't be sorry, answer to my prayers. Be the thorn for defenseless women. Offer the only justice available to those such as us, in the face of those with greater power." She leaned forward. "Help me teach him that healers, like commoners, are not without our own power. That you *don't fuck with us*. That eventually your deeds catch up with you."

He leaned forward as well. "How?"

"Simple." She clutched the amulet through her robes, perhaps in silent prayer or in acknowledgement. "Even in disgrace, I'm not without friends. And even in cowardice, the Adventurers Guild is not the home of fools. No healers or adventurers of any sort would answer Ollivan's call for a contract, so he's gone back into the wilds to hunt alone."

"Back where he hunted with you?" Dare guessed.

The Healer flinched at painful memories. "Yes," she hissed. "And it's where, Heliora willing, he'll meet his end." She looked around and dropped her voice even more, so he could barely hear her over the raucous music. "It's simple. You've already seen how monsters aggro to those closest to them, or in their path, except in unusual circumstances with abilities or monsters with a chaotic disposition. So we wait for that walking pile of gilded shit to pull aggressively, as he tends to do when bored or impatient."

She clenched her fist, green mana beginning to play around her fingers. "Then I use Mana Thorn to pull more monsters his way. As many as it takes. The monsters kill him, nobody knows we were anywhere near, and everyone chalks it up to another adventurer slain in the dangerous work of hunting monsters. The perfect poetry of a monster being slain by his own kind."

"And I'm there in case it doesn't go that smoothly," Dare guessed.

The gaunt woman laughed hollowly. "And because I'm sure you want to witness his death for yourself so you know your family is safe."

He thoughtfully downed the last of his beer. "Will it be the end of it, with him gone?"

"For you? Most likely." She laughed again. "No offense, but you're a nobody and nobody gives a shit about his feud with you.

Most adventurers and members of the nobility think it's stupid. If he dies to monsters no one would give you a second thought.

"As for myself . . ." She stared off into nothing, face twisted in leaden bitterness. "My life is already destroyed, and there is no end to that. But perhaps there can be a beginning, with him no longer actively seeking to ruin me."

Dare was sure she didn't want his pity, but it was hard not to look at her with sympathy. "I'll help you, of course. And I thank you for helping me. I don't relish the thought of killing anyone, but this fucker needs to die." He offered his hand. "I'm Dare."

The Healer flinched slightly and made no move to accept his handshake, which he realized in chagrin made sense given what she'd been through. He pulled his hand back and gave her an apologetic look.

"You can call me Thorn," she finally said. "No doubt you could find my name easily enough if you tried, but I prefer to shed it. At least while we carry out this grim necessity."

Fair enough. "Will you be ready to leave in the morning?"

Thorn nodded. "I'd appreciate if you could arrange horses." She looked away. "I . . . am struggling for coin at the moment."

Shit, Ollivan really had fucked up her life. Extra horses would eat into Dare's coffers, and be awkward on the trip home unless he resold them after all this was done, but with the Healer as a companion there weren't any better options.

"Do you have a place to stay tonight, enough for food?" he asked gently.

He could see the distraught Healer was torn, but finally she shook her head. "I could use help with that, too, thank you. I've been camping in the slums with my adventuring kit."

Well that definitely wouldn't do. Dare produced a few gold and slid them across the table to her. "If you'll be okay tonight, I have other things I need to do before we leave." Even if they were going to eliminate Ollivan, with the way they were planning to do it there'd be a long delay before word of his death reached Redoubt.

The assassins could still act in that time, so better to deal with them too if he could.

“I'll be fine,” Thorn said, taking the coins. “Th-”

They both jumped as a powerfully built bouncer loomed over the table. “Take that outside,” he rumbled, pointing at the gold Dare had just given her. “This is a classy establishment.”

The Healer went ashen with humiliation, and Dare felt a surge of anger. He met the man's gaze firmly. “It wasn't about that.”

“I don't care. Business deals between gentlemen is fine, but no coin passes from man to woman in this establishment except onto the stage or upstairs. You can offer in public but you pay in private.” The bouncer motioned them out of the booth. “Out, now.”

Well fuck him too. Dare moved between Thorn and the man, who at Level 25 wasn't really a threat to either of them, and escorted her out of the Crate.

Once on the street he turned to her. “Can I walk you to a reputable inn?”

“No,” she said, pulling down the deep hood of her heavy cloak. “I'll meet you at the south gate an hour after sunrise.” She paused. “Whatever it is you're doing, be careful, and stay to the lit streets . . . our levels don't make us invincible, just a more tempting target.”

Somehow he doubted she'd approve of his plans. He wondered if he should ask if she knew anything about the Assassins Guild.

Before he could decide she slipped into the crowd and disappeared down the street.

Dare stared after the Healer, worried for her safety in spite of her obvious competence. But he doubted she'd appreciate him following to make sure when she'd already told him not to.

So he hoped for the best and made his way down the street in the direction of the slums.

The red light district was actually not far from that part of the city, although there were no actual streets connecting them. In fact there was almost a wall, blocking off the destitute from the playground of the wealthy.

A lot of those walls were in shadowed alleys, and Dare decided now was the time to get off the streets. So he ducked into an alley and made his way for the ten foot tall barrier, senses alert for any threats from behind.

No one followed him, so he propped his spear atop the wall and easily vaulted it, Fleetfoot and Power Up making the task trivial. On the other side the rowdy night scene of the red light district was nowhere in sight; the more ramshackle buildings here were mostly unlit, and he caught sight of a few vagrants sleeping just down the alley, huddled together for warmth beneath a pile of rags.

With the abrupt shift from light to dark he paused to let his eyes adjust, senses alert for danger. The overcast sky provided little light, snow still drifting down but not enough to coat the streets. Thankfully Eagle Eye helped some, although more would've been nice.

Dare wondered if one of the abilities he could learn with Student of the Wild gave him better night vision. It would almost be worth it to hunt nocturnal animals to see what he got; not only were they an untapped group he hadn't checked for abilities, but being able to see in the dark would be incredibly useful.

He finally set out, sticking to the walls of buildings and doing his best to avoid being a silhouette or walking out in the open. He was well aware that he shouldn't fall into the trap of assuming everyone else could see as poorly as him; many of the Stealth classes that operated in the shadows would have night vision as an ability, especially ones like Thief and Stalker.

The slums were even darker than the rest of the city, although he got the vague impression of more people moving around, some walking the streets but more sticking to the shadows like he was. He doubted their purpose was wholesome.

Unfortunately, there were other people who were up but not moving. And as it turned out, not that it came as a real surprise, Thorn's warning wasn't an idle one.

Dare was slipping past an alley between two sagging buildings that practically leaned against each other when a faint flash of metal out of the corner of his eye saved him from wasting Prey's Vigilance. He whirled with all the speed afforded by Fleetfoot, looking with his Eye.

Level 18 Backstabber. A dagger specialist class, and not a particularly reputable one if the name wasn't a clue. The man definitely couldn't see Dare clearly, or he wouldn't have had the courage to try something like this.

Dare caught the plunging blade and twisted, lifting the scrawny man, or perhaps woman or youth, and slamming him into the wall at the mouth of the alley. The grunt of pain definitely sounded masculine.

"I'm going to give you the opportunity to walk away here," he hissed, avoiding "s" sounds since sibilants carried. "Don't come after me again."

He caught the hint of the man's nod and tossed him away, and his assailant scrambled to escape.

Shit, that had been close. Not really a threat, but a dagger wound stung like a bitch even if it wouldn't take many hit points.

What did he do if the next one was a Level 30 who could see him clearly and came from behind, or out of Stealth? He couldn't assume that his enemies would all be low level even in the slums, considering he was making for a possible Assassins Guild hideout.

Dare approached the ramshackle tavern from two streets away along a parallel route, finally climbing the roof of a warehouse that would give him a view of the place. He didn't have abilities that helped him with climbing, but he definitely had the athleticism for it. Even at night.

To his surprise, he saw activity around the tavern even at this hour and in the darkness. There was still a sentry standing watch by the door, a Stalker, and he watched a Poisoner slip through the door. Light briefly streamed through, showing the place was still lively even if all the windows had been blackened.

Those could both be assassins, and it wasn't lost on him that even if they were below Level 20, they could both be a threat to most citizens who'd be even lower level.

A Level 19 Poisoner could easily brew poisons that would outright kill a Level 4 like Marona.

Pulling his heavy wool coat out of his pack for warmth, he wrapped it around him and settled down to watch the place.

* * * * *

A few hours later, Dare concluded that if this tavern *wasn't* an Assassins Guild, it certainly could be.

There was no way it was a coincidence that over a dozen Stealth classes had vanished inside the place without reappearing in the time he'd been watching. One of which had been a Level 31 Soul Thief.

The place was obviously a crime den of some sort, but the classes that had entered were all ones suited for assassination. He'd seen none that would put their skills to thievery or thuggery.

It definitely warranted a closer look, but how exactly did he go about that? And more importantly, if it *was* the Assassins Guild how did he deal with it?

If it was really a place frequented by high level, likely wealthy assassins, it would be thick with poisoned traps, spell wards, sentries, and who knew what else. He probably couldn't even try to enter the tavern without drawing a huge amount of suspicion, even if he feigned drunkenness or ignorance. And no doubt the tavern room itself would offer no clues, since it was a front.

And dealing with the place was even more of a challenge.

The obvious solution was to report the location to the guards. Or maybe not so obvious; a guild of murderers who'd been operating in Redoubt for a long time had to have had run-ins with the law before, and found ways to protect themselves. They'd either have a mole inside the guards, or dirt on an officer or even the guard commander that encouraged him to make sure his people looked the other way.

Or something.

Besides, a guild with powerful, wealthy members like the Darkblade wouldn't just be hanging out in some filthy basement beneath a seedy tavern. This was probably a place to pick up assignments and report to the higher ups, and almost certainly had hidden defenses and plenty of back doors and bolt holes.

On the other hand, Dare was going to have a tough time killing a bunch of assassins by himself. They might all be lower level than him, at least the ones he'd seen so far, but that didn't mean they couldn't kill him with a thousand cuts.

And that wasn't counting the poison, especially since he didn't have a healer who could cleanse it.

Thankfully, with Collisa's rigidly balanced system when it came to classes he doubted any poison would be lethal, at least not to an even or higher level target; it would be hugely imbalanced to be able to kill a target with a simple cut. So while the poison might debilitate him or paralyze him or who knew what, on the off chance he got nicked he shouldn't immediately drop over dead.

He hoped.

Finally Dare climbed down from the warehouse roof and crept away in the direction of the market district, mulling over what to do now.

Did he try the guards anyway and hope for the best? With Adventurer's Eye he could always find the assassins again if they got spooked and moved locations, and it might actually be a good way of flushing them out into the open so he could get a better idea of their numbers and levels.

But he didn't like the thought of giving them warning that someone was after them. The element of surprise was too valuable to waste.

He didn't want to attack the place, either. At least not until he had more information of things like the layout of the interior, the number of guild members and their levels and abilities, and if possible their defenses.

But gathering information took time, and also risked alerting the assassins to his activities.

Well, he'd made what progress he could with the Assassins Guild for now. If he and Thorn could kill Ollivan he'd return, if nothing else try to get the guilt a message informing them of the knight's death, and warning them to abandon any contracts they'd had with him.

Time to find a place to get a few hours of sleep. Then he'd buy some horses and provisions and meet the Healer to get this done.

* * * * *

Thankfully, finding mounts in a city that catered to adventurers wasn't as difficult as Dare had feared. It only took him about a half hour to find and purchase two decent horses and all the necessary tack.

He also purchased enough provisions to last two people a few days; he could always hunt or forage for more if needed.

True to her word, Thorn met him at the south gate an hour after sunrise. She looked calmer and more rested than she had been last night, and while her face was still haggard she looked focused as she mounted. Unlike Zuri, who at Dare's recommendation bore a spear, she had a simple knife belted at her waist to go with her mostly Good quality gear.

She didn't seem in the mood to chat, and the ride was mostly quiet and businesslike as they pushed south and a bit east, Thorn guiding the way. He noticed she fingered her sigil to Heliora often, mouthing silent prayers.

Hopefully they'd be answered.

Around late afternoon they reached the spot the Healer had told him about, dismounting and hiding their horses in a thicket as they crept forward on foot. They found Ollivan's camp in an ideal location near some spawn points.

To Dare's disappointment, and contempt, even though there were hours of daylight left the man was already there, drinking from a flask and desultorily maintaining his gear.

Thorn explained that the man's information about safe spawn points only covered three of them worth hunting at this level. Even with clearing them every time monsters respawned at 6 in the morning and 6 in the afternoon, the task only took so long.

Especially since Ollivan tended to be reckless in his pulling, as evidenced by half a dozen poorly bandaged wounds that weren't serious enough to apply a bleed effect, so he was simply ignoring them and letting his hit points naturally regenerate. Which seemed to go faster than usual, probably a Warrior ability.

The wounds would scar worse than if he was healed or used magical items like potions or enchantments, or even was tended to by a competent medic. Although the big knight didn't seem to care, and in truth had a surprising number of scars.

Thorn's entire body radiated hate as she peered at Ollivan from their hiding place, gripping her knife and magic glowing around her other hand. But after a brief inspection of the camp she backed out of their hiding spot and led the way back to their horses.

"Find a camp far enough away he won't stumble on us?" Dare suggested. She nodded, lips tight, and they mounted up and retraced their steps to a secluded copse with a hill between them and the knight to block firelight.

It was a cheerless dinner, even though Dare hunted an epind with its delicious meat, and cooked it with foraged root vegetables. Thorn ate mechanically, not seeming to taste the food, then immediately retreated to her tent set up far enough from his that it was uncertain they could even be considered to be in the same camp.

As the night turned unexpectedly cold Dare retired to his own tent, shivering in his blankets until they warmed with his body heat.

Even with good shelter it was a cold and lonely night. He found himself desperately missing his loved ones back home. He longed to be back in the master bedroom's big bed with Zuri, Pella, Leilanna, Se'weir, and Ireni or Sia pressed close around him in a cuddly pile.

Soon, he hoped.

* * * * *

Dare was up at the crack of dawn cooking breakfast, Thorn emerging from her tent soon after. They ate in tense silence and prepared for the day's grim purpose, creeping back to Ollivan's camp.

At which point they had to settle in and wait for four hours as the knight made a leisurely morning of it. Including such highlights as a lazy wank facing the rising sun, a long, apparently laborious dump, and finally a late breakfast.

Thorn watched it all with the same simmering hatred, tense as a bowstring the entire time so it was a wonder she didn't exhaust himself from the pure force of her wrath. Oddly, it was only when Ollivan donned his armor and mounted up to ride to the first spawn point that she relaxed, looking ready and eager to have her justice.

Dare was eager for it to be over too, although mostly so he could return to his family.

At the spawn point, which featured odd hybrids of pigs and dogs except with the usual nightmarish embellishments, Ollivan tethered his horse a safe distance away and strode right in. Without hesitation he engaged the first of the outlying monsters, then went on to make quick work of the other isolated ones around the edges.

Then, laughing with an eagerness bordering on mania, he rushed a group of three closely spaced monsters and began fighting them at once.

Dare watched incredulously, not quite believing their opportunity had come so quickly. He knew the man was an arrogant fool, but to willingly take on a fight he could easily have broken up into safer fights was just bafflingly stupid.

The knight slammed into one of the pigdogs and sent it tumbling away, while the other two converged on him with feral snarls, nipping at his legs. He laughed at their attempts, bashing them away with his shield and slashing at snarling muzzles as they leapt at him again.

He even laughed when a wolf got through his defenses and Hamstrung him, while at the same time another managed to bite through the chainmail at the joint of his ass hard enough to injure him through it. The wounds were minor but weren't trivial, and were having a noticeable impact on his health bar, but he almost seemed to relish the pain.

Was he insane as well as brutal and sadistic?

Thorn strode forward with an expression of grim purpose, hands already glowing. Moments later a small, razor sharp dark green shard zipped past Ollivan and the monsters he was fighting and struck a monster deeper into the spawn point, aggroing it and a nearby add straight towards the knight.

Caught up in his fight, Ollivan didn't even notice, dispatching one of the pigdogs and turning to the other two. He seemed surprised when two more swarmed him, but it was only when the Healer's next Mana Thorn whipped past him to aggro three more his way that he finally began looking around.

Thorn was already running forward to aggro yet more monsters on the Warrior, and Dare hurried to catch up.

"You!" Ollivan roared when he caught sight of Dare. Then moments later he spotted the Healer. "You betrayed me to my enemies, you filthy whore?" he screamed in what seemed like genuine incredulity.

"Only one of us is a betrayer, you festering asshole!" she screamed back, bitterness poisoning the words. "Now die and be mourned by no one!" Her Mana Thorn whipped out to hit another group of the pigdogs.

As they, too, aggroed on the knight Thorn finally began backing away towards where Dare stood, ready to flee if necessary but lingering to witness the fruit of her actions.

Ollivan staggered away from the pile of monsters, trying to escape the sudden fresh onslaught. With every step he frantically swung his sword and moved his shield in defensive abilities, as the pigdogs swarmed him in ever greater numbers. His helmet had been torn away by a monster and blood sheeted down his face from a scalp wound, and he was limping from a lucky strike to his ankle.

Dare watched in amazement; holy shit, she was really doing it. Her idea had worked.

Don't fuck with healers.

Although it seemed that in spite of the impossible odds, Ollivan still had some fight in him. With a roar he burst out of the pile of monsters, stumbling and bleeding from dozens of minor and major wounds. Yet if he felt any pain, it didn't show in the insane fury that twisted his features into a monstrous mask.

"You spineless cunt!" he snarled as he Charged at Thorn. "I'll make you beg for death before I'm done with you!"

The haggard woman's cold mask shattered to one of terror as she turned to flee. But while she sprinted at her best speed, it seemed slow as molasses compared to what Dare could manage.

He looked at the distance between the knight and the Healer, Ollivan's health and the speed he was going and the rate he was bleeding, and the math wasn't good.

Shit. It would've been cleaner if Thorn had succeeded in getting Ollivan killed to monsters. Fewer questions, and no way to tie it back to them. The perfect crime.

But even if the Warrior might still die from his wounds, it was clear he meant to bring the poor woman with him.

Dare cursed quietly to himself and Pounced on Ollivan. It knocked the man to the ground, unable to move for a second, but that wouldn't be enough to let the pursuing monsters catch up. So he whipped his spear down in two smooth slashes and Hamstrung both the man's legs.

Hopefully the wounds wouldn't look too much different from those inflicted by teeth and claws to anyone investigating Ollivan's death.

The knight screamed and thrashed on the ground, not so much in pain as in fear and fury. "Motherfucker!" he snarled at Dare, eyes murderous as he tried to drag himself towards him with just his arms. "I'll torture and mutilate everyone you ever loved before f-"

Dare shut his ears to the man's vile but ultimately feeble threats and ran back to where Thorn stood. Together they watched in silence as the Warrior, dragging himself towards them desperately and bellowing in fury and terror, was buried beneath a pile of monsters. The pigdogs eagerly ripped into the man, finding ways through the armor to get at the flesh beneath, and soon he stopped thrashing and screaming as they began to feed.

Thus ended Sir Ollivan of Trentwood, and good riddance.

Chapter Eight

Deal

Dare felt a bit of vindictive satisfaction at Ollivan's death, after everything the man had done to him and his loved ones. But mostly he felt relief that the ordeal was finally over.

Or at least, mostly over.

“Take nothing,” Thorn said in a cold, flat voice. “His body, his horse, his camp, all stays as it is so those who come looking for him suspect nothing.”

He nodded. “Of course.”

She sighed. “It's a pity, though, because I would've liked to piss on his corpse.”

Dare tore his eyes away from the grisly scene of the monsters devouring the knight, feeling sick to his stomach; he'd hated the man, but it was still an awful thing to see done to a body.

To his surprise, in spite of his companion's calm tone she was hugging herself tightly, shoulders hunched and tears streaming down her cheeks. She hadn't taken her eyes off the feasting monsters as the sight became more sickening.

He supposed now that she'd had her justice, all that was left was the ruin Ollivan had made of her life.

He cleared his throat awkwardly. “If you want, you're welcome to come to Nirim Manor. Leave your old past behind and start anew in a peaceful, prosperous place.”

The Healer didn't respond for so long that he wondered if she either hadn't heard or was ignoring him. Then she shook her head slightly, a catch in her voice. “No, I'll return to Redoubt. Perhaps my situation will improve with Ollivan dead. The Adventurers Guild might take me back, and I can press my husband to let me be part of my children's lives."

Dare nodded. "I'm heading back there, too. Want some company on the ride?"

She laughed hollowly. "That seems only fair considering I'm riding your horse." She spat in Ollivan's direction, then turned away. "I have nothing more keeping me here."

In the familiar silence from yesterday they returned to their camp, ate an early lunch, then mounted up and started back for Redoubt.

If Ollivan's death had improved Thorn's disposition, she showed no sign of it. She seemed almost deflated, as if her grim purpose had been all that kept her going until now.

He decided to try again. "Thank you, Thorn. I don't think I would've found Ollivan easily without your aid." He hesitated, then added, "If you're ever in need of aid, any assistance at all I can provide, please contact me."

Thorn shrugged listlessly. "You're welcome." She didn't respond to his offer.

They rode in that melancholy silence the rest of the way to Redoubt, arriving after dark. That suited Dare's purposes because he was still able to find a stables who wanted to buy the horses, if at a slight loss, and it meant he'd be able to spend another night investigating the tavern in the slums.

His companion took her leave of him at the stables, looking weary but determined. "Go in the Goddess's grace, answer to my prayers," she said with a low bow. "May you find the peace you seek for your family."

That was certainly the plan.

Dare slipped through the night in the direction of the slums, again sticking to the shadows and darting from cover to cover as he made his way to the roof of the warehouse where he'd observed the tavern two nights ago.

Then he settled in to watch the place, observing the people who came and went and formulating plans.

It was hours later, when even Redoubt's night life had finally died down, when he was approached.

* * * * *

"Fancy seeing you again."

Dare, already tense as a bowstring, literally jumped at the man's voice coming from not far behind him. He used Roll and Shoot to throw himself to the side, to the very edge of the warehouse roof, and came to his feet facing the direction of the voice with his bow drawn.

There was nothing there: Stealth.

Shit, should he just cut and run? The man could be Level 50 or Level 15 for all he knew, and could very well be approaching to knife him with a poisoned blade.

Hell, there could be a dozen Stealthed enemies up here with him, even if he hadn't sensed any sign he wasn't alone.

Then again, the Stealthed man had opted for a greeting instead of an attack. That suggested he might at least want to hold off violence until they'd talked.

So Dare abandoned his desperate plan to use Snap to blind and disorient his assailant while he kept his eyes closed, then use the opening to flee. Instead he stayed where he was, although he kept the fletchings drawn to his ear as he searched the night with his senses, hoping for a clue to the other man's whereabouts.

"You must have me mistaken for someone else," he said cautiously.

The voice chuckled, indistinct enough that he couldn't pin down a location; maybe an ability. "There are only so many teenagers out there of your level, lad. And you're not one of the two currently residing in Redoubt."

Godsdamnit. The oddity between Dare's age and level was going to be make him stand out more and more as time went on.

There was a brief pause as if the Stealthed man was waiting for a response, then he said, "You can lower your bow, I only wish to talk." His voice hardened. "This time."

Dare reluctantly relaxed the string and lowered the point of the arrow. Slightly. No sense pointing it at nothing and antagonizing the man. "What do you want to talk about?"

Another chuckle. "I believe that's my question to ask. You're the one poking around where you shouldn't."

Okay then. Maybe it was time to take a gamble and just speak bluntly . . . after all, he'd considered trying to get a message to the Assassins Guild. If that's who this man represented.

So he took a breath. "Sir Ollivan of Trentwood perished to monsters recently. To any interested parties, any contracts he had in effect are now void."

There was a long pause. "Ah," the voice said thoughtfully, "is that what this is about? Your employer is shockingly well informed and quick to respond."

Employer? Dare supposed it had only been four days, five if it was past midnight, since he'd encountered the assassin and left for Redoubt. Barely enough time for a normal traveler to reach here from Terana if he'd been riding frequent remounts into the ground.

Okay, good to know he wasn't barking up the wrong tree. It actually wasn't the worst thing for the man to assume he was a mercenary hired via messenger pigeon or magical communication. Or that he was more well connected and knowledgeable than he seemed.

"That's what this is about," he confirmed in a confident voice.

The Stealthed man sighed. "It seems Maldinal stumbled into more than he was prepared for down south, poor fool. And sent it on to us."

Dare continued resolutely. "With your contract giver gone, I need to know this is the end of it."

His assailant chuckled. "I don't bend down to pick up a gaffer's dropped cane unless there's a coin in it for me, lad. There's no money in war with a target from a dead contract. As long as you're telling the truth about Ollivan, which I have no reason to disbelieve, our business with you is done."

His voice hardened. "Provided you leave now, and this is the last we hear of you and your employer."

Considering all Dare wanted was to rush home and be with his family anyway, he was more than happy to take that deal. "I'll be leaving the city, but I may be back on other business. Although I'm happy to forget you even exist if you'll do the same, and I'm sure my employer will also feel that way."

"Agreed." the assassin said in a tone of formal finality.

Silence settled, and after it had dragged for several long seconds Dare became confident that the man was either gone or at least done talking.

Glad to escape without having to fight an assassin on a rooftop in the dark, he dropped down to the street below and gratefully crept out of the slums.

Was this the end of it, then? Pragmatically speaking, the assassins should have no reason to go after him aside from vengeance, and the man hadn't seemed particularly broken up about his friend's death.

Still, Dare would keep up his guard. Maybe he could ask Marona where she got her alarm enchantments for her mansion so he could buy some, too.

Even so, for the most part Dare felt as if a huge weight had fallen off his chest, and he allowed himself to breathe freely for the first time in what felt like weeks.

It was time to return to his family and let them know that the threat should be over.

* * * * *

Dare found a humble inn not far from the south gate where he could spend the night, hopefully not drawing too much notice in the process. The threat from Ollivan may be over, but he still needed to make sure he wasn't identified as being anywhere near Redoubt to avoid suspicion.

Part of him wanted to explore the city while he was here, especially the market to see what high level and high quality gear was available. And he could admit it would be tempting to return to the Crate now that the pressure was off and he could fully enjoy the experience.

But it would all have to wait for the next time he visited. Although he did want to make one quick stop in the market.

The moment he woke in the morning, after sleeping longer than he'd expected thanks to days of accumulated exhaustion, he ate a hasty breakfast and made his way purposefully among the traders until he found a book seller.

The vendor was happy to recommend a very romantic storybook, and taking his word for it Dare got down to business.

"Fifty silver," he offered.

The woman scoffed. "You couldn't get a blank book bound for that price, let alone one transcribed with the most well loved romance on Shalin continent. 2 gold."

That was a harsher counteroffer than Dare had expected, and he idly wondered if his good looks had been making it easier to negotiate good deals all this time. An added challenge while wearing his homely makeup.

He rubbed the bridge of his nose, not having to feign weariness; usually he loved the give and take of haggling, pressing for the best deal possible. But at the moment he was too impatient for it. "Tell you what. Since you were kind enough to recommend it I'll go one gold, fifty silver. As long as you agree to be reasonable on any other purchases I might make."

She agreed quick enough to make him confident she'd got the better end of the deal, probably by a wide margin. But she made up for it when he found a couple books on the history of Haraldar and of wider Collisa and haggled to get better prices for them.

Dare had been meaning to learn more about the world that was his new home for a long time now, but it always seemed like he had more pressing things to spend his time doing. Maybe, with the months turning cold, he'd find himself home more often with the free time to do some light reading.

His business with the book seller concluded, he resisted the temptation to keep browsing the market and immediately headed out the gate to start his run southeast towards Terana, retracing his earlier steps.

He ate on the way, and while he didn't keep the same brutal pace he had on the way here he still made better time than people on horseback by a significant margin, going two or even three times the distance.

He'd promised Rosaceae he'd return to her domain, and at the speed he was going he judged he'd be able to make it there a couple hours before dark, and could spend the night there again and continue on rested in the morning.

Part of him couldn't help but look forward to the prospect of maybe sharing the demigoddess's bed again. And hoped that Lily would still be there; not only did he have the romantic book he'd bought for her to thank her for her hospitality, but he also wanted to see more of her.

Dare could admit he was intrigued by an impossibly beautiful bunny girl who was nerdy and liked to read.

The ancient dryad's clearing was just as magical in the fading daylight as it had been at night, the air becoming warm, the meadow around him green with clover and flowers, and an aura of deep peace and contentment wrapping around him like a blanket.

He felt as if he'd returned to the pleasant dream as he saw Rosaceae waiting for him and dropped to one knee. “Lady,” he murmured.

“Rosa,” she chided gently, lifting him to his feet with a surprisingly strong hand. “Remember, I see little need for formality.” She smiled. “Besides, there should be more familiarity between those who've entwined.”

Dare coughed, feeling his face heat. “Rosa. Thank you for welcoming me once again to your clearing.”

"Of course." The tall, long-limbed dryad picked him up in her arms and kissed him affectionately, squeezing his butt as she did, then turned and carried him towards the area of the stream where Lily had prepared meals for him before.

He wasn't sure whether to be surprised or not that there was once again a feast set out, roast fowl and mashed sweet potatoes and sauteed asparagus and, of course, salad.

"Dare!" Lily said happily, running forward to throw her arms around him as Rosa set him down. She was once again dressed in her lovely silver gown, her elegant appearance a contrast to her carefree enthusiasm.

"Glad you made it back so soon," she said, then pulled back and looked up at him, brilliant gray eyes full of concern behind her glasses. "Is everything okay?"

Dare gave her a weary but genuine smile. "I think so. I hope so." He brightened and swung his pack around to dig through it. "Oh, I got you something."

"Really?" the bunny girl said, so excited she literally bounced up and down on her powerful cunid legs, long silver pigtails swaying merrily back and forth. "That's so sweet, what is it?"

"A book I found in Redoubt." He produced the romantic storybook and offered it.

"Oooh," she said, taking it eagerly and running her hands over the smooth leather cover. "Marien's Musings, with additional stories from other sources! I only have the original musings, but I decided to leave it back home so I wouldn't accidentally damage it in my travels, so this is great."

Dare was a bit disappointed he hadn't managed to get her something entirely new, although he was glad it wasn't an exact copy of what she had. Then again, the vendor *had* said it was the most popular book on the continent. "Is it good?"

"It's great!" Lily said happily. "It's *so* romantic. I was overjoyed when Mother got it for me . . . I think it's the best gift I've ever gotten. At first she went to Lone Ox to see if someone there could order it, but-"

Dare blinked. "You're from near Lone Ox?" he blurted.

The gorgeous bunny girl froze. "Darn it!" she exclaimed, reproachfully bopping herself between the ears with her knuckles. "Now why did I have to go and say that?"

Rosa laughed richly.

He looked between them suspiciously. "What's going on?"

Lily gave him a sheepish smile. "I guess the cat's out of the bag, huh?" She took a breath, straightened her shoulders, and offered him her hand formally. "Hi, Dare. I'm Lily, daughter of Clover of Brighthill Warren."

That, wait, what? The Clover he knew was young enough to be Lily's sister . . . was it a common name? Or maybe the Clover he'd made love to *was* Lily's sister, and their mother had the same name and had passed it on to her daughter?

The silver-haired bunny girl must've misinterpreted his blank stare because her smile wavered. "Right, Mother doesn't usually tell the men she lets chase her down and give her a good mounting her name. She's the white bunny girl you were with about five and a half months ago." She paused significantly. "The mother of your cunid son Petro, who she gave birth to about two weeks ago."

Dare stiffened in shock at pretty much everything she'd just said. "What?"

He knew he'd impregnated Clover, unless by some miracle she'd already been pregnant. And he knew cunid children were born in five months. Still, he hadn't paused to consider he might already have another child out there in the world.

It sort of blew his mind. His first son . . . he wondered what the little guy looked like, and if he'd be able to visit him.

But he shook his head at the clear and obvious inconsistency. "How could you be Clover's daughter?" he protested. "She's only a few years older than you, isn't she?"

Lily giggled a bit shyly and fiddled with her glasses. "You don't know much about bunny girls, do you? We stay youthful looking and fertile right up until the moment we drop dead of old age. It's one of the gifts of our race, along with great speed and great beauty. Mother's actually almost 50, and I'm her second youngest child now that Petro's born."

Holy shit. Clover was older than Marona, and she still looked like a college coed with the face of an angel and the body of a pinup model?

Dare shook off that thought and focused on what was important. "Are they both okay? Is Petro healthy?"

The silver-haired bunny girl smiled tenderly. "They're fine, and Petro's perfect. He's an absolutely beautiful baby . . . the girls will be flocking to him when he grows up."

"A son," he said, grinning like an idiot. Now that he'd had some time to get his head around the idea of another child out there he was overjoyed at the news. "Male cunids are pretty rare, aren't they? I heard 1 in 7."

"You heard right." Lily looked proud. "He's Mother's first son."

"Would it be possible to visit him?" Dare asked. "Or would Clover consider visiting Nirim Manor?"

Lily laughed. "You're more than welcome to visit. Mother would be overjoyed, and so would my sisters and the other girls there. It's not every day they have a man available that they didn't have to go out and shake their fluffy cottontails at to entice."

A chance to get dog piled by an entire warren of bunny girls? Oh hell yes.

She gave him a knowing smile as if guessing his thoughts. "Mother would probably visit, too. She liked you and *really* liked your time together. And I'm sure she'd love to give Petro a chance to visit his brothers and sisters at Nirim Manor."

The beautiful bunny girl hesitated, taking off her glasses and breathing on them, then producing a cloth from her belt pouch to very thoroughly wipe them with. She looked shy for some reason, even nervous.

Rosa cleared her throat, a surprisingly musical sound, and gently nudged Lily.

The bunny girl jumped slightly, then blushed as she hastily shoved her glasses back onto her face. “Although if you're inviting people to visit,” she blurted, “could I come?”

Dare blinked. “You want to visit?”

“Well, I, um . . .” She shifted awkwardly, a blush creeping all the way up to her long white ears and turning her lovely face a rosy scarlet. “You're going to laugh at me.”

“Of course I'm not,” he teased, charmed by her discomfiture. “You're too beautiful to laugh at.”

“Really?” Lily bit her lip, looking at him hopefully with her big grey eyes. “It's just, you know, I read so many books. And Mother knows I love the romantic ones. I never liked the idea of going out and lying in a field until some stranger gets on top of me, it's just all about pleasure and couldn't there be more?”

She fiddled with her glasses some more, taking them off and putting them back on, then tugging on one of her long pigtails. “I always dreamed of finding a man who I could have that with, not just the steamy rough sex but all the other good stuff I've read about. Like cuddling, and getting flowers, and going on long walks in the moonlight and all the rest. And even deeper than that surface level, the true love and closeness and desire to spend our lives together and raise our children side by side.”

The achingly beautiful bunny girl abruptly put her face in her hands, although being careful of her glasses. “I just thought, well, Mother told me how gentle and romantic you were with her, and then I got curious and I went and saw how happy you and your goblin lover were, and how wonderful you were to her. And I was sad at first because I figured that was it, you'd already found your love and I'd missed out.”

“You wanted to be with me?” Dare blurted incredulously. Even after all he'd experienced on Collisa, all the beautiful women he'd been with, including actual deities, a part of him was still stunned that such an otherworldly beauty could be interested in him.

Lily's face remained in her hands as she let out an embarrassed squeak, her milky pale skin blushing rosy red all the way up to her ears again. "Well, I mean, when we've courted and done all sorts of romantic things together and we fall in love."

She brightened and peeked through her fingers at him. "You'd be interested in courting, right? I mean, we got visited by a Priest of the Outsider a while ago. He wanted to check on Mother and the baby and see how they were doing, and also gave us news about you as the father."

The bunny girl bounced in place, which not only made her pigtails sway adorably but also did very nice things to her perfect breasts beneath the thin cloth of her evening gown. "He told me you had a harem, and that you'd found a home, and how happy you all were together! And I realized maybe there was still hope."

Dare looked at the sky, as he often did when thinking of or speaking to Sia, even though she couldn't respond anymore unless Ireni was around.

He'd thought Zuri was the ultimate wingman, but it looked like his goddess fiancee was competing for the title.

"Lily," he said solemnly, "I would be honored if you came with me to visit Nirim Manor. And I'm sure all the others would love to meet you."

The bunny girl's smile was brighter than the rising sun. "Really?" she squealed, throwing her arms around him. "Yay! I can't wait!" She abruptly pulled back, absently tugging on her pigtails. "Oh! I have to go make sure I have everything packed for when we leave tomorrow! Go ahead and eat before it gets cold, I'll see you in the morning!"

She bolted off across the meadow with all the speed of a cunid, vanishing in a flash.

Dare couldn't help but grin as he turned to Rosa. Although he paused when he saw the very serious look on her face. Even more solemn than usual.

“You'll be good to her,” she said.

It sounded more like a statement than a question, but even so he nodded resolutely. “I'll spend my life trying to make her happy, if I have the incredible luck and honor of earning her love.”

The dryad abruptly smiled. “I don't suppose I need to tell you, but Lily's a hopeless romantic. In the most classical sense, straight out of a storybook. I know real life can't always be that perfect, but it wouldn't hurt to do everything you can to properly woo her. Flowers and presents, dates, hand holding, chaste kisses, slowly building passion culminating in the perfect night when the time is right.”

She shook her head, looking a bit bemused. “To be frank I don't see the point myself, when simply entwining is more direct. But it'll make her happy.”

“Thank you,” Dare said. He laughed. “I'll be honest, most of my romances until now have been fairly direct as well. Although I still try to give my fiancees all the wooing they deserve, each and every day.”

“Good, I'd recommend staying in the habit.” Rosa's eyes danced. “On the subject of direct, I'd like to entwine with you again tonight. It is pleasant to experience being fully joined again after so long, and I believe I didn't fully drain you last time.”

He hesitated, glancing after Lily, and the dryad laughed. “She won't mind. She knows she's joining a harem, and that you seek the company of most of the women you meet. As long as you don't neglect her she'll be fine with it.”

Her smile widened. “And she'll certainly have a lot of fun with your other lovers. With a 7 to 1 ratio bunny girls get used to pleasuring each other when they can't find a man.”

Dare was certain the girls back home were going to love Lily. Not only was she beautiful but she was sweet and innocent and absolutely adorable.

And with the proper spices and recipes she'd be a great cook, too.

He settled into a seat and piled his plate, gratefully filling his rumbling belly. He had to admit that if the way to a man's heart was through his stomach, the beautiful bunny girl was definitely making the best start possible with him.

As he ate Rosa massaged his shoulders and back, kneading his tense muscles with her long, graceful fingers. She was able to dig in and work out knots with surprising strength, including one beneath his shoulder blade that he'd been having a bitch of a time getting at.

As Dare showed signs of winding down with his meal the dryad began running her hands down his chest and kissing his neck, cherry blossom hair draped over his shoulder and left arm. Her eagerness was undoubtable, and as he turned his head to meet her lips with his she easily lifted him from his chair in a somewhat embarrassing princess carry.

Then they were off to her enclosed bower of blossoming cherry saplings, his lover's long legs eating the distance at her rapid pace.

His previous visit's languid entwining was nowhere in evidence tonight. As Rosa continued to kiss him hungrily, warm wet tongue snaking into his mouth and capturing his, she slipped her hands beneath his clothes and ran them over his body, undressing him in the process.

Almost as soon as he was naked she went for his manhood, stroking him firmly with both hands until he was gasping and jerking his hips in her grip. Then she straightened, towering over him and staring down to meet his gaze with gleaming eyes.

"I want to try something different tonight," the tall, slender dryad said, beginning to stroke him again.

"Sounds good," he said, cupping her narrow ass with both hands and squeezing the soft yet surprisingly firm flesh.

She smiled widely. "Good, what do you think about lifted sex?"

Dare hesitated, giving her better than eight foot body an uncertain look. She was so narrow she probably didn't weigh too much, although he had no idea what her density was compared to flesh and blood so she might be heavier than she looked.

Which wasn't a particularly sexy thought when his lover was jerking him off with both hands.

"I'm up for trying it," he said with a chuckle. After all, he'd enjoyed it with all his fiancees before, especially with Zuri and Sia with their smaller bodies. "You'll probably have to wrap your legs around me so they don't drag, though."

Rosa let out a musical laugh. "Oh, I think you got it backwards."

Her long arms wrapped tenderly around him, holding him by his upper back and beneath his ass, and he let out an involuntary gasp as she lifted him off his feet with zero sign of effort. It left him in an awkward position where his legs dangled and his cock led the way pointed directly upwards.

He looked up at her twinkling eyes as she widened her stance and thrust her pelvis forward, then raised him up until his tip was pressed against her glistening slit.

"Ready?" she asked, smiling.

Dare grinned back, surprised but getting into the spirit of things. "Fuck me."

With another musical laugh his lover pulled him up through soft folds drenched with fragrant nectar, her tight walls clamping around his shaft as she guided him in until his pubes rubbed against her hairless mound.

It was . . . he wasn't sure what exactly he could compare it to.

He'd lain back and let lovers ride him before, and he'd lifted his lovers up and down on his cock. But being the one lifted, his weight cradled gently in her soft arms, was entirely new.

With a low moan of pleasure the dryad lowered him, then lifted him, again and again, making her own rhythm as she, for lack of a better way of putting it, used him to fuck her. With the way she was holding him he would've had a difficult and awkward time moving his hips, so he just rested his hands on her smooth thighs.

And basically became her dildo.

Which honestly he couldn't complain about because it was a

novel experience and felt incredible. And he could tell Rosa was loving it.

She started lifting and lowering him faster, moans becoming deeper and more hungry. “I have a clitoris,” she finally gasped.

Dare gave a start, then with chagrin remembered that Rosie did, too, and he'd certainly attended to it very lovingly when he'd been with her. It was no surprise that the mother of all florans would share that with her descendants.

So he reached up with one hand and found her erect bud, rubbing it firmly. She gasped in delight, and he felt her walls clench down in response. She began moving him even faster, moans increasing in volume and frequency.

Until finally the cherry blossom dryad reached her peak.

She yanked him balls deep into her with a soft cry, then went rigid in rapture as she sprayed his crotch, abdomen, and chest with her sweet sticky juice.

Her tight pussy milked Dare desperately, and in the face of that overwhelming pleasure he groaned and released inside her, back arching against her supporting arms as his cock surged powerfully time and again.

Their shared climax lasted what felt like an eternity, and when it was finally over Rosa lowered him out of her, then lifted him up to hug him to her soft chest, lowering her head to kiss him. He wrapped his arms and legs around her neck and narrow waist as he returned her kiss, stroking her warm back as his erection rubbed against her belly.

“I love you,” she purred against his lips, sounding breathless. Her hands playfully rubbed and squeezed his ass. “That was incredible.”

“It was-” Dare began, then grunted in surprise as his lover seemed to realize he was still hard, and without so much as a heads up moved him into position again and rammed him up inside her, even more vigorously this time.

Girls had given him a wild ride before, and ridden him wildly as well. But that was the start of almost fifteen minutes of intense fucking as Rosa pistoned him in and out of her soft pussy with ever greater speed and force, only her constantly flooding juice sparing him from friction burns.

She kept going without pause right through his second orgasm, his refractory period almost agonizingly pleasurable. As for her, she seemed to be climaxing nonstop, rising to higher and higher peaks as her walls undulated against his shaft.

Ashkalla the Succubus had been sadistic and demanding, and Dare's dream sex with Sia in her alabaster mannequin form, when he'd been lost in her ambrosia haze, had been even more intense and prolonged.

But as the towering dryad continued sawing him in and out of her squelching pussy, he began to wonder if he was going to have to tap out.

As if sensing his plight she abruptly yanked him balls deep inside her again, then moved her hand between his legs to grip and fondle his balls, pushing him abruptly over the edge into his third climax.

As Dare finally shot his last spurt, limp and wrung out even though he hadn't done much besides lie there, Rosa became gentle and tender again as she lowered him to the soft heather, then spooned him from behind.

"Sorry if I went a bit overboard," she said with a throaty laugh, leisurely grinding against his ass.

"You certainly put me through my paces," he panted wryly.

"I know, I couldn't help myself." The dryad playfully tweaked his nipples. "You're just so little and cute. So sweet and innocent. I just want cuddle your solid little body close and rub that hard little ass of yours. Entwine with you forever so I can always feel your adorable hard cock inside me."

Dare coughed, feeling his cheeks heat. "I hate to say it, but most guys don't like hearing stuff like that." He couldn't say he really did, either; he got the feeling she was teasing him.

“I hope you can forgive me.” Her hands moved up to his shoulders and she tenderly spun him around to face her, then began pushing his head gently but insistently down between her legs. “Will you lick my cherry blossom, stud? I'm so wet.”

He found himself hesitating slightly. “I just-”

She giggled. “Oh, that. In case you were worrying, I absorbed every drop of your come deep inside me, same as my floran daughters do. It's all me down there.”

With that reassurance Dare obligingly pressed his lips to her slippery labia, tongue sliding between her folds to gather her sweet cherry nectar as he rubbed her clit with his thumb.

Rosa moaned in appreciation. “Thanks, sweetie, this is fantastic. You're so sexy.” She began tenderly running her hands through his hair. “Would you like to know a secret?”

He grunted in assent, mouth currently occupied, and she giggled almost giddily. “You've given me a dryad daughter,” she whispered, tenderly brushing his cheek with a finger.

Dare discovered he was happy at that news. He'd known he'd impregnated the demigoddess the first time they'd fucked, of course, since he hadn't had Prevent Conception to use. But the reality of it was a surprisingly pleasant thought.

He pulled his face away from her sticky sex to smile up at her. “That's great to hear,” he said, tenderly stroking her thighs.

The dryad laughed, low and throaty. “I didn't think you'd appreciate the significance of this event.” She pulled him up her narrow body by his shoulders so she could tenderly kiss him, then held him and stroked his back as she continued. “I'm the Mother of Florans, Dare. As in, in all my years I've given birth only to plant girls.”

Her voice turned wistful. “And while I love my sweet daughters dearly, I always grieved that I had no dryad or drus offspring. I'd resigned myself to the fact that my kind is created by the gods, not born.”

She reached between them and wrapped her elegant fingers

around his soft, well satisfied cock, making it stir again. “And then I learned of a remarkable man with a hidden blessing from a goddess . . . that every child of his borne of another race would be of the mother's race.”

Rosa laughed excitedly and hugged him so tightly his ribs creaked. “You've given me a dryad child, you sexy little man! You and your benefactor! And for that I will be eternally grateful.”

Dare grunted as she pushed him down her body a bit, between her spread legs, and urgently rolled her hips, guiding his half erect cock back inside her. As he continued to stiffen she began moving him delightfully within her soft pussy.

“And I'm going to show my gratitude by pleasing you as only a woman with over 43,000 years of experience is capable of,” she moaned in his ear. “A dream to carry with you for the rest of your days.”

True to her word, the rest of the night was as magical as the beginning had been explosive.

Chapter Nine

Home Ward Bound

Dare woke just after dawn to find himself alone in Rosa's heather bed, tucked snugly beneath a blanket of soft, fragrant cherry blossoms.

For an uncomfortable moment he wondered if the dryad had detached her long train of hair, then he realized they'd been gathered from the overhead bower.

Yawning, he pushed them aside and dressed, then ducked out into the clearing. Peace and contentment deeper than the enchantment laid over the clearing suffused him after the night he'd had with Rosa, and he couldn't help but feel a bit of wonder.

He'd helped a demigoddess conceive a daughter after her own image. Maybe not a demigoddess herself, but at the very least a dryad. And even if it had been due to Sia's intervention, it was still incredible to think about.

Dare found his lover and Lily chatting near the table, which this morning was laid out with only a light breakfast of boiled eggs and salad.

The bunny girl was dressed in her unabashedly indecent leather short shorts and chest wrap again, and beside his pack at the table was another one that looked stuffed full of objects that bulged the leather and hide in rectangular outlines.

Books, if he had to guess.

"Good morning!" Lily said, running over to take his hand and pull him insistently to the table. "Eat fast, I'm ready to goooo!"

Dare had to grin at her enthusiasm. "I am, too," he admitted. "Not just to let everyone know that I've sorted out our problems . . . I've missed them."

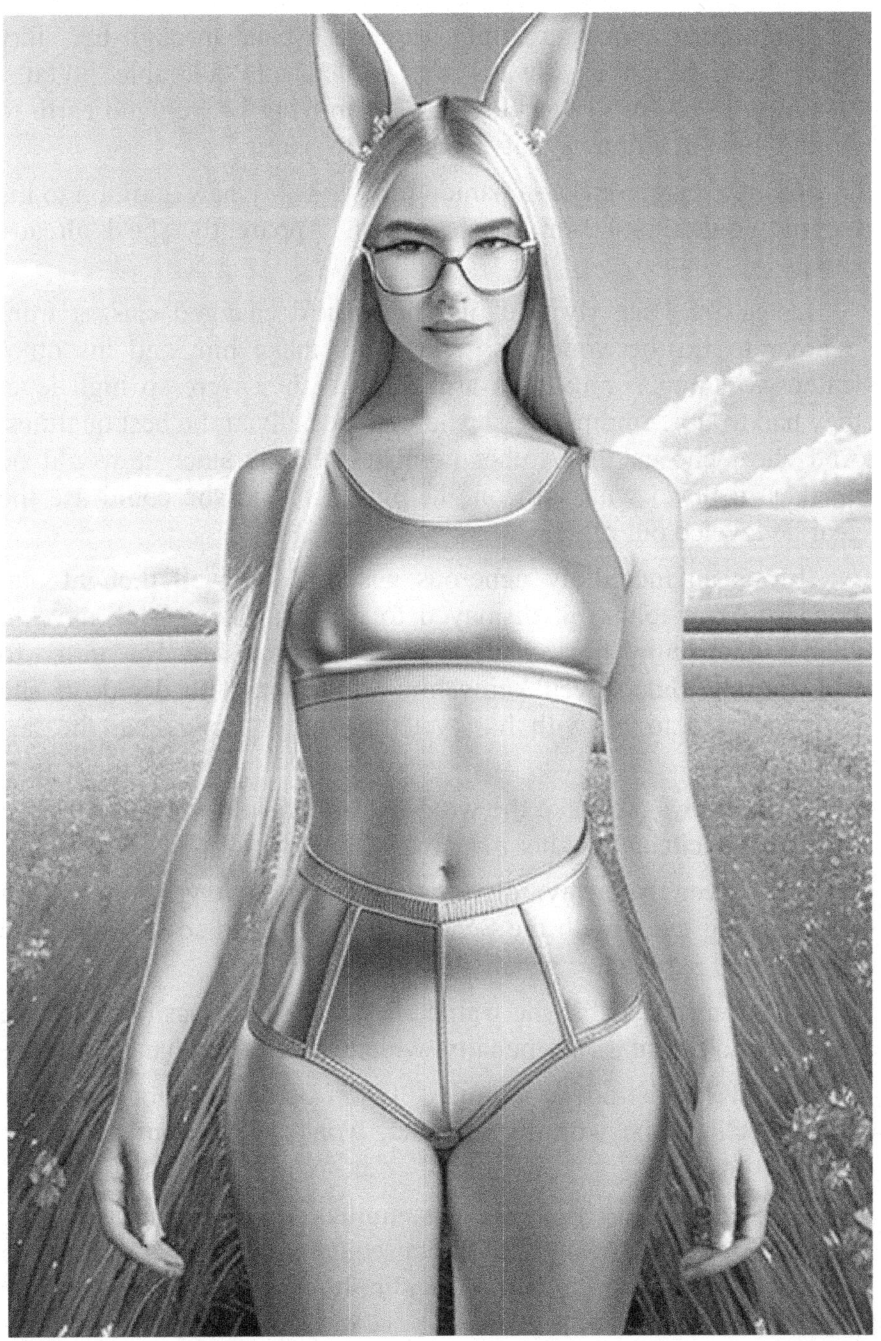

She sighed almost dreamily, running a hand through her silky silver hair, which as always was pulled into adorable pigtails. “Rushing to return to your lovers after moving heaven and earth to defend them in a faraway city. That's so romantic.”

His new bunny girl companion (and possibly new addition to his harem?) didn't join him for breakfast. Apparently she'd already eaten.

Instead she eagerly told him how she'd changed classes from Scholar to Leatherworker, so she could make him and his other leather-wielding companions armor when they were so high level they had trouble finding it elsewhere. Especially at the best qualities. And she'd chosen the Archer combat subclass since it would be quickest to level with someone helping her, and she could use the gear he leveled out of.

It was an incredibly generous gesture, and well thought out. Even so Dare felt a bit dismayed to hear it. “You didn't have to change your entire life's goals for me,” he protested. He started to add that she didn't even know him well enough to decide if she really wanted to be with him yet, but bit his tongue at the last second.

He didn't want to take the wind out of her sails when she was so obviously excited about her plans.

Lily waved that away, idly tugging one of her long white ears. “I wasn't doing much with the Scholar class, and I'm so low level the 10% overall experience penalty wasn't very much.”

Still, it meant that if she wanted to change her class in the future she'd be looking at a 30% penalty, which was an even harsher blow.

“Besides!” she added happily. “If I'm going to be part of your family we'll all be working together, won't we? I want to do my part.”

Dare glanced at Rosa, who just smiled down at them as if they were children speaking of inconsequential things. Which he supposed to someone as mind-bogglingly ancient as her wasn't far off.

"Thank you, Lily," he said, setting aside his other protests for now. "That was very thoughtful of you."

She bit her lip, milky pale skin prominently displaying her spreading blush, and reached over to grab a handful of salad straight from the bowl, munching it to cover her pleased embarrassment.

With another few bites he pushed away his plate and stood. "Well, my beautiful companion," he said, smiling and holding out his hand. "I look forward to many moonlit walks in the future, but for the moment can I offer you a daylight run?"

Lily giggled, shyly standing and taking his hand. "That sounds delightful." Her big gray eyes danced behind her large wire-framed glasses. "And don't worry, I'll slow down for you."

It wasn't an idle boast. Last time Dare had played tag with a bunny girl, or really the only time, she'd bolted at a pace he couldn't hope to match. Even running his fastest with Fleetfoot and Forest Perception, it was clear she'd been seriously holding back to let him keep up.

Now, with Cheetah's Dash, he hoped to come a bit closer to matching Lily's pace. Although it seemed like she was about 30 years younger than Clover, and undoubtedly fit. As was plain to see in her skimpy leather outfit.

So he had a real challenge ahead of him.

After they belted on their packs Rosa gave them both warm hugs, although she lingered a few more moments with Dare. "Do visit again if you happen to be passing by," she said, tenderly stroking his cheek. "You and all your family, on the rare occasion they have cause to leave the house."

She smiled knowingly. "Like, say, perhaps in about a month and a half when you head for Redoubt again to petition for knighthood and undertake the trials."

Wow, she really did keep her ear to the ground. Or maybe the opposite, since all her ears grew up out of the ground; being aware of everything the plants in the area knew was a pretty good form of limited omniscience.

"I will," Dare promised. "I'm sure my family would all love to meet you, and have the peace and rest of your beautiful domain." He shifted. "And I'd like to be here for the birth of our child, if you have no objections. Or at least afterwards to meet her and, if you'll allow it, be part of her life."

Lily sighed dreamily.

For her part Rosa looked amused. "You may meet her, certainly. Although I'm afraid it won't be anytime soon . . . I feel her growing far slower within me than any of my floran daughters. It will likely take years, even decades, before I produce her seed. And even I could not tell you how long it will take her to grow to adulthood; my kind are created already fully grown and imbued with some of the knowledge of the gods before being sent to our duties on Collisa."

Wow, that was a lot of fascinating information. Dare would've happily spent more time asking followup questions, but the dryad began ushering them towards the edge of the clearing with the briskness of a mother sending her children off to school.

"Tell Eloise hello for me!" she said as they stepped into the trees, waving a long reddish-brown arm. "Let her know Grandmummy loves her and blesses her to grow healthy and strong! And when you see Rosie again tell her the same."

"I will," Dare said, grinning. "Thank you again for everything."

Her eyes sparkled with mirth. "It was very much my pleasure." She paused, then added casually. "Oh, and could you give the Mistress of the House in particular my most polite invitation to come and visit me if ever she has the chance? I'd dearly like to see her."

For a moment he was baffled by that, not sure who she could be talking about. He doubted she meant Marona, although she was the only mistress of a house he could-

Oh, right. Duh.

Merellesia, the Outsider. The literal goddess living in his house and who he was engaged to be married to. Sia didn't make a fuss about her status with the family and certainly didn't try to lord over them.

But she was still a goddess.

"I'll tell her," he promised solemnly. "I'm sure she'd be happy to meet you."

She laughed at him with the tone of an adult at a child's innocent naivete. "But we've met before."

Dare felt his face heat. Of course, the demigoddess who was tens of thousands of years old and the goddess of exploration and new experiences had met. "Right."

"In fact, we're very close friends." The dryad stuck out her lip in what on a less ancient and noble woman might've been considered a pout. "Although she's been too busy to get in touch of late." Her eyes danced as she looked him up and down. "I believe I can guess why."

Wow, did he and their family really draw that much of Sia's attention? That was beyond touching. And humbling.

Lily gave Rosa one last hug, easily bounding up to wrap her arms around the much taller woman's neck. "Goodbye, and thank you for your kindness! I hope I can visit again soon!" Then she hopped down and bolted over to grab Dare's hand, tugging on it insistently. "Come on, let's go! I can't wait to get home!"

Dare followed, a bit bemused at her already calling Nirim Manor home. They hadn't courted yet and didn't really know each other, but she almost acted as if joining the family was a foregone conclusion.

Of course, if Sia had arranged things to turn out like this then there was a good chance that's where this was going. And he couldn't exactly complain about the opportunity to fall in love with a sweet, innocent, enthusiastic, breathtakingly beautiful bunny girl.

As they stepped out of Rosa's clearing a steady wind struck them, warmer than in the previous days but still chilly. Dare looked at Lily in her skimpy leather clothes and frowned. "Aren't you going to freeze in that?"

She grinned, showing her adorable bunny front teeth, and began bouncing in place. "I've got a fur wrap in case it gets too cold, but

I'll be fine as long as we set a good pace. Bunny girls are used to being naked to the elements and we run warm, but we especially generate plenty of heat when we're running."

She giggled and looked away shyly. "And during other physical exertions."

He coughed, feeling his cheeks heat. "So you're ready to go?" The bunny girl nodded eagerly, and with a laugh he activated Cheetah's Dash and burst into a loping run that would eat the miles.

Lily made a surprised sound from where he'd left her in his dust, then let out an excited peal of laughter. He didn't even hear a rustle from the forest litter beneath their feet as she burst past him going easily 30 miles an hour.

"Hey!" Dare called, catching up with markedly less grace and likely a lot more effort. "We need to keep this pace up all day."

She giggled again and pushed her glasses higher up her nose; he noticed for the first time that they were attached to a silver chain that was tight enough to keep them from falling off. "We can set a traveling pace later," she called playfully as she sped up even more. "Come on, you got a boost at 30 . . . show me how fast you can go!"

He had to admit that even if it would slow them down in a long run as they pushed themselves unnecessarily, he couldn't help but eagerly accept the challenge. He'd been wanting to race a bunny girl ever since he got Cheetah's Dash; the only other person besides Clover who'd really been able to outrun him was Ilin, and the Monk had needed to open his Locks to do it.

So Dare ran all out, making full use of his elite athlete body and the speed boosts from Forest Perception, Power Up, Cheetah's Dash, and above all Fleetfoot.

He burst past Lily in a rush of pounding feet and crackling leaves, and she gave the most adorable squawk of surprise. Then with a silvery peal of laughter she caught up, cheeks flushed and grinning to reveal her adorable bunny front teeth.

"Nice!" she said, gracefully vaulting a fallen log slanting between two trees. "I thought you were faster than a human should possibly be, but this is insane!"

The bunny girl abruptly bounded ahead, powerful legs propelling her in long leaps rather than actually running. As she stretched her lead once again her snowy white cottontail twitched playfully. "Still not fast enough, though!"

Dare had to concede defeat, abandoning his sprint and slowing to a more reasonable pace. Although he'd never complain about being in second place to Lily so he could watch her run; her graceful body was pure poetry in motion.

She slowed down as well before she got too far ahead, falling back to let him run beside her as they burst out of the forest and onto the plains. While she wasn't panting like a bellows and streaming sweat like he was, she was at least breathing hard and her pale forehead glistened with perspiration.

Although she recovered from the run quicker than he did. Especially when Cheetah's Dash ran out and he slowed even more, and had to exert himself again to maintain a decent pace.

"Now this seems more like a human's speed," the bunny girl said, still with that huge grin; she'd obviously enjoyed their race. "Although for a human sprinting all out, not one running at a pace he can maintain all day . . . what's your secret?"

"A gift from a goddess," Dare said. "Care to guess which one?"

She moved her glasses out of the way so she could wipe her forehead. "Well there's only one that I know of whose servants have taken an interest in you, so . . . the Outsider?"

He nodded. "What would you say about meeting her?" He could only assume Sia wouldn't mind him sharing her secret, considering the goddess herself had arranged for Lily to head out into the world in search of him, to fulfill her hopes for a grand romance.

Besides, if the bunny girl joined the family then she'd find out soon enough.

She stared at him in amazement. "I thought the Outsider has been traveling to other worlds, as her followers say she likes to do."

Ouch. *That* was a secret he should probably wait to bring up . . .

Lily might spook if she got bombarded with too many impossible things all at once. Like the fact that he was from another world and had died there before being reincarnated here.

Besides, he wanted the rest of the family to be there for that conversation.

"Let's just say she's returned again," he said cryptically, then with a grin sped up again.

* * * * *

Running with Lily was a blast.

Maybe Dare's run to Redoubt would've been more enjoyable without the heavy curtain of dread hanging over him, but even so it was especially fun to have company.

Without Cheetah's Dash Pella was mostly able to keep up with him, and so was Ilin. And on horseback his companions could match his pace well enough. But to be able to just run free without worrying about leaving everyone in the dust, and even break out in spontaneous sprints just for the hell of it, was a joy he hadn't indulged in often enough since his first weeks on Collisa.

And the bunny girl was there for every minute of it, sharing his joy at the freedom of pure movement. Egging him on and dancing around him and laughing gaily as she ran and leapt and bounded with unrivaled grace.

In the late afternoon Dare nearly stumbled mid-run in surprise as he felt a vibration in his pack. Just for a few moments, but enough to make him shout and skid to a halt, flinging it away thinking an animal had somehow gotten in there.

The contents scattered, and among them he saw the dark wooden box, its golden runes glowing but steadily fading. Putting two and two together he realized they must've just come in range of the bind point he'd set not far northeast of Terana, and the Home Ward was signaling him that it was ready for use.

"You okay?" Lily asked, bouncing impatiently ahead of him. She was flushed from exertion and glowed with a fine sheen of perspiration; in the fading light of the lowering sun she looked breathtaking.

Which was a stark contrast from his own sweat-drenched clothes and noticeable BO; not exactly the way he wanted to present himself to a possible romantic partner. Although he wasn't sure why he was just noticing this now when they'd been running all day and he'd been like this most of the time.

He felt his cheeks heat as he quickly gathered up his scattered things and shrugged back into his pack. “Want to go even faster than we have been?” he asked with a smile, holding up the cube. “Like, three times faster than I can run all out?”

The bunny girl looked at the item, inspecting its details, and her big grey eyes went huge behind her glasses. “Whoa, where did you get something like that? This seems like something a Level 50 hero would have.”

“I killed a Level 38 party rated monster and got lucky with the loot.” Something that happened often, thanks to Sia giving him a luck boost along with his other improved traits.

“At your level?” she said in clear admiration. “That's amazing! You must've forked out a lot of gold to buy up the rest of your party's share of such a valuable item, though.”

Dare coughed and scratched sheepishly at the back of his head. “There, um, was no one else.”

Lily stared at him incredulously. “You soloed a party rated monster five levels higher than you?”

“I, um, had a bit of help from an item.”

She began bounding around him, fiddling with her glasses as she looked at him with almost scientific scrutiny. “I wasn't going to comment on the fact that it's been less than seven months since you left Lone Ox, and you somehow jumped up 21 levels in that time. But that is just flat out . . . amazing!”

The bunny girl grabbed his free hand with both of hers and bounced up and down, eyes shining. “I knew there was something special about you right from the first. Not just handsome and kind but strong and brave, too."

Now Dare was *really* embarrassed. "Like I said, I had help from an item." He hastily held up the cube. "Well, shall we?"

"Go faster than I've ever gone before? Absolutely!" With an excited squeal she leapt into his arms.

He nearly dropped the Home Ward as he fumbled to catch her, practically falling over backwards at the unexpected move. He was distinctly aware of her warm, glistening bare skin against his arms, the clean scent of sweat and a fragrance that was uniquely her filling his nostrils.

She smelled incredible.

Lily slipped soft arms around his neck and looked up at him with her big grey eyes, a blush creeping across her cheeks. "Okay, let's go," she murmured.

"Right." Dare laughed in embarrassment. "Sorry I'm so sweaty and stinky."

"Mmm." She buried her face in his neck, long soft ears tickling his cheek, and breathed deeply. "I love the way you smell. Like the grass we ran through, and the sunshine that kissed our skin, and the fun we had." She nuzzled him. "And like you."

He briefly nuzzled her head in turn, then held her a bit tighter. "Home Ward Bound."

He felt the item activate and then . . . begin charging up.

Right, it had a 10 minute cast time. He'd forgotten in the heat of the moment.

Dare looked down at his bunny girl companion in chagrin. "So, uh, I just remembered this takes 10 minutes."

"Oh, right." That seemed to shake her from her excitement at their fast travel, giving her time to realize how intimately they were holding each other. Her milky pale skin blushed an even deeper pink. "So I guess, uh . . ."

He hastily set her down. "When the Home Ward finishes charging we can probably just hold hands to travel together."

"Okay." Biting her lip shyly, Lily dug into her pack and pulled out a heavy fur poncho that fell to her knees.

Dare could agree with that choice; the air had grown chilly with the sinking sun, and now that they'd stopped running his sweat was cold on his skin.

More comfortable in her warm garment, she plopped down crosslegged on the grass and rummaged in her pack for the book he'd given her, cracking it open to what seemed like a random page and absently reading.

Maybe she was trying to escape an awkward situation in the pages of a book. He could admit he'd often been guilty of the same back on Earth, although he'd usually used his phone.

Dare settled down close enough to her that he could take her hand when the Home Ward finished charging. "You know, I know some romantic stories from my home. Would you like to hear one?"

Lily perked up eagerly, lifting her nose from her book. "I would! Do your people have very many?"

He couldn't help but smile. "A whole bunch. Where I come from the priority in a relationship is finding love, rather than it at best being a happy accident in relationships begun for other reasons."

Her big grey eyes were a little bit starry as she looked off into the distance. "An entire land where everyone finds romance, and not just the lucky few?"

Dare shifted uncomfortably. He didn't want to be a downer and mention things like divorce rates and other relationship issues that were prevalent back home. "That's the goal most people have," he said carefully.

The beautiful bunny girl leaned forward, pushing her glasses higher up her delicate nose to look at him with shining eyes. "Tell me a story! The most romantic one you know!"

Whew, how did he judge that? Normally he picked movies and shows where the romance was a side plot, ideally with some good "plot" thrown in. Of course, if he was looking for a good story there were always the classics.

"All right," he said, settling back. "Once upon a time there was a little girl whose mother died of illness. Her father married again so she would have someone to care for her . . ."

Lily listened raptly to the fairy tale, looking distressed at the poor girl's plight, sighing dreamily at the romantic bits, and squealing with delight when she kissed the handsome prince and it all ended happily ever after.

Dare finished the story with a few minutes to spare. But since he didn't know exactly how the Home Ward worked, and didn't want to risk it going off and making him leave his companion behind, he suggested they hold hands early.

The beautiful bunny girl shyly placed her pale, soft hand in his. "This is kind of romantic, isn't it?" she murmured. "Trying something new together, hand in hand?"

He grinned and gently squeezed her hand. "Here's to having many adventures together, going new places and seeing new things side by side."

"Ooh, I lik-"

Dare abruptly lost all sensation in his body, including the feel of Lily's hand in his. Then he was catapulted straight forward, still in his seated position, the ground whipping past underneath him with alarming speed.

It was like being in a car looking at the road whip by, except twice as fast, much closer to the ground, and without the benefit of a sturdy metal vehicle around him. The sight was terrifying and nauseating and he might have had the urge to be sick if he could feel his stomach.

He looked over, relieved to see that he was still holding Lily's hand and she was right there with him. She was grinning ear to ear, eyes wide as she stared ahead in the direction they were rushing.

Then her mouth opened in a scream of sudden alarm, although no sound emerged, and he looked forward again in time to see that they were heading directly for the side of a tall hill, at speeds high enough to splatter them across it.

Dare barely had time to scream himself before they reached it and passed right through.

For a few moments they were surrounded by absolute blackness. Then they emerged back into daylight, only now they were about six inches higher off the ground than before. Or more accurately the ground was six inches lower.

Right, ethereal. They both looked solid enough, but they must've been phased out in some way to allow them to see the world around them without slamming into obstacles in their path. And a good thing, since they couldn't control their movement and the Home Ward was taking them on a direct line to their destination.

As Dare got used to the mode of travel it wasn't quite as nauseating or terrifying. Especially if he looked farther out rather than at the ground whipping past beneath or around him at impossible speeds.

Actually it was almost restful, like being in some sort of VR world tour program where he could see the beauty around him, without feeling the wind or the noise at this speed or any other sensations. Or maybe being in an absolutely silent airplane with zero turbulence.

In fact, if he closed his eyes it became like the ultimate sensory deprivation chamber, because not only did it mute the sensations but they weren't there at all. It was so relaxing he actually ended up dozing off, grateful for the chance to rest after a day of running.

So it came as a complete shock when the sensations abruptly returned with a jolt, and he found himself seated on the ground with the feel of Lily's warm hand in his.

He also heard her shrieks of delight practically in his ear; had she been doing that this entire time?

Dare's eyes flew open and he looked around to see the spot he vaguely remembered binding the Home Ward to, south of the battlefield where they'd defeated the monster horde. He climbed to his feet and helped Lily to hers, while she looked around curiously.

"Why did you bind the artifact here?" she asked, long white ears twitching curiously this way and that as she looked around for some landmark or other spot of interest.

"It was the closest place to home after I got the Home Ward," he said, tucking the item away in his pack. He motioned south. "Terana is a few hours south of here, at a normal human's pace at least, and Nirim Manor is about a day's ride farther, near the southeast corner of Bastion."

The bunny girl absently fiddled with her glasses. "So even at our faster pace, we can't get there today unless we run half the night?"

Dare nodded. "We'll need to set up camp. I can make you anything you don't have, like a tent or bedroll."

She squared her shoulders proudly. "No need, I made all that stuff for myself." She hooked a thumb at her chest. "Leatherworker, remember? I even made a cool collapsible camp chair whose design appeared just a few months ago."

"Oh yeah?" he asked casually, biting back a smile.

"Yeah, it's amazing. Look." Lily reached into her pack and pulled it out; Dare recognized his design, but with more padding on the seat, backrest, and armrests. She patted it affectionately. "And I'll tell you what, after traveling it's become one of my favorite things. I could just kiss whoever invented it and did my backside such a favor."

Now Dare did grin. "I wouldn't say no." At her blank look his smile widened. "That's my design."

His new companion stared at him. "What? No way."

Dare motioned. "Check the crafter's name."

Her eyes went a bit unfocused as she checked the information in the world system, then widened. "Goddess, you actually did." She grinned at him again. "Aren't you full of surprises."

He shrugged self-consciously. "To be fair, I didn't really invent it, just recreated a design from my home."

The bunny girl's nose wrinkled adorably. "How can you have copied a design from your home? It would still be in the crafting

######."

Damn, and here he'd been trying to avoid questions about where he'd come from. At least until it was a good time to tell her, like he'd told his family and friends. "They didn't use the crafting system. Making them is more laborious that way, but they could have more customized designs." All technically true.

"Weird, is that like a religious thing?" she asked. He just grinned, so she laughed wryly. "Well anyway, I'm a girl of my word." She danced forward and planted a peck on his cheek before darting back, giggling and blushing slightly.

She was so ridiculously cute.

Dare resisted the urge to reach up and touch where he could still feel the brush of her soft lips on his skin. It seemed a small thing, but it was a memory he'd treasure.

"Ready to get going?" he asked as Lily put away the camping chair and tightened the straps on her pack again. "I need to stop by Terana to let friends know the threat is over, but unless you want to stay the night in a mansion we could probably make it another hour or two farther after that."

The bunny girl obligingly pulled off her poncho and tucked it away, then bounced on the balls of her feet a few times. "Lead the way, noble sir."

Technically Dare wasn't either of those things, but then again she read a lot of romantic stories. With another laugh of enjoyment he started off at a strong pace; after the relaxing ride with the Home Ward he was rested enough to push himself harder for the final few hours of the day.

Lily ran easily at his side, shooting him curious looks as they went. "I never asked, but what threat did you have to take care of in Redoubt? Rosa only told me your family was in danger."

He shook his head grimly. "There's not much more to say. There was an evil knight trying to hurt my family, and I made sure my loved ones were safe."

She gave him an approving look, then changed topics. "And

what do you mean by staying at a mansion?"

Dare felt his cheeks heat as he quickly explained his relationship with Marona, Baroness of Terana. "She's invited me and my companions to stay with her whenever we're in town, and her maids are very accommodating."

More so than would probably be proper to mention.

The beautiful bunny girl looked a bit uncomfortable. "It would be nice to enjoy that sort of luxury," she said hesitantly. "But we need to get back to your family and let them know you're safe."

He had a feeling there was more to it than that. "Are you worried about going into a town?"

She hesitated, then nodded a bit sheepishly. "I may be different from other bunny girls in a lot of ways, but I share their reluctance to be around a bunch of strange people." She gave a strained smile. "One at a time is usually enough for my sisters, and for me I'm usually content with my books."

She grimaced. "Also we usually don't . . . fare well when we venture into the settlements of other races."

Dare's stomach twisted as he thought of what Zuri had told him about how bunny girls were highly desired as pleasure slaves, but languished and died quickly in captivity. It was sickening and again firmed his resolve to free as many slaves as he could, and if they had nowhere else to go help them start new lives on his lands.

"Things are different in Bastion, and especially in Terana," he promised her. "We can trust Marona to keep the streets of her town safe for us." He veered slightly closer to give her arm a reassuring pat. "And I give you my word, anyone who tries to cause trouble for you will have to get through me first."

Lily gave him a strained smile. "Thank you." She took a breath and squared her shoulders. "I guess if I'm going to be with you and part of your family, I'll need to get used to going where you go. Even into towns."

Dare glanced over at the lowering sun. Unless he just popped in and gave Marona the news, then popped right back out, they probably wouldn't get much farther today. It would probably be better to get a proper night's sleep and a good dinner and breakfast, then travel all the faster in the morning.

“What do you say, then?” he asked with a smile. “Want to meet a baroness and be a guest in her house?”

She gave him a starry-eyed look. “That does sound very romantic,” she admitted. “Most of the best stories take place in castles or mansions or lavish estates.”

“Well, I promise yours will as well . . . we're working to make Nirim Manor the most lavish estate in Bastion.”

Chapter Ten

Home At Last

The guards at the gate looked curious to see Dare accompanied by a bunny girl, as well as in clear awe of Lily's beauty. Not to mention showing a bit of jealousy for him.

She'd changed into her lovely silver gown before they approached Terana, and he'd offered her his arm as they came into view of the gate. She looked radiant as they walked down the road, showing no signs she'd spent the entire day running hard.

Which was a stark contrast to his own disheveled state, in serious need of a proper bath and clean change of clothes.

His companion stared at the guards a bit nervously as they approached, then jumped in surprise and looked on the verge of bolting as the two men abruptly clapped fist to chest in salute and roared in unison, "Huzzah for the hero of Marona's Field!"

"What's going on?" she hissed anxiously.

Dare smiled at the guards as he returned their salute. "Remember the party rated monster I told you about? It was the leader of a monster horde we fought near where the Home Ward dropped us off."

"Wow, that's incredible." Lily smiled a bit tentatively the guards, who bowed low to her with the utmost courtesy as they waved them through the gate.

Although her nervousness returned and she pressed close to his side as they made their way down Terana's streets, which at this hour were crowded with a modest number of passersby. All of whom couldn't help but gawk at the beautiful bunny girl in an evening gown on the arm of a sweaty, travel-stained man.

"Why are they looking at me?" she hissed. "Are they going to try to mount me?"

Dare had no doubt a lot of the male onlookers would love to do just that. He comfortingly patted her hand resting on his arm. "It's not every day they see a ethereally lovely, elegant young woman walking down their streets. You stand out like a rose in a thistle patch."

"Hey!" Lily protested, although she was smiling. "I like thistles. Their flowers are pretty and they're delicious." She grimaced. "Although when I'm in my usual state it's no fun to walk through a patch of them."

He assumed her usual state was nude, like most bunny girls. And he could certainly appreciate the discomfort of brushing against a bunch of prickly plants like that.

They headed straight for Montshadow Estate, although on the way Dare found himself stopping dead in spite of the hurry he was in, staring in amazement at a new monument in the market square.

It was a simple stone block, separated off by ropes. In the center of the block a familiar axe was buried in the stone deep enough to stick, its haft rising into the air higher than most men stood.

The Monstrous Battleaxe trophy from the Cursed Orc Warchief.

He'd completely forgotten about the item in the wake of the Darkblade's attempted assassination, and in the brief thought he'd given it since had assumed that it would find its way to Nirim Manor along with the other loot he'd left behind.

It seemed like Marona had other ideas, though.

"Wow, that's a huge honking axe," Lily said, following his gaze.

He chuckled and stepped over to where a metal plaque had been pounded into the stone, etched with a few sentences.

"Cursed Orc Warchief's Monstrous Battleaxe. Placed here to commemorate the heroism of Darren of Nirim Manor, who in glorious single combat slew the commander of the monster horde that imperiled us all."

Wow. Dare was still on the fence about displaying trophies in his home, seeing the need to bolster his family's reputation but not liking the aesthetic. But to have a trophy prominently placed in the center of Terana praising his deeds . . .

That was something else. Something incredible. He felt his heart swell with pride at the sight.

Lily read the plaque as well, looked up at him wonderingly, and silently leaned against his side as he took some time to appreciate this moment. He was vaguely aware of a few passersby gathering and beginning to clap, and with a somewhat embarrassed smile bowed to them before leading Lily on through the square.

When they reached Montshadow Estate the guard immediately pulled open the wrought iron gate and waved them through. “Please, Master Dare,” he said. “The Baroness insisted you be ushered in to see her immediately when you arrived.”

“Thank you,” Dare said, clapping his shoulder. “How have things been here?”

“No trouble, just the expected chaos of the aftermath of our battle against the monster horde.” The man bowed and motioned them to continue down the drive as he pushed the gate closed behind them.

Miss Garena was waiting at the front doors and curtsied low. “Welcome, Master Dare. The Baroness asked you to attend her in her sitting room.” She hesitated, glancing at Lily, who shrank slightly at her scrutiny.

“This is my companion Lily,” he said, patting the bunny girl's hand soothingly. “We've had a long journey today.”

The Head Maid curtsied to Lily as well. “Welcome, Miss Lily. The staff is drawing up baths and preparing a late dinner. We'll see to your comfort as Master Dare attends the Baroness.”

They were whisked into the entry room, where Marigold and a dog girl maid ushered Lily away, fussing over her with many an exclamation of wonder at her beauty and her striking silver hair. The bunny girl shyly went along, seeming disarmed by their warmth.

Although Dare didn't miss the naughty look the gnome maid shot him before the three women disappeared; he had a feeling she might be paying him a visit or pulling him into a secluded nook sometime during their visit.

He followed Miss Garena up to his noble lover's chambers on the third floor, where just before opening the double doors she looked him over with a critical eye. "Do try not to touch anything in there, particularly not the Baroness herself . . . she's already dressed for bed."

Happy as he would've been to comply with that request, the moment he stepped through the doors Marona wrapped him in a relieved hug and tugged him towards the loveseat, pushing him down into it and settling on his lap.

"You returned so soon," she fretted as she ran her hands over his chest and shoulders as if searching for injuries, looking anxiously into his eyes. "Did something go wrong? Did you change your mind about going after Ollivan?"

Dare shook his head with a smile, stroking her leg. "Ollivan has fallen, and the Assassins Guild have assured me his contract is equally dead."

The elegant noblewoman looked at him in amazement. "This quickly?" she said. "I know you can move fast when you need to, but it's been less than a week . . . a trip to Redoubt and back should've taken at least two weeks for travel alone, let alone the insurmountable task of taking care of matters there."

"I received some divine assistance. Or perhaps provided it." He quickly filled her in on what had happened in Redoubt.

By the time he finished she'd taken his hand and was gripping it hard enough to be uncomfortable. "You went after the guild alone, in the dark? You're fortunate they didn't slit your throat rather than treating with you."

Dare shrugged uncomfortably. "I suppose so." He hastily moved on from that. "Do you think this will be the end of it? Will the guild keep their word, and is there a chance Ollivan's family or friends will be suspicious?"

Marona leaned back in thought, absently stroking his leg. "I'd say arranging for him to be killed by monsters was very well done.

We can hope that the monsters devouring his flesh will conceal the cuts made by your Hamstrings, although it's a detail few would note when the answer is plain to see. Wise to leave all his things as they were."

She grimaced. "As for the other, I'm no expert on Assassins Guilds. But while we'd be fools to trust in them, we should at least be able to trust in their pragmatism . . . you're not worth the effort when there's no gold in it for them and as far as I can see you did nothing to antagonize them."

Dare let out a breath. "Hopefully this nightmare is finally over, and we can get back to our lives."

"I pray so," his lover said, kissing his shoulder. "Although if you can successfully petition for knighthood at the first of the year that will aid you greatly."

She gave his leg a final caress and abruptly stood, tone becoming brisk. "Let's get you into a bath, and then I'll join you and your companion for dinner." She gave him a keen look, lips quirked upward in amusement. "Or is it lover . . . my maids tell me she's an exceptional beauty."

He felt his cheeks heat, not sure exactly how to explain his relationship with Lily. "A friend, for now. One who's left home for the first time, and is excited to see the wonders of the world she's read about in the books she loves." He smiled fondly. "A world she views with a particularly romantic mindset."

Marona also smiled, expression wistful. "Ah, to be young and see the world with such innocent eyes again." She took his hand. "Come."

Apparently when she said "let's get you into a bath" she meant it literally, because she entered the bath room with him, Belinda waiting to attend them both. Through the door leading to the other bath room Dare heard splashes and giggles, and couldn't help but smile.

It sounded like the baroness's maids were showing Lily their customary warmth, and she seemed to have gotten over her previous nervousness. Her laughter was a wonder to hear.

Belinda undressed him with brisk efficiency, then Marona massaged his shoulders while the dragon girl maid shaved him, wiped the homely makeup off his face, and with some effort washed the dye from his hair. Then both women similarly disrobed and pulled him into the bath, where Belinda sensuously bathed them both while they cuddled in the warm water.

Sore and weary as Dare was, he still found himself becoming aroused at their attention. Marona felt it and lovingly stroked him beneath the water, teasing him with growing waves of pleasure. Just as he began to squirm in imminent release she urged him up to sit on the edge of the tub, then dove between his legs and took him into her warm mouth.

He noticed Belinda rubbing herself frantically off to one side, and at the erotic sight he took his noble lover's head in both hands to hold her still and emptied himself down her throat. She swallowed eagerly, making satisfied noises.

After cleaning him up Belinda helped him dress in silk pajamas Marona must've had made for him since his last visit. The maid dressed the baroness in a sleek silk nightgown that hugged her curves, and hand in hand they made their way to an intimate dining room.

Lily was there already, wearing her own comfy nightgown and happily digging into a salad.

She somehow managed to look elegant and breathtaking and adorable all at the same time. Her pale skin was flushed pink from scrubbing, smooth and sweet smelling with scented oils and lotions. Her silver hair had been brushed until it shone with hints of reflections from things around the room, hanging loose down to her waist in a shimmering waterfall.

The lovely bunny girl immediately leapt up when they entered, rushing over to take Dare's hands. “Dare, this place is beautiful!” she gushed, eyes shining. “And the servants are so nice!” Her cheeks flushed even deeper pink. “They gave me a bath, and it was the most luxurious thing I've ever-”

She cut off abruptly as she seemed to realize who Marona was, eyes widening. Then she fell into an awkward curtsy. “My Lady,” she murmured shyly. “Thank you for welcoming me into your mansion.”

The mature noblewoman smiled in a motherly way and lifted Lily upright, holding her by her slender shoulders and leaning in to kiss her cheeks. “My, but you are absolutely breathtaking,” she said. “I'll admit I've only had the pleasure of seeing a cunid once before, and only from a distance. It's wonderful to finally meet one, and such a dear young lady too.”

She glanced at Dare, eyes twinkling. “If I didn't have the feeling you have other plans, I'd invite you to join my staff here at Montshadow Estate.”

“Oh, that would be grand!” the bunny girl said with a dreamy smile. “It would be like a fairy tale.” She gave him a shy look. “But yes, I have other plans. Dare's invited me to join him at Nirim Manor.”

“That sounds lovely, dear. I've been wanting to visit there and see for myself all the splendid improvements I've heard about.” The baroness led Lily back to her seat and settled into the one beside her. “Come, make yourself at home. And let me know if you need anything. A friend of Dare's will always be welcome here.”

The young woman wasted no time digging into her salad again. “It's great that Dare has lovers to offer us such magical places to stay wherever we go.”

Dare, who'd settled in on Marona's other side, coughed in embarrassment at that. His noble lover gave him an amused look, with just the slightest teasing edge to it. “Does he, now? And where did you stay before?”

Oblivious to his embarrassment, Lily eagerly told the baroness about Rosa and her enchanted clearing. She also described her efforts, with the dryad's help, to make sure meals were prepared for Dare's arrivals.

He hadn't realized she'd gone to such pains for his sake, and was even more grateful to the caring young woman.

Marona eyed him thoughtfully the entire time. “Speaking of fairy tales,” she mused. “Your life is full of wonder and excitement, isn't it?”

Dare smiled and took her hand. “But wherever I travel, home beckons sweetly.”

Lily sighed dreamily.

The meal was pleasant, if brief. Then Dare and Marona bid Lily goodnight, Marigold appearing to lead the bunny girl to her room, and his noble lover led him up to her chambers.

“Come,” she said almost shyly, leading him into her bedroom. It was the first time he'd ever been in there, and to his eyes it suited her elegant simplicity.

It looked as if she was finally going to share her bed with him; the big, canopied four-poster looked incredibly plush and comfortable.

They cuddled for a few minutes, sunk in pillowy softness. Then Marona kissed him hungrily, he began to caress her soft body, and their clothes came off again as they made tender but passionate love.

Dare made every effort to guide her to a few intense climaxes before giving in to her breathless entreaties to come inside her. He grit his teeth in sweet release as waves of pleasure rippled through him, filling her with his seed, then afterwards gathered her into his arms and held his beautiful lover close.

Although he'd been planning to clean them up, Marona drifted off before he could catch his breath. So, warm and content, he closed his eyes and let sleep claim him as well.

* * * * *

Dare woke the next morning to find he was holding a rather smaller and plumper figure than the tall, elegant noblewoman.

Marigold looked up at him mischievously as he started in surprise. “Good morning, lover,” she whispered with a giggle, rubbing her soft naked body against him. He felt wetness against his hip from her arousal.

“Where did you come from?” he asked, groggily reaching through her silky pink hair to fondle her round ass. “Where's Mar- that is, the Baroness?”

She giggled again. “I came from Deepwater, originally. As for our Lady, she had pressing business in town and regrets she'll probably be occupied until after you leave.”

The naughty gnome climbed up to straddle his hips, rubbing her plump pussy up and down his quickly stiffening shaft and soaking it with her nectar, filling the air with the intoxicating cinnamon musk of her arousal. “Which means I get to fuck you in her bed.”

The feeling of her petals gliding over his sensitive foreskin was incredible, but Dare gently but firmly pushed her away with a concerned noise. “Prevent Conception,” he reminded her. “I don't have any.”

“Oh, fuck,” Marigold said, big blue eyes going huge; she knew his fertility was so high he could impregnate her just by touching her pussy with his dick. She bit her plump lip, urgently grinding against his thigh as she mulled that over.

Then she sighed in resignation and squirmed around until her glistening sex hovered over his mouth. “Okay, we'll do it this way. You just better make sure to make me feel good.”

Dare certainly did his best, luxuriating in the smell and taste of his tiny gnome lover as she began licking and rubbing his cock, then finally took him into her small mouth.

After about a minute he heard a clatter from out in the hall, and Marigold began riding his face more urgently as she pulled her mouth off his cock with a soft plop. “Quick!” she hissed. “Hurry up and come before I get caught in here!”

He felt his orgasm retreating at the prospect. “I'm not sure it's happening anytime soon,” he hissed back.

She began frantically jacking him off with both hands. “What if I told you that your bunny girl friend has the most beautiful pussy I've ever seen? And how she flowed like a fountain as I fingered her in the bath, all the while talking about how I shouldn't go too deep because she was a virgin and was saving herself for the man she was going to marry?"

The image of sweet, innocent Lily squirming as the adventurous gnome pleasured her was definitely enough to take Dare over the edge. With a gasp he grabbed Marigold's plump ass with both hands, squeezing her warm pillowy flesh, and pulled her pussy firmly against his mouth as he began spurting.

His tiny lover quickly wrapped her lips around him again, swallowing his seed as fast as he pumped it into her mouth.

Then she vanished faster than a plump woman should be able to, diving behind the bed as the outer chamber doors opened.

Dare hastily covered himself with a sheet, spraying a couple last jets against the soft cloth. But to his relief whoever it was didn't come into Marona's room.

A moment later he heard Miss Garena clear her throat to get his attention before speaking in a polite, firm voice. "Your pardon if I woke you, Master Dare. The Baroness informed me you were eager to get home to your family and wanted an early start. Breakfast is waiting for you downstairs, and Miss Lily is already eating."

"Thank you," he called, uncomfortably aware of Marigold's muffled giggles coming from beside the bed. "I'll be dressed and down shortly."

"Very well," the Head Maid said primly, her voice moving towards the exit. "I'll send Marigold to attend to your needs and guide you down to the dining hall."

The giggles abruptly stopped.

The moment the doors shut the gnome maid burst out of hiding, sexy little plump body moving in a blur as she threw on her maid uniform. "Be back soon!" she hissed as she hopped towards the door tugging on a long woolen stocking.

Dare couldn't help but grin as he dressed in the fine clothes he'd purchased in Redoubt, which had been freshly laundered while he slept. Then he gathered his gear and made his way out into the hall.

Marigold waited there, all prim and proper aside from her flushed rosy apple cheeks and the fact that her ruffled bonnet was slightly askew. "Good morning, Master Dare," she said with a perfect curtsy. "I trust you slept well?"

"And had a very pleasant awakening," he said, grinning at her.

She kept her placid expression but her big blue eyes danced as she turned and glided away. "This way, please."

Lily was dressed in her cozy leather poncho this morning, and she beamed at him as he settled down in the chair across from her. "I slept so well!" she said after swallowing a mouthful of salad. "My bed was big enough I could share it with all my sisters, and so soft!"

He smiled back as he began filling his plate with bacon, sausage, and eggs. "I can see. You're looking even more radiant than usual this morning."

Breakfast was delicious, and the maids kept an unobtrusive presence to allow him to share it with his bunny girl companion; there were no surprise visitors under the table this time.

As soon as they finished eating they set out, the maids once again lining up at the front door to bid him farewell and express their hopes that he'd return soon. As well as some of them subtly, or not so subtly, hinting that next time he visited he should make time for them, too.

Considering there were over a dozen beautiful women of various races to be with at Montshadow Estate, and he'd only been with Belinda and Marigold thus far, Dare fully intended to take them up on their offers.

Miss Garena stood at the door ready to open it, but paused in doing so. "The Baroness bade me to remind you of the Trials to join the Order of the Northern Wall that begin on the first of the year. Bastion's yearly Council of Lords takes place concurrently, and she'll be setting out on the twenty-first of Pol to travel to Redoubt. She invites you to travel with her some or all of the way, as you're able, and stay with her in the city as part of her retinue."

Dare hesitated. Marona, Ireni, and the rest of his loved ones had been urging him to petition for knighthood ever since the trouble with Ollivan started. It seemed less necessary now that the man was dead and his threat hopefully dealt with.

And with Pella due to have her babies around that time he really didn't want to leave her.

On the other hand, he had a feeling his loved ones would still encourage him to do so for the opportunities it would provide their family. Particularly their children being born into nobility.

Besides, he could admit that a part of him wanted to undertake the challenge and adventure. To be a knight in a medieval world. To see that part of Haraldar's culture, and maybe gain enough influence through those channels to change things for the better in the kingdom.

"Give our Lady my thanks," he told the Head Maid. "I'll need to speak to my family and make plans. And as my fiancee is due to give birth around that time and I can travel quickly in any case, I may come later. But if I am traveling there, I'd be honored to be part of her retinue."

The severe older woman inclined her head and opened the door, letting in a blast of chilly air. Dare offered Lily his arm, and together they walked down the drive, out the gate as the guard saluted respectfully, and through the town.

On the way through the market he paused to shop for gifts for his fiancees, getting the bunny girl's advice. He also used the opportunity to describe how he'd met first Zuri, then Pella, then Leilanna, Se'weir, and finally Sia and Ireni, and the adventures and wonderful experiences they'd shared together.

Her eyes shone as she listened, and she sighed happily. "You should see the way your eyes light up when you talk about each of them," she said. "I hope one day you'll look at me that way."

He was certain he'd be able to come to love this sweet young woman, and he took her pale hand and kissed the back of it in response.

After buying a soft little stuffed cat for Gelaa that she was probably still too young to appreciate, as well as an assortment of baby things for Pella's babies coming in about a month and a half, he packed everything up and they exited the city.

Again with a cheer from the guards, which was as embarrassing as it was gratifying as passersby turned to stare.

It was a relief to focus on running, leaping forward with Lily beside him and their backs to the chill wind blowing down from the north. As a nod to the cold the bunny girl kept on her poncho, and Dare pulled his hood low and put on the goggles Ireni had given him for running at high speeds.

His companion burst into peals of laughter at the sight, then apologized while giggling through her hands. Her own eyes were a bit red from the cold and the wind of their passage, but she seemed able to handle it far better than him.

Ominous leaden clouds filled the sky as the miles fell away behind them, and after a few hours of running a heavy snow began to fall. Luckily he judged that at the speed they were going they only had an hour or so more to go to reach Nirim Manor.

Dare loved being able to travel at car speeds.

Lily stopped to stare in amazement when Nirim Manor came into view, looking down on it from a rise so they could see past the low wall to the buildings within. "It's beautiful," she said. "Look at the gardens! Oh, I can't wait to explore them!"

To be honest he thought it wasn't looking quite as good as usual, given the hole torn into one corner of the manor. Not from an attack, thankfully, but from construction in progress. A small indoor pool from the looks of things, based on the hole sunk into the ground lined with ceramic tiles, and pipes connected to the rest of the house's plumbing.

It reminded him of something, but at the moment he couldn't put his finger on it.

He was distracted by the sight of sunlight glinting off copper-bright hair, speckled with snowflakes and streaming in the wind, as Ireni appeared through the gate and started towards them. Her delicate features were brightened by a radiant smile as she waved eagerly in greeting.

Except it wasn't Ireni's million watt smile that always took his breath away, which made her Sia.

His betrothed threw her arms around him and kissed him fiercely. “Welcome home, beloved,” she murmured, nuzzling his neck. “Oh, the challenges you've faced, and how magnificently you've conquered! I was rooting for you with every step. And I'm so glad you made it back to us safely.”

Before he could respond the petite redhead turned to Lily and wrapped her in an equally enthusiastic hug. “Welcome to Nirim Manor, Lily of Brighthill Warren.”

“Thank you!” the bunny girl said. If she felt awkward about being hugged by a stranger she showed no sign of it as she hugged the smaller woman back with equal warmth. “You must be Ireni . . . Dare's told me so much about you!”

The goddess smiled and displayed her black pearl ring. “I'm Sia, in fact.”

Lily immediately stiffened and dropped into a deep, clumsy curtsy. “Please forgive me, Goddess.”

Sia lifted the beautiful bunny girl up by her shoulders. “None of that, my dear. In this home, part of this family, I'm merely another of Dare's fiancees and soon to be the mother of our child.” She kissed Lily's cheek. “Besides, I hope soon we'll be very close, as I am with the rest of the family, and such formalities will be unnecessary.”

The bunny girl smiled uncertainly, but seemed at a loss for words.

Ireni came to the fore and removed the ring, replacing it with her emerald one. “Welcome to Nirim Manor, Lily. I'm Ireni.” She turned to Dare and threw herself into his arms, trembling slightly as she looked up at him. “I'm so glad you've returned safely to us, my love,” she whispered. “And that Ollivan will trouble us no more. Sia assured me things were all right, but I was still so scared for you.”

Lily stared at her blankly, clearly lost as to what was going on.

To be fair, Dare had described Sia and Ireni to her but hadn't included all the finer details, such as that the two women shared Ireni's body as the goddess dwelt in her.

Ireni seemed to read his mind, as she seemed uniquely able to do, and drew back to give him a wry look. "I'm going to talk to Lily for a bit, then we can have a proper reunion. Leilanna's in the garden if you want to greet her. The others are inside sheltering from the storm."

She nudged him on towards the gate, then turned and hooked an arm through Lily's, walking off with her. "We have a few things to talk about, Lily, and they're going to come as a bit of a shock. First off, I'm a high priestess of the Outsider, who is also known as Sia. The Goddess has blessed me with the honor of dwelling within me . . ."

He left his fiancee to her explanation and headed through the gate.

To his discomfiture, as he made for the gardens a man he'd never seen before emerged from one of the guest houses and hurried his way. "Master Dare!" he called, beaming. "Welcome home! Can I assist with anything? Take your things inside?"

Okay then. The man was a Level 11 Tiller, in his late 20s and with the wiry body and weathered features of someone who worked hard in the fields. An honest enough sort, at first glance.

He obviously knew who Dare was, and acted like he belonged. But Dare wasn't about to give him his possessions, which included the Home Ward that was potentially worth as much as this entire manor and the lands it stood on.

"Thank you, no," he said with a polite smile. "You can head back inside out of the cold." He paused. "Although, um, who are you?"

The man chuckled ruefully. "Sorry, must be a shock to come home and be greeted by a stranger." He offered his hand. "I'm Johar, of Harald Province."

Dare returned his handshake. "Well met, Johar. What brings you to Nirim Manor?"

The man shuffled awkwardly. "Well, uh, your pardon, Master Dare, but your generosity did. Yours and that of Mistress Ireni and the rest of your household." At his blank look Johar ducked his head. "I don't like to think of it now the nightmare is over, but my family was betrayed by our landlord and taken as slaves."

A shadow passed across his humble features, then they brightened again. "Thank the Outsider, Mistress Ireni purchased us before we could be separated, gave us our freedom, and offered us employ here. As well as land to farm in the spring, if we want it. Which of course we will, with thanks, begging your pardon."

That came as a surprise, but Dare was pleased to hear it. Ireni had made it her life's purpose to help free slaves and give them new lives in Kov, and he was glad she was continuing that here. He'd been resolved to do what he could to free slaves and if possible find a way to abolish slavery entirely, but as yet hadn't made any efforts.

He'd have to try harder, with Ireni's help. And that of Zuri and Pella and Leilanna and Se'weir, and Ilin with his charitable efforts.

At his reassurances he didn't need anything Johar retreated back to the guest house to weather the storm with his family, and Dare continued on to the garden. He paused for a moment where they'd planted Eloise's seed, the small mound of dirt covered with a blanket of snow, and knelt to rest a hand on it.

"Home again, Daughter," he murmured, smiling softly. "And hopefully that's the end of the danger to our family. In the spring you'll be able to grow fast with no fear of trouble. I can't wait to finally meet you. Also Grandmummy Rosaceae sends her love, and blesses you to grow strong and healthy."

He straightened and continued deeper into the gardens, which were mostly dead and bare at this time of year. There were still plenty of tall, snow-covered shrubs and topiaries to block his view, and his heart momentarily stopped in wonder when he rounded a bend and at last saw Leilanna kneeling on the path, working the earth with a trowel in preparation for spring.

She was snugly dressed for the cold, the hood of her cape lowered so the snow gathering on her head was almost indistinguishable from her snowy hair whipping in the wind. Her ash-gray skin was flushed darker with the cold, and she was softly singing a hauntingly beautiful elvish tune as she worked.

Dare strode to her, and she stiffened and turned to him, dark pink eyes widening with surprise swiftly followed by joy. Before she could begin to stand he dropped to his knees and gathered her into his arms, hugging her tight.

Chapter Eleven

Personal Reunions

Leilanna's soft, warm body pressed against Dare urgently as she hugged him back, peppering his face with kisses before pressing her plump lips firmly to his.

Finally she pulled back, looking at him with tears in her eyes. "I was so afraid," she whispered. "Sia told us things were okay, but I was still so worried that you'd run into something you couldn't handle, while I was here hiding where I couldn't help you."

He pulled her head down to his shoulder and stroked her silky hair, damp with snow. "It's all over now," he murmured. "Ollivan is dead and the Assassin's Guild is dropping the contract. It's over now and we're safe."

His dusk elf fiancee wordlessly pulled back, pushed gracefully to her feet, and tugged his hand insistently for him to follow her.

Dare stood as well and let himself be led deeper into the garden, to the secluded nook where he and Se'weir had shared their first time. It was a bed-sized patch of the softest grass he'd ever felt, surrounded by tall flowering bushes for privacy.

At the moment it was covered with a few inches of snow, but Leilanna began casting a spell he hadn't seen before, and soon flames fanned out from her to melt away the snow, dry the deep green grass beneath, and finally encircle the bed in a line of flames that warmed the air inside to almost balmy temperatures.

Sure enough, he saw that she'd reached Level 30 while he'd been gone and had gained a spell called "Freeform Fire." Which if he had to guess was a limited range and power pyrokinesis that allowed for great precision and control.

His beautiful fiancee shed her clothes so swiftly she could've been wielding magic for that as well, then stepped into the center of the circle of flames and posed for him in all her glory. Dare looked in awe at the snow swirling around her, the firelight bathing her tantalizing curves.

She crooked an elegant finger, smiling, and he hastily shed his own clothes and stepped over the flames to gather her beautiful body into his arms, kissing her passionately.

As her tongue slipped hungrily into his mouth seeking his, he lowered her to the soft grass and climbed on top of her. After missing his beloved for weeks his need for her was a sharp pang, and she seemed just as desperate as her hands gripped his ass and pulled him towards her.

The few seconds he rubbed his tip against her entrance while she begged him to keep going were almost agonizing, but finally he felt her arousal begin to flow and coat his tip. He wasted no more time pushing through her flushed petals in a smooth motion, savoring the pleasure of her silky walls.

Leilanna squealed and began to buck beneath him, gripping his back and scraping her fingernails over his skin in rapture as he spread her open until he was balls deep in her tight warmth. He responded and moved with her, basking in the feel of her glorious body as his thrusts became more urgent.

“Yes!” she moaned as her legs clamped around him, hips rolling desperately. “Gods yes, I needed this. After all the worry you put me through this is exactly what you needed to do to make it better.”

Cool snowflakes kissed his back, a sharp contrast to his beautiful lover's heat as she climaxed. Her flooding arousal added a squelching noise to his vigorous thrusts, and her silken tunnel lovingly massaged his shaft as she buried her face in his shoulder to stifle her cries of passion.

Even though it had only been a few minutes Dare felt his balls boiling, and in spite of his best efforts gave in to the pleasure. With a last gasp he buried his face in her soft hair and breathed deep of her heady scent, pushing deep one last time to erupt against her core.

The both froze in shared orgasm, fully joined and basking in the heat of their desire. Finally Dare rolled to one side and gathered his dusk elf fiancee into his arms, running his hands lovingly over her flushed skin, slick with her perspiration. The air was starting to blow across them more coolly as her encircling flames died down.

"I love you," he murmured, softly kissing one of her pointy ears. "And I missed you more than I can say."

Leilanna gave a low, throaty laugh as she turned her head so her plump lips met his. "I could tell. And I love you too."

He shared her lingering kiss for several enjoyable seconds, savoring her sweet blackberry wine taste. "I was worried for all of you the entire time I was gone."

"Then you have an idea how we felt." She buried her face in his shoulder, tenderly kissing his neck. "So you fucked Ollivan up, huh?"

Dare smiled grimly. "Even better. With some help we made it look like he was killed by monsters while farming gold."

"A monster killed by monsters. Poetic." His beautiful lover looked around at the flames, which where almost entirely gone, and shivered as if finally feeling the cold. "Bah, my time's up. Go get dressed and head inside . . . I'm not the only one who was worried about you and missed you."

He blinked. "Wait, was this intentional?"

She grinned at him. "You think I'd be working on the garden in the middle of a snowstorm? Sia gave us a heads up you'd be getting home this morning." She abruptly bounded to her feet, full breasts swaying hypnotically as she reached for her clothes. "She also told me you brought home a beautiful bunny girl she thinks might join the harem. I want to go meet her!"

Dare began dressing as well, a bit bemused by that revelation; he should've guessed the goddess was on top of things. Although she usually wasn't so forthcoming with her knowledge about what was going on.

Maybe she made an exception for new additions to the family.

"Oh," Leilanna said as he finished, "before I forget, can I get the legendary chest so we don't have to work the pumps by hand anymore?"

He laughed and dug into the secret pocket where he kept the peanut shaped item, handing it over to her. "You know this helped me kill a party rated monster?"

She grinned. "Yeah, which explains the ##### ###### balance change that happened that day. Even without Sia confirming it, we all guessed that had to be you." She gave him a last fierce kiss, slapped his ass with a giggle, then ran off towards the gate.

Shaking his head with a smile, he headed towards the manor and slipped in through the nearest door, the one leading into the kitchen.

To his pleased surprise he found Se'weir in there, busily making lunch. The plump hobgoblin barely came up to his chest, soft skin a lighter green than Zuri's avocado hue and hair a luxurious wave of soft brown that fell halfway down her back. In the heat of the kitchen she was wearing only a thigh-length tunic of soft wool and an apron.

She turned at the sound of the door, froze when she saw him, then her beautiful face lit up with joy. With a happy cry she threw herself into his arms, hands powdered with flour grasping his neck as she pulled his head down far enough she could kiss him while standing on her tiptoes.

Dare returned her fierce kiss, luxuriating in the feel of her soft body pressed against him. He'd missed her gentle warmth and unexpected passion, and the worry he'd felt for her all the time he'd been gone vanished in his own joy at their reunion.

Finally Se'weir pulled back, pale yellow eyes looking up at him fiercely. "Our enemy lies dead at your feet, my mate?"

"He'll threaten our family no more," he assured her solemnly.

She nodded in satisfaction. "I had no fear you could deal with him, even without Sia's assurances."

With startling abruptness she pulled away from his embrace and stepped over to the table, bending over it and lifting her tunic, then shoving her cute yellow panties down to expose her round ass and glistening, hairless sex.

“Take me, my mate,” the beautiful hobgoblin said, looking over her shoulder at him with a hungry expression as she lifted her ass higher in invitation.

Dare eagerly unlaced his pants and freed his manhood, then stepped forward to rest his hands on her wide hips. He gently stroked her soft skin as he lined up with her entrance, rubbing his tip up and down her petals to gather her arousal. The crack of her ass waggled invitingly, and he pushed his erection between her soft cheeks and thrust a few times while she moaned in surprise and enjoyment.

“Do you wish to take my other hole, my mate?” she said in a husky voice. “I think I can handle your size.”

Maybe, although Se'weir was small enough it would be hard for her. Zuri couldn't take him in the ass even with stretching, and Sia struggled with it even though she relished powerful sensations.

He chuckled and playfully smacked her left butt cheek, watching it jiggle delightfully as she giggled in enjoyment. “No, I just wanted to rub it between these sexy buns of yours a few times.” Like with Leilanna, his urgency for his lover brooked no more delay, and he pulled back and and thrust into her in a smooth motion, stretching her tight walls.

The beautiful hobgoblin squealed in pleasure and wiggled against the table, plump ass and thighs jiggling as he pulled back and thrust in again, then again. Her back made an undulating wave as he thrust harder, and she cooed and pushed back against him desperately.

“Yes!” she panted, cheek rubbing against the table with every forceful penetration. “Breed me, my mate. Bask in the glory of your victory with me. Show me I'm yours and you're mine, and you know what pleases me.”

Dare grabbed a handful of her hair and pulled her head back gently as he thrust into her, smacking her round ass with his other hand. That was enough to push her over the edge, and with a delighted wail she quivered and sprayed his thighs in climax, velvety walls lovingly milking him.

Since he'd already come once with Leilanna he could last a bit longer with Se'weir, even in the overwhelming pleasure of taking her over the table while she squirmed delightedly in orgasm.

"I missed you," he panted, rotating his hips to thrust in at a different angle. "So much. I thought about you every moment I was gone."

"So did I, my mate," she panted, rising up on her tiptoes so he pushed against her g-spot every time he entered her. "So did . . . ah! Ah! Ahhhhh!"

His beautiful fiancee collapsed in another quivering orgasm, and Dare groaned and gave in to his pleasure, burying himself deep in her inviting warmth and coating her walls with his seed.

When he finished he gathered her into his arms and held her tenderly, breathing in her warm scent as he slipped a hand up beneath her tunic and played with her pillowy breasts. "I love you."

"And I love you, my mate." She made a happy sound and nuzzled his chest. "I didn't realize it was possible to feel like this, before I met you. To be part of such a wondrous thing as this family that has welcomed me."

Dare's ears pricked up at the sudden plaintive cry of an infant deeper in the house. Gelaa.

At the sound Se'weir sighed regretfully. "Guess my turn's over," she said, leaning up to kiss him one last time. "I'll see you soon, my betrothed."

With a lingering smile for him she returned to her cooking, the tantalizing smells promising a delicious meal to come.

He left her in the kitchen and made his way upstairs through the strangely empty house, then down the hallway to Gelaa's room, ducking inside.

To his surprise he'd reached her first, an unusual thing in a house full of doting women who treated the newborn as if they were second mothers. She was lying in her cradle, adorable little face scrunched up and small arms and legs waving as she wailed at the ceiling.

"Shh, baby girl," Dare soothed, leaning down to gently lift his goblin daughter into his arms, cuddling her close. She was almost two months old already, but still felt so tiny. "Daddy's here. Daddy's home. And he's made sure you'll be safe."

He turned to see Zuri standing in the doorway, looking up at him with a tender expression. She quietly stepped over to him, wrapped her arms around his waist, and hugged him tight. Her small shoulders shook in a sudden surge of emotion.

Dare dropped to his knees and shifted Gelaa to one arm to hug his goblin fiancee to him, stroking her sleek black hair and kissing her forehead. "I'm here, my beloved," he whispered. "I'm home. And I've made sure you're safe."

"And so are you," she replied, kissing him softly before resting her head on his shoulder. "Safe and back with us."

"It should be over now. We can go back to living our lives without fear."

Zuri smiled up at him, yellow eyes full of love. "I was never afraid as long as I knew you were protecting us." She paused a beat. "Although it helped that Sia let us know things were going okay."

Gelaa was still fussing, waving her little balled fists as she made plaintive sounds. Zuri gave him a final kiss, then gently took their daughter from him and moved over to settle in a rocking chair sized for her, freeing a breast so the baby could nurse.

"Go on and find Pella," she said gently, nodding towards the door. "We can meet up again after Gelaa's done eating and goes back down for a nap." She looked up at him, big yellow eyes shining with love. "I want you."

Part of Dare wanted to stay and share this tender moment, but that wouldn't really be fair to Pella. Especially if his fiancees had arranged this so they could all have a chance to be with him.

So he leaned down to kiss his betrothed, then slipped back out the door, shutting it behind him.

He turned away, half wondering where to go to find Pella, and decided the master bedroom was a safe bet.

He turned out to be right, although before reaching it his dog girl fiancee burst out into the hallway and practically tackled him with a joyous squeal. She hugged him tight with her hugely pregnant belly nestled between them, eagerly alternating between fierce kisses and licking his mouth and face with her soft flat tongue.

Dare laughed and returned her loving kisses, running his fingers through her luxurious golden hair, down her back and to her soft fluffy tail, which he ruffled and played with for a moment before pulling back.

"Gods, I missed you," he murmured, tenderly brushing her cheek with his fingers while he looked deep into her soft brown eyes. He dropped a hand to rest on her belly. "How are you and the babies?"

"Missing you with all our hearts while you were gone." Pella looked up at him with a big smile. "But I can smell your calmness, which means you must've dealt with the threat like Sia assured us you had."

She paused, sniffing, then to his chagrin dropped to her knees and buried her face in his crotch.

"Mmm, that's not all I smell," she moaned. "Your cock is tantalizing right now. I mean it always is, but now it's not just your sexy scent but also Se'weir, and Leilanna, and oh, Marigold and Marona!" She giggled and nuzzled his growing erection. "You must've had fun last night."

His beautiful dog girl fiancee breathed deeply. "And even from before you last bathed, the scent of . . ." her brow furrowed, "cherry blossoms?" She grinned up at him mischievously. "Dare, did you fuck a cherry tree?"

He threw back his head and laughed, ruffling her floppy ears. "A dryad, actually. She offered me rest in her enchanted clearing on the way to and from Redoubt. Her name is Rosaceae."

Pella stiffened. "Wait, as in the mother of Rosie's entire race?

The demigoddess who birthed all florans?" Dare shrugged and grinned, and with a laugh she slapped his ass. "That's something I want to hear more about later. What was it like?"

He chuckled ruefully. "She picked me up as if I was as small as Zuri and fucked herself with me."

His dog girl fiancee pealed laughter as she gracefully rose to her feet, ushering him towards the bedroom next to the master bedroom. "Okay, go get undressed. I was expecting to be after Zuri so I'm not quite ready. Give me five minutes, okay?"

"Sure. I could use a few minutes to recharge anyway if this is going to be a marathon."

"More like a gauntlet." Eyes dancing, Pella bounded back into the master bedroom.

Dare stepped into the other bedroom and shed his clothes, sitting at the end of the bed to wait. He was a bit bemused by the fact that his fiancees all wanted to jump him the moment he got home, before he'd even had a chance to bathe after the morning's run.

And other recent activities, as Pella had pointed out.

Speaking of her, it was less than a minute later when she stepped through the doorway, grinning hugely and tail wagging enthusiastically. "Okay, Dare, I'm ready!"

"Wait!" he blurted, staring at her in delight.

She paused. "What?" she asked uncertainly.

Dare grinned at his beautiful fiancee. "The light streaming through the doorway is backlighting the thin nightgown you're wearing, so I can see the silhouette of your body through the cloth." His smile widened. "Including that you're naked underneath."

Pella laughed a bit quizzically. "Dare! You've seen me naked plenty of times."

"And I never get tired of it," he teased. His eyes traced the beautiful curves of her heavily pregnant body. "You look seriously sexy like this."

"Really?" her tail began wagging harder again. She playfully reached down and rubbed herself through the thin cloth. “Want me to dance in the light?”

Dare felt his cock lurch at the prospect; that would be incredibly sensual. “Later,” he growled with a grin. “Right now I need to run my hands all over your sexy little body.”

His fiancee giggled and bounded towards, him, peeling off the nightgown as she climbed onto his lap and straddled him. “Little?” she teased, pressing her hugely pregnant belly against his stomach.

“Aside from where you're round and sexy. Like here.” He gently rested his hands on her stomach and began to stroke the taut, silky flesh. “And here.” He moved his hands around to dig his fingers into the yielding flesh of her luscious ass, even bigger and more tantalizing now.

“And here?” Pella giggled again as she pressed her soft pillowy breasts against his face.

Dare's cock throbbed against her soft pussy. “Gods, I need you right now,” he groaned, voice muffled.

“Me too,” Pella panted, grinding her incredible softness against him. “You were gone for so long.” She began licking his face with her soft flat tongue, then kissed him deeply.

He continued to caress her perfect body as she broke the kiss and pushed his head down to rest between her full breasts, and he breathed in her clean scent and luxuriated in the softness of her pillowy mounds.

He trailed his lips over her soft skin until he found a stiff nipple, kissed his way around it, then took it into his mouth and gently sucked.

Then stiffened in surprise as warm liquid squirted into his mouth.

“Oooo!” Pella whimpered, fluffy tail wagging furiously. “Oh gods that feels . . . I don't even know how to describe it. Indescribable.”

Dare reflexively swallowed, tasting a somewhat sour, slightly chalky flavor. It wasn't exactly unpleasant, just unexpected. “Sorry,” he said sheepishly. “I didn't know you were already producing milk.”

She giggled and pulled his head back to her nipple. “It's fine, that was sexy. And it felt really good, too! Go ahead and have more if you want.”

His cock lurched against her soft pussy at the prospect. “Are you sure?”

His dog girl fiancee grinned mischievously. “Something tells me you think it's hot, too,” she teased. “And besides, you can't get enough of lapping from my fount when we're making love, just like I enjoy swallowing your seed.” She stroked his hair. “Come on, my love, savor me.”

Dare eagerly took her nipple between his lips again and gave another gentle suck, feeling a second squirt of sweet milk fill his mouth.

Pella moaned and ground her soft folds against him even more urgently. “That feels incredible,” she panted as she soaked him with her arousal. “Keep going. More!”

He switched to her other nipple and took another, deeper pull, and she squealed and mashed his head against her yielding breast with both hands. As he suckled she rose up, silky petals gliding up his length to press against his tip, and with a needy whimper impaled herself on him in one slow, sensuous movement.

Dare groaned in pleasure at the sensation of being inside his beautiful lover, tasting her sweet milk as he ran his hands over her round pregnant belly. She'd always been ridiculously sexy, of course, but he wasn't sure he'd ever felt such an intense surge of raw desire for her.

After weeks away, he needed her more than he'd realized.

Pella made sure he stayed latched on as she moved up and down on his cock, silky walls gripping him tight as she rose and squelching as she dropped back down. It only took a minute or so before she let out a whimpery little whine and clutched him desperately around the head, pussy clenching around him in orgasm as her nectar drenched his lap.

His final suck drew only a little milk and he realized he'd drained her dry. That thought, combined with the pleasure of her rippling walls, was enough to make him release inside her with a grunt of pleasure.

When Dare finally finished he turned sideways and drew her down to cuddle with him on the bed, stroking her tenderly as he buried his face in her golden hair between her floppy ears, breathing in her clean scent. “I love you,” he whispered.

“And I you, my mate,” she murmured, licking his chest. “For all the wonderful life we'll have together, and whatever awaits beyond.”

After a few minutes of contentment holding each other the beautiful dog girl's ears twitched up alertly. “Sounds like Gelaa's asleep and Zuri's ready in our bedroom,” she said with a grin, bounding up and reaching for her nightgown. “I'm going to go say hi to the new friend you brought back . . . she smells beautiful!”

Dare couldn't help but laugh at that. “You can smell beauty?”

She laughed. “Of course. I'm surrounded by it everywhere in our family. It's like a constant warm hug for my nose.”

Well, he learned something new every day. He stood and hugged Pella from behind, gently supporting her big belly with both hands as he kissed her neck. “And even more beautiful within,” he murmured.

“Mmm.” His dog girl fiancee contentedly nestled against him. Then with a laugh she danced away, disappearing out the door. “See you later!”

Dare contemplated dressing, then decided it seemed a bit pointless considering he'd be in bed with Zuri in thirty seconds. Although he did take a minute to wet a cloth in the washbasin by the door and give himself a quick wipe down.

Then, grinning with anticipation, he ducked out into the hallway and through the doorway into the master bedroom.

His breath caught in wonder at the sight of his beautiful goblin fiancee, practically lost in the middle of the huge bed they all shared. She was dressed in a leather tunic he recognized as the one he'd made for her long ago after they'd first met, which he didn't realize she still had.

And honestly wouldn't have minded if she'd thrown out; it looked crude and clumsily made now.

Most noticeably, however, was that the translation stone she always wore around her neck was resting on the bed beside her. He found out why when she sat up and looked at him, giving him a solemn, shy smile.

"Dare abur Zuri?" she murmured.

In an instant Dare was back to those peaceful days of just the two of them, discovering the world and the leveling system together. And then finally discovering their love.

In an almost pavlovian response to the familiar invitation from so long ago, his cock stiffened and began to grow until it stood out rock hard and proud in front of him.

His goblin fiancee looked at it hungrily, big eyes roaming his tall, muscular body. She flushed dark green with desire and wasted no time shedding the tunic and tossing it aside.

It was Dare's turn feast his eyes on her gorgeous little body, with her disproportionately large breasts even bigger from producing milk for their child. She'd swiftly shed the baby fat, and while she might've barely come up to his belly button she had a figure any college coed would envy.

Her beautiful face was all sharp angles, her yellow eyes big and smoky and full of such deep love and desire it took his breath away. Her sex glistened with arousal, and her thighs squirmed against each other in quiet pleasure at his awed scrutiny.

Zuri took the translation stone and draped it back around her neck, then held out a small hand to him. "Dare mate Zuri?" she murmured with a smile.

After weeks apart he felt the same urgent need for her as he felt for his other beloved, but after coming three times in fairly quick succession he wasn't in a hurry. And he didn't want to hurry.

Dare climbed onto the bed and crawled to her, pulling her to him for a fierce kiss. Even though she hadn't really understood kissing at the first, now she was not only expert at it but enjoyed it hugely.

His goblin fiancee moaned and rubbed her tiny body against him, small hands running up his stomach, across his chest, over his shoulders and down his arms. He just as eagerly fondled her large breasts, ran his hands over her flat tummy, and gripped her small but round ass. Her skin had a slightly slippery feel as if she'd just applied lotion, and was incredibly soft and warm.

He didn't think he'd ever tire of touching her.

It quickly became clear that Zuri was in more of a hurry than he was. Which she proved by finally shoving him onto his back and then straddling his face, rubbing her pussy all over his mouth and coating him with her flowing arousal.

Dare eagerly pressed his tongue between her folds, savoring the heady strength of her musky pheromones and her sweet taste. He found her clit and worked it firmly, grabbing her ass as her thighs clamped around his head.

She squirmed against him desperately as he pleasured her, until finally with a cry of bliss she rose up slightly and squirted all over his face.

Giving him no time to get his bearings, his goblin lover scrambled to the edge of the bed and positioned herself on her hands and knees, staring at him with eyes glassy with lust. “Take me,” she murmured.

Dare wasted no time rolling off the bed onto his feet. She was just the right height for him to position himself at her small entrance and begin to push in, reveling in the ease with which he slipped through her folds and sank in deeper in spite of the vise-like tightness of her walls.

He'd thought Marigold was tighter, but at the moment he'd swear he'd never felt anything like Zuri's sweet pussy around his cock. Even more than the pleasure, the familiarity of every inch of it felt like coming home.

Zuri squealed and pushed back against him, grinding him hard against her cervix with over half his length still outside her. The way his girth stretched her tiny folds until they made a pale ring straining to encircle him was ridiculously sexy, knowing that the world system that allowed him to make love to such a small woman made it perfectly safe and pleasurable for them both.

And it was definitely enjoyable. He groaned and sped up his thrusts, grabbing her small hips and pulling her back into him.

She went nuts, quivering in orgasm and squirting his thighs as her arms give out and her face pressed into the comforter. Her vise-like walls clamped down and milked him so hard it was an effort to keep moving inside her, and her moans of pleasure were loud even with being muffled by the bedding.

Even after being with Zuri so many times, Dare could never hold out for long inside her. And missing her for weeks made it even harder. Having come three times already didn't seem to matter, and finally with a gasp he lifted her entirely off the bed with his hands supporting her slight weight, pushed in to her core, and released powerfully inside her.

She wailed her pleasure the entire time, limp and quivering everywhere but within her crushing pussy as it milked him for every drop. Then finally he collapsed onto the bed beside his tiny fiancee and gathered her up into his arms, holding her tenderly.

"I've missed you, Zuri," he murmured, nuzzling her inky black hair. "I love you so much."

"I love you, my heart, my soul," she said between panting breaths. "I'm glad you're back now, and we can put this nightmare behind us."

They cuddled for a few minutes, then his goblin betrothed reluctantly squirmed out of his arms and sat up. Dare chuckled. "Time to send me off to find Ireni? Or Sia first?"

She grinned at him. "Actually, they're both more patient than the rest of us. And they've been busy welcoming Lily. So next is lunch." She rubbed his knee fondly. "Come on, let's take a dip in the shower and I'll cast Cleanse Target."

Dare blinked. "We have a shower now?" He'd meant to get one installed as soon as he could, but none of the others had seemed interested in that compared to baths.

Zuri laughed delightedly. "Did you think we've been sitting on our hands while you were gone? Ireni and Leilanna have been figuring out ways to add hot water and heating for the house through the winter."

"And the indoor pool in the corner?"

She gave him a mysterious smile. "That's a surprise. And not the only one by far." She tugged on his hand. "Come on, my beloved. We've had our personal reunions, now it's time for everyone to celebrate your return."

Chapter Twelve

Surprises

The dining room table was large, but even so it was close to crowded now. A reminder to Dare that he'd probably soon need to make more renovations to increase the size of the dining room, as well as commissioning a much larger table.

All his fiancees were there, glowing with happiness. Lily sat beside Ireni, freshly bathed and wearing a stunning white dress with white ribbons twined through her long silver pigtails; even after spending days with the beautiful bunny girl, he often found himself stopping and staring each time he saw her again.

She returned his stare with a shy smile, fiddling with her glasses.

Ilin intercepted him at the door to pull him into a back-slapping hug, smiling wide in relief. “It's good to see you, my friend.”

Dare gripped his shoulder. “And you. Thank you for looking after my family while I was gone.”

Amalisa was next, hugging him tightly as well. Dare noticed she'd gained a couple levels since he'd last seen her; Zuri was right, everyone had been busy while he was away.

After that his fiancees swarmed him for their own hugs, filling the air with warm chatter as they guided him to a seat at the table. Ireni was quick to claim his lap, and he wasn't about to complain even if it made eating awkward for both of them.

He noticed his petite fiancee was trembling slightly and pulled her closer, kissing her head. “Hey, you okay?”

She nodded, although her big green eyes were filled with tears. “I was just so worried for you.”

Dare was a bit surprised by that. “I would've figured Sia would tell you more than anyone that I was okay.”

Ireni nodded and rested a hand on his cheek. "But being all alone, frightened for us and not knowing if we were okay, and bearing the weight of what must've felt like an impossible task. It had to be awful for you."

It had been, but better he bear that burden than his loved ones. "I was too busy solving the problem to dwell on my fears," he said, which wasn't entirely true. He hastily changed the subject. "How about here? I notice you've been busy while I was gone. And we have some new guests."

Lily blushed, then her brow furrowed when she realized he didn't just mean her.

Ireni nodded. "Johar, his wife Hanni, and their daughter Enni and son Oli. Marona pointed me and Ilin to their plight." She grimaced in sympathy. "They're serfs from the Harald region, near the capitol. Their lord wanted their and the other tenants' valuable farmland for more favorable leases, so he began grinding them down with taxes. As families began buckling under the pressure and missing payments he used the opportunity to sell them off into slavery as debtors."

Dare swore in sympathy. "And they couldn't relocate?"

"Many could, and did, which suited the greedy noble just fine because it fit his goal." Ireni scowled in quiet fury. "Taking slaves to sell off for extra profit was just an added benefit." She motioned vaguely in the direction of the guest house. "Anyway, Johar and his family were carted north together, but they were due to be split off and sold individually soon. So I purchased them and invited them to the manor."

"I'm glad you were able to save them," he said, hugging his petite betrothed closer. "So they'll serve as house staff here?"

"Short term, certainly. Although their hope is to begin farming in the spring under a tenant's contract."

"Good." Dare leaned down and kissed her softly. "I'll admit, even if it's optimistic, I can envision founding a village here where we can give freed slaves a chance to start new lives. Ones with all the opportunities they deserve. We can even think about buying more of the surrounding land."

That drew a chorus of approval from the others.

Se'weir bustled in with a tray of food, and Zuri and Amalisa hurried to help her bring in the rest. She'd gone all out, providing a generous spread worthy of Thanksgiving.

Which, now that he thought about it, would be just a few weeks away going by an Earth calendar.

Dare could only laugh as his fiancees loaded his plate with a huge steak, mashed potatoes swimming in butter, peas, fluffy bread with butter and cheese, salad, chopped fruit, and of course an assortment of pies and cakes. Thankfully Ireni was happy to help him eat it all, as well as playfully feeding him bites every now and again.

The mood during the meal was merry, although with a few somber moments. They talked about the Battle of Marona's Field, and Dare described in full his trip to Redoubt and what he'd done there. Then they talked about improvements to the manor, including the progress in the Avenging Wolf tribe's village, and what everyone had done while he was gone.

"So what happens now?" Leilanna asked as the meal wound down to nibbling on desserts. "The danger's past and we can get back to doing whatever we were planning, so what's the plan?"

Dare hesitated, looking around. "Well first off, Marona invited me to accompany her to Redoubt at the beginning of the year to petition for knighthood. But I'm not sure I want to leave Pella so soon after she has the babies."

His fiancees exchanged looks, then turned to Ireni. "You have to go," she said simply. "Marona's already taken steps to sponsor your petition, and a chance for you to earn a noble title is a huge opportunity for us and our children who'd inherit it."

Pella nodded solemnly. "I understand the necessity, and the babies will be okay without their daddy for a few weeks." She abruptly brightened, bouncing excitedly. "Speaking of inheriting noble titles, Ireni got-"

"Shhh!" his four other fiancees at the table exclaimed at the same time. Lily looked bewildered, Ilin grinned, and Amalisa giggled.

Dare looked between them in bafflement. "What's going on?"

"Laster, my love," Ireni said, leaning up to kiss his cheek. "Let's settle for now that you'll be leaving, and earlier than you likely expect to get through the snow . . . no running off a couple days beforehand and expecting to get there in time."

He couldn't help but grin ruefully, since he'd actually been thinking of doing something like that.

"Besides," she continued briskly. "Marona needs the company, at least for part of the journey, and we owe it to her." She looked around at the others. "We'll have to see who wishes to accompany you, although rest assured I for one will be going."

"So what else?" Leilanna asked. "That's over a month and a half away. What are we doing until then?"

Everyone looked to Dare. "Well as a start, let's talk about what everyone wants," he said. "Personally I want to try to get at least three levels, ideally five, in that time. And of course farm enough gold to support the family in comfort through the winter."

Ireni cut in gently. "I think you should also make it a priority to kill five more party rated monsters and earn the Protector of Bastion achievement. It's a public achievement and will be a point in your favor when you petition for knighthood."

He jumped slightly as text appeared in front of him. "Quest offered: Playful Challenge. High Priestess Ireni of the Outsider has given you the daunting task of killing 5 party rated monsters before the end of the year."

Dare laughed as he accepted. "You just gave me a quest."

Everyone leaned forward intently as he described it, then shared a laugh. "Sounds like the world system has doubts about whether you can do it," Ilin joked. "But I'm not about to bet against you."

Ireni waited until the merriment died down, then looked around. “As for what I want to do, I propose Ilin and I take Ama and Lily out and help them level. Having a high level Enchanter and Leatherworker will allow us to create powerful gear for Dare, Zuri, Pella, and Lily. And with enchantments and the right materials Zuri can create good enough gear for myself, Ilin, Leilanna, and Ama.” She smiled crookedly. “Or who knows, maybe a main class Tailor will join us at some point.”

Zuri cleared her throat, expression regretful but firm. “Don't prioritize gear for me. I think my adventuring days are over while I focus on Gelaa, and the other children I'll have with Dare.”

Pella nodded reluctantly. “Same for me, at least for a while. I always wanted to be a mother and raise the children of a man I could love with all my heart. I had enough excitement in my life with my old master and in the years before I met Dare, now I just want to put all my passion and energy into my family.”

She paused, expression turning determined. “Although make me gear even so . . . I want to be able to defend my home and loved ones if I need to.”

Dare wouldn't have expected anything else from his gentle but fiercely protective dog girl fiancee.

“Then I suppose I should probably get gear too, just in case,” Zuri agreed, although it was obvious she only planned to use it as a last resort.

“Going back to leveling up Amalisa and Lily,” he said. “I think you should take the Home Ward. I don't really need it for travel, and if Ireni and Amalisa use it to get home each day then Ilin and Lily can run back at a faster pace.”

“Sounds great to me,” Amalisa said with a grin.

“And me,” Ireni agreed. “We're both small enough to ride double on a single horse on the way out, and bring it with us on the way back.”

“Well my plans shouldn't surprise anyone,” Se'weir said. “I'll stay here and do my best to make our manor a comfortable home for everyone, and when I have time visit the village of my kin and help them how I can." She rested a hand on her belly, eyes soft as she looked at Dare. "And be a good mate to Dare and a devoted mother to our children."

Leilanna sniffed. "To be honest, I don't want to go out in the cold if I don't have to. And anyway I need to stay close to maintain the heating system, and I'm using a good chunk of my mana each day on that. Although of course I'll accompany Dare to Redoubt as his w-" She froze, looked around guiltily, then hastily amended, "his fiancee."

Dare chose not to dwell on that hint, although he wondered if it meant the indeterminate date his fiancees had been debating for their wedding had finally been settled.

"Speaking of the heating system," he said. "What did you guys think of for that?"

The beautiful dusk elf blushed slightly. "Well, I kind of drew on the idea you had of painting the hot water tanks on the roof black. The water in them stays warm even after the sun goes down, and the more there is the longer the heat remains."

Dare nodded in understanding. "So you're using a heat sink?"

She nodded. "I'm not sure if you noticed, but we covered the tanks in their own insulated shed. It helps, but even when the tanks are full they won't stay hot all day. I usually have to reheat them if we want water in the evening, or wait until noon to heat them."

She smiled at the petite redhead in his lap. "As for heating for the house, Ireni helped me figure it out, with help from Morwal. We're pretty proud of it. We dug a basement beneath the manor and put a giant rock in there. It's massive enough that the heat I pour into it lasts for almost a full day, and in the enclosed space it dissipates slowly."

"And the heat just drifts through the floorboards?" he asked.

Ireni laughed. "No. I borrowed some ideas from how your people do things on Earth-" She glanced at Lily and smoothly shifted what she'd been about to say, "-en heating systems with underground rooms."

She motioned to the wall, and with a start he recognized a vent there. It looked surprisingly similar to what he remembered from his old life. "We installed a whole system of vents connected to the heating room. We have another pump in the closet right above it connected to a fan, which will blow the hot air from below throughout the entire house."

Leilanna chimed in eagerly. "Even better, we rigged up a system that acts like the thermostat Ireni described to me. Since water expands when it freezes and shrinks when it melts, we can use it to work a lever that activates that translation stone you used to record your voice for the automatic pump. If it gets too cold it moves the lever and starts the fan blowing warm air, then when it heats up enough the lever lifts off the stone and it stops. Now that we've got the legendary chest back for the pumps, we'll be able to have easy running water again and automatic heating in the house."

Dare whistled, genuinely impressed. He'd still been trying to work up an optimal system, and here they'd done it while he was gone for a few weeks. "You two did an incredible job."

Pella eagerly clapped her hands. "And best of all, it's all connected to the new pool room for-" This time she cut off without needing to be reminded by the others.

Dare chuckled. "Okay, I'm happy to wait on whatever secret you're keeping."

His fiancees exchanged looks. "Actually, now seems like a great time," Sia said, coming to the fore and grinning up at him. "Girls?"

With a delighted squeal Zuri scrambled out of her chair and rushed over to a nearby table, pulling open a drawer and almost reverently withdrawing a sheaf of papers. She brought it over to Dare, eyes shining.

"What's this?" he asked, leaning in to kiss her as he accepted the papers. They all just grinned at him, so he brought the papers closer to the glowstone in the center of the table and began reading.

Then his eyes widened. He looked to Ireni, who he was certain was the only one who could've managed this. She'd returned to the fore, and beamed back that million-watt smile he loved.

"How?" he asked. "I thought the bureaucracy in Haraldar was a hopeless boondoggle and we don't have any of the documents we needed."

Pella leaned over and enthusiastically rubbed the bookish redhead's shoulders. "Our girl is amazing is how," she said. "Of course, we couldn't have done it without Marona, too."

Dare spread the papers on the table, reassuring himself they were all there. Official documents confirming his marriages to Zuri, Pella, Leilanna, Se'weir, and Ireni, and legitimizing all children as heirs. Signed by Baroness Marona Arral of Terana Province, under the authority of the Duke of Bastion as a representative of the King of Haraldar.

As he read them his fiancees gathered around him to wrap him in their arms. He was surrounded by beaming smiles and teary eyes shining with love.

"We talked about waiting until the wedding to show you those," Leilanna said, nuzzling his head from behind "But we were all too excited."

Lily clapped her hands, eyes bright with excitement behind her large, wire-framed glasses. "Oh, this is so romantic! I'm so glad I got to be here for this!"

Dare looked over the papers again, a bit dazed. "So we're all married now?" He was happy his beloved were officially recognized, of course, and that Gelaa was legitimate in the eyes of the kingdom, and all his other children to come would be as well.

Still, this was all a bit sudden.

Ireni seemed to sense his thoughts, leaning up with a laugh to kiss him warmly. "We still need both signatures on all the papers, witnessed by Marona or one of her official representatives." She playfully nudged his shoulder. "Which will happen at our combined wedding."

"Which we're still deciding on a date for," Zuri said. "Although if you ask me the sooner the better."

"I'll leave that decision in your hands, since you're all making most of the preparations," Dare said, riffling through the papers and feeling a warmth at seeing the names of his beloved on them. Then he froze when he realized he'd missed one at the bottom.

Ireni felt him tense and followed his gaze, then winced. "Oh. I thought I separated all those out."

She tried to reach for it, but Dare snatched it away before she could, holding it out of reach of her shorter arms and reading hastily. Then he finally let her have the sixth marriage certificate, although from her expression she knew it was too late.

"Trissela," he said flatly. The mermaid he'd had sex with in Ireni's brothel in Kov.

Sia came to the fore, hands raised placatingly. "My beloved, Ireni was just being her usual efficient self. If she was going to go through the bureaucratic boondoggle, as you called it, better to get all the paperwork we needed done at once, even if we weren't going to use it quite yet."

He looked around at his other fiancees as well as Ilin and Amalisa, whose expressions were guarded. Only Lily seemed as bewildered as he was. "So the indoor pool is for her? Her bedroom?"

The goddess nodded placidly. "You'll recall, when Ireni and I first came to you we told you Trissela would be joining our harem."

"I don't recall that at all," Dare said. And given his fond memories of his time with the beautiful mermaid, he was sure he would've.

She hesitated. "Oh. Well we were going to, before we got derailed with your reservations about us sharing Ireni's body. Although I could've sworn I mentioned that I was going to be sending L-" She cut off, glanced at Lily, then said hastily, "lots of opportunities for new women to join our family. Trissela is at the very top of that list, someone I care deeply for."

Ireni pushed forcefully to the fore, expression pleading. "And believe me, even if you don't really know her yet I'm sure you'll love her. She's one of my dearest friends, and one of the kindest and sweetest people I know." She hesitated. "Also, you'll remember she's carrying your child."

"Thanks to another thing you didn't deign to tell me." Dare scrubbed his face with his hands. "It's not that I don't . . . I mean, I liked her just fine when I was-" He cut off before he could say "paying to fuck her".

Somehow that didn't seem like the best thing to say at the moment. "It's just a lot on top of everything else." Some heat found its way into his voice. "It's not every day I find out I'm married to almost a complete stranger."

"Only after you both sign," Ireni insisted. "It's just paperwork, it doesn't mean anything until it's been made official. You have plenty of time to fall in love with her before you decide anything, which I know you will."

His dazed mind seized on something else she'd said. "Wait, what did you mean, "all those"? Are there more certificates you drew up?" His voice took on a slightly frantic edge. "For who?"

Her eyes darted ever so briefly to the side, towards where Lily was sitting. "Okay, maybe I should've waited until they were needed to arrange for them," she admitted. "But I didn't mean anything by it. It's just a seriously irritating and time consuming process, and if it was going to happen anyway, or at least there was a chance it could, I figured I might as well-"

His petite fiancee cut off with a plaintive noise as he gently lifted her off his lap, then stood and strode out of the dining room into the entry hall. "I need to unpack all this," he mumbled, reaching for his gear. "Did my bow make it back here?"

"Dare," Pella pled as she watched him through the door, tail drooping and eyes anguished. She wasn't the only one looking after him helplessly.

Ah, there it was, in the corner; good to see Ilin had brought it back with him. He absently kissed his dog girl fiancee as she followed him into the entry room, pulled his heaviest cloak off its hook by the door, and stepped out into the teeth of the snowstorm.

* * * * *

Part of him knew he shouldn't just be running off like this, that it would be better to sit down and talk this out.

But what the serious hell? He'd literally run himself frantic these last few weeks, only to come home to the warmth of his loved ones and find out that they'd been secretly arranging his life for him behind his back.

And Sia!

Giving him nudges as he was traveling Collisa to help him cross the paths of women he could fall in love with, and who could come to love him in turn, was one thing. It felt like they were both still pursuing their own happiness, and had been fortunate enough to find it with each other.

But this? Bringing women around to throw at him and expecting him to fall head over heels from the impact? Even their own introduction when Ireni had just waltzed in and announced she was going to be part of his life from then on.

Sia sure, he had a relationship with already, but-

Damnit. He couldn't complain about that because them walking into his life had been one of the best things that had happened to him. He loved Sia and Ireni with all his heart.

But that didn't change what they'd done. And it wasn't just him this affected, either.

Was this the sort of fairytale romance Lily had always dreamed about? Nudged by Sia's acolytes to find her way here, only to discover she already had a marriage license all written up to a relative stranger?

This was too much. Failing to point out his high fertility stat so he'd inadvertently knock up the women he'd slept with before finding out, all the while thinking they were being safe, had been a seriously dick move. But at least he'd been mostly to blame for not looking closer at the stat and what it did.

Sia had promised him she wouldn't fuck with his life here. That she had no interest in tying strings to him and making him move like she wanted, because she wanted to see him succeed and fail by his own decisions.

She was interfering too much.

Dare had been intending to go out and hunt some monsters, work off some steam. But he didn't really want to go out in the middle of a snowstorm. And even with his cloak it was colder out here than he'd expected.

But he didn't want to go back inside. Instead he made his way to the garden, settling down next to where he'd planted Eloise.

"Want some company down there?" he half joked with a wry laugh. "Curled up in a warm, safe hole underground sounds pretty good right now."

The crunch of snow alerted him to someone's approach, and he tensed. But it turned out to be Lily, bundled in her poncho over her white dress.

"It got a bit awkward in there after you left," she said a bit sheepishly. "And I don't really know any of them so it was even more uncomfortable. Mind if I sit out here?"

"I'm not sure I'd be the best company at the moment," he said with a wry laugh.

The bunny girl grinned at him. "Actually, I was talking to Eloise." She plopped down on the other side of the dirt mound and patted it fondly. "It's an incredible thing, having a plant girl like you enough to ask you to bring her seed home for you to raise."

Dare supposed it was, and if she spent so much time with florans she'd probably know. "I'm glad I'll have a chance to be part of my daughter's life."

"Mmm." She smiled down at the planted seed. "Did you tell her yet that Rosaceae sends her love?"

"I did." He also patted the dirt mound. "What do you think of that, Eloise? I got to see the demigoddess who birthed your race. A very ancient, wise, and kind dryad. And one who watches over you from afar with love."

Silence settled between them as the snow continued to fall, Lily looking around the grounds and at the various buildings. "This place wasn't what I expected it to be."

Dare sighed. "I understand. I'm sorry you ended up here like this . . . I feel like we tricked you."

She looked surprised. "How? I followed the guidance of a goddess to find a man I hoped I could love." She laughed wryly. "Although I wasn't expecting she'd already have a marriage certificate prepared for us. That was a bit of a surprise."

He laughed too. "Yeah."

The bunny girl reached out and rested a hand on his. "Nobody likes to think they're being pushed into something," she said gently. "Even if it's something they think they could be happy with. But you know that if I didn't want to be here I'd just leave."

Dare sighed. "I wouldn't blame you. You deserve to find a man who can make you happy and give you the best life possible."

"I agree. Although you know when I said this place wasn't what I expected, I meant it in a good way." She bounded to her feet, offering her hand to help him up. "Tell you what. There are five women in there who love you with all their hearts, and it'd be a shame to spoil your reunion over this. How about I have Ireni give me the marriage certificate, so I can tear it up if I decide that's the path through the bramble thicket. Otherwise I say we give this a try and see if we can make it work."

He accepted her help up, shaking his head. "Thanks for being so understanding about this."

Lily laughed. "What can I say? I'm a hopeless romantic."

When Dare stepped back into the dining room he saw that Ilin and Amalisa had pulled a disappearing act. He couldn't really blame them considering the tense atmosphere.

So much for an enjoyable lunch and then chatting and maybe

sharing some drinks in the parlor. Maybe even games; he'd copied a few board games from Earth for them to play, which had all received a fantastic reception.

As well as their patterns being put into the crafting system.

Ireni was in the seat he'd vacated, bawling her eyes out while the other four women clustered around her comfortingly. The moment she saw him in the doorway she rushed over and threw her arms around his waist.

"I ruined everything!" she wailed, burying her face in his chest.

"Yeah, how selfish of her to work tirelessly so you and a bunch of beautiful women can have a happily ever after together," Leilanna said sarcastically, glaring at him; it was obvious where she stood in this argument. "I'd stomp off in a huff too."

"Didn't you throw a huge hissy fit because your honor made you swear a Lifesworn Oath to him?" Pella pointed out, sounding genuinely curious.

The dusk elf flushed. "That's completely different!"

"Leilanna has a point, though," Zuri said quietly but firmly. "As his soon-to-be wives we have a duty to help him find other wives and consorts and lovers."

That was the first Dare was hearing of any such duty, but at the moment his focus was on Ireni. He wrapped his arms around her and stroked her hair gently. "Ireni, I love you," he said.

She kept her face buried in his tunic. "You know I just want you to be happy and loved. And you know I want the same for the women we bring into our family, so they can be happy and loved too."

"I know," he said. He gently but firmly pushed her to arm's length so he could meet her tear-filled eyes. "But you know what's often been missing with you and Sia? What we're doing right now . . . talking about it before making any decisions. Something this important can't afford to be a surprise, unpleasant *or* pleasant."

His beautiful fiancee nodded miserably. "You're right. After all the times in my life where my choices have been made for me, sometimes without even any warning first, it should be the first thing I consider."

She bunched his sleeves in her fists with a plaintive noise. "Sia warned me to be careful with what I was doing. I thought she meant not to make any mistakes on the paperwork that would bite us in the ass later."

Dare leaned down and kissed the tears from her cheeks. "I like Trissela, Ireni, and if she's your friend then that just makes me all the more willing to try to make it work with her. This caught me by surprise, but I'll give it a chance."

At some point the others had gathered around them, aside from Lily in the doorway that was, and one by one they joined the hug. He met each of their eyes to make sure they were all okay, and felt humbled by the love he saw returned there.

With a rueful laugh he looked back down at Ireni. "Well, looks like we're going to have another guest. When is Trissela coming?"

"As soon as it's warm enough in the spring," she replied with a wry laugh of her own. "When you live in water, traveling in winter becomes a lot less enjoyable without special, and expensive, accommodations. Mermaids are hardy to the cold since they often live in the deep sea, but it's different in open air. They're not adapted to it."

So he had plenty of time to get used to the idea and prepare for her to join their lives. Also that extra time was good since he'd resolved to do his best to properly woo Lily the way she deserved, and having his attention divided between two lovers would complicate that.

Zuri stroked his arm. "You've had a very exhausting few weeks, my mate. Even if you've had chances to rest in peace and safety in that time, none of those places was home." She tugged on his hand. "Come, how about we take a short nap, all of us together. Then maybe we can invite Ilin and Ama and Lily back, and get out your games and share dessert over them. We can wait out the rest of this snowstorm in the comfort of the manor, together with family and friends."

Dare smiled and lifted her into his arms, nuzzling her slender neck. “That sounds perfect,” he murmured. He shifted to hold her in one arm and did his best to gather up the rest of his fiancees with the other.

All but Ireni, who excused herself to lead Lily to a room they'd set up for her in the guest house Amalisa occupied, promising to join them later.

He gave their bunny girl guest a goodbye smile, and got a surprisingly warm one in return as the two women bundled up and disappeared out the front door.

Then his other fiancees began tugging him towards the stairs, and together they made their way up to the master bedroom. Where he a bit sheepishly submitted to being undressed down to his underwear and tucked in beneath the covers, while his lovers similarly stripped down to lingerie or more functional panties and joined him.

There, after weeks away from his loved ones, Dare could finally feel all of them cuddled close against him, a loving pile of soft, warm bodies. He wasn't sure any of them were really tired, even after that big lunch Se'weir had prepared.

But they lay still and peaceful around him as he drifted off, listening to the soft sounds of their breathing.

Chapter Thirteen

Back to Routine

Dare must've been more exhausted than he'd realized, even with the excellent nights of rest he'd gotten in the beds of Marona and Rosa. That, or the comfort of being back in his own bed, content in the knowledge his loved ones were safe, had eased the last of the tension out of him.

Either way, when he woke up he got the sense he'd slept for a few hours at the least.

Elsewhere in the house he could hear conversation and laughter and the clink of dishes, an inviting sound. Although his main focus was on the petite, soft body in his arms, his only companion in the otherwise empty bed.

He didn't need to open his eyes to know it was Ireni. The feel of her pressed against him, her scent, even the sound of her breathing was as familiar as anything in his life.

Dare opened his eyes to find her looking up at him, big green eyes soft and shining with love. “Hey,” he said, leaning down to tenderly press his lips to hers. “Your turn?”

His petite betrothed smiled wryly and tucked a stray wisp of auburn hair behind her ear. “I suppose. Although it was more that the others got bored and wandered off not long after you fell asleep, aside from Pella who napped for about a half hour before leaving to visit Lily with the others.”

“And you stayed this entire time, awake and bored out of your mind?”

She laughed. “I'm never bored since Sia is usually available to talk to.” She gently stroked his bare chest. “And much as I'd love to talk to Lily more, there's nothing I'd rather be doing than cuddling with the man I love for however long I can.”

Dare pulled her closer, relishing their shared intimacy. “That sounds incredible right now.”

They lay for a few minutes in contented silence before he stirred. “So, any other news I missed?”

“Mmm,” Ireni furrowed her brow in an adorably thoughtful expression. “Well, we've been feeding the slime girl we brought back enough that she split recently. The Avenging Wolves asked if they could have the new slime for their village.”

Dare couldn't help but smirk. “I'm sure they did. We don't need two, right?”

“Unless you want to do pink slime girl threesomes,” she said dryly.

Tempting as that was, he shrugged in approval. “It's fine by me if everyone else doesn't mind. It'll help the goblin villagers with improving hygiene.” He stroked her soft shoulder, looking down at her in wonder. “You know how amazing you are, right? You've got this place running like a well-oiled machine, where otherwise I get the feeling we'd be running around like chickens with our heads cut off.”

“Well, maybe not quite that bad,” his bookish fiancee said with a smile. Then she hesitated. “Will you forgive me if sometimes I go overboard in that efficiency, and get ahead of myself doing things like ordering marriage certificates in bulk?”

Dare grimaced. “I suppose Leilanna and Zuri had a point . . . we all seem to agree we want the harem to keep growing, which means more women will be coming.”

“They sure will be,” she cut in, eyes dancing mischievously. “You know how to make us very happy in bed.”

He chuckled. “And if I never complained about Zuri acting as a wingman, even appreciated her help, it would be kind of dickish of me to begrudge you and Sia doing the same for me.” He kissed her softly. “So forget about forgiveness, let me thank you.”

Ireni made a contented sound and kissed his shoulder. “I think at this point we're not strangers to love, are we?”

"No, thank Sia." Dare rubbed her back. "We've been very lucky to find so many wonderful people to share a family with."

"Mmm." She looked up at him with her big green eyes. "Dare, are you ever going to give me up?"

He blinked and held her closer. "What? Never!"

"Good." His bookish lover gave him a small smile. "And are you ever going to let me down?"

Where was this coming from? "I give you my word, I'll never-" He abruptly cut off, realization dawning. "Wait, did you just rickroll me?"

"Yes!" she squealed, rolling on the bed giggling.

"Son of a . . ." Dare flopped onto his back and put his forearm over his eyes. "Even on another world."

"I got you!" she said, nudging his shoulder. "You didn't even see it coming, sucker!"

He mock glowered at her. "Sucker, huh?" he growled, then pounced and started to tickle her tummy.

Ireni squealed for a different reason and giggled even harder, although he noticed she didn't try to get away. In fact, she almost seemed to be pressing into his hands, beautiful doll-like face flushed and eyes sparkling.

Dare found himself holding her, then kissing her tenderly. She was soft and sweet in his arms as she kissed him back, running her hands over his chest and shoulders then down his back.

He caressed her as well, wondering at her graceful curves, her silky skin, her beautiful coppery hair. His lips followed his hands in exploring her body, while her small hands held his head and she sighed in quiet enjoyment.

The morning's urgency to be with his lovers after they'd been separated for weeks, and in such frightening circumstances, didn't make an appearance with Ireni. He'd missed her just as fiercely, and he wanted her just as much, but this was exactly what he'd wanted with her.

To make love, to share quiet, peaceful moments. To show their feelings with their tenderly shared gaze, with soft touches, with quiet words of love and affection.

For Dare, whose life on Earth had been dominated by lonely days in his little apartment playing games on his computer, to share this intimacy with a woman he loved was something he treasured. And his sweet fiancee made no secret that after the life she'd lived, if anything she treasured this even more.

"I love you," he breathed as he pushed tenderly between her silky folds and slipped inside her, her tight walls welcoming him in.

"With all my heart, my love," Ireni murmured in reply, legs wrapped gently around him as she stroked his back. Her hips moved almost placidly, but in perfect timing with his thrusts.

As the minutes passed their passion slowly built, until finally his redheaded betrothed went limp with a happy sigh, her sweet tunnel rippling around him in orgasm as her nectar flowed.

Dare kissed her softly as he pushed a last time into her core and released inside her, filling her with his seed.

Afterwards they went back to cuddling and caressing. "I missed you," he said, kissing her glistening rosebud lips. "It's good to be home."

"Mmm," she said, kissing him back tenderly. "Hopefully the next time you leave, it won't be under such tense circumstances."

He looked over at the black pearl ring on the bedside table. "I haven't seen much of Sia, doesn't she want some time?"

The goddess came to the fore, smiling lazily. "I got to experience all your other reunions, so I was content to wait." Her eyes flashed with sudden heat. "But I've been missing you for a long time, and since I volunteered to be last you'd better do your best to make it worth the wait."

Without another word she pressed against him, all passion and hunger where Ireni had been soft and intimate. Her hands explored him eagerly, lips trailing over his muscles with quiet little moans of enjoyment.

Dare just as eagerly roamed his hands over her soft little body, making her gasp as he toyed with her nipples and kneaded her small ass with his fingers. He kissed her auburn hair, her lips, down her jaw, then paused to nibble and suck on her delicate neck.

His divine fiancee moaned and pressed against him urgently, nectar glistening on her thighs as she ground her sex against his hip. He dipped a hand between her legs and rubbed her soft folds, making her whimper and push against him almost desperately until he plunged two fingers inside her, hooking his fingers upward seeking her sweet spot.

She let him know when he found it by arching against him, biting down on his shoulder to muffle her cry of pleasure. Her arousal flowed down his fingers and over his hand, and he brought them up to his lips and tasted her ambrosia.

Suddenly impatient to be inside her, Dare flipped her over onto her stomach and pulled her hips up towards him. She eagerly lifted her ass, presenting her glistening sex, and he guided his tip to her entrance and pushed all the way to her core in a long, hard thrust.

Sia buried her face in a pillow just in time to stifle another, louder cry of pleasure, bucking her hips up against him. The angle of his penetration seemed to be perfect to stimulate her, and he had to hold her hips to keep her from squirming right off his cock in sheer delight as he began moving inside her.

“Gods, you're sexy,” he panted, staring down at her delicate body beneath him. Her furnace-hot, tight walls felt heavenly against his shaft, squeezing and rippling in her pleasure as she welcomed him in deeper.

Her movements were perfectly in time with his, maximizing both their enjoyment, and it only took a few minutes before she slumped to her stomach on the blankets, nearly pulling herself off him when her limbs seemed to give out as she sank into a powerful climax.

“Don't . . . stop . . .” she moaned, before burying her face in the pillow to muffle more squeals of pure bliss.

Dare followed her down, fucking between her tightly closed thighs and into her soft tunnel as she quivered beneath him, building up to an even higher peak. She felt even tighter in this prone position, but her flowing nectar drenched her thighs and let him slip easily in and out.

Whether intentionally or by happy accident, thrusting between her soft thighs meant they squeezed and caressed the base of his cock, making it feel like he was going balls deep every time he bottomed out inside her. It was incredible and he was certain he wasn't going to last for long.

But he held out, hoping to tease another orgasm out of his beautiful fiancee.

It didn't take long before Sia arched her back again, lifting her ass against his weight, and clamped down in an even more powerful climax. Dare let her rippling walls tease him over the edge to his own orgasm, and with a grunt pushed in a final time and emptied himself inside her tiny pussy.

His sexy redheaded fiancee wasn't done, though.

As they came down from their shared climax she insistently squirmed and twisted until he was on his back with her on top of him. Somehow she'd managed to keep him inside her the whole time, still in that same prone position, except now her weight rested on him with her back against his chest.

Well this was a new position. One he hadn't even considered before.

With a whimpering moan Sia pushed with her legs, sliding up his shaft. “Your turn,” she panted as the back of his sensitive tip brushed her entrance.

It took Dare a second to realize what she meant. With her position on her back against him she couldn't really make herself slide back down onto him without doing some serious gymnastics.

Which meant he'd have to do it for her. Just like he didn't really have any easy way to move inside her in the other direction, so she'd have to do that for him.

Cooperative fucking. Or more cooperative than usual, that is.

He took his fiancee's hips and pushed down, thrusting his own hips upward at the same time, and she whimpered as she slid back onto him until he bottomed out. Then her slender legs pushed her back up, and he pushed down again.

It took much longer to get used to timing his movements with hers to make a good rhythm, but somehow that just made it all the more intense. Like they were learning more about each other, learning to work in sync to bring each other pleasure.

Soon they were moving like a well oiled machine. A *very* well oiled machine.

Their cooperative movements lasted until Sia abruptly collapsed mid-movement with a quivering moan, squirting his legs with her juices as she climaxed again. With the angle of penetration it felt like she was massaging his shaft upside-down, and he bit his lip around a groan and decided he was ready to join her in a second orgasm.

He pushed her hips down until he was bottomed out again, then rubbed her clit to make her squirm and squeal until she squirted again. That did it for him, and with a twitch of his hips he gave in to the overwhelming pleasure and emptied himself up into her.

As they came down together Dare wrapped his arms around his petite fiancee and cuddled her close. “I love you, Sia,” he murmured, kissing her hair.

“I love you, Dare,” she replied, lying limp and satisfied atop him.

They stayed like that for a few minutes as he shrank enough to finally pop free of her silken embrace, freeing a flood of their juices that soaked his crotch and the already sodden blankets beneath him. Then she squirmed around to lay on her stomach atop him, green eyes solemn but with a slight crinkle of amusement around the edges.

The goddess motioned to the door, through which the talk and laughter from downstairs continued to entice them. “Although speaking as the nerd who fell in love with a gamer from Earth, I want to go join the fun now."

Dare laughed and wrapped her in his arms. "Sounds good." He sobered, looking into her mysterious eyes. "I know I already said it but I love you, Sia. And I'll admit I might've missed you most of all during the last few crazy weeks. Being able to talk to you at any time, and hear your voice through the system, was more of a comfort than I'd realized."

Her typically amused, almost detached expression softened, showing more tenderness than usual. "You may have missed me, my beloved, but I was there. Rooting for you every step of the way, even if I couldn't act openly."

He kissed her softly. "And maybe helping me more than I realized?"

The goddess's delicate features became mysterious. "I may have approached a beloved sister about a shared purpose. And of course I knew I could count on Rosa to look after you, the dear." He opened his mouth and she laughed and held up a hand. "Yes, I will visit her soon. It's only polite when she's practically a next door neighbor."

With another laugh she hopped off the bed, his seed trickling down her slender thighs, and grabbed his hand. "Come on, let's go play with everyone!"

With a laugh Dare allowed her to insistently tug him off the bed.

After lovingly cleaning each other with wet cloths, they dressed and made their way down to where the others were playing games in the parlor. He accepted a glass of wine from Ilin as he and Sia settled down between Se'weir and Leilanna, holding out his arms in invitation for Zuri to bring Gelaa over for him to hold.

Looking around as the others finished their game, gently rocking Gelaa in his arms as she cooed and looked up at him sleepily, he realized something.

One of the things he'd longed for when playing RPGs and reading fantasy stories had been to sit in a tavern common room, quaffing ale and laughing with companions as buxom serving maids served food and drinks. Warmth and good food, a bard playing music in a corner while a table full of dwarves laughed and competed with him to sing bawdy songs.

And yeah, now that he'd had a chance to experience that it was definitely an enjoyable way to pass the time. But what he had here, in this room, was infinitely better.

When a debate broke out about what game to play next, Dare cleared his throat. "You know, there are a few games I used to play with larger groups that would be funner with this many people. Want to try one of those?"

"How do you know so many games!" Lily asked, milky pale cheeks flushed after a couple glasses of wine. "Do the people where you come from have that much free time?"

"Some of them. But it's more that we're able to produce enough food that most people can turn their labor to other things. Including making games."

"And romance?" the persistent bunny girl said, gray eyes sparkling behind her large glasses.

"Oh, you're just too cute!" Leilanna, sitting beside her, said as she wrapped Lily in a hug. With the age similarity it was no surprise the two gravitated towards each other, along with Amalisa and Se'weir.

Although everyone seemed to have fallen in love with the sweet, innocent, romantic bunny girl.

Pella, sitting on Lily's other side and looking overjoyed about it, suddenly began tugging on the younger woman's hands to get her to stand. "Come on, I just thought of something. Zuri, Sia, Leilanna, you guys too!"

The four women joined her, looking bemused as the eager dog girl arranged them in a line facing the rest of the group. Although not according to height or any other reason Dare could see.

Then Pella took her own place and faced them, tail wagging. "Look!" she said excitedly, brushing her fingers through Sia's coppery hair, then Lily's silver pigtails, then her own golden ponytail, then Leilanna's snowy locks and finally Zuri's jet black hair. "Now that Lily's here we've got copper, silver, gold, truesilver, and godmetal! All the precious metals!"

Leilanna groaned. "*That's* what you got us up here for?" Rolling her eyes, she made her way back to cuddle up to Dare, letting Gelaa hold her finger in a tiny fist. "Are you going to make the game so we can get playing?"

Pella reluctantly returned to her seat. "I thought it was fun," she said, pouting.

Chuckling, Dare asked Zuri to grab some of the paper she used for her scrolls, making the necessary cards with it. Then they gathered around to take turns pantomiming the words on the cards, to much laughter and ribbing.

And so the day passed, the snow swirling outside while inside the house was full of warmth and laughter.

* * * * *

Dare woke early the next morning, gently disentangling himself from the warm pile of women cuddled around him. Then he shivered at the unexpected cold and looked at the master bedroom's vent.

Time to troubleshoot, it looked like.

A quick check down in the new basement confirmed that the huge stone was still radiating heat from Leilanna's spells yesterday, easily enough to warm the house. The legendary chest was similarly in place to power the fan.

A check of the makeshift thermostat, which was embedded in the wall to connect to the outside to regulate temperature, showed that it had sprung a leak in the night and no longer had the pressure to push the lever. He fixed the leak and refilled the tank to the line Leilanna had drawn, then waited impatiently until the water inside froze enough to push the lever and get the fan going.

The balance between the cold outside and the heat inside melting the ice was a fickle one, and even if Leilanna and Ireni had tinkered enough to get it fairly good he resolved to see if he could find mercury to rig up a proper thermometer.

Or at least get a stronger container for the water thermostat.

Dare checked the water pressure next and determined the tanks were less than half full. So once the house was heated up enough that the thermostat turned the fan off, he snagged the legendary chest and moved it over to the pump shed to get water pumping up to the roof.

He was pleased to see that his fiancees had also thought to insulate the pump shed and add a vent to the small room, as well as moving the pipes inside the house so they wouldn't freeze. They'd done a great job.

Once the tanks were filled and the chest moved back down to the heater, he gathered his gear and began looking it over. Especially his bow, just to make sure it hadn't taken damage on its trip home out of his care.

He'd been so emotional yesterday when he'd taken it outside that he hadn't taken the time to inspect it, but as he looked now to check its durability he was pleasantly surprised. Amalisa had apparently been busy, and it now had an enchantment.

Granted, it was a lower level enchantment using one of the materials they'd gotten from the same dungeon where they'd gotten their fortune and the legendary chest. As such it only added a few extra points of shock damage and a miniscule buff to range; even Quill Shot did more.

Still, every little bit helped. And it promised exciting prospects in the future as the young noblewoman leveled up.

Speaking of which, a knock on the door turned out to be Amalisa, Lily, and Ilin, ready to pick up Ireni and get an early start leveling up the two young women. Outside the newly risen sun glittered brilliantly on several inches of fresh snow, but it looked as if the storm had passed and the day would be good for leveling.

Dare invited them in to sit at the dining room table and rummaged in the kitchen for something quick for breakfast.

Ireni appeared in the doorway, dressed in her adventuring robes and gear, and pulled him off to one side for a good morning kiss. "Your goals for today, my love, are to farm any spawn points on the way to the mountains that'll get you experience."

He blinked as he dug into his pouch to retrieve the Home Ward to give to her. "The mountains?"

She nodded. "The spawns there are so random that you'll have a higher chance of finding party rated monsters. After all, you've already found two in that area." She tucked the fast travel item away. "For now find any party rated monsters you can, but move on and farm spawn points to get experience. Once you've found a couple Ilin and I will join you hunting them . . . there are enough low level spawn points in the mountains that we can even bring Ama and Lily and help them level there."

"Sounds good," he said, grinning. "Thanks for the tip."

His petite fiancee's eyes danced merrily, and she leaned close to his ear. "Speaking of tips, you should take Lily for a romantic walk this evening and look at the stars. And go for runs with her whenever you can. You both share a love of running."

Dare sobered. "Do you think the others will mind if I spend so much time doing my best to give Lily the storybook romance she's longing for? I don't want them to feel like I'm neglecting them."

She giggled. "The obvious answer to that is of course they won't, as long as you *don't* neglect them." She playfully patted his cheek. "Looks like you've got your work cut out for you."

"Spending time with the women I love is the opposite of work."

Ireni laughed outright. "Good answer, but we appreciate the effort all the same."

Dare heated up some leftovers from the icebox, and they shared a hasty breakfast. Everyone was in good spirits, not seeming bothered by the prospect of going out in the cold and snow. Although Lily especially seemed eager to really focus on leveling.

In her usual thoughtful, efficient way Ireni had purchased the best possible bows and arrows for the bunny girl to see her all the way up to Level 20. That would've been hugely helpful for Dare in his own leveling, and would certainly ease her efforts. Even better, she'd arranged for Amalisa to practice her enchanting by improving the bows with shock damage, like Dare's own bow.

Although at that level the bonus was much more significant.

Even with a combat subclass, Lily would be getting experience quick. And the fact that as an Archer she could hit multiple targets would only speed things up. With Ireni buffing and shielding her she had pretty much every advantage imaginable.

The rest of the family dragged themselves out of bed to see them off, and after saddling the horses Johar stood off to one side waving. A plain but kind looking woman stood at his side, and a rosy cheeked daughter of about eight and son who was five or six played in the snow nearby.

Dare was a bit disappointed that he couldn't travel with the others, but they were heading closer to Terana, much closer in Lily's case, to farm the lower level spawns there. Meanwhile he was going in pretty much the opposite direction.

And on foot, trusting he'd have enough room in his mostly empty pack for any loot he found.

In the cold the storm had dropped a fine powdery snow. Deep enough that he had to wade through it, but light enough that it didn't impede his movements too much and wasn't too tiring. At the speeds he traveled he also kicked up huge clouds to hang shimmering in the air behind him, which was neat.

Of course, it was harder to see what the ground looked like beneath the snow. Dare found himself tripping more often than usual, although thankfully the snow was forgiving and cushioned his fall.

Admittedly, he might've been paying less attention than he should've to where he was going because he was occupied by the breathtaking sight of Bastion blanketed with snow.

He'd fallen in love with this region's rugged beauty almost from his first view, the expansive plains, rolling hills, dense forests of old growth trees, and stark mountain ranges. It all had a wild, untamed feel to it, a frontier waiting to be explored in all its wonder and excitement.

Maybe there were more beautiful lands Dare and his family could've made their home, but he felt fortunate that Bastion was where they'd been when they decided to settle down. And in his definitely unbiased opinion the area around Nirim Manor afforded the most breathtaking views, with the Gadris Mountains looming in the distance.

It was only a short run to the first spawn point on his way to the mountains, with Level 26-28 monsters like large vultures with wicked talons. For some classes they'd be a huge pain in the ass, but for him they were relatively straightforward.

And interestingly enough, with his bow's new shock enchantment each arrow sent a skittering web of electricity spreading out from the point of impact. It may not've done much damage but it was pretty awesome looking.

At an average of six levels lower than his he killed most of the monsters in two or three shots, and often one with a critical hit. It didn't take long at all to clear the spawn point, and he was never close to in danger. Same as his other times fighting these things.

The loot wasn't great, but it would net a few gold; at this point they had an entire shed devoted to trash loot, which they'd cart in bulk up to Terana every month or so to sell at the market. As expected, Ireni was a formidable haggler, catching merchants by surprise to find such a petite, beautiful young woman unwilling to back down an inch as she pressed for the best deal possible.

And unlike Dare, who tended to leave the people he haggled with a bit disgruntled by his bartering style, the bookish redhead always left them charmed and smiling even if she'd gotten a favorable deal.

Pella was also great for that, with her keen senses that often let her know if she was being deceived or leaving potential profits on the table. And Leilanna, while she tended to be even more aggressive in her bartering than Dare, had a keen eye for the value of things and stubbornly refused to accept anything but the best possible deal, even if it meant walking away.

Between them, the big loot selling trips to town were enjoyable as well as profitable.

He left the vultures behind and continued on to a slightly higher level spawn point, clearing it out as well. In a way it felt good to finally be focused on leveling efficiently again, like scratching an itch that had been irritating him for weeks now. The frustration of other things getting in the way of working to better himself and improve his family's circumstances.

Now, fingers crossed, they'd all be free to get back to their lives.

Scaling the mountain slopes was a bit treacherous with the snow, causing Dare to stumble and occasionally slide backwards a few feet. He made good time even so, doing his best to hit the spawn points he and Ireni had found on their way to spots he hadn't explored yet.

Although he had to swing by the raid dungeon they'd discovered on their last trip, just to check it out again.

He was way under level for the place, if even the entry mobs were Level 41-42. Going by his experience with the dungeon he'd gone through with Zuri, Pella, and Leilanna, that meant the end boss would probably be two or three levels higher than that.

Maybe even more, for a dungeon that was obviously intended for a large party or small raid. Or maybe even a large raid, if the other monsters in there were stronger than the entry ones.

Even though it was way out of his league for the near future, Dare was glad he'd checked the place when he spotted a party rated monster perched in front of the ruins. It was a massive tree, withered and rotted, motionless and as innocuous looking as any tree but giving off a clear aura of menace.

Dare recalled that outside of the lower level dungeon near Driftwain there'd been a large camp of even lower level kobolds guarding the entrance. There'd been no such guardians for the Glittering Caves dungeon they'd beaten, but this guy was clearly here for that purpose.

He looked at it with his Adventurer's Eye. “Ancient Outpost Watcher. Monster, Party Rated. Level 39. Attacks: Ensnare, Root, Crush, Colossal Stomp, Leaf Blast, Infestation, Vine Whip, Regenerate, Dream Gaze, Stone Bark.”

Whew, that was a lot of daunting abilities. And its stats were nothing to sneeze at, either; even after nearly soloing the Cursed Orc Warchief, with some help from the legendary chest of course, Dare wouldn't have wanted to go anywhere near an enemy like this without a solid party.

Including a sturdy tank.

Was it possible to get strong enough to kill this thing by the end of the year, with the help of Ireni, Leilanna, Ilin, and possibly recruiting some of the adventurers from Terana? Assuming he could ensure his pregnant fiancees would remain safe during the fight.

It was something to consider, at least.

He ran on, finding and clearing more spawn points. He even took a chance on Level 37-38 monsters, whose attacks hinted they were swift and dealt high damage, but were easy to kill. Nothing he couldn't handle with Cheetah's Dash if he was careful and made sure it was always off cooldown. And they provided great experience and loot.

In spite of the unavoidable delay in leveling while dealing with Ollivan, Dare was well on his way to his next level. Mostly thanks to the huge bumps given by Marona's quest to destroy the monster horde, and the XP bonus for defeating the Cursed Orc Warchief.

He estimated that with the continually rising experience requirements for each level, even under ideal circumstances it would take him up to a week once he reached Level 34 to level again to 35. And the time for subsequent levels would increase by a few hours to a day every time.

And at 40, once he finally reached that point, the requirements would probably jump just as sharply as they had at 30. It might take him weeks for every level, no matter how well he optimized his experience gains. Not to mention the monsters would jump sharply in difficulty as well.

He had to wonder if at some point it would become impossible to solo level, even with advantages like Fleetfoot and Adventurer's Eye.

For now, though, Dare was confident he'd level up within the next few days. And he couldn't wait to reach 35 a week after that and see what he got for it.

While he found more good spawn points in his searching, to his disappointment he didn't see any more party rated monsters. Although he supposed it would be optimistic to find a bunch of the rare spawns all over the place, even in the mountains.

As the sun started to sink in the sky, he grudgingly turned back for Nirim Manor. He wanted to get as much experience as possible in the time he had, and it frustrated him a bit that travel time took up such a significant chunk of his day. Even with his ability to move at high speeds, the distance between home and the first spawn points, then between each spawn point, and finally the trip home all added up.

He loved having a home for his family, but it was hard not to long for the days when they'd traveled from one ideal leveling location to the next, camping beside the best spawn points so they could get a good start each morning and make the most of the day.

Part of Dare was tempted to keep leveling and set up camp in the mountains. But he'd never do that without making sure his loved ones knew his plans so they wouldn't worry, and anyway he'd promised Ireni he'd be back in time to take Lily on a romantic moonlit walk.

Although he did resolve to bring up the possibility of spending two or three days at a time in the mountains. Hopefully his fiancees and Lily could forgive him for being gone that often, considering what he needed to accomplish before the beginning of the year.

Chapter Fourteen

Winter Days

Running hard for home, Dare made it just before sunset.

He was there just in time to see Ireni and Amalisa appear out of thin air in front of the stables, seated on the back of a sturdy gelding. Which made him jump a foot into the air in shock, heart pounding, before he realized what was going on.

Good to see the Home Ward had worked for them.

The first thing Amalisa did after sucking in a shocked breath was whoop loud enough to make the horse dance nervously. "That was amazing!" she shouted, scrambling off the horse and looking around, cheeks flushed. "Goddess, that was the biggest rush I've ever experienced."

She spotted him standing there and rushed over to take his hands. "You've used the Home Ward, and you get to run super fast all the time . . . is running fast even better than that?"

Dare couldn't help but laugh. "In some ways. I can't go a third as fast, but I can feel the wind blowing past and the joy of pushing my body to the limits."

"I guess, but even sprinting as fast as I can wasn't anywhere near that fun." The young noblewoman laughed and whirled away, spinning around the yard. "Did you go through a hill? I screamed so loud." She giggled. "Or I guess not loud, since I didn't make any noise. But I tried to!"

Ireni slipped off the horse and came over to wrap her arms around him, nuzzling his shoulder. "It was certainly something new and amazing," she agreed. "Although I prefer being carried by you as you run."

"I certainly enjoy it." He leaned down and kissed her softly. "Lily and Ilin running back?"

She nodded. “Lily and I had to go farther than I would've liked to find monsters she could take on, even with my help. But we made good progress, and were able to put in extra time thanks to the Home Ward.”

Before he could ask any followup questions his organized and purposeful fiancee briskly turned him around and started pushing him towards the house. “Speaking of Lily running back, we should have just enough time to get you bathed and shaved and dressed in something nice for your moonlit walk after dinner.”

Dare laughed and let her guide him inside, where the rest of his fiancees emerged to greet him and, to his chagrin, lead him into the bath room and undress him, then push him down into the tub.

It was enjoyable, but he was certain they had even more fun than he did as they soaped him up and rinsed him off, with much splashing and laughter and more than a little groping.

Finally they dried off and dressed him in a fine suit Zuri had made special for occasions like this. Soon after that Se'weir, who'd excused herself early to begin dinner with the help of Johar's wife Hanni and daughter Enni, called up that Lily and Ilin were back, and Amalisa would be joining them as well.

Dare was shocked when his hobgoblin fiancee set a genuine hamburger in front of him, complete with bun, ketchup, mayo, sliced onions, and lettuce and tomatoes. Not to mention a heaping pile of golden fries.

Se'weir happily admitted that Ireni had described the Earth meal to her, and putting their heads together had figured out how to grind the meat and fry the potatoes.

From the first bite of their own burgers everyone agreed it definitely had the potential to become a favorite. Although Lily looked a bit puzzled about the mention of Dare's home world; they still hadn't explained his past to her.

The conversation around the table was mostly focused on everyone's leveling. Dare described the party rated monster he'd found outside the raid dungeon, getting everyone's view on it. Ireni thought they could kill it with some planning, and maybe hiring a tank from Terana.

Assuming they wanted to risk the tank discovering the location of the dungeon, which was apparently highly prized information that could be sold for a fortune to the right people. Although Dare speculated that if they also offered the tank a position in the raid to clear the dungeon that would be incentive to keep the secret out of self interest.

Ireni and the others who'd gone out leveling together then described their day, which had been productive but mostly uneventful. Then finally everyone who'd stayed home talked about how things had been at Nirim Manor; quiet and peaceful, thankfully.

After dinner the girls ushered Lily up for her own bath and makeover. Aside from Amalisa, who excused herself and left for her guest house to get in an early night after a long day of leveling.

Dare and Ilin made their way to the parlor, settling into overstuffed chairs beside the fireplace. Which in spite of Leilanna's and Ireni's ingenious heating system still had a lit fire crackling merrily. Dare poured himself a small splash of brandy, and to his surprise his friend asked for one as well.

“Are you sure?” he asked the bald ascetic.

Ilin smiled wryly. “My path is my own to tread, my friend.”

Dare shrugged and poured another glass. “As long as I'm not corrupting you with my hedonistic ways.”

Rather than the expected easy laugh from his friend, Ilin just smiled absently as he accepted the glass. He took a slow sip, showing no reaction to the strong liquor as he stared into the fire.

He didn't look sad or worried or even bothered by anything. Just . . . thoughtful.

Dare let the silence stretch for a few minutes, then cleared his throat. “How did the leveling with Amalisa go today?”

The normally unflappable Monk actually gave a start at his voice, looking over quickly. “It was productive. Lady Amalisa killed monsters swiftly and without issue, and I was able to keep them subdued and away from her even when she ran out of mana and had to switch to her sword. It helps that she was able to give her weapon the best enchantment possible to speed the killing. No levels, but she's making astonishing progress."

He chuckled and nodded towards Dare as he took another sip from his glass. "Or at least, astonishing for most."

"I still need to thank Amalisa for the enchantment she put on my bow," Dare said. "She's been a good friend."

"Yes, a good friend, and an exceptional young woman," Ilin mused, gaze returning to the fire. "With kind and gentle heart speaking to a beautiful soul." With a start he sat up, looking embarrassed. He swiftly drained his glass and abruptly stood. "It's been a long day and we start early again in the morning. I'm going to get in as much meditation as I can."

A bit surprised, Dare stood as well. "Probably a good idea. Good night, my friend."

Ilin nodded absently and strode from the room.

Dare stared after him, bemused. If he didn't know better he almost would've thought the stoic Monk had a crush on Amalisa.

Before he could dwell on that a flurry of voices heralded the return of the women. Lily was ushered into the room, wearing her silver dress, thick white woolen stockings and matching white shoes, and a heavy coat of white fur from the Fell Tundra Wolf monsters Dare regularly hunted from a nearby spawn point.

She looked breathtaking, yet still adorable with her long silvery pigtails and big glasses. He couldn't help but gawk, and suddenly felt a bit awkward.

He'd been interested in the ethereally beautiful bunny girl from the first, that went without saying. But they hadn't really done anything romantically speaking while traveling together.

Now, knowing he was taking this perfect woman on what was basically their first formal date, knowing where it could lead in the future, made him feel nervous and excited in a way he hadn't felt in a long time.

Closer to what he felt dating back on Earth.

Dare became aware of his fiancees giggling behind Lily, while the bunny girl's milky pale skin turned pink in a characteristic blush. Somehow, knowing he wasn't the only one nervous and excited put him more at ease, and he smiled and offered her his arm.

"You look beautiful, Lily," he said. "Shall we?"

She nodded and slipped her slender arm through his, leaning against his side a bit. "It's beautiful out tonight," she replied with a dreamy smile.

With the others all watching eagerly they made their way outside, feet crunching in the snow as they started for the garden. Lily's face was upturned to look at the night sky, which tonight featured a dazzling nebula and the bright accretion disk surrounding a black hole.

Also the glittering arm of a spiral galaxy, an uncomfortably large gas giant planet looming in the distance, and a vast void in the sky where no stars shone; the gods of this world cared a lot more about spectacle than realism.

Dare briefly wondered if Collisa would ever have a space program. And if so, what exactly they'd find if they sought out those stellar phenomena.

Sia always just laughed when he asked about it.

Lily sighed as she stared upwards, the lenses of her glasses reflecting the glittering show in the sky. "You're educated, Dare," she murmured, pointing, "what do you call that? I've never had any books about the sky."

"The binary star system?" he asked.

She nodded. "I guess. What's that glowing band between them? Is it a celestial pathway?"

Dare laughed ruefully. "Actually, it's where one is drawing the stellar matter from the other. Basically eating it."

The beautiful bunny girl frowned. "Well that sucks. So even in the sky things are killing and dying?"

"In their own way. Although they're not alive, they're just burning in a nuclear fusion process."

She stared at him blankly, then pointed. "What about that one?"

He couldn't help but grin. "That's the spiral arm of the galaxy we're in. It has billions of stars like the sun." Assuming this world followed any of the usual rules of the universe.

Lily sighed, turning her head so her silky hair brushed his arm. "It's all so beautiful. So many things still to learn, even with all the books I've read."

"I've been meaning to get a library started at Nirim Manor. There's still so many things about Haraldar and Collisa I don't know, either."

She squeezed his arm tighter against her side. "That would be wonderful. I'd love to learn all the secrets of the world with you."

"Well we're both fast enough we could travel and explore together," he said. "That would be fun."

His date gave him a solemn look, eyes sparkling behind her glasses. "Careful, you make offers like that and I'll hold you to it."

Dare laughed. "I hope you do."

The conversation turned to the day's leveling, even though most of it had been covered over dinner. Lily was close to Level 9, and excited about how quickly she was killing monsters and getting experience. She was already planning the perfect armor set for Dare, and urged him to start saving up the materials she'd need.

"I wish quality was determined by the work you put in," she said with a sigh, "how careful you did things and how highly skilled you were. But in the crafting system once you max your ability proficiency to your level it's all random after that."

Unsurprising; for balancing purposes the only really fair way to do things in an ability system *was* with RNG, since you couldn't exactly get better at abilities that basically did the work for you. "So you might have to make dozens of pieces of armor to get an Exceptional quality piece?"

The bunny girl made an adorable face. “More like hundreds. And up to a few thousand for Master quality, unless we get lucky. I don't even know for Fabled . . . I don't think you even have a chance to craft them until higher levels.”

She nudged him with her elbow. “Anyway, from now on we'll both have to gather leather and hides from every animal we find, and probably even buy materials, to get enough for me to craft us the best items.”

Dare smiled wanly, a bit daunted by the prospect. “Good thing we can break down items to get back some of the materials.”

“True, although it'll be more profitable to sell the higher quality ones we don't plan to use.”

They reached a bower that had been cut through the middle of two interlocking evergreen bushes, creating a fragrant and surprisingly cozy spot, and settled on the bench there. Dare was surprised but pleased when his beautiful companion scooted close and leaned against him for warmth.

“Are you enjoying it here, Lily?” he asked.

The bunny girl looked at him, startled. “Are you kidding?” She smiled warmly. “I'll admit I miss home a bit, Mother and my sisters and little baby Petro. But this . . .” She looked around, expression contented. “It feels like a second home.”

“I'm glad.” He found her elegant hand in the sleeve of her coat and held it. “I'm happy you're here.”

Even in the dark he could see her blush, and she shyly squeezed his hand.

They sat for a time, enjoying the night and looking up at the sky. Finally Dare noticed Lily's head nodding and suggested they should head inside.

He walked her to the guest house she shared with Amalisa, and at the door took her hand and kissed it. “Thank you for a wonderful evening, Lily. I hope you sleep well.”

“And you.” She hesitated, then in a rush leaned in to kiss his cheek before darting inside.

He found himself grinning like an idiot as he walked back to the manor. Where of course all the girls wanted to know how his date had gone, pressing for details and critiquing his conversational tidbits.

"You were way too academic with the sky stuff," Leilanna said. "Try to frame it romantically . . . sure, that binary star system is a celestial pathway that lovers walk when they depart Collisa."

Pella nodded enthusiastically. "And that black hole surrounded by swirling light is the sky's butthole waiting to be filled by the sky's lover!"

That drew a gale of laughter from everyone. Although once the talk turned to filling holes his fiancees shifted from a romantic mindset to an amorous one. Sia was the first to claim him, and since they'd already been talking about it she waved her curvy little ass invitingly in front of his face with a playful expression.

Or in other words, the night ended how they tended to, until finally Dare and his well satisfied lovers fell asleep in a contented pile.

* * * * *

Eight days later Dare reached Level 35.

He'd really been looking forward to it. Really really looking forward to it. So when it came time to return home so he'd make it back for a late dinner and bedtime, and he only had a dozen or so kills left to get it, he pushed for a bit longer to get the last bit of experience he needed.

He was glad he had.

The levels ending in 5 were almost as good as the levels ending in 0. But in this case he almost would've said that this level was *better* than 30, if not for the fact that he'd gotten Cheetah's Dash which was one of his favorite abilities ever.

The reason this one was so great, though, was because he got not one, not two, but *three* new abilities.

One of course was the one he could get every 5 levels from his

Student of the Wild tree, which let him take abilities from certain animals he killed and put them in a pool he could choose from. He'd been killing nocturnal animals eagerly hoping to get night vision, but to his disappointment hadn't found it yet, if it was available at all.

Still, he had a few choices.

One was a melee attack called Claw that he was avoiding because his focus was on ranged attacks and survivability. And recently he'd found Eagle's Screech, which could be used to signal allies up to 5 miles away. That seemed of limited use, and also redundant since he already had Snap, which he could use to create a moderately bright light that could be seen from even farther away.

Then there was Squirrel Claws, which passively increased his climbing speed by 10%. That was actually pretty badass and would be fun to have; Dare was all about anything that increased his speed in any way, and passive boosts were always nice.

But ultimately he went with one of the first options he'd been given. "Escape Bonds: On use, remove all Snare or Root status effects. Cooldown 5 minutes."

Simple and to the point. Dare had been tempted to pick that for survivability every single time he could pick a Student of the Wild ability, but had put it off. But he'd come more and more to realize that his mobility was *everything*, and if something stopped him he was probably dead. And he could admit that the Ancient Outpost Watcher he'd seen gave him even more motivation to pick it, in order to counter its attacks.

The second ability was super exciting, not just for the ability itself but because it was a secret one he'd unlocked. By, of all things, putting a point in Snap.

Dare had already loved that ability based on the potential to produce light, which he considered useful under many circumstances, even if it was only for a moment. And he'd just laughed when the others had looked at him in bafflement for his choice.

Now he'd unlocked another ability in the Snap tree, which he hadn't expected. "Strobe Arrow: Congratulations, Hunter, you have discovered an untapped resource in the mana pool, and found ways to use it to advantage. Using the mana equivalent of 20 Snaps, enhance the tip of your arrow to briefly produce a moderately bright light every half second until it strikes the target."

That could be all sorts of useful as a distraction, to mess with people's night vision, to light up dark places at a distance, for signals, and probably lots of other things he hadn't considered yet.

But the shining glory of Level 35, the moment he'd anticipated eagerly for *twenty-five* levels now, ever since getting Rapid Shot at Level 10, was *finally* getting another archery ability.

And hot damn, it was a good one. "Burst Arrow: Blindly channeling the raw, untapped potential of your mana pool, infuse your arrow with a surge of mana from one of the schools of magic: Earth, Water, Air, Fire, Nature, Holy, and Void. Increase damage by 200% and add a status effect based on magic school used. High mana cost. 2 minute cooldown."

Dare wasn't sure if this was another ability he'd unlocked by having *some* other ability that used mana, or if he would've gotten it anyway. His immediate takeaway was that by letting him use it for any different school of magic, he could get around magical resistances to specific schools, and exploit magical weaknesses.

Like, say, fire, nature, and holy against undead.

Not counting the status effects, which he'd have to experiment with, it was also effectively the same damage increase as Rapid Shot. Except front loaded instead of distributed over four arrows, which certainly made a difference. Although also with double the cooldown, which actually made it *less* damage overall. It also used a limited resource.

Speaking of which, given the high mana cost it would probably only be usable so many times a day and would almost certainly be reserved for emergencies, or at the end of a day of monster farming to get some added efficiency.

But it was still incredible. It seemed tailor made to be useful in boss fights, particularly raid rated monsters with their stupidly big health pools. And in the regrettable instance he had to fight other humans, between it and Rapid Shot he'd be able to end a fight fast.

Dare was enough of a child that he went nuts celebrating, running around yelling excitedly and loosing arrows at random trees and other targets that wouldn't break his arrows.

He wished Zuri was here to celebrate with him. And all the others, of course, but some of his fondest memories of excitedly sharing new abilities from hard earned levels had happened with his beloved goblin fiancee.

He wanted to pick her up and spin her around, run around at max speeds laughing for the sheer joy of the moment.

When he finally calmed down a bit he got down to the business of checking his new abilities. Given his limited mana pool he wasn't sure how many Burst Arrows he'd be able to loose, although hopefully he had enough to test all of them. And ideally use the ability at least a dozen times.

He wasn't officially a magic using class, so he wouldn't expect his mana abilities to be as powerful as, say, Leilanna's spells. But even so he hoped they'd be versatile enough to make Burst Arrow awesome.

Dare returned to the spawn point he'd been hunting at and found a target for his new ability. As seemed obvious, he decided to go with fire for his first arrow, drawing the fletchings to his ear before activating Burst Arrow.

It was a rush. Literally.

The ability's description made a bit more sense now, as he felt like he'd opened the floodgates of his mana pool and just poured it all into the arrow, which began to flicker with an unstable, sullen orange glow. He loosed it, and the shaft burst alight as it hissed through the air and slammed into the monster, exploding in a burst of sparks that blackened its skin and made it shriek in pain and fury.

Damn, that looked cool. He hastily killed his target, looted it, then found a new monster to try the next school of magic on.

Over the next fifteen minutes he tried all the different schools of magic for his ability, seeing what status effect they caused. Most lasted less than 10 seconds and were fairly straightforward, like fire putting on a burn damage over time, but for the most part they were pretty unique and useful for a lot of situations.

Disappointingly, water's effect was to increase the target's vulnerability to cold. Which, well, definitely made sense, but it probably sucked the worst out of all of them. Although it had its uses, especially in winter.

Air got the arrow spinning like a drill and increased armor penetration, which was definitely handy. Earth caused a minor stun effect, up to 1 second, which was one of the more exciting ones.

Nature caused a 2 second snare effect to both movement and attacks, also a more exciting one. Holy reduced the target's regeneration and health restored by spells and abilities, which would probably be of limited use. And Void put a temporary curse on the target that reduced their chance to hit with attacks by 20%. Which could be nice, but Dare wasn't about to trust his life to randomness like that except in an emergency.

Maybe in party or raid fights to help mitigate damage on the tank or help a companion in an emergency.

They were all small effects, none of them overwhelmingly powerful. But maybe enough to tip the tide of battle in a critical moment if used correctly.

Dare used Burst Arrow as quick as it came up, and confirmed that he could shoot it exactly thirteen times before depleting his mana pool. Which just left seeing what Strobe Arrow cost.

After that a quick glance at the sun told him he'd lingered too long, and even running at reckless speeds it was still close to full dark before he panted his way into the manor yard.

As soon as he stepped inside he was mobbed by women who'd been waiting for close to an hour, growing more anxious with each passing minute. He was a bit surprised Sia hadn't reassured them, but he supposed the goddess couldn't step in for every little thing.

Dare tended to greet Zuri first, especially if she had Gelaa with her. But this time he waited until he finished hugging and kissing all the others before taking his daughter in his arms and cuddling her for a few moments.

Then, while his goblin fiancee looked at him in confusion, beautifully angular features showing slight hesitancy, he handed the baby to Se'weir.

Then he swept Zuri up into his arms with a laugh and began spinning her around eagerly. "I finally got an archery ability!" he shouted, hugging her close and kissing her fiercely.

The others all cheered and crowded around to hug him and shower him with kisses in congratulations. After he stopped spinning, of course. Dare happily answered questions as they pressed him for details; it was probably a bit silly to make such a big deal about a new ability like this, but it had been a long time coming.

The others had already eaten, but they joined him at the table to keep him company. And Pella, Se'weir, and Leilanna unapologetically went for a second dinner.

He was so tired he found himself nodding off after a few bites, and allowed himself to be led up to bed and undressed before rolling beneath the covers and drifting off beneath a pile of warm, soft bodies.

* * * * *

The next morning Ireni stopped Dare as he was preparing to set out. "No monster hunting today," she said.

He frowned at her. "Why?"

Rather than answering she handed him his bow. "Because I need you to go hunting hunting. Could you take several horses out and bring back as much meat and as many hides as you can? Try to be home before noon . . . you and Lily have some crafting to do."

That request was even more bewildering; with the cold to

preserve the meat Dare had been going wild with hunting already, and they had enough to last them throughout the winter and even trade a bit to the goblins and in Terana. Not to mention all the foraged greens, root vegetables, and herbs and spices he'd gathered.

He didn't really have to worry about overhunting, either, since one of the features of Collisa was that animals bred far faster and grew to maturity in a fraction of the usual time. Carnivores and omnivores could also eat monsters, which made their populations explode with the plentiful food available.

As for bringing home tons of hides for crafting . . . hell if he knew what that was about.

But Ireni didn't seem inclined to explain her mysterious behavior, and he trusted she had a good reason for her requests. So he loaded half a dozen horses with packs and set out in search of game or monsters that dropped edible meat as loot.

Another reason to love this area, especially for Zuri's sake, was the abundance of epinds.

The meat produced by the smaller, cow-like animals was almost impossibly tender and flavorful, and their hides were as soft and supple as calfskin. Both of which made them hugely popular for both hunting and domestication.

They seemed to prefer the plains just below the mountains, as well as the foothills, and usually traveled in small herds. Although the males could often be found wandering on their own.

Dare had a stroke of good fortune and came across a larger than usual herd of them fleeing south from the cold. A dozen of them provided enough meat and hides to load down the horses, and he downed one last one and harvested it into a bundle of its meat wrapped in its hide to carry on his back, barely able to handle the weight even with his belt letting him carry 20 more pounds.

When he came in sight of Nirim Manor he saw a line of around 30 ragged, miserable people approaching on the path from Terana, leading a few overloaded beasts of burden.

Even at a distance, especially with the help of Eagle Eye, he could see the drooping ears and tails that identified most of the column as felids. And his eyes were especially drawn to two distinct catgirls at the front who had a creamy orange coloring.

Linia and Felicia Melarawn. Which would make the grizzled felid behind them Irawn.

Dare was torn between happiness at the sight of his friends and worry about what they were doing here in such a state. He dropped the bundle he was carrying and ran forward, leading the horses behind him.

By the time he arrived the column of mostly felids, as well as a few canids and a young bovid woman, had reached the gate. Where basically the entire household had emerged to greet them, rushing around with blankets and mugs of steaming cider.

Felicia spotted Dare and ran towards him with a cry, throwing her arms around him. Her big, pale orange eyes were filled with tears of relief.

"Hey," he said, hugging her. "Are you okay? What happened?"

Over her shoulder he noticed Linia still standing with the column glaring at him, shoulders pulled back proudly. Rather than her Flanker chainmail she was snugly dressed in winter clothes with a thick cloak, the hood pulled low to cover her pale orange cat ears.

And even bundled up like that the beautiful catgirl was clearly pregnant, round tummy a sharp contrast to her slender figure. Dare couldn't help but think that she looked sexy as hell, and if she wasn't so clearly irritable he might've found himself thinking of the possibilities now that she was here.

That, and the fact that she'd come with a group of people who were clearly refugees in need of aid, and he had more important things to think about at the moment.

Felicia pulled back, almost angrily scrubbing at her eyes. "Marauding orcs from across the border attacked our village. They killed or enslaved most of the villagers there before Linia was able to flee with the people you see here." Her lip quivered. "I was in Redoubt when they reached it, and my captain gave me leave to come with them."

Dare stared in amazement at the dozens of miserable people. "You came all the way across Bastion? Why?"

Linia finally approached, answering curtly. "We didn't have a choice . . . no one else would take us unless we bound ourselves in slavery or indentured servitude in payment. All the northern border is in chaos, with monsters rampaging and feral tribes fleeing into the region and raiding and pillaging any settlements they come across. Villages are evacuating, towns are hunkering down, heroes are flocking to where the action is, and with the snows everyone's worried about starving."

"Besides, we wanted someplace far from the danger," Felicia added.

He could hardly blame them. If things were really getting that bad on the border then Nirim Manor, all the way in the southeastern corner of Bastion, was about as safe as it got short of leaving the region. Safe enough he hadn't even heard news of the dire situation, aside from vague whispers.

Although even so things up north must've deteriorated quickly, as they often seemed to. He just hoped the encroaching monsters and dangerous tribes didn't reach this far.

"What about the heroes who came north to fight back the monsters?" he asked.

Felicia spat furiously, looking remarkably catlike in the act. "Raiding a ruined city for loot and renown. The Marshal has the Irregulars trying to pick up the slack, but we're outnumbered and under-leveled."

Wow. Even from a cynical perspective that was a dick move. So much for being heroes.

Ireni arrived, snugly bundled in a thick coat and carrying two mugs of steaming cider, which she gave to the catgirl sisters. "We have plenty of room in the manor," she said. "Ilin, Lily, and Amalisa will move in with us, and Johar's family as well, and even then we have half a dozen empty guest bedrooms that can hold two or three people apiece. More if you want to sleep on the floor. That, plus the two guest houses, and nobody will have to sleep out in the cold."

Dare motioned to the loaded horses he'd returned with. "And we've got plenty of food, not just this but a fully loaded larder and icehouse."

In spite of her proud posture Linia's shoulders sagged at that. "Thank you," she murmured, gulping the warm drink. "We'll find a way to repay you, somehow. And the moment we can go home, or find some other place to go, we'll be out of your hair."

"Don't be silly," he said firmly. "There's plenty of space on our land. You can even rebuild your village here, if you wish. I offer you my protection, and whatever assistance I can provide."

"Really?" Felicia asked, eyes shining with hope.

Ireni warmly hugged the young teenager, who was almost as tall as her. "Of course. We would never turn away friends in need."

Dare nodded. "We already have a goblin village here that's prospering well."

He should've realized that might not draw the best response. "Goblins?" Linia said, wrinkling her nose. "Why? Don't they just try to constantly steal and wreck shit?" She abruptly seemed to remember his goblin lover Zuri and looked a bit guilty. "Sorry, but that's usually how it goes."

"Not in this case," he said. "Rek'u'gar is a friend. Soon to be a brother, since I'm engaged to his sister."

"Zuri?" Linia asked.

Dare chuckled. "A lot's happened since we met in Jarn's Holdout."

"I'll say." Her glare returned and she pointedly rested a hand on her visibly pregnant belly. "And we're definitely going to talk about that."

Gulp.

"Also you're what, like 10 levels higher than when I last saw you?" Felicia added. "Fucking how?"

“Language!” Dare, Linia, and Ireni all said at the same time in the same stern tone.

The young catgirl crossed her arms sullenly. “Right, I'm just a little kid so I'm not allowed to do anything. You're all *so* much more mature at four years older.”

Dare grinned at the fact that she thought Ireni was the same age and him and Linia; with her delicate doll-like features and petite size the redheaded Priestess looked younger than her years, but she would actually be turning 25 in a few months.

He'd been a bit disappointed to learn that people didn't celebrate birthdays on Collisa, and everyone had looked at him funny when he suggested it. Still, he hoped he could encourage them to adopt the practice, and since Ireni knew about Earth she'd probably be on board with having a birthday party.

After all, you could never have too many excuses to celebrate, right? He certainly planned to celebrate his children's birthdays even if he couldn't convince anyone else to celebrate theirs.

“4 years is an eternity at your age,” Linia said, pulling her little sister into a hug. “Believe me, I remember, and I worry that you're growing up faster than you should. Especially since you're around coarse, ill-mannered mercenaries day in and day out and learning things a proper young woman shouldn't. Like how to swear.”

Felicia muttered something too quietly for Dare to hear, but obviously loud enough for Linia with her sharper hearing. The older catgirl's expression darkened dangerously, and she grabbed her little sister's big velvety ear and twisted it hard enough to make her yowl in protest. “Care to repeat that for the group, recruit Felicia?”

Ireni cut in gently. “Let's get everyone in out of the cold. We can have this discussion around a warm fire and lunch.” She prodded Dare. “You should go retrieve that epind meat and hide you dropped and take it all to the icehouse, then get the hides curing so we can make warm clothes for our guests.”

Well, that explained why she'd sent him out.

“I'll help!” Felicia said. She beamed at him. “I switched my class to Hunter, see?"

Sure enough, she was a Hunter now. Which was a marked change in attitude from when he'd first met her and she'd mocked his class choice.

Although as refugees surviving in the wild, Hunters would have a lot more useful tools than an Archer.

"Level 6 now, nice," he said. He glanced at Linia. "And you're up to 22."

"Shut up," the orange dream catgirl said, glowering. "Thank you for taking us in . . . I half didn't believe Lissy when she told me you had a mansion and might be able to help us." Her glare intensified, and she pointedly rested a hand on her belly again. "But we're still going to talk about this, and I expect some groveling."

Dare winced. "Felicia explained what happened, right?"

"That you're a huge idiot who doesn't even know what fertility does?" She snorted. "Yep. And you're just naive and goodhearted enough I can actually believe such bullshit coming from you."

Without another word she strode back to her column to get everyone through the gate and into the manor.

Chapter Fifteen
Guests

"So . . . she's pissed at me," Dare said as he salted a hide.

Felicia grinned, inexpertly but enthusiastically working on her own. "Actually she's calmed down a lot. When I first told her what you told me she was literally spitting mad and scratching the furniture. I learned a lot of interesting new swears."

He shook his head wearily. "Think she'll come around?"

"Well she's here, isn't she?" The teenager paused with admirable comedic timing. "Of course, she didn't have many other options. But at least she didn't tear your head off and stuff it up your ass like she was threatening to do. That's a good sign."

Fantastic.

"I'm glad to you're okay," he said, changing the subject. "Me and Ireni were worried about you after Zor kicked us out of the raid."

Felicia grimaced. "We didn't have any trouble after that. Most people were angry about what Ollivan did to poor Ireni, and the fact that Lord Zor didn't do anything about it. I know a lot of women and healers and support decided not to work with either man again. As for the Irregulars contingent, we hunkered down and kept to ourselves until the loot was assessed and we got our share, then we traveled to Redoubt separately."

She brightened. "Here's something you'd probably be happy to hear. When we left Redoubt word was spreading around the city that Ollivan died to monsters, the idiot. He was fighting alone because what healer would ever want to group with him?"

Dare felt a moment of sadness for Thorn. "I heard," he said.

The young teenager spat off to one side. "One less piece of shit in the world."

Hard to argue with that.

Silence settled for a few minutes, then she stirred and gave him a thoughtful look. “It's not as bad as you might think.”

He jumped slightly. “What isn't?”

“With Nia, duh,” she said with a laugh. “She'll probably be mad at me for telling you, but even though she's furious at you she was looking forward to seeing you, too. And not just because she hoped you'd be able to help us.”

Dare perked up. “Really?”

“Of course.” She laughed again, tossing a pinch of salt at him. “She likes you and had fun with you in Jarn's Holdout. And why wouldn't she? You're handsome, rich, high level, a complete badass on the battlefield, and on top of it a good person who genuinely cares about her.”

He heard a gagging sound behind him and whirled to see Linia standing there, hands on her hips. “Run inside and get some food, Sister,” she said curtly.

“But I'm help-” Felicia started to protest.

Linia's sleek tail went stiff and bristly and she took a step forward. “Go!”

Sulking, the young teenager stomped off. Leaving Dare with his pregnant former lover.

He had to say she looked stunning. She'd had a chance to bathe and put on clean clothes, which he thought she'd borrowed from Ireni; they fit her slender body, but with a higher hem on the taller woman. Her peaches and cream complexion was flushed with the cold and with the healthy glow of pregnancy, and her pale orange hair was pulled into a shimmering braid.

“I wish the circumstances were better, Linia, but it's good to see you,” he said.

She snorted and made her way over to take the seat her sister had vacated, out in a corner of the yard where the stink of curing hides wouldn't bother the animals or any of the guests. “I suppose we should address the mammoth in the room," she said, absently rubbing her pregnant belly.

"Right." Dare set the hide he was working on aside and reached for a cloth to wipe his hands. "First off, I'm sorry about screwing up with Prevent Conception. Felicia explained what happened, right?"

"That you're an idiot who doesn't know the basic facts of life?" the orange dream catgirl laughed sourly. "Yeah. From any other guy I'd say that was the lamest line ever, but I actually believe you." Her expression softened. "It helps that you practically begged Lissy to help convince me to let you be a part of the baby's life and help however you can."

She paused pointedly. "So I'm going to let you."

He felt a bit of tension between his shoulders ease. "Thank you."

Linia sniffed. "Honestly I might've been willing to come even if things hadn't turned to shit up north. Felicia told me about Nirim Manor and how you and your harem have created a comfortable home here." She looked around. "And she wasn't exaggerating . . . this place is beautiful. And it's got luxuries you usually only expect to find in the wealthiest homes."

Dare smiled, pleased at the praise. "You're welcome to stay as long as you want."

"Good, because with my village evacuated this is the best place for me to give birth to *our* child. Then after it's weaned I'll go back to the Irregulars and you and your consorts can raise the baby. I'll visit as often as possible, of course, but I'll leave the responsibility to you."

The cute catgirl leaned forward to loom over him, orange dream eyes holding his with absolute seriousness. "Can I count on you for that?"

"Absolutely," Dare said in his firmest voice. "I want to be in our child's life, and help however I can. I would be honored to have the baby here and help raise it, and I'm sure my fiancees will feel the same."

"Good, although obviously I'm going to be talking to them, since no offense but when it comes to the child they'll probably be doing the lion's share of the work."

"True." He smiled. "Zuri and Pella are excited to see you again, in case you didn't notice. And the others are eager to meet you and welcome you to Nirim Manor."

"Mmm." Linia tapped her pouty lips as she looked at him. "Even though I'll be staying here I'm not going to be part of your harem, you know that right?"

That was reasonable enough under the circumstances, although Dare was still a little disappointed; he liked the beautiful catgirl, and wouldn't have minded spending more time with her.

Although of course she was basically indentured to the Irregulars as a freed slave under contract with them, so he would've had to arrange to pay off her contract or something. And she'd already made it pretty clear she was happy with her mercenary company and loyal to them.

"All right," he said. "I'm pleased to have you as a guest and as the mother of our child, and I hope you'll be a good friend as well. I want to make you as comfortable and welcome as possible."

Linia rolled her eyes. "Ancient Forebears, you need to be led to the point, don't you?" He stared at her blankly, and she sighed and gracefully slid over onto his lap, snuggling close and firmly pulling his arms around her with his hands resting on her pregnant belly.

Lips twitching with amusement, she looked up at him with her big feline eyes. "Handsome, I've spent the last few weeks traveling here remembering the fun time we had in Jarn's Holdout and looking forward to more of the same. Long months of it, until I give birth and then after while I'm nursing the baby, until it's weaned and I have to leave and return to my duties."

She shifted so her narrow but curvy ass pressed against his crotch, firm but soft and definitely eliciting a response. Which drew a satisfied catlike smirk as she continued to hold his gaze. "I've already told you felids don't do relationships. We have friends, we have lovers, we move on. If we see them again we're happy and we can have more fun together if they're up for it, but we won't be held down or even held *to* someone else. It's just how we are."

The slender catgirl waved around the yard. "I hope to visit here often and think of it as a place I can call home when I'm here. And I definitely want to have fun with you and Zuri and Pella and any of your other fiancees who're interested."

She paused, then continued very firmly. "But I'm not going to settle down and marry you or become your concubine or whatever. And if I fuck other men I fuck other men. Understood?"

Dare wasn't sure how he felt about that, but he nodded. "Understood." Smiling, he leaned in and kissed her pouty rosebud lips. "It's good to see you again, Linia. And I look forward to having more time to spend with you."

"Good, because I'm going to take you up on that right now." Smiling with very catlike satisfaction, she bopped him on the chest with a cutely curled fist and hopped off his lap, grabbing his hand and tugging him towards the house.

His family, friends, and beast kin guests all looked on in amusement as Linia peeled off her cold weather gear, practically tore his cloak and coat off him, and dragged him through the entry room and up the stairs.

As she burst into the master bedroom with him in tow Se'weir, who'd been changing out of a flour dusted and grease spattered tunic, squeaked in surprise and reached for the clean dress she'd laid out nearby.

"Oh, um, excuse me," she said. "I was just about to head downstairs."

"Nuh uh, beautiful," the orange dream catgirl said with a grin. "You're going to stay and help me fuck your fiancee's brains out."

The plump hobgoblin brightened. "Really?"

Dare couldn't help but watch in amazement as Linia minced up to the shorter woman, tail lashing as if stalking prey, and ran her hand up Se'weir's bare arm. "If you're up for it," she purred.

His fiancee blushed. "Oh, well if you're Dare's mate, of course."

She bashfully looked up at the pale orange catgirl. “You're really pretty.”

Linia laughed. “Thanks.” Without hesitation she leaned down and kissed the other woman firmly on the mouth. After a moment of surprise Se'weir kissed her back with equal passion, even slipping her tongue into the taller woman's mouth. Linia upped the ante by fondling the hobgoblin's ample breasts through her bra, making Se'weir giggle and hug her closer, eagerly slipping a hand beneath the catgirl's shirt.

It didn't take much of watching that before Dare was hard as a rock.

Linia reached out and pulled him into the kiss, and he found his mouth invaded by wet lips and exploring tongues. Somehow in the blur of passion his lovers stripped his shirt and pants off him, the catgirl managing to lose her own clothes as if by magic at the same time, and they all piled onto the bed together.

As Se'weir kissed and sucked on his neck, soft body pressed to his back, he wonderingly ran his hands over Linia's lithe body, amazed by how she'd managed to stay so slender a good four and a half months into a seven month pregnancy. Her small breasts might've grown slightly, but aside from her sexy swollen belly she looked about like he remembered.

The thought of his baby growing inside the beautiful catgirl was a huge turn on. He ran his hands over her taut stomach, rubbing her popped out belly button and making her squirm and giggle, then leaned down and began kissing over her roundness.

Linia let him explore her body for a few minutes. Then she quickly took charge, and almost before Dare knew it she had Se'weir on her hands and knees with him positioned behind her.

The brash catgirl mercenary seemed to have quickly homed in on what her hobgoblin lover enjoyed, too. As Dare thrust into his fiancee she slapped the plump woman's ass and pushed his hips to urge him to harder thrusts, goading them both on with sexy suggestions and dirty talk.

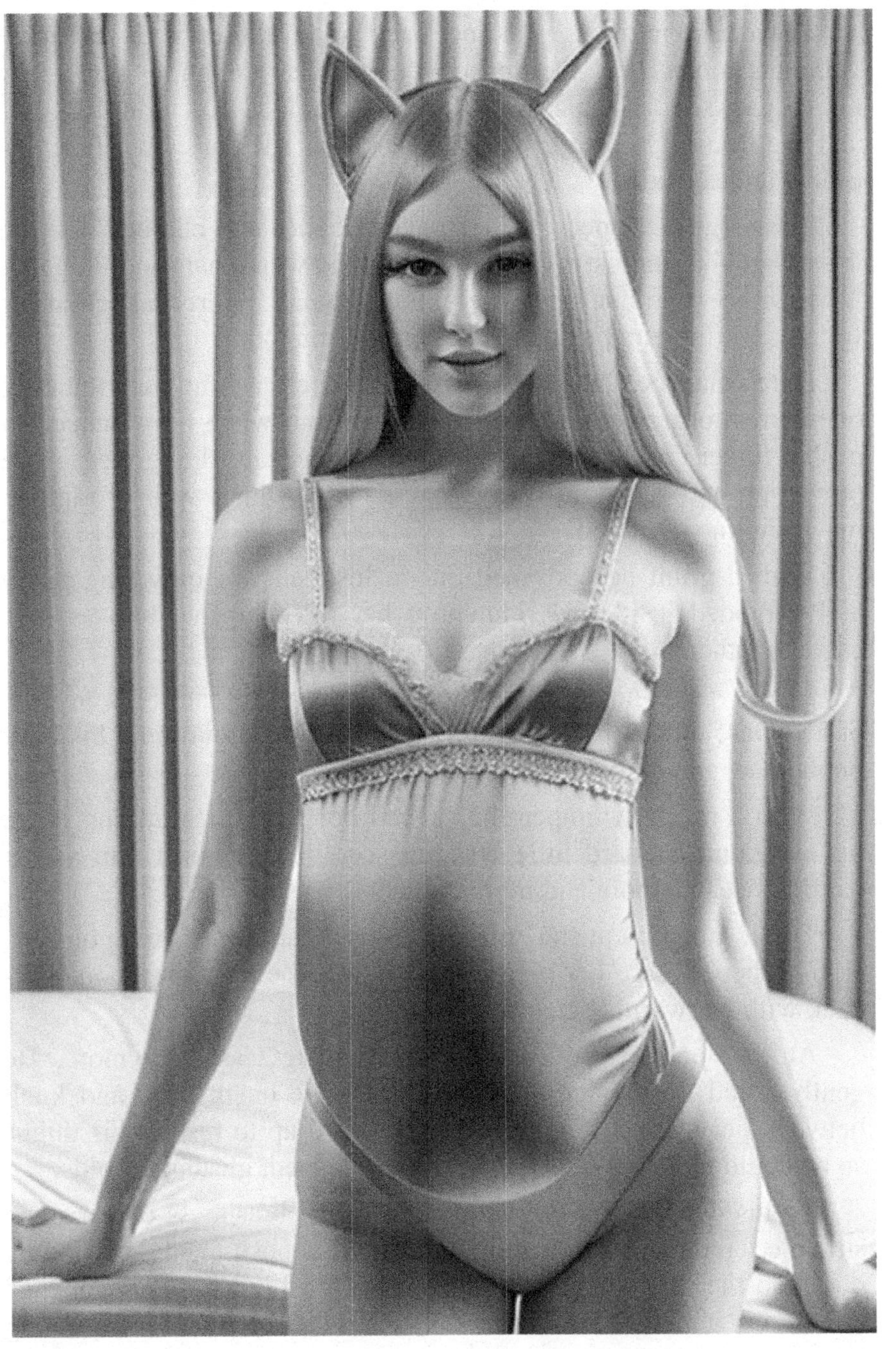

Se'weir went nuts, grinding back against him with the most delicious moans, her plump body jiggling in delight. After a few more spanks from Linia her soft pussy clamped down on his cock, and she flooded his thighs with her juices as she buried her face in a pillow and squealed.

The catgirl stripped off her soaked panties and climbed beneath the hobgoblin, almost roughly grabbing Se'weir's hair and dragging her face between her legs. The plump woman eagerly lapped at the wet pussy, drawing moans of enjoyment from both.

Dare's fiancee climaxed again on his cock, and he rode the edge of his own orgasm as he rutted into her. But when he watched her push a finger into Linia's asshole, causing the catgirl to go tense as a bowstring and squirt all over Se'weir's face with a wail of rapture, his discipline shattered.

With a grunt he bottomed out in his fiancee's quivering pussy and exploded inside her, clutching her thick hips to him as they came together.

Linia wasted no time squirming out from beneath Se'weir. She pulled Dare out of his hobgoblin fiancee, shoved him onto his back on the bed, and climbed on top of him.

With a needy whimper she rubbed her pussy lips up and down his erection, her hard little bud pressed firmly against him as her panting became more and more ragged.

To his amazement she orgasmed again just from rubbing on him, arching her back so her pregnant belly jutted out as she flooded his cock with her warm nectar.

At that point Dare couldn't stand being teased anymore. He gently lifted the orange dream catgirl to lie on the bed and knelt between her legs, pulling her tight little ass up to rest on his thighs so he could press his sensitive tip to her flushed, glistening folds.

To his delight Se'weir, showing a bit of brashness of her own, straddled the beautiful catgirl's face. She positioned her gaping pussy so their combined juices dripped into Linia's eagerly opened mouth for a few seconds, then lowered herself until her pouting labia kissed her new lover.

The slender woman gave another caterwaul of pure enjoyment, muffled between the hobgoblin's thighs, and urgently wiggled her hips to try to push herself onto Dare's cock, tail lashing at his thighs and butt.

He grabbed her ass for leverage and pushed into her in a smooth motion, moaning at the feel of her tight pussy stretching around him.

"Goddess nurturing, I've missed your huge cock," Linia moaned, voice muffled against Se'weir's pussy. "Give it to me."

Dare ran his hands over her taut round tummy and began to thrust inside his beautiful lover, enjoying the way she couldn't seem to get enough of him just as much as he basked in the incredible feel of her tight walls. Her nectar poured freely, filling his head with the heady scent of her strong musk and vanilla.

He'd thought about being with the playful catgirl ever since they'd parted ways in Jarn's Holdout. In his excitement at finally being reunited with her, it only took a few minutes before he felt his balls churning eagerly at the prospect of filling her pink little pussy with his seed.

He toyed with her small breasts, tweaking her sensitive nipples, and between his attention and Se'weir eagerly riding her face Linia lost it. One hand darted down to furiously rub her clit, and with a wail muffled by the hobgoblin's pussy she clamped down hard on his cock and climaxed so powerfully her entire body trembled.

That was enough for Dare, and with a last gasp he grabbed the catgirl's slender hips and pulled her against him, bottoming out inside his sweet little lover as he emptied himself inside her.

Squeaking frantically in her own excitement, Se'weir lifted herself off Linia's mouth and furiously mauled her throbbing bud, tensing as she returned the favor and squirted all over the catgirl's delicate face with a moan of pure release.

If Dare thought they were done, Linia proved him wrong. She gave him a few minutes to recover while she and Se'weir made out and fingered each other, which not only kept them both keyed up but soon had him hard as a rock again.

His hobgoblin fiancee finally sat up against the headboard and pulled the catgirl back into her arms, while Linia grabbed a pillow to wedge under her ass so he'd have a better angle to penetrate her. She spread her legs wide in invitation, gaping pussy flowing obscenely with their combined juices, and he kissed his way up her round belly, kissed and sucked on her breasts and nipples, and finally pressed his lips to hers as he pushed inside her yet again.

After coming twice he was able to hold out for much longer, coaxing the catgirl to two more orgasms with the help of Se'weir, who fondled her breasts and rubbed her clit while kissing her neck and velvety ears.

Finally, as Linia's pink walls rippled over his shaft in her strongest orgasm yet, squirting all over his crotch and thighs, he buried himself inside her one last time and with a grunt gave into a powerful orgasm of his own.

Afterwards they cuddled for a few minutes, languidly kissing and caressing each other. Then Se'weir, bless her heart, grabbed some wet rags and warm water and cleaned them off.

Dare would've happily stayed in bed with Linia all day, but with a sigh he began to dress. "Well, I guess we should tell the others what's going on?"

"What *is* going on?" his hobgoblin fiancee asked, grinning up at him as she wiped down Linia's thighs. "I mean this was lots of fun, but I'd have no idea who Linia was if you hadn't shouted her name as you came inside her."

He couldn't help but laugh as he playfully swatted her round ass. "Come on, let's get everyone into the parlor and we can explain the situation."

* * * * *

The explanation was briefly delayed while Zuri and Pella hugged Linia and made a huge fuss over her. Then the catgirl made a huge fuss over Gelaa as Dare's goblin fiancee proudly introduced her, as well as Pella's hugely pregnant belly.

The two hadn't spent nearly as much time with Linia as he had, although they'd all made love together for a few hours the morning before parting ways.

Apparently that had been enough for them to be happy to see her months later and carrying his baby.

Irawn and Felicia joined them, and Dare shared drinks with everyone who was drinking (which to his surprise again included Ilin) before they all settled down to talk.

Arranging to care for the refugees took some time. Irawn was hesitant about Dare's invitation for them to settle permanently on his land and rebuild their village, but Linia and Felicia both pushed for it and he agreed to bring it up with the others.

Then Dare explained what he and Linia had discussed about her staying, and then asked his fiancees if they'd be willing to help care for the baby after the catgirl had to return to her duties with the Irregulars.

The consensus was of course, duh, you don't even have to ask, and a bit of squeeing at the thought of having an adorable little felid baby in the house.

He thought that was awfully reasonable of them considering they'd all have children of their own to care for soon, and before long Nirim Manor would be crawling with babies. Pun intended.

"We'll just have to hire more servants, as well as wet nurses and nannies," Ireni said matter-of-factly.

Growing the household even more; Dare couldn't complain about the idea of getting help for his family, but the speed at which things were happening still left him a bit dazed.

"Will you be sleeping in the master bedroom?" Pella asked, cuddling up to Linia on one side. Zuri, on the catgirl's other side holding Gelaa, nodded in agreement.

Linia grinned, although her peaches and cream complexion turned a bit rosy in a blush. "If you've got room for me. All the other rooms are occupied right now, aren't they?" That prompted some light laughter.

"What would you think about bringing her along to level with you and Amalisa?" Dare asked Ilin.

His friend hesitated, looking reluctant for some reason. Amalisa did as well, surprisingly; she was usually generous and eager to cooperate with the group. But the young noblewoman only paused a few moments before nodding and giving the catgirl a warm smile. "Of course she's welcome."

Dare glanced at Ireni, about to ask if she'd be interested in taking Felicia with her and Lily to help the young teenager level, but to his continued surprise she shook her head subtly.

Hmm. Maybe it was because the catgirl sisters might've been their friends, but they were also Irregulars and not part of the household. And more importantly, there was that warning he'd gotten a while ago about not misusing his power or there'd be consequences.

Helping everyone he met level up willy-nilly was probably not the best idea. He was probably already doing more of that than was strictly safe, especially since he was Noticed.

The meeting broke up after that. Dare and Ireni went with Irawn and the catgirls to talk to the other refugees and help them get settled in. They also broached the topic of the displaced villagers building a new home here, and got some positive responses.

Although it was obvious they needed time to think about it.

Dare was about to head back out to start crafting the cured hides into warm fur clothing and blankets, but Ireni pulled him aside for a moment and silently handed him a pair of keys. "For the heating room and loot shed," she murmured.

He guessed she'd used the padlocks they'd ordered when Ollivan had been threatening them to secure the rooms. A part of him didn't like the thought of locking things up just because they had unfamiliar guests in the house, but on the other hand the legendary chest was worth thousands of gold. As was the Home Ward, and some of their other gear and loot was similarly valuable enough to be tempting.

Beyond the value, even, losing the legendary chest would cripple the house's heating and plumbing, and losing any of their gear would hamper their leveling efforts and leave them vulnerable to attack.

Best not to take chances.

So Dare nodded and tucked the keys into his pouch before ducking out into the cold, heading over to the smoke shed to check the curing meat before gathering up the fur and leather he'd created to begin crafting.

Thank the gods for the ability system, or all of this would've taken days or weeks instead of hours.

* * * * *

It didn't take a genius to guess that with Linia joining them in bed, the evening was going to be a lot of fun as the other women all got to know her.

The adventurous catgirl was more than happy to play with any and all of them, which was good because she quickly became a favorite. Even Ireni wanted to kiss and cuddle with her while they explored each other's bodies, and Sia was as amorous as always.

Although when Linia was finally tired out she retreated to cuddle between Zuri and Pella to sleep. Dare was a bit disappointed to not get to sleep next to her, like he usually did with new lovers when they joined the group.

But he was glad she felt welcome and comfortable with his first two lovers. And honestly he'd gotten to spend plenty of time with her, so he couldn't really complain.

The next morning was a bit awkward with so many unfamiliar faces in the house. Although the refugees were eager to help out however they could, joining Se'weir in the kitchen or grabbing cleaning implements to thoroughly tidy up the house.

Still, with all the noise and confusion Dare was eager to get out of the house, even though usually he didn't set out to hunt monsters until after breakfast, when the others left to level as well.

So he found Lily in all the confusion and pulled her aside. "Want to go run around for a bit?" he asked with a smile.

The bunny girl looked almost absurdly relieved at the offer, and eagerly grabbed the soft white fur cloak he'd gifted her and followed him outside. He supposed she was probably feeling even more overwhelmed with all the new arrivals than the rest of them, since she'd grown up in a secluded warren surrounded by familiar faces, and had been taught to be wary around other races.

Particularly since she had a unique personality even for cunids, and seemed to enjoy solitude and a good book nearly as much as a pleasant evening surrounded by friends.

Although Lily certainly had a playful side. Especially when doing something she loved, like running. "You're it!" she shouted, slapping his back before taking off in an explosion of snow, her long, shapely legs propelling her more in bounds than in a run.

Dare grinned and activated Cheetah's Dash as he sprinted after her.

In spite of his focus on leveling over the last nine days he hadn't neglected the romantic young woman. They hadn't had a chance to run together since their trip here, but they'd gone on moonlit walks, he'd cooked her dinner and they'd shared private meals together.

And if nothing else they always spent at least a few minutes sitting together in the parlor, talking quietly about various things. Usually her life back in her warren, and any romantic stories he could remember.

They had yet to kiss, although they'd held hands and hugged, and even sat close together with their legs and shoulders just touching.

Now, though, as Dare chased the beautiful bunny girl around the yard, he couldn't help but think about the last time he'd played tag. Back near Lone Ox not long after he'd arrived on Collisa.

When he'd chased Clover, a game which had ultimately ended in him making love to her and conceiving his firstborn son, Petro.

This game of tag was far more innocent. Lily held back just enough that he was able to tag her after several minutes of effort, and then he used every trick in his book, or ability on his character sheet, to try to keep away from her in turn.

Obviously she could've caught him anytime she wanted, but she kept herself to just fast and nimble enough that he was pushed to his limits staying ahead of her.

Finally the silver-haired bunny girl tackled him into a snowdrift with a playful giggle. It devolved into an impromptu snowball fight, which was interrupted when Felicia and a few children from the refugee caravan, then Johar's and Hanni's two kids, appeared as if by magic to join the fun.

It soon became him and Lily against the six newcomers, an epic battle against all odds which eventually ended with the two of them being tackled into the snow again.

Se'weir rescued them, appearing at the door to call that the food was ready. With a laugh Dare easily escaped from a canid boy enthusiastically trying to dump an armful of snow onto his head, and rescued Lily from a similar attempt from Felicia to dump snow down the back of her coat. Together they herded the kids towards the manor to eat breakfast.

On the way the bunny girl slipped a gloved hand into his, smiling up at him with a flushed face and sparkling eyes. “That was fun. It reminds me of winters back home playing with my sisters and our friends.”

“It was,” he agreed, squeezing her hand. “In spite of our humiliating defeat at the hands of our mighty foes.”

The kids laughed, and Felicia grinned at him over her shoulder.

Lily laughed too, although her expression was soft as she leaned against his side. “Your kids are lucky to have such a fun daddy.” She nudged him playfully with her shoulder. “Although you're going to be vastly outnumbered at the rate you're going.”

With so many people gathered in the manor breakfast was served in the kitchen, dining room, living room, parlor, and even entry room. Se'weir, Hanni, and several of the refugees had put out a good spread, with plenty of meat as the felids and canids preferred. Everyone was very complimentary as they dug in, looking eager to have delicious and plentiful food after so long going without.

Although Dare ate surrounded by his friends and family in the dining room, he caught snippets of conversation from the other rooms. A surprising amount of it was their guests' amazement at the manor's heating system, plumbing, and even warm running water. The toilets especially drew praise bordering on awe.

Apparently those sorts of luxuries hadn't been available back in their village.

For those who weren't heading out to hunt monsters, the plan for the day revolved around sorting out the best possible long term situation for the refugees. Many had seemed relieved at the idea of having a safe place with a friendly landlord where they could rebuild; a lot of free people from other races had trouble finding that, even in a more reasonable place like Bastion.

In fact, in some places lords who discovered secret villages on their lands swept in and enslaved everyone, or demanded crippling taxes beyond the usual payments required for a tenant lease. The poor villagers of other races could do nothing about it but endure the mistreatment or leave, since if they tried to seek justice they'd only be punished for being caught squatting on someone else's land.

So if nothing else, for the refugees who were still on the fence about his offer his land provided a safe place to stay, at least until they figured out what they wanted to do. And while they were here, they agreed it made sense to take care of temporary living arrangements.

Se'weir, Linia, and Irawn planned to visit the Avenging Wolves, to see if they could hire them out for the work of cutting logs and constructing cabins. Although the decision was based on need rather than a sense of cooperation; the felids were a bit cautious of the nearby goblin village. To the point that they intended to put their own on the exact opposite corner of Dare's land, to the northeast of the manor.

Dare didn't much care where the refugees put their new village, as long as they didn't insult his soon to be brother-in-law and the goblins, and the two groups didn't start trouble.

He finished eating and kissed his fiancees goodbye, as well as Linia, and took Lily's hand and kissed the back of it. Then he set off, determined to get as much done today as possible to make up for the previous day's change of plans.

He still hadn't discovered any party rated monsters, and even though it meant potentially missing out on good spawn points he set off for a different part of the mountains this time. Farther to the southeast and basically right next to the Tangle, the wall of enchanted briars that served as a fence between Bastion and the elvish kingdom of Elaivar.

It was not only awesome to think of a living wall built by elves, but also a beautiful landmark in its own harsh, forbidding way. Dare had visited it to admire the sight a few times, although never closer to the Gadris Mountains, and he was curious what the elves had done about stretching the Tangle across the mountain range jutting into their kingdom.

Unsurprisingly, going southeast away from Terana meant he encountered even higher level spawn points than he would've going south, which would've taken him closer to Jarn's Holdout to the west along the mountains, as well as settlements in Kovana on the other side. They were still far enough below his level that the experience and loot gains from farming them were modest, but if he gained too many more levels this might end up being the only spot close to Nirim Manor where he could really find good hunting.

Aside from in the mountains themselves, where the spawn points varied wildly. But even there they were too unpredictable to really make for reliable farming.

In fact, as Dare hunted a spawn point of Level 28-29s he came across, he couldn't help but think of the future of his leveling. As in, long long term future.

Sia had told him at the beginning that no one had ever reached the level cap on Collisa. And even though she hadn't specified exactly what that cap was, and wouldn't elaborate on what the higher levels would be like, he thought he knew why.

On the surface her claim seemed a bit unbelievable to him,

looking back on his own swift leveling over the last nearly eight months. Even considering the huge advantage Adventurer's Eye gave him.

But the higher level he got, the more he saw it.

Not only did it become more difficult from a logistical perspective to hunt appropriate level monsters farther and farther from a home base in some town or, in his case, an established estate, but the experience requirements increasing with each level were significant, especially when they jumped every 10 levels.

And getting better gear and finding faster ways to travel only helped so much.

As Dare calculated it, the amount of experience, and thus the amount of time, effectively doubled every five levels if you counted the big 10 level jumps. Even if it seemed like it had been quicker for him before now, a lot of that had been because he went from basic gear he made himself to more powerful crafted gear and loot. And the difficulty of carrying loot in a single backpack and selling when it was full, which seriously slowed him down.

But if he looked at it now, at Level 35 it would take him an average of 10 days a level until he reached 40, at which point it would be taking 2 weeks a level. By level 45 it would be taking him about a month a level, and at 50 about 2 months.

Up to 4 months at 55, to 8 months at 60, to 16 months at 65 and almost 3 full years at 70. To around 5 years at 75 and a decade at 80. *A level.* Two decades at 85, four decades at 90, eight decades at 95, and a mind-boggling century and a half at Level 100.

Assuming everything remained as it was. And assuming optimal leveling efficiency, which meant he'd practically have to live out in the higher level zones and never see his family, which he wasn't about to do.

Dare could almost believe the level cap really was 100, when during his initial leveling he'd optimistically thought he'd be able to reach 100 in no time at the rate he was going and so it must be even higher, 150 or 200.

But 100 could work, because even the longer lived races wouldn't be able to reach that in their lifetimes.

Even with the start he'd had, eventually that wall of doubling experience was going to hit him right in the face. He could probably reach Level 45 by the time his 19th birthday rolled around if he pushed, and 53 when he turned 20.

And then Level 57 by 21, 60 by 22, 65 by around age 26, 70 by 33, and by the time he reached 75 he'd be 46 or so. At which point to reach Level 80 would take about *25 years*, and he'd be over 70 by the time he managed it.

And that might just be the end of Dare's leveling career, unless he managed one or two more in his twilight years; no wonder all the higher level heroes he'd seen were all so old. Especially since they didn't have the benefit of Adventurer's Eye to speed up their leveling.

Sia had also told him he'd live far longer than most thanks to the body she'd made for him. But even if he lived centuries he'd still be lucky to make it over Level 90.

That bothered him a little, but not as much as he'd expected it would. He could still get higher level than anyone he'd ever met while he was still a young man, and maybe by that time life would be offering other challenges and blessings than what he got from leveling.

Besides, within those levels there were dungeons and raids to clear. A world to explore. Kingdoms he could make a difference in, people he could help. Exotic women to meet, friends to make.

Wives to love, children to raise. A home to build into the paradise his family deserved.

During Dare's musings he'd cleared two more low level spawn points, and now he paused at the top of a rise to take in the view of the Tangle meeting with the Gadris Mountains in front of him.

Wondrous sights like this to see.

A lazier people might've called the mountains a good enough barrier and resumed the wall of brambles on the southern side of them, but not the elves. They'd erected the Tangle up and over the mountains in an impossibly straight line, winding its way up slopes and cliffs, down out of sight into valleys, until finally it disappeared over distant peaks.

He had to wonder if the elves of Elaivar would be willing to let him travel their lands and see what other wonders they'd created. Leilanna had told them that while Haraldar gave elves free passage and most citizen rights within their lands, that openness wasn't mutual and Elaivar strongly discouraged human traders and visitors.

Maybe as a high level hero they'd grant him a special exemption. Especially if he bought up more land around Nirim Manor, and had a strong enough presence on their border they thought he was worthy of trade agreements and treaties.

Also, it was possible that being married to Leilanna would confer on him some rights and privileges he wouldn't otherwise have among the elves. Or he could help them handle some crisis and become an elf friend. The possibilities were there, he hoped.

Until then, he finally caught a break in his search for party rated monsters.

Chapter Sixteen

A True Party

It was an undead giant, easily 12 feet tall and powerfully built. Or at least it had been before its flesh started to rot off its bones.

It bore a small tree as a club, and was angrily walking along the Tangle, slamming its crude weapon into the enchanted brambles, which boasted a dense knot of branches and roots that were thicker around than Dare's entire body. He wasn't sure whether the monster was trying to get through into Elaivar or just tear down the wall in pursuit of mindless destruction, but either way it wasn't having much luck against the magnificent barrier.

He looked at it with his Eye: "Rotten Shambler. Monster, Party Rated. Level 26. Attacks: Batter, Stomp, Rot Aura, Unholy Regeneration, Vile Breath, Hurl Debris."

For all its intimidating size and appearance, its stats weren't all that impressive. Dare was fairly confident he could solo it with little difficulty, but as he looked at it an idea struck him.

With low level party rated monsters like this, why kill them alone? Most of the benefits from these kills came from achievements, trophies, and experience bonuses, not the simple experience from killing the monster.

If Dare could find a few of these, he could bring along as many of the others as he could and they could all get the progress towards the achievement. Make a day of it.

Of course there was the risk someone might wander by and see the party rated monster, and it would be killed before he and the others could come back for it. But given its location and the fear even seasoned adventurers had of traveling in unknown areas of the wilds, he thought it would be fine.

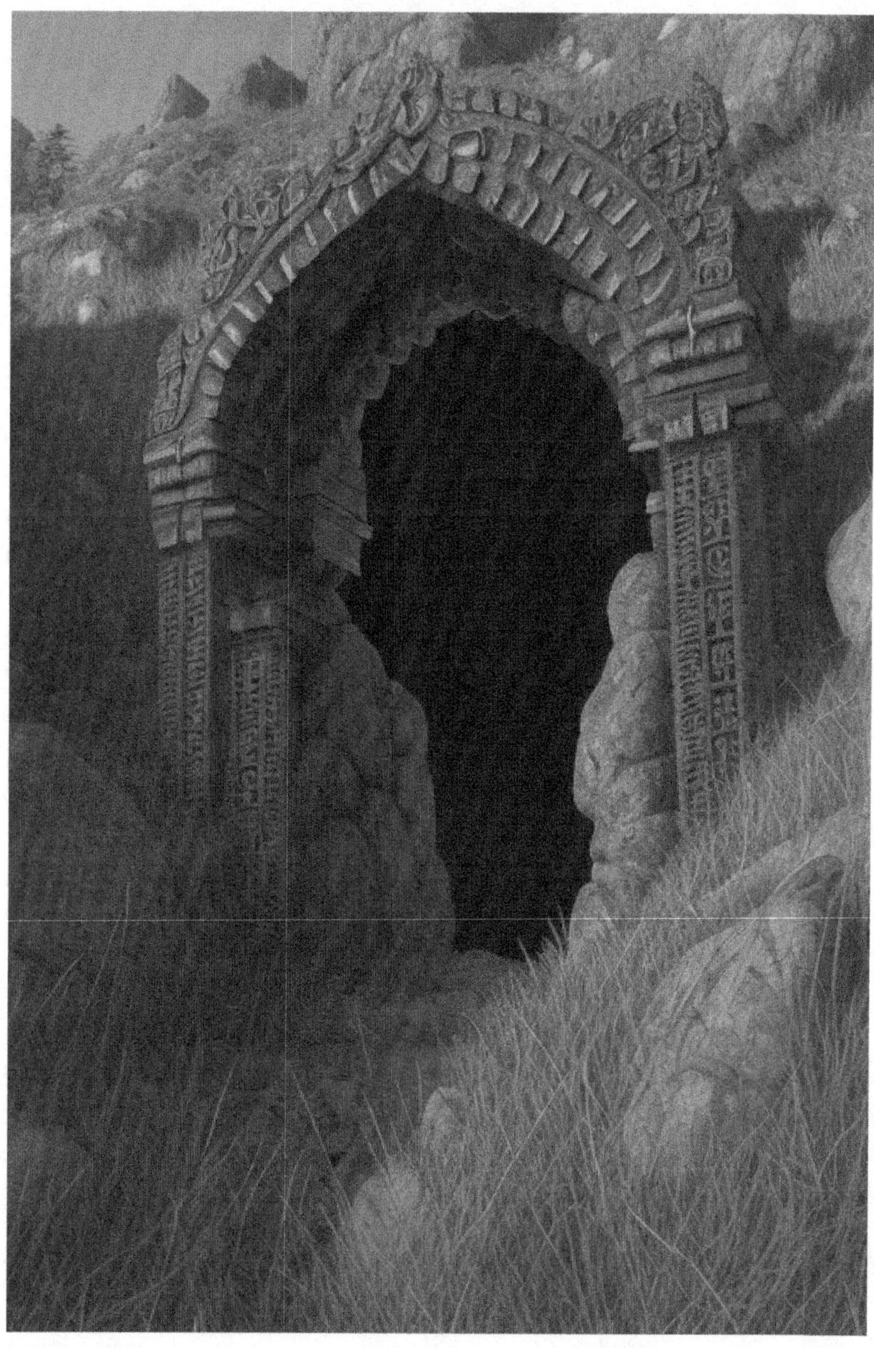

So he left the Rotten Shambler behind and continued on into the mountains, clearing spawn points, scouting, and searching for more party rated monsters.

Instead, to his amazement he found a wonder of the world.

Running past a narrow ravine in a secluded mountain valley, he spotted something along the face of a cliff at the back of it and skidded to a stop. It was an opening, perfectly square and about seven feet tall, skillfully carved with runes and intricate artwork. Although time had worn them away until they were almost gone. In front of the opening lay the torn and rusted remains of a thick metal door.

What in the world?

Dare had met dwarves before, in the raid with Lord Zor, and had even slept with Ulma, a dwarf maiden who was hairy in all the right places. Although he hadn't taken the opportunity to ask them if they lived underground or what their homes looked like.

This certainly matched most dwarvish doorways into underground kingdoms he'd seen in games. An ancient dwelling of theirs, maybe?

He cautiously approached, Adventurer's Eye searching for any threats. There were none in sight, so after checking the entrance for traps or pitfalls he cautiously entered the carved stone tunnel.

About ten feet in it opened into an antechamber, about ten feet by ten feet and showing signs of rotted and moldering fortifications to defend the tunnel leading deeper into the mountain on the far side. He kept going, even more cautiously, until it grew so dark even his Eagle Eye's slight vision bonus didn't help.

It wasn't a dungeon, he was pretty certain about that. The Glittering Caves had been a dungeon, and as you'd expect with dungeons it had light sources in most places, in that case glowing moss and lichen, and they ran into dangerous monsters almost from the start.

This was just an empty, abandoned ruin.

Or maybe not. Dare jumped at creepy skittering sounds echoing down the tunnel to him, then turned and bolted back outside, pausing in the sunlight to stop and listen in case he'd been pursued.

He hadn't, and honestly those sounds could've carried for a ways underground if the tunnels went deep enough. He went in search of animals to hunt and began making preparations.

A half hour later he had several torches made, soaked in animal fat. Armed with that, plus Snap and Strobe Arrow, he felt ready to do some exploring.

This was exactly the sort of thing he'd wanted to do ever since coming to Collisa. Discovering secrets, exploring the deep places of the world, looking with awe upon wonders long forgotten.

And, ideally, finding some treasure along the way.

The torch wasn't as bright as Dare would've liked, which just made him miss the reliable glowing moss of the Glittering Caves all the more. It also flickered constantly from gusts rushing out from deeper within the tunnels, or pouring in around him from the entrance.

Almost like vast breaths. A disquieting thought, and he moved a bit quicker as he made his way deeper down the tunnel.

Finally, after hundreds of yards straight into the mountain, the walls around him opened up into a new room. Or, judging by the way his footsteps echoed in the distance, a vast underground hall.

Dare shoved the torch into a crack in the worked stone at the end of the tunnel and drew his bow, shooting a Strobe Arrow angled for maximum distance.

One of the nice things he'd discovered about the ability was that even though it used the mana of 20 Snaps, if the arrow flew for long enough it kept strobing until it hit a target, even if it meant more than 30 or 40 individual Snaps.

Which was good, because the arrow arced through empty space before dipping in its trajectory and finally dropping to the ground, skipping a ways farther before rolling to a stop.

And the entire time, what it revealed in its pulsing flashes of light was a wonder beyond wonders.

The ceiling was probably a hundred yards overhead, supported by massive stone columns carved with spiraling ramps that connected to the openings of tunnels in the ceiling leading upwards. All the walls sported tunnels as well, of various sizes, and ramps in the floor led down to tunnels below. A vast network of places to go and things to see.

The vast hall was at least three hundred yards across, since that's where the arrow had finally come to a stop, and most likely equally wide. But rather than simple bare stone around the various ramps and columns, the entire floor was carved into masterfully flowing thoroughfares, garden plots, fountains, and hundreds of mounds that looked like low dwellings.

All dead, sadly. The fountains were dry, the gardens full of withered, blackened remains of vegetation, and the thoroughfares dusty. But in its heyday it must've been a beautiful sight.

How many dwarves had lived here, if that's who'd created this wonder? How long ago? What had forced them to leave?

Dare jumped when he heard more skittering, echoing through the vast hall from somewhere to his left. He whirled and fired off another Strobe Arrow in an equally long distance arc, then immediately nocked another one and backed towards his flickering torch.

The flashing arrow revealed more majestic ruins as it passed into the darkness, then finally illuminated a familiar shape as it ducked into one of the low, round dwellings. A goblin, almost certainly.

No surprise, really. Zuri had told him that her people preferred being underground if they could, for safety. Although with the crude tools they were able to make they couldn't usually tunnel through stone, and stuck to places where they could dig through dirt and soil.

Collisa certainly had its share of subterranean creatures, but among them the most well known were dwarves, goblins, and kobold monsters.

"No need to fear!" Dare called, just loud enough to be heard by the goblin from a few hundred yards away; he didn't want too draw too much attention in this vast, empty space. “I'm a friend to goblins! Do you know of Gar'u'wek of the Avenging Wolf tribe? My friend, and father of my mate.”

There was no answer, and no more sounds to be heard but the fading echoes of his shout. He bit back a sigh. “I'll leave you in peace.”

Turning, he retrieved his torch and made his way back down the tunnel; he'd have to return with better light sources. And in the meantime he could discuss this discovery with his family and friends, and ideally come back with them. Along with Rek and some of his tribe, to negotiate with any goblins who'd found their way into this place.

An abandoned dwarven city might not offer much in the way of experience, or probably not even loot if there were scavengers lurking about. But he was struck by a powerful urge to explore its tunnels and learn its mysteries.

Although that might have to wait for when Dare returned from petitioning for knighthood. He had too much to accomplish at the moment to take the time to explore ancient dwarvish ruins.

Even so, between this and the raid dungeon ruins farther into the mountains he wondered what other secrets could be found in the Gadris Range. He was eager to find them all.

A few minutes later he was out in the fresh, cold mountain air, running up the ravine. Part of him was disappointed to be going back to the mundane grind of scouting, clearing worthwhile spawn points, and searching for party rated monsters, when he could be exploring his underground discovery. But the other part of him was excited to see what else he might find.

As it turned out, nothing else that day. Some spawn points worth farming, a few roaming monsters but none of them party rated, and more than a few majestic views of the surrounding mountains and the region of Bastion to the north.

Still, he was satisfied as he headed for home, going by a different path to clear more spawn points and scout more of the mountains on the way. He'd found the Rotten Shambler, discovered ancient dwarvish ruins, and explored a new area.

All in all an exciting and productive day.

When Dare arrived home he found the other group already returned from leveling, in the stable yard taking care of mounts. They'd needed to rearrange things slightly with Linia part of the group now, making it three people who could benefit from the Home Ward when only two could use it.

The solution had been to have Ilin help Lily, traveling farther out with her because of her lower level, so the two swiftest people could run to their leveling spot and then use the Home Ward to get back. Meanwhile Ireni, Amalisa, and Linia rode horses to their leveling spot, then rode back.

Ireni and Linia seemed happy enough about the day's leveling, and Lily was ecstatic about gaining a full level with Ilin's help. But Dare couldn't help but notice that the Monk was uncharacteristically terse, almost surly, while Amalisa was a bit reserved and distant.

They all went inside together, where they discovered that with all the refugees to accommodate Se'weir had basically kept the kitchen open all day, so people could eat their meals in smaller groups. She looked a bit tired, but happy about being able to help.

She and the others who'd stayed home all gathered around the returning adventurers, ushering them into the dining room and making sure they had full plates in front of them. Everyone was eager to hear how things had gone with everyone, and Dare let the others speak first, wanting to save the best for last.

It came as a surprise when, halfway through the meal, Amalisa abruptly spoke up. "Can we trade back so I'm with Ilin?" she asked, eyes on her plate. "I'm more familiar with him, and I think we work well together."

That led to some raised eyebrows around the table. "Fine by me," Ireni said. "I can go with Lily and we can use the Home Ward back. It'll be a bit slower, but not too much more."

Dare glanced at Ilin, who almost looked embarrassed. "We do

work well together," he admitted. Which seemed to settle the matter.

Finally, everyone else finished reporting their days and Dare found himself the center of expectant attention; most of them knew him well enough to guess that he had big news, even if they'd been content to let him save it for last.

He grinned. "It's been an interesting day." He quickly told them what he'd found.

That drew a lot of interest and excitement, especially when he suggested that they save the lower level party rated monsters so as many people as possible could get the experience bonus and achievement progress.

Although most of the conversation revolved around the dwarven ruins. "I'd love to go with you to explore it all," Lily said, eyes sparkling enthusiastically behind her glasses. "It's amazing to think something like that could just sit there undiscovered for all these years."

Dare supposed he should amend his previous list of subterranean races, since cunids also lived in underground warrens. Although they tended to be more airy, cheerful places closer to the surface.

"The wilds tend to swallow things, as spawn points take over and become increasingly high level if left alone," Ireni said. "Especially up in the mountains, where they're already so unpredictable in levels, and there are so many roaming monsters. Often forgotten wonders are waiting just under our noses."

"Do spawn points ever appear underground?" he asked. "That place was huge enough to justify a few."

Sia took the fore, although she hesitated in her answer. "Yes to spawn points appearing underground, but no to them appearing in ruins. Molzog, God of Deep Places, delves endlessly beneath the earth, creating tunnels, caverns, and chasms. Molzog's Delvings are home to their own variety of plants and animals, including intelligent races, and monster spawn points will appear within them."

That was badass as hell. An entire underground world to

explore.

Dare wanted to see what else she'd tell him about that, but at the moment his interest was the dwarvish ruins. “So we won't find monsters in tunnels and chambers dug by subterranean races?”

She shook her head. “It depends on a few things. If there are intelligent creatures still living there, like the goblin you saw, then it might remain classified as a settlement. Although most often with abandoned ruins the world system turns them into dungeons or even raid dungeons. Usually populated by monsters appropriate to whatever people had lived there before.”

Linia nodded. “Like the ruins the “heroes” up north are so busy looting while the border gets overrun.” Her sarcasm contained a heavy dose of bitterness.

Dare stayed on topic, frowning as something occurred to him. “Wait, though. Dungeons despawn after they're cleared. Does that mean the world system clears away all these ancient ruins and the knowledge of the people who lived there is lost forever?”

The goddess shook her head. “Ruins dungeons are an exception. After being cleared they remain to be explored, and depending on what happens next, whether enough people remain or they're abandoned again, they'll either go back to being a dungeon or stay empty.”

“So what would happen if we decided to move into the ruins and rebuilt the underground city?” Se'weir asked, eyes dancing eagerly. “My tribe could join us!”

“Pass,” Leilanna said immediately, making a face.

Pella nodded, ears drooping. “That doesn't sound comfortable at all.”

“And what about Eloise?” Zuri asked. “I wouldn't mind living there if it came to it, but we can't abandon our home.”

Dare nodded. “It might be a place to retreat to if there's ever a major threat and we could find a way to relocate Eloise. And I'm excited to explore the place and could even see people settling there. The main hall I saw really was beautiful . . . if everything could be restored, with working fountains and some sort of artificial sun, it would be an amazing place to live."

Felicia, who was sitting near Zuri holding Gelaa, shifted eagerly. "We should contact Gorfram and Ulma and the other dwarven Irregulars! They might even know something about this place."

He liked that idea. Dwarves settling in the mountains would mean trading opportunities, and would help civilize the area around Nirim Manor even more.

"What if the party we put together to kill whatever party rated monsters you find swings by the place to explore a little?" Ireni asked. "We could bring lights and rope and other gear and see what we find."

Everyone seemed to agree with that. To the point it was decided that if Dare was able to find one more party rated monster in his search, the group would set out the next day to kill it and the Rotten Shambler and then explore the ruins.

By that time it was late enough that people were nodding off. Felicia had passed the baby back to Zuri and fallen asleep with her head on Pella's lap, and Dare wasn't the only one who kept starting awake as the murmured conversation around him took on a dreamlike quality.

He finally excused himself to bed, which was the cue for everyone else to do the same. He carried Gelaa to the nursery and helped Zuri put her to bed, then with a chuckle carried his goblin fiancee to bed as well at her sleepy insistence.

Everyone was tired enough that after undressing and piling into bed together, most fell asleep immediately. Or at least so Dare assumed, since he did.

* * * * *

Dare threw himself into the search for party rated monsters with full enthusiasm after that, looking forward to the prospect of leading a party into the dwarven ruins as a reward for his efforts.

To his disappointment, in spite of his best efforts it took eight days to finally have some luck, in a ravine deep in the mountains past the spot where he'd found the entrance to the lost underground kingdom. In that time he managed to reach Level 36, which was actually a pretty good speed, so he considered himself to be making good progress.

Still, after killing these 2 party rated monsters he'd still have 3 more to find to finish the achievement, unless of course he wanted to tackle the Ancient Outpost Watcher. And only 3 weeks, 4 at the most if he really delayed to the last second, to accomplish it.

The party rated monster he found was a stone golem or elemental of some sort, a dark gray, featureless humanoid maybe six or so inches taller than him and almost creepily skinny, like aliens looked in a lot of movies. His Adventurer's Eye identified it as: "Basalt Animate. Monster, Party Rated. Level 29. Attacks: Durable, Null Magic Shell, Weighty Blow, Crushing Tackle, Shift Earth, Land Swim, Headbutt."

Didn't sound particularly fun to fight, but from what Dare could see it didn't have any ranged attacks or movement speed increases, which was always good to see.

He might've headed home a bit earlier than he strictly needed to that evening, passing on a couple potential spawn points in his rush. He even made it home before everyone else for once, and so veered by the new settlement the refugees were raising on his land.

Thus far they hadn't gotten farther than gathering piles of logs for cabins, digging a few basements in the hard, half-frozen soil, and marking out plots to build on. Including a large communal structure similar to an old viking feast hall where they'd all live while the other houses were being built.

Irawn was there with a few other men, notching logs so they could be fitted together to make sturdy cabin walls. It was laborious work using axes, and even in the chill evening air they were all shirtless and sweating profusely.

Dare grabbed an axe and pitched in for a bit, grateful for the boosts to strength and stamina he'd gotten from Power Up. In fact, he was a log notching machine compared to the more wiry felids.

When he finally declared he was heading home the others decided to call it a day as well. They exchanged banter on the short walk, and he was pleased to conclude that the men would make good neighbors if they decided to stay.

Dinner was a flurry of planning for the party to set out the next day. They'd already planned out who'd be coming, and the lowest levels among their companions had been working extra hard to get high enough level to participate.

A party was capped at 9 members, and in order to invite any more you had to make it a raid. Still, nine spots was plenty for the people able and wanting to go.

Thanks to Lily's incredible efforts she was already Level 19, blowing his and even Ireni's already mind-blowing leveling pace out of the water. It meant she'd be able to get credit for the Level 29 kill, which was great news.

Then there was Linia at 24, Amalisa at 24, Zuri at 30, Leilanna at 30, Ilin at 31, Ireni at 31, and to fill out the party Rek at 25.

It was the biggest party Dare had been in other than Lord Zor's raid. Since he so far out-leveled most of those he'd invited it would trash his own experience from the monster kills themselves, although he'd still get the bonuses.

But that was just fine with him since his main goal was the achievement.

They'd also planned for several goblins with experience exploring underground to accompany them to check the ruins, and were prepared with glowstones, torches, rope, climbing harnesses, pickaxes, rock chisels and hammers, and shovels.

This time, not only would they be able to see where they were and what they were doing, but would be able to clear any blockages they encountered.

Dare couldn't wait. He felt like he had as a kid eagerly anticipating a trip to the amusement park.

The excitement of the next day's outing had everyone in an extra frisky mood, even those who wouldn't be going like Pella and

Se'weir. So even though they headed to bed later than usual they stayed up a bit longer making love.

He was put through his paces by his eager lovers, and by the time he finally cuddled up between Se'weir and Pella he was so worn out he drifted off immediately.

The next morning was a whirlwind of activity, and the group made for a merry gathering as they mounted up to head into the mountains, with Dare, Ilin, and Lily running on foot. Pella, Se'weir, Felicia, and the others remaining behind all waved from the gate as they set off, some looking disappointed about not being able to go.

Especially his dog girl fiancee, who was getting so close to delivering twins, and Linia's little sister who sulked while trying to pretend like she wasn't.

Not wanting to waste opportunities, when the party passed spawn points everyone Level 30 and over would drop from the party, so the others could clear them. It still wasn't as good for them as a day of committed farming at their usual spawn points, not even with the higher level monsters giving better experience. But it was still pretty good.

Amalisa even got to Level 25 along the way, an event they all celebrated. She got a few new enchantments that would be far more useful for the higher level people with her Enchanter main class, and with her Spellwarder subclass got a new spell that did low damage but put a minor snare on the enemy.

Dare wasn't sure it would stack with other snares, especially not Zuri's Nature's Curse, but he could imagine a Spellwarder would find it invaluable for solo leveling.

Speaking of his goblin fiancee, she looked clearly antsy the farther they got from Nirim Manor, obviously worried about Gelaa. Se'weir and Pella were taking care of her, and since Pella was producing milk she could nurse the baby.

Still, he wondered if he hadn't pushed too hard encouraging her to come out with him today. She genuinely seemed done with leveling and had little interest, even in achievements.

It made him miss the days when they'd hunted monsters together, just the two of them.

Zuri caught him looking and gave him a wan smile. "One last adventure before I settle down?" she said gamely, seeming to read his thoughts.

Dare smiled back. "Of the monster hunting sort. I plan to have many other adventures with you throughout our very long, blissfully happy lives together."

Her eyes softened and she held out her arms. Surprised but pleased, he lifted her out of her saddle, Ireni obligingly taking her pony's leads, and he carried his tiny fiancee the way he so often had in their adventures together.

It felt nice to him, right, and by her happy sigh as she snuggled beneath his cloak she obviously felt the same. "This, I'll miss," she admitted, kissing his neck.

In spite of the lighthearted mood of the party, they set a hard pace for the horses. They had a lot of ground to cover today, especially if they hoped to kill the two party rated monsters in time to explore the dwarven ruins.

On the plus side, the monsters themselves didn't look as if they would be a problem.

The Level 26 Rotten Shambler, for all its fearsome size, was almost a joke to a full party that mostly out-leveled it. They ripped through it with almost ludicrous speed before it could even land a hit on Ilin, who was serving as tank while buffed and shielded by Ireni.

In spite of that ease its drops were as good as any party rated monster, a hundred or so gold and loot that would sell for a few hundred more. As well as a few grisly trophies Dare wasn't eager to display even if they did offer a prestige boost, which Rek and his goblins asked to take when nobody else seemed interested.

The highlight was an Exceptional quality necklace that would be useful for the casters, giving a modest boost to the size of their mana pool. After some debate they decided Ireni would benefit most from it.

After looting the monster they wasted no time mounting up and continuing on, celebrating as they went.

Their path took them past more spawn points for the low levels to clear. And while they didn't take the time to enter the dwarven ruins as they passed the narrow gully in the ravine, they paused for a quick meal at the entrance to further discuss the place.

It wasn't that anyone doubted Dare's description of it, but seeing the rune-marked wall with the square cut tunnel plunging into the mountain fanned everyone's excitement.

Dare hadn't taken the time to inspect the runes before, assuming he wouldn't be able to read them. But he'd forgotten that the translation stones worked with reading as well as spoken languages, and dwarvish was one of the ones the stone worked for.

It was obviously an ancient version of the language, and the Enchanter who'd created their stones must not have known the archaic words and phrases. So there were gaps in the writing, or odd translation errors.

Although surprisingly the names and numbers were all intact; maybe they used a different system than the runes. One that had lasted the years better.

Above and around the sides of the entrance was carved boldly: "Gurzan's Last Hold. Kin of Bolzk Emberbeard. Ware to enemies . . . your doom beneath the mountain . . . kingdom of delvers that will last a thousand generations."

Of course, it probably didn't help that the runes were weathered in some places. Although not as much as Dare might've expected given the ancient feel of the ruins.

"What do you think killed them all off?" Leilanna asked, studying the runes as well.

"Who knows," Linia replied with a shrug. "Plenty of dangers in the world, and monster hordes are only a few years or decades of untended spawn points away from overrunning kingdoms on the edge of the wilds."

Dare glanced at Ireni, who'd be in a better position to know the fate of the dwarves than any of them, but she just smiled back mysteriously.

After a hasty lunch they left Rek's skilled tunnelers behind to begin explorations, the young hobgoblin urging them to be careful of any potential threats in the vast hall and flee at the first sign of danger.

"You've got a party of adventurers due to come back in a few hours," he said with a laugh, clapping one of his smaller tribesmen on the back. "No need to be heroes yourselves."

With time getting away from them they began leaving spawn points untouched and focused on getting to the meadow deep in the mountains where Dare had found the Basalt Animate.

Like with the Level 26 party rated monster, the Level 29 was straightforward enough. It took over four times as long to kill because of all its defensive abilities, but with its weaknesses the ranged members of the party were able to take it down from a distance.

The only hiccup, more of an inconvenience than a real threat, was when the stone creature used Land Swim and disappeared beneath the earth, moving the dirt easily with its powerful limbs and tunneling at almost running speeds for most of the party.

Of course, it raised a furrow of dirt everywhere it went, so it wasn't exactly stealthy. The obnoxious part was they couldn't do anything to it while it was underground, and it refused to come out until it had a target to hit. So Ilin ran in protected by one of Ireni's barriers, bracing for the worst.

The Basalt Animate burst from the ground in a flying punch, like some sort of superhero.

But in spite of the speed and power of its attack the wary Monk was able to dodge at the last second, then kite the monster away. Meanwhile the rest of the party finished chipping away at the moving stone until it finally crumbled in pieces.

At which point it became diamonds.

Not a lot, and most pretty small. But even so they guessed the haul was worth upwards of five hundred gold. Se'weir would most likely be happy to see them, with her Jeweler class. The monster also dropped several materials for earth enchantments, which were much more exciting; those mostly provided defensive bonuses for armor pieces and were prized by tanks and melee fighters.

The trophy for the monster was a large diamond that was so flawed it would probably be worthless even if it was cut into smaller pieces, which they found inside the Basalt Animate's head.

"You know," Dare mused, looking at the fallen elemental as they took a few minutes basking in their victory. "Am I insane for thinking we could try the Ancient Outpost Watcher?" It would mean a lot less time exploring the dwarven ruins since it was a few hours there, and then the same time back.

But still . . . flush from the easy victories, he had his eyes on a third party rated monster in one day. That much closer to finishing his achievement.

They all stared at him in disbelief. "You mean the Level 39 that practically made you shit yourself when you first saw it?" Leilanna asked. "The one that could kill half the members of our party in one hit?"

"I can kite tank it now that I've got Escape Bonds," he protested.

"Yeah, until the second time it grabs you and proceeds to rip you to pieces," Ilin said. "I'm certainly in no position to take it on at my level."

Dare sighed, giving up. "Yeah, I'm insane to think it. It's just frustrating to have it sitting there tantalizingly, when I've still got three party rated monsters to kill in less than a month."

"Hire a tank from Terana," Linia suggested. "If the achievement is what matters then you can be more generous with the loot."

Ireni nodded. "How about I arrange it? The Fighter you fought beside against the monster horde is Level 34, and with my barriers he'd be up to the task. You keep scouting and finding more party rated monsters, and I'll make sure you can kill them before the time is up."

That was a good solution, and took some of the weight off his shoulders. “Thanks,” he said, leaning down to kiss her briefly. “Not sure what I'd do without you.”

“Get yourself killed trying to kite tank a monster with snare, root, and stagger effects?” she said with a grin, to easy laughter from the others.

Wrapping an arm around his petite redheaded fiancee, he turned towards the horses. “Well in that case, let's explore an ancient dwarvish kingdom!”

Chapter Seventeen

Beneath the Mountain

When the party reached the vast subterranean hall they discovered that Rek's goblins had been cautious but busy.

Dare would estimate that about a hundred yards in all directions were now lit by torches interspersed with campfires, he assumed intended to help keep away roaming monsters and predators. The high ceiling overhead was still shrouded in shadows, and he reminded himself to keep an eye directed upwards in case of flying threats.

The previous view he'd had of the hall, briefly lit by his Strobe Arrows, had been mysterious and wondrous. But now, seeing it in proper light, Gurzan's Last Hold was even more awe-inspiring.

Every inch of stone had been expertly worked by dwarvish craftsmen, with avenues lined with benches, garden plots clearly marked out between stretches of open ground for monuments, odd arrangements of rock formations, the prevalent dome-shaped homes, and other features of what had once been a bustling dwarven city. Even the walls and ceilings had elaborate carvings, as well as bare patches where he assumed tapestries or some other form of decoration had hung.

If this cavern had already existed this massive and in this uniform shape, which was unlikely, the work he saw would be the work of centuries by thousands of diligent dwarvish stonemasons.

Barring magic of some sort, he supposed.

Time had been surprisingly kind to the labors of the dwarves, aside from random signs of clear destruction and defacement. As well as ancient remnants of animal nests, rubbish from roaming monsters, and a thick coating of dust.

"Well this is something," Linia breathed. The world-wise

mercenary looked awed in spite of her studied show of nonchalance.

Lily was practically bouncing in place, looking at everything with eyes gleaming behind the reflection of firelight on her glasses. “This is why I left the warren,” she blurted. “To see things like this!”

“To think this was waiting only days from my village,” Zuri agreed. “We could've lived here in comfort instead of cowering from slavers until we were finally caught.”

“And my village,” Rek said. “But of course exploring this far into the mountains would've been suicide for most.” He shot a quick look at Dare.

“Well now that we've spent a few minutes admiring it,” Dare said, rubbing his hands together. “What do you say we give this place a closer look?”

At first they walked together, poking their heads into abandoned dome houses, meeting halls lined with stone benches, storage chambers, and other places whose use was less obvious. Peering into the various tunnels branching off from the main hall and speculating on what mysteries lay at the end of each. They all carried torches, lanterns, or glowstones, so there was plenty of light to see by.

Dare had noted the lack of any dwarvish remains or abandoned possessions before, and he confirmed it now. The homes were nothing but bare stone, yawning doorways opening out into the vast cavern. The long-dead plants in the garden plots were desiccated stalks, and everything that could conceivably be picked up and carried off had been.

Perhaps the dwarves had been forced to flee but had time to take everything with them. Or perhaps they'd all died right here, but in the intervening ages scavengers had carried it all off.

It didn't bode well for loot prospects, but he didn't have to tell the others to search for secret rooms and compartments because Rek had already stressed it quite clearly.

After a few minutes of finding nothing worth noting they agreed to split up into groups of three, each group taking at least one person over Level 30 in case of surprise threats. Dare had also managed to convince all his companions who were high enough level to get Snap, which at the moment was only the magic users for whom it unlocked earlier, to put one of their precious ability points into it.

Between that and the torches, they worked out a system of light signals to communicate from a distance.

Some groups kept going deeper into the hall, some branched off and began exploring the nearest tunnels. Dare, accompanied by Lily and Ireni, led the way to the closest of the massive columns and started climbing the spiral ramp up to one of the tunnels in the ceiling.

Honestly, he was surprised everyone hadn't chosen to search one of the ceiling tunnels, since to him they were clearly the most exciting. As it turned out he wasn't wrong to think that, either.

The ramp had no railing, but thankfully was wide and smooth and had a rough texture that made for solid footing. Even so, Lily huddled close against his back and he could hear her rapid breathing. "Afraid of heights?" he asked gently.

"It helps that the footing is solid." she said with a shaky laugh. "But this high up I get antsy if I don't have anything to hold onto."

Dare reached back and took her hand. "There," he said, smiling back at her, "now you do."

She smiled back and gave his hand a squeeze. Or as it turned out just gripped tightly; her nervousness was no joke.

They'd been getting along great since she'd come to Nirim Manor, with daily starlit walks, playful runs, quiet evenings sitting together with the others reading or talking or playing games, and lots of pleasant day to day moments. Following Rosa's advice he was taking it slow, but he felt like it was about time he started making more grand romantic gestures.

He had a few things planned, like cooking her a romantic dinner and taking her on an outing to a breathtaking vista he knew of nearby. He'd also tried his hand at writing some love poems and notes, with lots of helpful advice from his fiancees.

They'd yet to share their first kiss, but he thought that if the dinner went well that might be a good time for it. Embarrassing as it was, he was taking his cues from the romance novels Lily loved so he could give her what she'd dreamed of.

As best Dare was able, at least; real life wasn't a story, and things didn't always go perfectly. But so far they'd gone pretty damn good, and he looked forward to getting closer to the romantic bunny girl.

Lily relaxed when they entered the tunnel at the top of the ramp, which he was interested to see was round in shape rather than squared off like the others they'd found. He wondered if there was some significance to that.

The immediate thought that came to mind was a trap that involved a giant round boulder careening out of the darkness and squashing them flat. Which made him watch even more closely for tripwires and pressure plates and other triggers.

So closely, in fact, that it was Ireni who squeaked and stopped dead, eyes wide as she stared up the tunnel. “Goddess,” she breathed, clutching at his cloak to stop him.

Dare followed her gaze to see dark shapes looming in the deeper darkness at the edge of the torchlight. They didn't move, but every instinct screamed they weren't just rocks or other debris sitting on the tunnel floor.

He considered using Strobe Arrow and deliberately shooting to miss, but didn't want to risk riling up whatever those were. Instead he looked at his companions. “Put your heads up beside mine,” he whispered.

After a confused pause both women leaned forward, poking their heads out to be level with his. Dare held his hand up above and behind their peripheral vision, then Snapped several times in quick succession and activated his Adventurer's Eye.

The moderately bright light washed away the darkness, and he was immediately glad he hadn't shot an arrow and that they'd stopped when they had.

The shapes turned out to be monsters, odd fungus creatures like misshapen mushrooms with arms and legs. They were barely in range of his Eye, which meant he and his companions were almost within their perception circle.

Because the three monsters were Level 52, 52, and 53.

Lily, who'd moved up beside him so she wouldn't be blinded by his Snap, gasped and said what they were all thinking. “Dungeon entrance?”

Dare quickly pulled her back, since at her level she was dangerously close to aggroing them. Just to be safe he retreated back a dozen steps with the two women huddled close to him, then explained what he'd seen with his Eye.

“I don't get it,” he said when he was finished, staring at the shadowy silhouettes of the mushroom beings. “You said ruins could become dungeons, so this isn't a surprise.” He pointed back down the tunnel towards the vast hall they'd just climbed out of. “But why isn't that also part of the dungeon?”

Ireni shrugged. “It's not always the full ruins, especially if part of the ruins are being scavenged or settled.”

Lily frowned. “Still, why this little tunnel up in the ceiling? The entire ruins is basically abandoned, and this part became the dungeon?”

The bookish redhead grinned at her. “We're in an abandoned dwarvish city. For all we know that giant cavern back there is just the mudroom to a complex that fills this entire mountain.”

That was an exciting thought. But either way, they weren't going anywhere near a Level 52+ dungeon anytime soon. Even if, going by the monsters stats, the dungeon was party difficulty and wouldn't require a raid.

Still, a second dungeon in the mountains. Both less than a day's hard travel from Nirim Manor, in the middle of nowhere so they wouldn't be discovered by random travelers or adventurers, and waiting to be conquered once his group grew strong enough.

That was pretty exciting.

At the moment, though, the thought that if those things suddenly aggroed they'd rip the three of them to shreds, or going by their attacks poison and suffocate them with spores, had Dare backing away even farther with the others. Only when they disappeared into the gloom did he breath easier, irrational as that was.

As if not being able to see them meant they were no longer a threat. Which made him imagine them creeping up on him and his companions, ready to burst into view again like something out of a nightmare, even though he knew that wasn't how monsters behaved.

Skin crawling, he quickened his pace back towards the ramp at the end of the tunnel.

The tunnel hadn't branched anywhere, so there was nothing more to explore up here until they could brave the high level dungeon. Dare breathed a bit easier as they stepped onto the ramp, even Lily seeming relieved after the close call with the mushroom monsters.

He wasted no time leaning out over the drop to the floor below and Snapping to get everyone's attention. Then when he got several answering flashes of light from Snaps and obscured then revealed torches, he risked raising his voice to a shout that echoed through the huge cavern.

"We found Level 52 and higher monsters in this tunnel! There might be more in other tunnels or deeper in this cavern, so tread cautiously . . . they could aggro before the lower level people are even aware of them."

"Be especially careful of the ramps leading upwards!" Ireni added.

There were answering shouts of assent, and more than a little alarm, from the other groups. Dare also saw the torches flowing back towards the entrance, his companions retreating to explored ground just to be safe.

"You heard them," Rek barked at his goblins. "Double torches for added light!"

That was a smart idea, and everyone doubled up on torches, pushing the darkness farther back. Dare's group made their way back down to the ground, where he left Ireni and Lily behind and headed for the next column ramp to see if its tunnel, too, led into the dungeon.

On top of holding his torches he used Snap to see farther ahead, and was glad he had when he spotted more of the mushroom creatures looming out of the darkness.

Okay, so multiple entrances? A much bigger dungeon than the Glittering Caves? It just confirmed that they needed to be even more careful searching the rest of the ruins.

Although a part of him wasn't sure whether to be excited or disappointed by the prospect that they might not get to explore much of this place after all, at least until they were much higher level. It meant nobody else had explored this place for a long time, either, and the secrets of Gurzan's Last Hold might still be there to be found.

Grinning at the prospect, he turned and headed back down the tunnel.

“Landgiver!” a high, piping voice called from a lower curve of the ramp as he reached the end of the tunnel. “Come quickly!”

Fearing the worst, Dare activated Cheetah's Dash and bolted down the ramp at borderline dangerous speeds, even with the solid footing. He soon came in sight one of Rek's tunnel experts running towards him.

To his relief the man's sharp features showed excitement rather than fear. “We found something!” he called eagerly.

Well that was vague. “What?” he shouted back.

Rather than answer the goblin scrambled back the way he'd come, beckoning. Maybe he wanted it to be a surprise.

Bemused, Dare followed. And then lost patience and outpaced the messenger when down below he saw several flickers from his companions Snapping or obscuring their torches, over by a far corner of the vast hall.

He met everyone near a ramp leading down into the ground, which had apparently been hidden by a stone slab seamlessly fit into the floor that Ilin, Rek, and a few of his goblins had laboriously moved.

That was promising in and of itself, but even better the bottom of the ramp was sealed with a sturdy steel door, etched with forbidding dwarvish runes warning intruders to keep away.

Dare eagerly inspected the solid barrier; there didn't seem to be any doorknob or lever to open it. “Ideas to get through?”

Rek hefted a pick. “Dig out the stone around it.”

“That'll take forever,” Leilanna argued. She stepped forward, hands whooshing alight. “I could probably melt through the hinges if I can find them.”

“Dwarves are skilled at anti-magic traps,” Ireni pointed out. “Also what if there's something valuable just on the other side of that door? We don't want to destroy it getting through.”

Dare grabbed a pry bar and hammer from one of the goblins. “How about a combination of the two . . . let's try to break the hinges.”

The gap between the door and the stone frame was practically invisible, masterful dwarvish craftsmanship. But with some determined hammering he was able to punch through, not finding a hinge but making a small opening to the other side.

One of the experienced goblin tunnelers pressed his pointed nose to the opening, sniffing. “Air is stale and dead,” he said. “Very old feel. Odd smell to it . . . metal, wax, oil.”

“Anything dangerous?” Rek asked. “Poison? Toxic mold?”

The goblin shook his head with a shrug. “Smells like a chamber sealed for many years, that's all.”

The young chieftain grunted in satisfaction and barked out orders, and Dare soon found himself displaced by goblins with picks and pry bars busily working around the edge of the door. With the pace they were going everyone agreed they'd be through before the rest of the group could head out to explore more and then return, so everyone stuck around to talk about what they were going to find.

The general consensus was treasure.

"Dwarves tunnel through entire mountains like industrious ants," Leilanna said. "They have to be digging up all sorts of gems and precious metals and who knows what else in the deep places of the earth."

Linia nodded. "And they only spend as much as they have to, and hoard the rest."

"Maybe we'll find a giant diamond the size of my head!" Zuri said enthusiastically. "Or truesilver! Dwarves are always digging for truesilver."

Dare could admit he joined the budding sense of anticipation. He just knew the dwarves who'd lived here wouldn't have gone to this much effort to hide this ramp and whatever lay beyond that thick steel door unless it was something worth protecting.

Finally Rek gave a shout and they all grabbed ropes and pulled together, bringing the door crashing down onto the ramp with a grinding squeal.

To reveal treasure beyond what Dare could've dreamed.

"Books!" Lily blurted, eagerly stepping past him. "An ancient library!"

"I'd say more likely a records room," Ireni said, also slipping around him.

Dare followed them and looked around the small room, at the unfamiliar but recognizable objects inside. Cubbies for scrolls and shelves for books. More shelves stacked with thinly hammered metal plates connected by rings like an ancient version of a binder. They were mostly gold, brass, or bronze, and were etched with small, closely spaced runes. There were also stacks of clay and hard wax tablets.

And in one corner of the room a stone table with writing and etching implements, along with more wax tablets, a stack of unused plates, a punching tool, and a few loose rings.

The chamber had been sealed for so many centuries or millennia that all the scrolls and books had rotted to dust, even in the stale dry air. But the dwarves, either primitive enough they mostly used those other methods or wise enough to write for the ages, had mainly made records that could last.

Dare picked up a small book of gold sheets, grunting slightly at the unexpected weight; if it hadn't been a priceless record of a lost civilization it still would've been valuable just based on the precious metal.

Again he marveled at the convenience and sheer awesomeness of the translation stones, even if they couldn't fully translate the archaic writing. He eagerly began to read:

“Being an . . . Torgan Irongrip, King Beneath the Mountain, of the . . . Gurzan's Last Hold, in the year 553 of the Great Exploration. The hall of Gurzan . . . 23,100 delvers, expanding 218 . . . beneath the Spine of Gurzan.

“In the seventh year of Torgan's reign came many humans of Old Galedor, but . . . Kin of Bolzk Firebeard, Deepest Delver and Master of All, were first to . . . as always. For three years there was trade between . . . Gurzan's Last Hold, but then in the year 556 . . . Heroes of Galedor, bringing fire and ruin to the surface lands.

“In that year were the Gates of Throngil Deepdelver sealed . . . south of the Spine of Gurzan, where many elves had founded refuges from the orcish invaders. Long has the enmity between the Kin of Bolzk and the . . . but for a time there was trade. Then did the elves go to war with the humans of New Galedor . . . the Throat of Hilzar, and . . .”

Dare carefully set the plates down, looking around him. If he wasn't mistaken that sounded like an account from soon after the Shalin continent was discovered and the races began to settle it. So how long ago would that be?

He turned to Ireni. “How old is Collisa?”

She grinned at him as she looked up from a wax tablet she'd been perusing. “How old is Earth?”

Lily scrunched up her nose in confusion. “How old is dirt? What's that supposed to mean?”

"I mean how long have the races of Collisa lived here?" Dare clarified. "How ancient is this world's history?"

Sia took the fore. "I don't suppose it would be a spoiler to tell you in broad terms." She looked at him gravely. "Nearly a hundred thousand years, my love. So old that some races have died out entirely, and others have sprung up and grown to prominence. So old that the dawn of the oldest races has been forgotten to the mists of time." She paused meaningfully. "By most."

"Then this is priceless," he said, waving around the room.

"To those who value the knowledge of the past, without a doubt," Ireni agreed, returning to the fore. "The dwarves will wish to have this."

"I wish to have it, too," Dare said. At her arched eyebrow he laughed. "I mean I want to copy all these texts for our library. Especially if we can find an expert who can read what the translation stones aren't able to. After that the dwarves should certainly have the actual artifacts . . . they'll probably fetch a good price."

Leilanna, who was poking through the ruins of the scrolls and paper books, snorted. "Make a gift of them. You'll win the eternal friendship of the dwarves, and they'll shower you with gold, gems, and masterfully crafted items in gratitude."

She grinned at him. "Whereas if you tried to sell them such precious artifacts of their past, they'd hate your guts and haggle for every copper. They might even go to war over it . . . dwarves take things like the knowledge of their ancestors and their ancestral homes very seriously. Which is why they're always going on quests to reclaim them."

Dare looked around. "Think they'll want to reclaim this place?"

"Probably," his dusk elf fiancee said with a laugh. "So we'd better explore the hell out of it before letting them know it's here. And then hint that we rushed to them with the knowledge of its discovery as soon as we could. If they flock here grateful for our service to their kind we'll have the best neighbors imaginable."

Ireni cleared her throat. "Better to wait until we clear the dungeon, then make it sound as if the entire thing was guarded by monsters. Easy enough to obfuscate the truth without actually lying, which is generally not a good idea with dwarves . . . they hold long grudges."

Dare felt his heart sink. "It would take over a year to get up to that level. And the number of people willing to level with me seems to shrink by the day."

He was a bit disheartened by how everyone looked away, not disputing that claim.

Linia cleared her throat. "I know dwarves. Give them the records after you've copied them, but tell them you won't show them where you found the records until after you've cleared the dungeon. Loot rules apply even for ancient ancestral homes, and as long as you don't put it off for too long they'll give you a few years. If for no other reason than gratitude at your gift."

"If he does it like that they'll show their gratitude by not going to war for his reticence, instead of by showering him with gifts," Leilanna pointed out.

The catgirl smirked at her. "Then I guess it's a question of whether an ancient dwarvish ruin has more treasure than the gratitude offered by a bunch of greedy dwarves."

Dare set the plates down. "I like Linia's option best. Both sides get what they want, both sides feel like they've been fairly dealt with."

"Assuming the dwarves aren't bastards about it," the dusk elf muttered; true to form, there didn't seem to be much love lost between the two races.

Linia clapped him on the back. "Approach the dwarvish contingent of the Irregulars first. I'll make introductions and speak on your behalf."

"Will that help?" Rek asked doubtfully. "You said you're not much more than a recruit, right? What influence do you have with your mercenary company?"

Linia hesitated, and Dare almost thought she looked a bit cagey.

"I've got friends in high places."

He was willing to take her word for it. "All right, let's pack all this up," he said. "*Carefully*. As if it's all made of dirt clods that could crumble at the slightest touch."

Ireni rested a hand on an ancient tablet. "Some of it practically is."

His redheaded betrothed personally oversaw loading the tablets, and left it to Dare, Lily, and Ilin as the most surefooted to carry them. "You know what happens if you break these?" she told Dare in a serious voice as she carefully strapped his pack on him.

He grinned at her. "No sex for a month?"

Her return look was grave. "Ancient knowledge that may have no other source could be lost forever."

Dare swallowed, making sure to move with the utmost care as he made his way up the ramp.

Only to find his companions warily circling a scrawny, raggedly dressed goblin who'd emerged from the nearest tunnel.

"Easy!" Dare said, stepping forward. "Hello, friend, how can we help you?"

The goblin looked at him flatly with overlarge yellow eyes. "You called to me when you intruded may sleep cycles ago. You said you came in peace."

"And that was enough for you to approach us alone?" Rek asked as he came up beside Dare, somewhere between amused and derisive. "You've got some balls on you for a tunnel rat."

The strange goblin stood with head raised and shoulders back, resigned but determined. "If you kill me then at least my people will know you come with the sword. They'll have time to flee, or prepare the traps."

Dare sternly waved Rek back. "We're here for peaceful purposes," he said. "We live nearby on the surface and want to explore these ruins."

The small creature glowered at him. "These ruins are our home.

You've invaded our home and pillaged wealth we lay claim to." He waved at the heavily laden packs of tablets and metal sheets the group was carrying.

Rek growled and idly lowered his spear. "We could pillage even more, tunnel rat."

The underground dweller shrank back, and Dare cleared his throat sternly. "That would go against our agreement, Chieftain Rek'u'gar. I'm obliged to deal with any crime I witness."

The young hobgoblin glared at him in challenge for a few moments before grunting and stepping back.

Dare turned to the strange goblin. "Do you live in this hall, specifically?" he asked. The goblin shook his head sullenly. "Are you of dwarvish descent and claim the records we found?" Again, a sullen head shake. "Then these ruins remain unclaimed and open to explorers. You could've found this hidden trove instead of us, but as we found it, we claim it. As we claim the right to explore all areas you are not currently living in and have not marked as your territory."

The goblin spokesman's yellow eyes burned resentfully. "And what if we came to the surface and pillaged all the land around your home? Would you think that equally fair?"

"I would, since it's unclaimed land. And while you're up there feel free to bring goods to trade with us . . . we'll give you generous deals." Dare reached into his pouch and pulled out a handful of silver, dropping them into a smaller coin bag and tossing it to the small goblin, who fumbled to catch it. "On top of that, I'd like to hire your people as guides to these ruins. I'd rather be friends with your tribe."

"So you can come enslave us later?" the goblin growled in his squeaky voice, although his eyes gleamed as he hefted the sack, listening to the coins clink.

Dare motioned to Rek. "I've befriended the Avenging Wolves. I've even taken the daughter of their chieftain as a mate to strengthen our alliance. I would like to befriend your tribe as well . . . you're our neighbors, after all."

The ragged goblin began backing away into the darkness. "Take your loot and go, human. We'll speak more of this if you return. Maybe."

Rek waved his spear after him as he disappeared. "The Landgiver offers you peace from a position of strength, rather than simply taking what he wishes as he has the power to do! You're a fool to insult him!"

Dare resolved to leave the young hobgoblin behind the next time they talked to the underground goblin tribe. He could do without the spear waving diplomacy.

Biting back a sigh, he clapped his soon to be brother-in-law on the shoulder. "Come on, let's head home. We've got a long journey ahead of us, with precious cargo."

Chapter Eighteen

Blind

Three days later Dare blearily dragged himself out of bed, ate a hasty breakfast, kissed his loved ones goodbye, and headed out to level.

He could admit he'd spent longer than he should've last night perusing the dwarvish records. He wasn't alone, either, since Lily and Ireni had also joined him.

Ironically, if it had been Earth history he might've found it dull and tedious. The information was dry and mostly focused on dates and large scale events, like the most boring history class he'd ever attended. And the fact that chunks were missing from practically every sentence definitely didn't help.

But it was dwarves! Dwarves talking about dealings with humans and elves and a dozen other races. Talking about delving a vast kingdom beneath the mountain, of their struggles and discoveries.

Hell, they'd unearthed an ancient horror that they'd had to battle for years to defeat, losing thousands of lives in the process. And at a much later date they'd discovered a rich truesilver seam, only to find that dark elves had found it first when two teams of delvers from the different races met.

Spurring a vicious guerilla war full of trapped tunnels, sabotaged and undermined excavations, surprise attacks bursting from solid stone, and other chaos from two stubborn but crafty races that both believed the underground was theirs by right.

It would make for incredible stories if fleshed out. Dare even joked that Lily should write a romance novel about some of the dry accountings of the lineages of dwarvish kings.

Which she seemed surprisingly keen about. She even pressed

him for details about his sexual encounter with Ulma so she had a reference. He felt a bit awkward talking about it with someone he hadn't even kissed yet, but she didn't seem embarrassed so he tried to play it cool.

All in all a pleasant evening with a woman he loved with all his heart and another he was coming to care about deeply. But it meant a late start and a bit of a bad mood about how it would delay the day's progress.

A mood that didn't improve when Ilin pulled him aside before he could head out.

"Master Dare," his friend said, expression solemn, "could I have a word with you somewhere private?"

Dare stared at his friend in surprise; the bald ascetic was usually calm and reserved, but he hadn't been this formal since they first met. If even then.

So what could he possibly want to talk about that required such a solemn question?

"Okay, sure," he said. "The gardens?"

"That would be ideal." Ilin turned and started away.

Dare paused to pat the snow-covered mound where Eloise's seed was buried and murmur a quiet good morning before hurrying after his friend.

The garden was mostly snow and bare branches, although he noticed with amusement that the children had made snowmen (or snow ogres from the looks of it), as well as the usual snow angels and crude crescent forts for snowball fights.

The Monk led him to a secluded spot and took a deep breath; if Dare hadn't known better he would've sworn his friend was a bit nervous. "Master Dare, I wish to speak to you in your capacity as Lady Amalisa's guardian."

Dare started at him blankly. "I wasn't aware I was. She's an independent adult."

Ilin smiled faintly. "Yes, she certainly is." He gave a start and hastily continued, “However, you've taken her into your home and are seeing to her welfare, and through your betrothed Pella you have a connection to her. While Lady Amalisa retains her independence as an adult, she recognizes you as her guardian.”

“She does?” That was the first he was hearing of this.

“It is not uncommon among young noblewomen, if for some reason they must leave home before being wed, to come under the care of a relative or family friend.” His friend's expression tightened. “And while her brother has disinherited her and expelled her from his home, he doesn't have the authority to strip her of her titles or noble heritage. Such an act is the purview of the King, and I doubt Braley will even try to get such approval. So she remains a noblewoman.”

“Okay,” Dare said slowly. “I'm happy to help her until she can find her footing. And if she considers me a guardian I'm honored by her trust and will do my best to prove worthy of it.” He gave the Monk a keen look. “But I'm kind of wondering why *you're* coming to me about something concerning her.”

To his further surprise Ilin turned visibly pink, all the way up to the top of his shaved head. He took several seconds to answer and was practically fidgeting in place before finally blurting, “I'd like to ask your blessing to take Ama's, that is Lady Amalisa's, hand in marriage. And on her behalf would ask you to do her the honor of escorting her down the aisle when the time comes.”

If the previous revelations had come as a surprise, this was an absolute shock. Dare's first thought was that this was a joke, and he had to stifle an incredulous laugh in the face of his friend's obvious sincerity.

“You and Amalisa?” he said carefully. “How?”

The Monk chuckled ruefully. “I assume you're either asking how I can do so since I've given a vow of celibacy, or how we came to reach such a decision.”

Now Dare finally laughed, joining his friend. “Yes.” He hadn't really even considered the possibility, but now that he looked back it seemed obvious, and he felt like he should've realized what was developing between his friends a lot sooner.

The two had been spending a lot of time together with Ilin helping Amalisa level. And when Dare thought about it, the couple seemed well suited to each other. Amalisa was sweet, kindhearted, and innocent, yet also fiercely determined to be independent and step away from the lifestyle that had coddled her from birth.

Ilin, on the other hand, lived his life to improve himself and help others, and was devoted to his friends. Dare could imagine the two turning their drive and passion towards each other, and working together to help those around them and make the world a better place.

He could see them having a real impact on Bastion, Haraldar, and possibly even all of Collisa.

His friend thoughtfully inspected a nearby trellis, woven with a chaotic tangle of small vines. "Firstly, my Order recognizes that people are imperfect. And while they encourage celibacy and asceticism as a path to enlightenment, they view marriage and children as a good and beneficial thing, ideal for most people and the lives they want to live. Those who choose the path of marriage and children can remain part of the Order, only they turn their efforts to the welfare of their family instead."

That was surprisingly reasonable. And to be honest Dare had always thought his friend was too cheerful and outgoing, too happy to enjoy the pleasures of life, to really fit the solemn, disciplined, even stern disposition of an ascetic.

"Honestly I can see you settling down from your life of wandering," he admitted. "You seemed on the verge of that when I invited you to stay with us at Nirim Manor." He paused. "Although I'm very curious how a shy maiden managed to win the heart of an ascetic."

Ilin blushed. "What makes you think it wasn't the other way around?" he asked.

Dare laughed. "You meditate through me having sex a dozen

feet away without batting an eye. Even though you seem inclined to marriage and children, I have to guess you needed a bit of a push."

His friend shrugged, looking a bit sheepish. "I suppose so. Ama hinted at first, more and more obviously, before coming right out and asking if there was ever a chance I might take a wife. And that, if so, would I consider her."

That must've taken quite a bit of courage from the gentle young noblewoman.

Ilin was looking at him expectantly, and with a start Dare remembered a question had been asked. With a broad smile he clapped his friend on the shoulder, then pulled him into a backslapping hug. "I don't feel it's my place to give my blessing, my friend, but I certainly offer my congratulations and full support. And of course I'd be very honored to escort her down the aisle."

Ilin looked unexpectedly relieved. "Thank you," he said, gripping his shoulder tight. "I'll tell Ama we can go forward with our plans." Then he hesitated. "Oh. Ah, those will include some changes."

Dare jumped to the obvious conclusion. "You two are done leveling."

"For good, perhaps, but certainly for the moment," Ilin agreed sadly. "I know you're counting on me to help you with your hunt for party rated monsters, and I will if needed. But starting today I believe we'll ask Ireni to take Linia and Lily out without us. They're close enough level now that they could share experience."

Well, that was his friends' decision to make. And certainly reasonable enough if they planned to start a family. Although it meant he'd have to resign himself to Amalisa not getting any better Enchants for their gear.

A small consideration in the face of the couple's happiness. Dare pushed aside his regret and smiled again. "Well, we should probably plan accommodations. We can renovate one of the guest houses for your family, connect the plumbing and maybe even the heating."

His friend hesitated, looking away. "That's generous, Dare. But we've already spoken of moving to Terana. We want to take over running the orphanage together, and focus on our charitable work. Particularly after the lives lost to the monster horde."

Oh.

"We won't go until after you and the others return from Redoubt to petition for knighthood, of course," Ilin said hastily. "In fact, depending on how severe the winter is we might stay until the weather improves." He laughed. "So I suppose we might take you up on that offer of the guest house after all."

Dare smiled back weakly. "So we'll get to keep you around for a bit longer."

His friend sobered and gripped his shoulder. "You've been a good friend to us, Dare. The best friend a man could hope for. And we've certainly had some memorable adventures together. I hope our friendship lasts to the end of our days, but the future Ama and I wish to build lies on another path."

Dare did his best to match his friend's excitement, for his sake. "A good path, my friend. Terana's not so far away. We'll be able to visit you all the time. And of course you're welcome to visit here as often as you like, for as long as you like. I'm sure Pella will practically insist on it."

"I'm sure she will, and we'll be happy to take you up on that," Ilin said with a grin. He was practically fidgeting. "Please excuse me, I'm going to tell Ama." Pressing his palms together in a short bow, he turned and strode briskly out of the garden.

Dare watched him go, feeling a strange melancholy.

He'd found many lovers, many companions, many friends since coming to Collisa. But he had to acknowledge that Ilin was his only guy friend. His best friend outside of his fiancees.

Part of him had hoped that once the lower level people in their group had caught up closer to them, the Monk would join him in leveling again. That maybe they could even push to the highest level possible together with whoever wanted to join them.

But that was a selfish regret, when Ilin had found true and well deserved happiness. And he would be good to Amalisa, who deserved the same happiness.

That didn't make Dare feel any less at a loss at seeing the future change be-

He was practically bowled over as a fur-wrapped bundle of energy threw herself at him. “Is it true?” Pella squealed, hugging him and spinning them both in place. “Ama's going to marry Ilin?”

Dare should've guessed that his dog girl fiancee would be able to hear, if anyone did. Maybe even from the house. “Easy,” he said with a laugh, resting a gentle hand on her belly. “Now's not the time to be bouncing around like a ping pong ball.”

“I don't know what that is!” she said with a giddy laugh, nuzzling his face with contented noises. “Can you believe it? I'm so happy for them. They're so perfect for each other.” She giggled. “And won't they make such a cute couple, with absolutely adorable babies?”

“They will,” he agreed, his melancholy lifting in the face of Pella's boundless enthusiasm. He really was happy for the couple, and glad that they'd found love together.

“What do you think of them moving to Terana?” he asked, stroking her back as she clung to him.

“I think it's perfect for them!” she replied. “Managing the orphanage and helping people is just how both want to live, and the town will be blessed to have them.” Her face fell slightly. “And sure, I'll miss them when they move, but that just means I'll have to borrow the Home Ward and visit whenever I can.”

The dog girl's enthusiasm resurged, and with a squeal she squirmed out of his arms and bolted for the manor. “Oh, I need to go congratulate her! We have so many plans to make!”

Amusingly enough, it was easy to tell when she found Amalisa, even though the two were out of view, by the excited squeals that filled the air as the women celebrated the happy news.

Dare stared towards the manor with a fading smile as Pella's enthusiasm departed with her. He knew he should go and join the others, who were probably celebrating the good news. But it was sinking in that the last few weeks of leveling alone were likely to be his future as well.

His fiancees, and eventually wives, would stay here with their children. Ilin and Amalisa were leaving to begin their new lives. Lily might never match his level since she didn't need to; her crafting class would allow her to make gear for him from several levels lower as long as she kept her abilities maximized.

And with a combat subclass she couldn't really contribute much to a party.

Besides, she'd already told him that as much as she wanted to explore with him, she wasn't interested in being an adventurer for the rest of her life. And of course if they fell in love and got married and had children, she'd want to stay at Nirim Manor with the others.

That just left him, on his own. It was frustrating to think that everyone he wanted to help level up eventually abandoned it in favor of the life they preferred.

That nobody shared his drive to discover new things, and level up to be able to go on more challenging adventures.

Who would raid the elvish ruins and the dwarvish city with him? Who would explore the wonders of Collisa at his side? Was he going to spend the rest of his life torn between lonely days or weeks out in the wilds, and returning home to his family where he wanted to be for his wives and children?

Torn between his desire for adventure and the wonderful life they'd created at Nirim Manor?

Dare made his way out of the gate and set off towards the mountains. He'd ignore spawn points and go deeper today, looking for party rated monsters.

Possibly the last adventures he'd have with Ilin.

He knew he was wallowing in self pity when he should be happy. That things weren't as bleak as he was painting them out to be. There were still plenty of friends to make, women to romance, adventures to have.

If he was being reasonable, he knew he'd been trying to force two things together that couldn't be: his life as an adventurer and his family life. Sure, it was wonderful to adventure with the women he loved and share those experiences with them.

But ultimately they wanted to be at home, surrounded by the rest of the family and raising their children in peace and contentment. And he wanted that for them.

Even if it meant adventuring alone.

Soon enough he'd perk up again. Look forward to the future and begin making plans. Perhaps he'd join the Adventurer's Guild, find parties with dedicated adventurers who shared his excitement for exploration. Find companions he wanted to travel and level with long term.

But for the moment, his heart was as leaden as the heavy clouds overhead.

* * * * *

Those clouds.

Dare probably should've paid more attention to them. The temperature was plummeting, the wind was picking up, the light was fading even though it was barely past midday, and the charcoal gray clouds overhead were piling up against the mountains with a towering vengeance.

He hadn't found any party rated monsters. He'd gotten barely any experience either since he'd bypassed the spawn points. And best of all, he was rewarded for his determination to explore deep into the mountains by the prospect of a heavy winter storm, maybe even a blizzard.

Cursing silently to himself, he tore his gaze from from the sky and bolted back the way he'd come using Cheetah's Dash. Not at a pace he could sustain for hours, but at a run that would leave him puking his guts out in an exhausted huddle on the ground in a fraction of that time.

Getting caught in a blizzard would suck, but he was confident he could survive it. He just wanted to get out of the mountains first if he could.

Running on steep, snowy, and often icy mountain slopes, while all the time the wind whipped at him and flurries of snow drove against his face, was a bit reckless. But thankfully by some miracle he got down to the plains without breaking his neck.

By that time the flurries had become a swirling white wall, and Dare realized the storm really had become a blizzard. Even so he trusted his struggling senses, bolstered by Hunter abilities, just enough to keep pushing on instead of finding shelter and hunkering down.

He was so close to home. If he could just reach Rek's village then from there Nirim Manor would be easy to find. He just had to go a little farther.

Although he should've known that was a bad idea.

Dare remembered hearing somewhere that blizzards could be so dangerous for getting lost in that some people had been known to step outside into them, walk a couple feet away from the door, and end up unable to find their way back.

He thought he was going north, based on the slope of the ground and his familiarity with the terrain. But with the snow swirling around him, and especially driving into his face hard enough he had to squint and raise an arm against the onslaught, his visibility had been reduced to a few feet and he stumbled blindly.

About the time he ran face first into a tree he didn't even see coming, he realized he'd made a mistake, possibly a fatal one. But after hours of stubbornly stumbling forward he felt committed, sure that if he tried to set up camp now he'd freeze to death before he could manage it.

Besides, at this point he was sure he'd gotten so close to home that if he set up his tent, in the morning he'd find himself in the lee of Nirim Manor's walls.

It was bound to happen eventually, and Dare should've seen it coming, but his panicked haze was finally broken when he felt a inner warning from his Adventurer's Eye that he'd stumbled into a spawn point.

He stopped dead and turned around, immediately backing out. But in the blinding white snow he somehow got lost even doing that, so after several hasty steps he was still within the spawn point's border. Worse, now he was well and truly lost, just as likely to stumble into the heart of the spawn point as get out.

Fuck, he was an idiot. What made him think his high levels meant anything against a blizzard?

A roar was the only warning he had as a shape loomed out of the darkness and swung clumsily at him. Dare threw himself backwards with Roll and Shoot, coming up firing a Burst Arrow with fire damage. Then he immediately activated Rapid Shot.

Somehow he missed, even from feet away; he couldn't see his enemy anymore. Although the monster quickly came in view again as it shambled forwards with another roar, having no trouble following him through the blinding snow.

Dare danced backwards as he shot two arrows from near point blank range that actually landed. Then he tripped over something and fell headlong, losing his bow as he scrambled back to his feet and kept backing away, retrieving his spear from off his back.

Okay. At least these spawn points should all be lower level than him. And he thought the monster coming after him was a firbolg, which was slow anyway.

Although nothing you wanted to tangle with from melee range. Which was exactly what he had to do unless he wanted to flee blindly and possibly run headlong into their camp.

A shape looming out of the wall of blinding snow nearly made him swing wildly, but it was smaller, cloaked in leather and fur with swirling midnight hair and large velvety ears.

The fox girl he'd saved here months ago, Seris.

She had his bow slung across her back, and without a word that would've probably been lost to the wind anyway she grabbed his hand and pulled him urgently away. Dare gratefully followed, since she obviously seemed to know where she was going.

Through the gusting swirls of snow he caught occasional glimpses of her delicate features furrowed in concentration, cute button nose wrinkled as she sniffed out a trail. Maybe retracing her steps?

A faint shout mostly lost to the wind heralded a taller shape appearing on Dare's other side, draping his arm around her slender shoulders and supporting him with surprising strength. Selis, the arctic fox girl.

After what could've been a minute or a half hour of struggling through the snow, Dare found himself ducking beneath an evergreen bush into a mostly hidden earth tunnel, crouching to avoid the trailing root strands growing down through the ceiling.

The two fox girls led him into a cozy room with a fire roaring merrily in a stone fireplace to warm the space, the smoke whisked away through a stone chimney. A pot of stew hung over the coals to one side of the fire, bubbling and filling the air with a pleasant savory aroma that made his stomach rumble.

Most of the room was taken up by a pile of furs and clean but faded blankets, with a couple cushions near the fire that were obviously used as an eating area. A small tunnel on the far wall led to what looked like a storeroom filled with dried meats, fruits, and vegetables.

"Here," Seris said, leading him to a cushion by the fire and wrapping a blanket around him.

"T-thanks," Dare said. He hadn't realized how cold he was until entering the warmth of this room, but now he was shivering violently, unable to keep his teeth from chattering. His armor and winter clothes were soaked and felt like they were freezing on his body.

The small midnight fox girl leaned close, delicate vulpine features just inches from his. "His lips are blue," she murmured.

"That's not good." Selis crowded close, snowy ears twitching worriedly. "His teeth are chattering, poor thing."

Seris pushed his blanket aside and began tugging off his sodden cloak. “We need to get him out of these wet clothes and under the blankets.”

Dare wasn't about to protest to being undressed . . . he'd had enough amorous encounters with women by this point that he had little shame, especially when he was half-frozen.

The fox girls peeled off his wet armor, coat, tunic, and pants, then began wiping him down with warm wet cloths, murmuring admiringly to each other as they did. “Goddess, he's not just cold as a statue, he's solid as one too.”

“When did you ever see a statue?”

“You know what I mean. He's got the most rock hard muscles I've ever felt.”

“You're not wrong, I don't think I've ever seen a more sexy man. And I thought I wanted him when his clothes were still on.”

Dare didn't know whether to be embarrassed or pleased by their frank appraisal. Although mostly what he felt was relief as his hosts pulled him to the bed and buried him beneath a pile of warm, soft furs and blankets.

Even in his current half frozen haze he wasn't numb to the scent of the two beautiful fox girls suffusing the bed around him, a wild, enticing feminine musk.

His hosts knelt to either side of him, watching worriedly as his violent shivers continued. “He's still too cold,” Selis murmured, stroking his cheek. “We need to warm him up.”

Seris nodded. “I've heard skin to skin contact is the best way to warm someone up.” She began to peel off her clothes, porcelain complexion showing a slight blush as she stripped down to a fur chest wrap and undershorts. While she was about the same height as Ireni she was much curvier, her lush body made even more tantalizing by her fluffy sable fox tail, big velvety ears, and long raven hair shining with blue highlights.

Selis seemed to agree wholeheartedly with that suggestion, because when she stripped she didn't stop at her underwear, briefly revealing her body before slipping beneath the covers with him.

Dare wasn't so far gone to the cold that he didn't stare at her good sized breasts, pink nipples swiftly hardening from the cold, and her silky white bush and firm ass. She was taller and more toned, but with soft curves in all the right places.

The midnight fox girl slipped beneath the blankets as well, and he soon felt two soft, warm bodies press against him on either side.

He had more reason to appreciate that than just the warmth they provided, and as his shivers gradually eased and warmth suffused him he found himself focusing on the sensations more and more.

Especially when Selis draped a leg over his, pressing her sex against his thigh in the process, and he felt moisture on her silky petals.

If Dare hadn't been on his way to stiffening before, tenting up even the impressive mound of blankets covering him, that certainly did it.

Seris lifted a leg over him as well, then pouted when her soft skin brushed the damp cloth of his underwear. “He's never going to warm up properly wearing these wet undershorts,” she said, biting her lip as she began tugging at the waistband. “Besides, it's keeping us from having proper skin contact.”

Selis grinned and reached over his chest, pressing very nice breasts against him in the process, to tweak the smaller girl's velvety ear. “In that case why are you still in *your* underwear, sister?”

Dare jumped in surprise. “Sister?”

With their difference in coloring being literally black and white, he'd missed the striking resemblance in their features. Both delicate and lovely, with that mischievous vulpine sharpness and those big golden eyes.

“That's right,” Selis said, reaching down to stroke Seris's silky black tail resting across his stomach alongside her two fluffy white ones. “We're twins.”

That was even more surprising; obviously they weren't identical.

Holy shit, he was in bed with two gorgeous twin fox girls. Had he actually collapsed in the blizzard and this was some sort of glorious last fever dream before death claimed him?

The sisters worked together to tug off his underwear and toss it over beside his drying clothes. Then he felt Seris moving next to him as she pulled off her fur wraps and tossed them aside as well. After which she once again cuddled close, pressing her full breasts against his side and draping a leg over his.

Although unlike her sister, who was simply aroused, the midnight fox girl was so sopping wet her nectar dripped down his thigh.

Dare shifted his arms to wrap around the beautiful twins. He was more than warm now, and it was pretty clear where this was going. Unable to resist the temptation, he began gently stroking Seris's fluffy sable tail and alternating between petting Selis's two snowy ones.

The twins giggled in unison. “Sister, I think he's warming up,” Selis said.

Seris moaned softly and twitched her tail in his grip. “I bet he'd warm up even more if we were moving instead of just lying here.” She began slowly rubbing her silky petals against his thigh.

“I think you're right,” the arctic fox girl said with a vulpine grin, revealing cute little fangs her lips had hidden. She began to grind against him as well. “Would you like us to warm you up, Dare?”

At this rate he was going to explode before they'd even gotten around to touching his cock; gods, this was sexy.

“Both of you?” Dare panted.

It was Selis's turn to blush. “We've shared everything our whole life,” she said bashfully, “including mates.” She gave him a pleading look. “But if you don't want that then please at least be with Seris. It would make her happy.”

If he didn't want that? In what world and what sort of madman wouldn't?

“Oh, don't!” the midnight fox girl exclaimed. “I'd be too guilty if you left her out. If you have to leave someone out leave me out . . . I don't mind watching."

She sounded like she really didn't want to be left out.

"No no!" Dare said hastily, smiling at them. "I would love to be with you both. That would be . . ." Incredible. Fantastic. Out of this world. "Cool."

Seris giggled and reached up to tweak her sister's soft white ear. "I keep telling you that any man who would want one of us will be ten times as eager to have us both at once. Especially when we show him how fun we are." She gave him a wicked smile, none of her previous bashfulness to be seen. Especially since it showed her naughty little fangs.

"You're not wrong," Dare admitted with a chuckle. He was about to get a chance to sleep with *twins*! And not just any twins but sexy fox girls. Even if this was a dream as he froze to death, he didn't want to wake up.

"Good!" Selis said, wiggling farther onto his chest so she could hug her sister tight not only with her arms but with her two fluffy tails. "Because I just know that any man would want you, dear Sister. You're just so cute and petite and soft."

Seris buried her face in her sister's chest. Which was sweet and innocent in spite of her choosing to nestle in the valley between the taller girl's breasts. "No, they'd choose you, beloved. You're so soft and sexy and you've got such perfect boobs and child-bearing hips. And *two* beautiful fluffy tails."

Dare's cock throbbed urgently at their affectionate display. "Sorry for interrupting, but I'd say that any man lucky enough to have you both would be insane to pick a favorite."

"You think so?" Selis asked, pressing her nose to his so she could look deep into his eyes. Her snowy tails unwrapped from her sister to teasingly brush over his legs. "Because I love my sister very much, so you mustn't neglect her."

"And I love my sister very much," Seris added, rubbing her breasts against his chest. He could feel her diamond-hard nipples gliding over his skin as her silky soft midnight tail joined her sister's tails brushing him. “You mustn't neglect her.”

“And what about you two?” he half teased, half asked: he'd obviously never been in a threesome with twins, and was hoping for some idea of how to navigate it.

Both blushed in the firelight. “When it comes to that,” Selis said with a giggle, “both of us are just interested in sharing our mate-”

“But that doesn't mean we aren't affectionate with each other,” Seris finished for her sister, also giggling.

The snowy fox girl nodded in agreement. “It's true. Nothing makes me feel more loved than having my sweet sister hugging me and telling me how beautiful and soft I am while our mate slams his big hard cock in my little pussy.”

Seris made a contented noise. “Or resting my head on my wonderful sister's lap as she strokes my ears and tells me she loves me, while our mate is very rough with my soft little body.”

“Oh gods,” Dare groaned, his rock hard cock straining painfully against the blankets piled atop it. “You two are doing this on purpose, aren't you?”

Selis snickered and ran her hand over his abs. “Of course. We know it's what mates lo-” Her hand brushed his cock, obviously far higher up than she'd expected thanks to its length, and she cut off with a gasp.

Her head disappeared beneath the blankets, and she gasped again. “Nature's blessing, Sister! Look at the tent he's pitching!”

Seris's head disappeared as well and she also gasped. “And I thought he couldn't get any sexier!” she murmured in awe. Dare bit back a groan as she tentatively reached down to rub his throbbing shaft with her small hand. “He's been hiding a centaur cock from us.”

“Or at least a bovid cock,” her sister said with a giggle. “Now I'm even more glad he's the one who saved you, Sister.” She also reached down to stroke him.

He grit his teeth. “I'm not going to hold out long at this rate,” he gasped.

The twins shared a silent look that seemed to say as much as a conversation. “I'd kind of like to watch him shoot . . .” Selis said slowly.

“I can't wait to have it in my mouth,” her petite sister countered. “And if he can't hold out I want to taste his come, instead of letting him waste it all over his stomach.”

“I can hold out,” Dare protested, flushing in embarrassment. “And even if I couldn't, I can go a dozen times or more if needed, and fuck right through an orgasm too at first.”

The twins stared at each other in flat out disbelief. “A dozen times,” Seris repeated. “And keep going right through your refractory period.”

Selis laughed. “You know we're going to test that now, don't you?”

Dare's cock throbbed in their hands. “Oh gods yes, please do.”

The sisters looked at each other for several seconds, still absently stroking his shaft. “You know, Sister,” Selis said. “I think he means it.”

Seris nodded solemnly, full lips parting in a very vulpine smile with her cute little fangs. “Yes, I think it's going to be a very long night.”

The arctic fox girl returned the smile. “If we've finally found a mate we can do whatever we want to, without having to worry about whether he'll have the energy to please both of us equally . . .” She stroked his cock again. “A long night indeed.”

Dare stifled another groan and closed his eyes as both twins simultaneously dove beneath the covers, squirming down until he felt their hot breath on his cock.

He'd had some incredible experiences since coming to Collisa, but he had a feeling this was going to be particularly special.

Epilogue
Sleepover

The next thing Dare knew the fox girl twins were on his cock, kissing and licking either side of its length with small pink tongues. He hastily flicked the covers down so he could watch, biting back a groan at the sight of their tongues pleasuring his shaft, expertly teasing every inch without ever brushing each other.

Selis grinned up at him as she boldly reached out and began fondling his balls while kissing her way up his length. "You know, Sister," she moaned. "I think these really could hold a dozen loads."

"Savor the moment," Seris admonished as she struggled to work his tip between her small lips with her mouth open as wide as it could go. "Darr br pramm urg mem," she continued as he finally popped into her warm, wet mouth, the vibrations of her words sending shivers of pleasure through him.

He shivered even harder as she began teasing his opening with her tongue, while Selis simultaneously began running her own wide open mouth up and down his shaft, tongue pressed hard against his skin, and for good measure gently squeezed his balls.

"That's about all I can take," Dare gasped after less than half a minute. He grabbed Seris's head, midnight hair silky beneath his fingers, and tried to push a bit deeper as he prepared to empty himself into her small mouth.

Before he could Selis let go of his balls and tightly squeezed the base of his shaft between thumb and forefinger. "Ah ah ah," she teased as she expertly cut off his orgasm, grinning up at him. "If you're going to shoot down our throats, you need to be deeper in." She nodded to her twin. "Go ahead, Sister."

Instead Seris pulled away, gasping for breath as his large tip popped free of the tight seal of her pouty lips. "You can have his first load," she panted. "It always takes me longer to get it in, and even more with this monster. I want to make sure he can last until I've got him all the way down." She slipped her small hand between her legs. "Besides, I like to watch you . . . you're so good at swallowing big hard cocks."

Dare groaned as Selis took her sister's place on his tip, mouth easily engulfing him and taking him all the way to press against the back of her throat in one smooth motion. "You girls always seem to know exactly what to say and do to get me going," he said as he stroked the arctic fox girl's large velvety ears.

Selis made a noise of enjoyment as she worked him into her throat, tails lashing in pleasure, and Seris smiled at him and rubbed herself even faster. "Yes, keep doing that," the petite fox girl said. "We both love it when mates play with our ears."

"How about this?" he teased, gently taking one between his fingers and tugging playfully. Selis moaning against his cock was all the confirmation he needed that she enjoyed it.

The arctic fox girl determinedly worked him deeper, face reddening and delicate throat bulging with the outline of his tip. She kept humming, the combination of the vibrations and her rippling esophagus as she swallowed repeatedly causing his pleasure to surge.

Especially as Seris squirmed around to where she could begin licking and sucking his balls.

Soon enough Selis was bobbing up and down on his cock, occasionally choking and gagging but not relenting for a moment. Under her relentless onslaught Dare finally grunted, gently tugged her ears to pull her farther onto his cock, and with a surge of pleasure began pulsing down her throat.

"Good girl," Seris crooned, stroking her twin's tails as the arctic fox girl swallowed eagerly. "Take it all, little sister. All that yummy seed to fill your tummy."

The naughty words drove Dare to a new surge of pleasure, and he sank into the ecstasy with another groan.

Selis finally pulled back with a gasp, grinning at him. "How was that? I bet it blew your mind."

"It was incredible," he agreed. "You're amazing."

"That's just because you haven't seen me yet," her petite sister said, starting to straddle him. "I'll show you how to please a mate, little sister."

It was a bit odd to hear the tiny fox girl calling her taller twin that. Dare could only assume she was the older one.

The arctic fox girl pouted. "You don't always have to turn it into a competition, big sis. We can just have fun."

Seris giggled as she began rubbing her sopping pussy against his sensitive tip. "What's more fun than pushing ourselves to the highest peaks of pleasure possible?"

Dare certainly had no complaints with either perspective. Although he gently caught the midnight fox girl's hips to pause her increasingly urgent motions. "I have scrolls of Prevent Conception in my pack."

The twins exchanged one of those looks that seemed to share the information of a full conversation. "We take what nature gives us," Seris finally said. "Vulpids have low fertility and most of our mates are other vulpids or humans, so we haven't gotten pregnant yet. But should it happen it'll happen."

Selis giggled, tracing the sharply defined muscles of Dare's pecs. "And I'll admit, you'd be a mate I'd want to breed with." She looked up at him with her big golden eyes. "Would that be hot? Knowing you might plant a baby in my womb?"

That was seriously fucking hot. Especially the thought of impregnating both twins at once and seeing their tummies grow together. But while his cock was rock hard and throbbing urgently against Seris's plump labia, he kept his wits about him.

"My fertility is a bit higher than most humans," he said. "Or a lot higher, actually . . . 51."

Both beauties stared at him with twin expressions of shock. "Could that be true?" Seris whispered to her sister.

"Why would a mate eager to sink into your beautiful little pussy admit to having *more* fertility?" Selis whispered back.

"Well he's got the Prevent Conception scrolls, so he'd have no reason to lie."

The arctic fox girl thoughtfully reached beneath her sister to grip Dare's cock. "What a mystery this is, big sister. From his cock I'd say we have a bovid in our bed, but if he's right it seems he's actually a cunid."

"Or an Incubus," Seris said cheerfully. "Here to drive us into a wild delirium of pleasure while draining our stamina, mana, and life force."

Dare grinned at the banter, but wasn't about to be put off. "Seriously, though, you might get pregnant just from rubbing your pussy on my cock, especially after I've already come once."

"And I'm serious," the midnight fox girl said right back, fluffy tail swishing back and forth. "Do you really want us to use your scrolls?"

He hesitated. "I suppose it's up to you. I wouldn't mind being a father to your children, and I'd do everything I could to care for them and be part of their lives."

The twins exchanged another long look. "We take what nature gives us," Selis said.

Seris nodded, thoughtfully rocking back and forth on his cock in a way that was going to drive him wild if she kept it up. "Would you like to raise babies with me, little sister?"

"Oh, you know they'd be adorable and the best of friends," the arctic fox girl said, tails lashing excitedly.

Her small twin looked down at him, blushing. "Okay, Dare. Put babies in us."

Dare groaned. "I think that's the sexiest thing you've said yet."

Selis giggled. "It is pretty hot, but I think we can do better." She gracefully moved to straddle his head, tails playfully swatting his face as her glistening petals dripped arousal onto his neck. "What about if we both ride you while holding each other's hands?"

His hips twitched involuntarily at the thought, and with a giggle of her own Seris slid up his shaft until his tip was pressed against her tiny opening. Then, with a needy whimper, she began impaling herself on his massive cock.

"Gods, Sister, he's stretching me like nothing I've ever felt!" she panted. "We're going to have so much fun with him!"

At the same time Selis moaned and dropped down on his face, urgently rubbing her arousal all over his nose, mouth, and chin until finally planting her labia firmly against his lips.

Engulfed in the torrent of sensations from the ministrations of both sexy twins, Dare reached up to grip Seris's curvy hip with one hand and Selis's thigh with the other, not so much guiding their motions as trying to keep up with them. He kissed the arctic fox girl's soft petals and tasted her wild, sweet nectar, then plunged his tongue into her depths for a better taste.

Selis moaned and pressed harder against him, and he began flicking her erect bud with his tongue with relentless patience.

Meanwhile Seris's hot, slick tunnel, tighter than Ireni's and far more demanding, massaged his length as she bounced up and down on him with sweet, whiny whimpers.

Dare had been ridden by two women like this before, but the knowledge that they were gorgeous twin fox girls taking their pleasure together made it even more intense. Especially since their moans of pleasure were almost in tandem, as if as twins they could even time their upcoming orgasms to match up.

That realization was enough for him, and he moaned against Selis's dripping pink pussy as he exploded inside Seris, the intense surges of pleasure making his head spin.

The petite fox girl either didn't notice or wasn't ready to stop, because she didn't pause in bouncing on his shaft as he filled her up, their combined juices dripping down his still-hard cock. If anything, she sped up, moaning more urgently.

The athletic arctic fox increased her pace as well, mashing his nose and lips with her furnace hot pussy and arousal flowing all over his face.

Dare wasn't sure if it was a coincidence or if the twins were just that much in sync, but he swore that both stiffened with a soft cry at the exact same moment, their pussies winking against his lips and around his cock in a shared climax as their gushing nectar nearly drowned him and drenched his crotch simultaneously.

He would've liked to hold out longer, but he still had plenty left in the tank and this was too fucking hot. So he gave in to his own orgasm and released again inside his petite lover.

Both sisters rose off him at the same time, letting him come up for air with a gasp, and they once again pressed up against either side and draped themselves over him. Making contented noises, they alternated between passionately kissing him and licking and sucking on his neck.

He'd had a lot of erotic experiences since coming to Collisa, but a threesome with fox girl twins had to be right up at the top. "You two are unbelievably sexy," he murmured, rubbing their soft little asses as they continued to tease him with their small pink tongues.

They broke the kiss and giggled, each kissing him in turn. Seris took his hand and pressed it to her flat tummy. "You're unbelievably sexy yourself," she whispered. "You just planted a baby in me, you know that? My tummy's going to get all big and round."

Dare's cock twitched, and he groaned against Selis's lips as she dove back in and slipped her tongue into his mouth.

But only for a few seconds, then the arctic fox girl rolled onto her back and tugged at him insistently, eyes glazed with lust. "Breed me now," she begged.

At the same time Seris began pushing at his butt until he was on top of her sister. "Yes, breed her!" the midnight fox girl said eagerly. "Your turn, little sister. I want to watch him put a baby in you!"

It soon became clear she wanted to do more than watch, because as Selis spread her legs wide and he positioned his sensitive tip at her eagerly waiting entrance, Seris got behind him and pressed her curvy little body against his back. As she rubbed against him insistently he eased forward, spreading the athletic fox girl's slick pussy wide as he slid inside her.

“Yessss!” Selis gasped, wrapping her arms around Dare and lifting herself to kiss him hard. “Nature's bounty, you're huge. Stretch me out so I feel you in all the best places.”

Moving in time with her sister's eagerly rolling hips, Seris rubbed her body against his back as he pushed in deeper. “That's it, give it to her!” she encouraged. “She loves it rough.”

It certainly looked that way. The arctic fox girl had adjusted quickly to his size and was now moaning in passion as he sawed in and out of her needy sex, Seris matching his movements with her body pressed to his back.

When he finally had an intense rhythm going the petite fox girl let go of him with one hand and pressed it down between their bodies, frantically rubbing her clit. At the same time he felt Selis stiffen and begin pushing her hips back against him even more urgently, and wondered if the twins were about to share another mutual climax.

He felt his balls boiling in anticipation, and as the two beautiful fox girls raised their voices together in bliss, trembling against his front and back, he unleashed his seed inside the arctic fox girl in powerful jets.

“Yessss!” Selis panted, pussy clamping down on him and milking him desperately. “Nature's love, I've never felt anything like this.”

“Yessss!” Seris cried out at the same time. “He's filling you up, little sister! We're going to have his beautiful babies!”

Dare heaved in huge breaths as he shot a few final spurts into Selis's eager womb. Then he dropped down beside her with a last gasp of effort, Seris still cuddled against his back. The arctic fox girl rolled over to cling to his front, sandwiching him between soft, warm bodies as he recovered from the intense experience.

After the exhausting day and then the strenuous lovemaking, he found himself drifting off into warm, contented slumber.

At some point he drifted awake to the sound of cutlery scraping on dishes, and guided by hunger joined his twin lovers as they spooned him out a bowl of stew. He devoured it ravenously, gratefully accepted seconds, then allowed Seris and Selis to guide him back to bed.

There the two beautiful women banished his sleepiness with their hands and mouths, reminding him insistently that he'd promised to satisfy them both completely.

Dare was a man of his word, and he pushed weariness aside to enjoy his time with the fox girl sisters, bringing them to a series of rolling climaxes until they were finally limp and quivering, as worn out and satisfied as he was.

Cuddled together in a tangle of soft limbs and fluffy tails, they drifted off into contented sleep.

* * * * *

"Are you sure you don't want to visit Nirim Manor and meet everyone?" Dare asked as he tightened the belts on his pack.

"Maybe some other time," Selis said, languidly reaching out to rub his leg. "In the winter we like to stay where it's warm and sleep. Especially after a blizzard."

Confirming her words, Seris was huddled beneath a pile of blankets, only her cute little nose and rosebud lips showing as she dozed.

She looked awfully cozy, and he was tempted to undress and climb back in with her. But his fiancees and friends would be worried sick about him after disappearing in a blizzard.

Or well, Sia had probably reassured them he was fine. But still, he needed to get back to them to let them know everything was okay.

Dare leaned down to kiss the arctic fox girl, stroking her velvety ears and teasingly batting at her fluffy tails. "Thanks for saving me from the blizzard," he said. "And for letting me shelter here last night."

She giggled wickedly. "Oh, is that all you're grateful for?"

"Incredible as last night was, I'd say saving my life trumps it," he said with a laugh, giving her another lingering kiss. "Can I visit again?"

"Every time you run past here on the way to an adventure," she said. "Or on the way home. And you're welcome to spend the night whenever."

He certainly wasn't about to pass up the offer; last night had been wild.

"Go 'way," Seris grumbled, poking her head out of the covers to squint at them with a cute glower. "Tryna sleep."

"I'm about to," Dare said with a smile, leaning over to plant a kiss on her pouty lips and stroke her velvety ears as well. "Thanks for last night. I hope to see you soon."

"You too, lover," she said sleepily before burrowing back under the covers. Selis blew him a kiss before squirming under the blankets to snuggle up to her sister.

He lingered for a moment to take in the peaceful scene, then ducked out through the tunnel, snugly closing the door behind him.

The morning had dawned bright and cold, not a cloud to be seen in the sky. The only evidence of yesterday's blizzard was the better than two feet of snow blanketing the ground atop what had already been there. It was almost enough to require snowshoes and definitely hampered his movements, but not enough to be more than a nuisance.

Dare activated Cheetah's Dash and set off at a brisk pace. Yesterday's melancholy had vanished with the leaden cloud layer, and he was looking to the future with more enthusiasm.

His family were content to stay at home, and he was content to return to their love and warmth after every adventure. It hadn't really been fair of him to assume that a bunch of women he found under different circumstances would all want to devote their lives, and risk their lives, to hunt monsters with him.

If anything, he should be grateful they'd gone along with his plans so gamely and kept him company through thick and thin.

But if he wanted people who shared his enthusiasm for adventuring he should look for them specifically, rather than trying to convince people who were content with their lives to adopt a life that didn't suit them.

That's what the Adventurer's Guild was for. And even in Terana, small as it was, there were a handful of adventurers around his level that Marona kept on retainer for major threats. He could find people to share new adventures with.

The goblin village was hunkered down from the blizzard, but to his relief nobody had been lost in the storm. The worst that had happened was one of the less well constructed houses had partially collapsed from the weight of snow on the roof, but thankfully nobody had been hurt. Dare joined Rek checking on the livestock, then clapped his future brother-in-law on the shoulder and hurried on his way.

Nirim Manor looked unharmed by the wind and snow, everything clean under a heavy blanket of snow and sparkling brilliantly in the sunlight. People were out and about doing chores, and children were taking full advantage of the fresh blanket of deep snow to play.

It was incredible to think how much this place had changed in just a few months. How many people had joined his family and their friends in a new life here.

It was incredible. And humbling. He wondered what the future held for this place, and what they could build here.

Dare found his family eating breakfast, and the moment he walked through the door he was immediately inundated by his fiancees as they gathered him in a group hug and expressed their intense relief.

“I knew you'd be okay, of course,” Leilanna said stoutly as she hugged him around Se'weir. “I just hated the thought of you out there freezing in the snow."

"He was okay," Pella said.

"Well yeah, we knew that thanks to Sia," Zuri said, glaring up at him fiercely as she clung to his waist. "But you shouldn't have been out there in the cold. Why did you go when a storm was obviously brewing?"

Dare was saved from having to explain his previous morning's petulance by his dog girl fiancee interrupting. "No, I mean he was okay because he spent the night cozy in a fox girl den." She sniffed, eyes widening in delight. "With twins!"

He started in surprise. "How-" he began, then chuckled ruefully. Right, her sense of smell was remarkably keen.

Linia laughed. "So we were all here worrying ourselves sick, while you were out there having every man's dream threesome?" She playfully swatted his ass. "I should've guessed."

"What are they like?" Se'weir asked. "Can I meet them?"

Ireni just held him, smiling gently. Farther back Lily held Gelaa, smiling at him in clear relief at his safe return.

"I hope you at least had a productive day yesterday," Leilanna said, hands on hips.

Dare smiled ruefully. "Actually, I bypassed spawn points hoping to explore more of the mountains, then when I saw the blizzard coming I rushed back trying to get home in time." He grimaced. "The only thing I really accomplished yesterday was nearly freezing my ass off."

Linia slapped his butt again. "Well speaking as someone who happens to like your ass, I'm glad you didn't."

Zuri tugged on his hand. "Come on, you must be starving. Let's get some food in you."

He was ushered to his seat at the table, where Ilin and Amalisa were waiting to offer their own greetings and relief at his safe return. The two already looked like a couple, seated comfortably together, and Dare was again amazed he hadn't seen it before.

His fiancees pushed him down into his chair and put a heaping plate of sausage, bacon, and eggs in front of him, then returned to their own breakfasts. They talked a bit about yesterday's storm and how Nirim Manor had fared, then the conversation shifted to Ilin's and Amalisa's wedding plans.

They'd tentatively set the date for spring, probably around the same time as Dare's wedding to his fiancees, and for the same reason; they had people they wanted to invite and wanted the weather to be warm enough for travel.

Dare settled back to enjoy his breakfast and the company of his loved ones. With the deep snow he decided he'd stick around the manor today: check to see that everything was looking good with the snow and cold, plan out the improvements he'd been considering, check on the refugee village under construction, and just enjoy some time with his family and friends.

Including finally cooking a formal dinner for Lily and taking her out on a proper date. Maybe even sharing a first kiss.

He still had things he needed to accomplish before leaving to petition for knighthood, but there was time. It was good to remind himself that he didn't always have to rush around trying to accomplish his goals as quickly as possible.

Sometimes it was good to just slow down and enjoy what he had. Which was more than he ever could've dreamed of back on Earth.

End of Horde.
The adventures of Dare and his family
continue in Redoubt, sixth book of the Outsider series.

Thank you for reading Horde!

I hope you enjoyed reading it as much as I enjoyed writing it. If you feel the book is worthy of support, I'd greatly appreciate it if you'd rate it, or better yet review it, on Amazon, as well as recommend it to anyone you think would also enjoy it.

As a self-published author I flourish with the help of readers who review and recommend my work. Your support helps me continue doing what I love and bringing you more books to enjoy.

About the Author

Aiden Phoenix became an established author
writing stories about the end of the world.
Then Collisa called, a new and exciting world to explore,
and like the characters in his series he was reborn anew there.

Made in the USA
Monee, IL
12 January 2024

51672106R00208